HAWTHORN ACADEMY

HAWTHORN ACADEMY

YEAR TWO

D.R. PERRY

DISRUPTIVE IMAGINATION

LMBPN Publishing supports the right to free expression and the value of copyright. The purpose of copyright is to encourage writers and artists to produce the creative works that enrich our culture.

LMBPN Publishing
PMB 196, 2540 South Maryland Pkwy
Las Vegas, NV 89109

First US edition, June 2020

ebook ISBN: 978-1-64971-022-2
Print ISBN: 978-1-64971-023-9

THE HAWTHORN ACADEMY YEAR TWO TEAM

Thanks to our Beta Readers

Rachel Beckford and Mary Morris

Thanks to our JIT Readers

Veronica Stephan-Miller, Rachel Beckford, and Kerry Mortimer

Editor
SkyHunter Editing Team

GLOSSARY

People

- **Changeling**- A mortal child of either one or two faerie parents. Most changelings choose a monarch sometime in their twenties, although some do it earlier than they have to.
- **Dampyr**- The mortal offspring of two vampires. They aren't as rare as many suspect, although because their blood is exceptionally sustaining to vampires, they keep their status secret. Dampyr sometimes have magic or psychic powers that work unreliably.
- **Faerie**- A term used to describe either a changeling who has tithed to a monarch and spent a year and a day in the Under or the pure creatures such as Gnomes and Pixies who were created by the king and queen.
- **Ghost**- A dead person with unfinished business becomes a ghost. If a mortal makes a contract before death, that gives them unfinished business and lets them linger. When ghosts finish their business, they move on, but no one knows where they go from here.
- **Magus**- A mortal who can use magic. Magic comes from

energy in the world. Most magi can only use one type of magic. However, a rare few can do more than one kind. Those are called extramagi.

- **Merfolk**- People who can live on land with legs or in the sea with fins and tails. They only emerged from the ocean after the Big Reveal and are still extremely rare outside of harbor towns.
- **Psychic**- A mortal with psychic power. Psychic ability comes from a person's own body and mind.
- **Vampire**- An unliving person who drinks blood to survive and enhance their abilities. Only regular mortals, psychics, and magi can get turned into vampires. Shifters, changelings, and faeries won't turn, and most of those won't survive an attempt.
- **Shifter**- A mortal who can take an animal's shape. Shifters have one form, with coloring similar to what they have while human. They usually have an enhanced sense while human-shaped, which goes along with their animal. For example, an owl shifter might have keen eyesight and a wolf shifter, a great sense of smell.

Shifter Varieties

- **Dragon**- The only shifters who can see both magic and psychic abilities, though only while shifted. The most powerful ones can partially shapeshift. Dragons are immortal and reproduce infrequently. There are so few of them since the Reveal that they've started taking other magical shifters as mates.
- **Kelpie**- A magical shifter who gets their abilities from an enchanted faerie pelt that bonds with their soul. The Kelpie pelts were created by the Goblin King, so they have Unseelie energy and restrictions. A Kelpie's animal form is a horse. Families pass the pelts down through generations,

and part of each ancestor lives on to help their descendants. The ancestors can get distracting, however.

- **Selkie**- A magical shifter who gets their abilities from an enchanted faerie pelt that bonds with their soul. The Selkie pelts were created by the Sidhe queen, so they have Seelie energy and restrictions. A Selkie's animal form is a seal or sometimes a sea otter. They can use water magic as long as they wear the pelt. Families pass the pelts down through the generations, and part of each ancestor lives on to help their descendants. The ancestors can get distracting, however.
- **Tanuki**- A magical shifter with enhanced speed and the ability to see all types of magic while shifted. They are also the only creatures who can manipulate luck, causing it to turn from good to bad or the other way around. They stop aging if they own a charm infused with luck from humans. Very few of those charms exist, having been either used up during the Reveal or locked away.

Powers

- **Air magic**- The power to conjure, control, and banish wind or air.
- **Earth magic**- The power to conjure, control, and banish earth, sand, or rock.
- **Empathy**- A psychic power to sense and influence emotions in other people.
- **Fire magic**- The power to conjure, control, and banish flames.
- **Ice magic**- The power to conjure, control, and banish ice.
- **Lightning magic**- The power to conjure, control, and banish lightning.
- **Poison magic**- The power to conjure, control, and banish poison. Each magus has a slightly different type of toxin they produce. Some are even antidotes to others.
- **Precognitive**- A psychic power to foretell future events.

- **Spectral magic**- the power to conjure, control, and banish light.
- **Spectral Affinity**- A trait some spectral magi have that makes them charismatic and believable.
- **Summoner**- A psychic power that lets the user make contracts with pure faeries, letting the summoner call them in times of need. Each creature has an anchor, some item symbolizing the bond. Mastery of summoning takes decades of study, which is why the most powerful are either vampires or past middle age.
- **Seelie**- The Sidhe queen's court. The Seelie way is about following the letter of the law, even when it's hard or cruel. They have a hard time reconciling faerie rules with the new mortal laws since the Big Reveal.
- **Solar Magic**- The power to conjure, control, or banish sunlight. Some of the most powerful practitioners can find hidden objects or discover long-kept secrets.
- **Solar Affinity**- A trait some solar magi have that makes them beacons for coincidence.
- **Space magic**- The power to move the self or objects instantly across distances. Some can even move other people.
- **Space Affinity**- This space power comes with an ability to locate people or things important to the magus.
- **Telekinesis**- A psychic power that moves objects.
- **Telepathy**- A psychic power to read minds.
- **Tithe**- The process of pledging to either the queen or king, making a changeling choose to be either Seelie or Unseelie.
- **Umbral magic**- The power to conjure, control, and banish shadows and veil or camouflage objects or people.
- **Umbral Affinity**- A trait some umbral magi have that makes them difficult to remember without psychic ability, faerie magic, or a shifter pack bond.
- **Undeath magic**- The power to conjure, control, and banish unliving energy.

- **Unseelie**- The Goblin king's court. The Unseelies bend the rules and often navigate mortal society more easily than their Seelie counterparts.
- **Water magic**- The power to conjure, banish, and control water.
- **Wood magic**- The power to conjure, banish, and control wood. It takes extreme power to influencing a living plant.

Creatures

- **Basilisk**- A venomous serpent that also has poison magic.
- **Dragonet**- A tiny dragon-like creature, always associated with one or more element which powers their breath attacks later in life. They have scales but are warm-blooded like birds. Most don't get much bigger than a small cat.
- **Familiar**- A magical or mythical creature who makes a bond with a magus.
- **Gryphon**- A chimera which has the head of a bird and hindquarters of a predatory mammal. They come in several combinations of base species, and habitat influences their choice in magi to bond with.
- **Karkus**- A crab that can change its shape. They're said to be the offspring of the crab that pinched Hercules as he battled the Hydra.
- **Lightning Bird**- A familiar from South Africa with an affinity for lightning. Its beak can jump-start a car.
- **Mercat**- A shapeshifting feline with fur for land and scales in the water. They can live in lakes, rivers, or in the sea as well as on land. They must never completely dry out, or they will die.
- **Moon Hare**- A magical rabbit that gets power from its particular moon phase. They commonly bond with umbral magi.
- **Pharaoh's Rat**- These natural predators of dragon shifters are the size of ferrets and resemble a mongoose with more

fur. They have an affinity for space magic and can use it on occasion.

- **Pigeon**- Not as mundane as most think, some pigeons have an uncanny sense of direction due to their affinity for air magic.
- **Pricus**- An aquatic goat said to be descended from Capricorn. They can warp time even better than Gnomes.
- **Pure Faeries**- Creatures who spring to life from magical sources in the Under. They are genderless, and their type and ability depend on place of origin. They're associated with only one court, although they will work together to defeat a common enemy.
- **Sand Cat**- A feline that lives in the desert, able to go for weeks without water. Earth magic lets them do this.
- **Sha**- A magical desert dog from Egypt. Sha are the size of mundane toy breeds with short hair and small pointy ears. They could pass for mundane except for their blue tongues. They are attracted to anything undead.
- **Sphinx**- A magic cat with an affinity for fire. The reason they're hairless is that they're resistant to flames.
- **Strix**- A venomous owl with an affinity for poison. Female striges have rounded tufts on their heads, while males have pointed ones.
- **Sumxu**- A lop-eared cat found only in northern China. They are masters of camouflage and have an affinity for several kinds of magic.

Places

- **The Academy**—Something between a community college and a military academy for extrahumans, the Academy is geared toward helping extrahumans who don't play well with mortals get ready to join a blended society. It's got divisions for learners of all ages, though they are housed separately.

- **Cherry Blossom School**- A dojo geared toward teaching extrahumans self-restraint, meditation, and how to temper their enhanced physical abilities with more mundane skills. It's been around for close to a hundred years, run by the Ichiro family. Mundane classes used to be offered as a front but now are a separate division.
- **Ellicot City Magitechnic**- A prep school for magi and psychics specializing in magipsychic technology. It's located outside Baltimore.
- **Gallows Hill School**- Traditionally for shifters, this prep school in Salem recently opened its doors to changelings and other extrahumans not categorized as magi or psychics.
- **Hawthorn Academy**- A preparatory school for magi in Salem. Its campus is in the space between the mortal realm and the Under, giving it unrivaled privacy. They specialize in teaching familiar magic.
- **Providence Paranormal College**- A school founded just one year after Brown University and located right in its shadow. Providence Paranormal used to admit only magi and psychics, but it's been accepting all types of extrahumans ever since Henrietta Thurston became headmistress. There has been trouble since then for students and faculty, leading people to believe dissenters are sabotaging the school.
- **Trout Academy**- A prestigious preparatory school for changelings with magic, recently open to magi and magical shifters. Its campus is located in South County and has been operating in some form or another since Rhode Island Colony was founded.
- **The Under**- The faerie realm. It's been divided into two parts ever since the Sidhe Queen and the Goblin king split up thousands of years ago. Mortals don't age in the Under, but it's a dangerous place for them to be. Getting lost means never being seen again, and it's easy to get indebted to

something nasty while trying to get through or out of the Under.

- **Wolf Messing Prep**- An institute for psychics to learn to control their skills before heading to college.

Events

- **The Big Reveal**- The term used for the 1990s, when the world discovered magic was real and extrahumans existed. The decade was marked with fear as everyone adjusted to the changes. Since the 21st Century, law and technology work for both humans and extrahumans.
- **Boston Internment**- A reaction by Boston government officials to the disappearance and suspected trafficking in extrahumans, especially shifters. All registered extrahumans in Boston lived on barges for close to a month under guard by the Boston Police. The traffickers got their hands on some magical gadgets, rendering the protection useless. Few survived.

CHAPTER ONE

"I'm heading out!" I hollered up the stairs to my parents, who were still in bed on this lazy Sunday afternoon.

"Drop by Bubbe's first. She's got a gift for you," Mom called back.

"Okay!"

Since I was already almost out the front door, that meant I'd have to go down, out, and back in again through the front entrance to my grandmother's extraveterinary office. It was no big deal; I'd done that a million times over the years.

In the waiting room, I had to stop until Bubbe let me in. It only took a few seconds, but it felt longer than that. I had places to go and friends to see because it was June fifteenth, my seventeenth birthday. Probably, that was why Bubbe wanted to see me too.

Or it could be bad news—about a number of unpleasant things.

"Shush, you."

Yes, I was talking to myself, to a piece of my mind I called the Evil Inside Voice. It had shown up last fall and hadn't gone away since. Personality-wise, it was totally a pessimist and super annoying.

"Aliyah?" Bubbe opened the door behind the counter.

"Hi." I waved. "Mom said you wanted to see me?"

"Yes. I have something for you for your birthday."

1

My grandmother looked down instead of at me, not her typical behavior. Holidays and special occasions almost always brought her joy. Bubbe usually loved any reason to celebrate, but this day was different, and I should have known why.

"Are you okay?" It might have been my birthday, but I loved my grandma. She's always been there for me and was an amazing person, so I didn't want her suffering.

"A little maudlin is all." Finally, she looked up, the corners of her mouth tilting slightly in a faint grin that didn't touch her eyes. "Come along now."

She held the door open, so I walked through, then stepped aside to let her lead me down the hallway that made up her workspace. Examination rooms lined the hall, each sectioned off by a bisected dutch door. But she didn't bring me into any of those, heading instead into the kitchen.

The space was clean and well-kept as usual, except for the table in the middle. Boxes from the basement covered its surface, ones I recognized from the storage areas down there. Until now, these had been strictly off-limits. Somehow all their surfaces were clean instead of covered by debris, despite long years languishing down in the dust-bunny farm.

Either Bubbe had kept it tidy in the storage space, or she'd used some magipsychic device or enchantment to prevent dust from collecting on these. If that was it, the boxes and their contents had to be important to her.

"I promised to tell you all about my brother, the first Noah Morgenstern. We ought to sit down."

I sat, thinking she'd join me, but instead of taking the seat on the other side of the table, my grandmother fiddled with a pair of tall glasses on the counter. She'd prepared iced tea, the kind she often made in summer from the fresh mint in Dad's herb garden.

Patience wasn't my strong suit, but I could manage it for a short and select list of people. Bubbe was first on that list. I sat gazing down at the cover of one scrapbook on the table. It had neon streaks against a deep purple background, reminding me for all the world of the trapper keeper Professor Luciano used in the magipsychic lab at Hawthorn Academy.

I reached out, thinking surely my grandmother wouldn't mind if I had a peek at the photos before her explanation. Her nod as I ran my fingers over the plastic cover confirmed my hunch, so I went ahead and had a look inside.

I recognized my great-grandfather immediately from the many photos on the wall in our apartment upstairs. Unlike the ones in that collection, he stood beside two children instead of just one. Grandma's brother Noah was considerably older than her, unlike the small age difference between my sibling and me.

The first Noah had almost nothing in common with my Noah— physically anyway. The two were practically opposites in that regard. Great Uncle Noah was broad-shouldered instead of beanpole-thin, his smile full and genuine instead of half and ironic, and he was fair-haired instead of dark. He reminded me of someone, in fact.

Me.

You resemble your uncle Richard more.

I rolled my eyes, then noticed that my grandmother had her back to me, thank goodness. I'd let my family in on nearly every secret I'd kept last year at Hawthorn Academy, but not the Evil Inside Voice because I still hoped it'd disappear once I'd spent more time living authentically. Also, I suspected my inner turmoil had more to do with it than any magic.

"Sugar in your tea, Aliyah?" She held the teaspoon over one glass.

"No, thanks. I'll take honey, though, if you have it."

"Of course." Bubbe switched the spoon for the dipper from the honey jar.

A few moments later, after clinking long stirrers around the two tall glasses, Bubbe brought them to the table and sat, pushing the one with honey across to me. I wrapped my hand around it, letting my palm cool against the sweating glass. Even though Bubbe's office had air conditioning, she didn't crank it up until July. She always said it helped the animals in her care know the seasons had changed.

"I hadn't imagined he was so much older than you." With my dry hand, I reached out, tapping the photograph. "Your Noah."

"He might look much older, but he wasn't really." Bubbe pointed at another picture, one where I immediately spotted the difference. "Only four years."

"Oh. So he was big for his age?"

"An early bloomer is what our parents said." Bubbe reached for the page. "I think you'll see something else of interest here."

She'd flipped it over carefully so as not to disturb the pictures pasted in it. They all had that matte look, almost pebbled in true vintage fashion. Glossy wasn't the preferred finish in those days.

I noticed the photo she wanted me to see right away. Great Uncle Noah sat on the beach, just above where the ocean wet the sand. It was dawn, and the person taking the picture did nothing to shield the sun. I saw little besides a silhouette, but one part of it struck me.

"He had a dragonet. Like me." I blinked.

"Yes. A huge surprise to our parents. They thought for sure he'd bond with a tannin, but one day he was out taking a walk, and, well," she said and shook her head, grinning mildly. "It was quite similar to how it happened for you, actually."

"Was he a fire magus? To start with, I mean."

"Solar, like the rest of us Morgensterns. The fire came in later, during his Coast Guard training, so he discovered he was an extramagus later than you did."

"He was in the service?" I sipped my tea.

"Yes. He introduced me to your grandfather. Brought him home for shore leave right after I graduated from Hawthorn. He ended up winning our wager because of that, too."

"Wager?"

"I said I'd never marry. He bet me two dollars I would fall in love eventually." She smiled softly. "I bet him two more that I'd stay a Morgenstern for the rest of my life. We ended up breaking even."

"Because Grandpa insisted." I returned her smile, remembering stories from my childhood about him saying there were plenty of folks named Smith but almost no magi named Morgenstern.

"That's right."

"Even back then, before the Reveal, your parents were okay with your brother bringing a mundane friend around?"

"He knew about extrahumans. One boat squadron at the Coast Guard was in the know. Back then, with the rise of technology, things had almost gotten untenable. Most of the Salem community figured keeping extrahumans secret wouldn't be possible for much longer."

"I know we'll cover it this year in extrahuman history—the twentieth-century stuff, with the Reveal and everything. Noah said I'd have to do a report on what someone in my family did. Can I use these and make my report about your brother?"

"Yes." She nodded her head once, then held it still. Was this too painful for her? I wanted to take the request back, but she continued, "I'll put them in the spare supply closet so you can get them as needed, but bear in mind, your brother will be jealous."

I sighed. "Why?"

"He didn't have access to any of this last year." Bubbe stared at her hands, laced around the glass of tea. "And that was my mistake. He should have. He's the namesake, after all."

"So, who did he write about?"

"Perhaps you ought to ask him."

"But Bubbe, you know he's not—"

"I know, and you're aware of how I feel about that. The two of you should make up, and this time it's more on him than you."

"I don't understand." I twirled the stirrer in the glass. "Last time you said we both made mistakes. And now, after I got punished for lying, you're saying our issues are his fault?"

"Aliyah, your brother has to learn forgiveness sometime." She shook her head. "Grudges break the person who holds them forever."

"I don't think that'll happen." I shook my head. "Not for a while yet."

"It'll take time, but keep trying." She gazed out the window behind me.

"Do you want to stop talking about your Noah, then? For now, I mean."

"I think I can manage for a while longer. Was there something specific you wanted to know, Aliyah?"

"My brother and yours don't seem much alike. Were you surprised? That I turned out more like him than Noah did?"

"He came late to his abilities, which saved him a good deal of turmoil when he was your age. I wasn't expecting any similarity between the two Noahs, but they are alike in one way. The first Noah Morgenstern had a long and passionate correspondence with a fellow from overseas he met at Hawthorn Academy during an exchange program."

"He was gay?"

"You can read them if you'd like, but yes, they're love letters." My grandmother took a shoebox off the table and opened it briefly to reveal a row of envelopes, then replaced the lid and handed it to me. "Share them with your brother if he asks. He's proud of who he is, but..."

I nodded, studying my grandmother's face. Her eyes were shinier than usual, though not bright. Instead, they reminded me of deep water under moonlight. I imagined the extra reflection in them was hiding grief not given voice for far too long.

"I'll have a look at them eventually." I glanced at the clock on the wall behind her. "My friends are waiting, Bubbe. Sorry, but I gotta go."

"One thing before you leave." My grandmother picked up the smallest box and plucked something from it before closing it again. The item fit so completely in her hand I couldn't see what it was at first. Then she opened her hand, letting part of it drop.

The object dangled, gleaming gold, red, and orange with a hint of blue at the center. She ran the chain through her hand, pulling up the slack until the pendant rested on her palm, then showed it to me. I read the Hebrew inscription twined between the gemstone accents.

"*Shema Yisrael*. Was this his bar mitzvah pendant?" I glanced up at her.

"Yes, it was. And I'd like you to have it," she said, her voice hushed as if she spoke at a graveside.

"Bubbe I couldn't possibly take that from you. It should be Noah's since he's the namesake."

"It's a gift, one I've wanted to pass on for years now. I hope as you explore your great-uncle's past through these letters and photographs, you will understand why it belongs with you and not your brother."

All at once, it made sense. This was a matter of the heart, important to Bubbe, and by extension, important to me because I loved her. If I could honor her this way, I would. I was the one who'd insisted on learning about Great-Uncle Noah. Instead of nodding and turning to leave, I reached out and ran a finger over the pendant.

"It's beautiful." I lifted my gaze, looking my grandmother in the eye. "Thank you. I'll wear it today."

She nodded, swallowing. She'd been on the verge of tears. It reminded me of last year when I tried empathizing with my room-mate Grace, who'd lost her parents, imagining how I'd feel if Noah had died. All this time, my grandmother had carried a similar burden, secret from her grandchildren—heavy stuff to ponder on a birthday.

I turned and let her clasp the pendant around my neck. It hung just below the top of my shirt. Before turning around again, I pulled it out from under the fabric.

We hugged briefly but tightly. The moment brightened.

"Thank you, Bubbe." I pulled back enough to look her in the eye. "I love you."

"Happy birthday, Aliyah. I love you, too."

The whisper of shuffling papers and closing albums followed me out of the kitchen and down the hall toward the veterinary office's exit. Soon I'd be out in the bright light of day, in the company of friends and celebrating. I'd appreciate it all the more after the somber start to my day.

CHAPTER TWO

"You're not going to tell us to beware the Ides of June this year, Aliyah?" Izzy raised an eyebrow, then rolled the Skee ball up the lane to score five hundred points. "It's practically a Salem Willows tradition."

"No. After last year, my birthday's nothing to worry about." I chuckled.

"There was a problem last year?" Grace blinked. " I wasn't around, but it couldn't have been that bad, right?"

"Aside from a certain dragonet getting tangled in her hair and Aliyah fleeing the premises after flipping the bird at Noah, everything was great." Dylan smiled, eyes twinkling.

"You didn't tell me she got stuck in your hair." Grace shook her head, reaching down to pat her moon hare's back. "That's a bond right there. Lune practically burrowed into mine the night we met, but nobody saw. Where *is* Ember, anyway?"

"Sleeping in. Bubbe says it's because she's having a growth spurt. And the day we met was pretty embarrassing." I rolled my eyes. "Thanks for sharing, Dylan, even if you left out the part where you almost had to kick me out of here."

"Hey, it's practically my job," he stated. "Someone's got to fill in for

Noah. And Gale's slothful, too. Catching zees like they're endangered or something."

"Making sure we've got plenty of tokens isn't your job anymore, so I guess you've got to do something while you're here." I shrugged.

"How's the job at Walgreens?" Cadence changed the subject. She'd been doing that an awful lot since the end of the school year.

"Boring, but less trouble and way more air-conditioning than I ever had working here." Dylan grinned. "At least campus is climate-controlled."

"You'll appreciate that by the end of July." Cadence nodded at Grace. "It's nice out now, but later on, it can be downright brutal. Figured I'd warn you since you haven't experienced Salem summers. I imagine it gets hotter here than Québec."

"Oh, yeah. I checked the almanacs." Grace fanned herself with a flier advertising open mic night on Sundays at the Witch's Brew. "I could have gone back and worked for my aunt, but my bank account said I couldn't turn down Mr. Ambersmith's job offer. And I get to explore more of the town."

The corners of Dylan's mouth turned down briefly, but the moment he caught me looking, he wiped that look right off his face. I raised an eyebrow, but he turned.

What's he hiding?

"When do you start?" Izzy aimed another Skee ball and threw, missing the five hundred score but managing a hundred and fifty points this time.

"Monday." Grace shrugged with one shoulder. "I'll work eight hour days, but I don't care. It's something I love."

"I think it's awesome, creating works of art people can wear." Cadence clapped her hands. "Will you design your own stuff too? Your costume at Halloween was incredible, and Aliyah tells me your Valentine's dance dress rocked harder than Night Creatures."

"Maybe. I can sketch, draft, and craft whatever patterns I want after hours. They'll even let me use their equipment if I bring my own materials."

"Hey. Why isn't anyone else playing?" Izzy turned, putting her hands on her hips. I noticed she was all out of Skee balls. "I'd like some competition. Why isn't Noah here? He was always good for a couple of rounds."

"He's still not talking to me. And I can't blame him." I sighed and shook my head. "My brother can't abide lying."

"Seriously." Cadence glanced at the open doors. "He's always been a stickler about that. Used to get in the middle of our games in grade school. He'd go nuts if we bent a rule."

"I'll give it a shot." Grace cracked her knuckles. "It can't be harder than Bishop's Row."

As Grace and Izzy set up their Skee Ball games, I turned toward the door to get a breath of fresh air. The light caught my *Shema Yisrael* pendant, flashing a multitude of colors from the gemstones practically in Cadence's face. She squealed, her typical reaction to shiny things.

"Omigod, Aliyah! I can't believe it! Why didn't you show me this? It's gorgeous!"

"Guess I forgot." I winced. "Sorry."

Dylan gave me a look that could have wilted daisies. I'd known Cadence my entire life and she could barely read me, but Dylan, who I'd only known for a year, picked up on my nonverbal cues as adeptly as Izzy. He knew there was no way I'd have forgotten what could only have been a birthday gift.

"It's awesome!" Cadence smiled. "Was it a birthday present? Did it come from your parents?"

"Bubbe, actually. It's a hand-me-down, sort of."

"Wow. Can I take a closer look?"

"Sure, knock yourself out." I leaned against a support beam in the arcade, moving my hair aside so Cadence could examine my pendant.

"It's a hand-me-down, you said? Because it matches your fire magic, like, totally. I can't imagine Bubbe owning something that wasn't all solar."

"Her brother did fire magic, but he passed during the Reveal."

Are you sure nobody suspected he was an extramagus? He was thirteen at his Bar Mitzvah. How could he have had this?

I cleared my throat, which my friends misinterpreted.

"Oh. I didn't know, sorry." Cadence took a step back.

"It's okay. I didn't know about him either until just before school ended." My face felt warmer than the day's temperatures merited.

"What was his name?" Dylan tilted his head.

"Noah." I sighed. "Dad named my brother after him."

"Wow." Cadence shook her head. "I always wonder about my extended family, but my parents never talk about them."

"Are they all, you know, under the sea?" Dylan looked at his shoes, probably trying to think of some less awkward way to phrase the question. Or maybe he couldn't help but make the too-obvious jest and didn't want to come across as mean-spirited.

"I guess." Cadence shrugged. "Anyway, are you ever going to go back to the UK? London, right?"

My eyes widened as I realized Cadence was pulling a Grace. That meant she wasn't cool answering questions about herself, a fairly recent development for my mer-friend. I'd realized last year the best way to avoid giving details about yourself was asking for other people's, and here Cadence was, doing it.

Perhaps she'd learned it working on the school paper at Gallows Hill, or maybe she was hiding something. I'd met her parents, and they were pretty normal for extrahumans. If I didn't know they could grow fins and gills in the ocean, I'd have thought they were shifters or Fae.

"I'm not sure." Dylan shrugged. "Flights are expensive. I can't afford tickets and tuition, even if I work three jobs all summer. Anyway, how's Gallows Hill? Will you ever bring friends from there around?"

"Oh, most of them are nocturnal and don't like being out at this time of day." Cadence looked at just about everything in the arcade except Dylan's face. "Anyway, you'll meet them eventually. Or ask Brianna. You two work together."

Cadence's smile was as brittle as a sea glass orb. Neither friend was comfortable with the other's questions. Pushing them to hash it out in public would have been a jerk move, so I didn't. Eventually, they'd discuss whatever was eating them.

"Anyway, let's go see who's winning Skee Ball." The laugh I attempted sounded more like a nervous titter. "My money's on Grace."

12

"Oh no, you didn't." Cadence narrowed her eyes, snorting. "You'll catch it if Izzy heard that."

"I'd rather piss off Izzy than Grace, honestly." Dylan winced.

"Come on, guys." I beckoned them toward the Skee Ball lanes, where we spent the rest of the morning watching our friends compete.

After getting home from the Willows, I felt exhausted. Grace and Izzy had gone overboard, competing so intensely that I walked slightly apart from the group on the way home. It was easy to make excuses and leave because my parents and I had dinner plans, just not as early as I let my friends believe.

I couldn't force my friends to get along, but that hadn't been a problem last year. What had changed? I wracked my brain, trying to think of an answer. That was why when I opened the door at the top of the stairs, I almost hit Noah in the face with it.

"Sorry!" I stepped back, blinking.

"Whatever." Noah sailed past me, his elbow colliding with my shoulder. It had to be intentional since he was the same height as me.

"No, I mean it. I'm sorry. About everything." My voice cracked. "Wait, Noah."

Noah said nothing. His footsteps echoed in the stairwell, hollow like the pit of my stomach. All he did last year was run away from me, but somehow, this was worse. We were in our own home, not a campus half-full of bullies hell-bent on dividing us. Now instead of running, he just power-walked like I wasn't important to him anymore.

It was all I could do to keep from sobbing as I shut the door behind me and locked it. Even the familiar weight of Ember landing on my shoulder to greet me didn't offer much comfort.

"Peep?" My dragonet craned her neck until she could look me in the eye.

"I don't know, girl." I sighed and shook my head. "Sorry I didn't bring you out, but you were fast asleep, and I didn't want to wake you."

Ember didn't peep at this, only rubbed her cheek against mine. During the school year, she was always up before me, but lately, my familiar had been sleeping in. I thought it'd be no big deal.

I missed having my little friend around, and apparently, Dylan did too. I stopped in the kitchen, for once not because I was hungry. Out with my friends, it felt too people-y, but being home alone wasn't much better.

"Dad?" I raised my voice, calling through the house. "Mom?"

The door to Mom's home office opened just as I walked past it. That startled me, so I jumped backward, bumping into the counter and knocking over a stool. And here I'd thought I'd outgrown the clumsiness that had plagued me last summer.

"Aliyah. I'm glad you're here. Something came up that I wanted to mention to you." Mom stepped out into the kitchen, closing the door behind her. This was usual because sometimes the stuff she looked at on her computer was confidential.

Mom worked in the Magical Academics Department for the entire state of Massachusetts. She helped with standards and common practice in extrahuman education for both public and private schools, but she also coordinated transfers and special education accommodations for extrahuman students.

"Oh, really?" I blinked. "Me?"

"It seems you'll have a transfer student in your year at Hawthorn come September."

"I guess we have room for one, all things considered." I shrugged, glancing away. The last thing I wanted to do was have another in-depth chat about my dating life.

"Yes. The one fellow who got held back." Mom refrained from uttering his name out loud. That was nice of her, but I'm a big girl and should be able to handle hearing the name of my toxic ex-boyfriend.

"You mean Alex Onassis." I raised an eyebrow, refusing to give him the Lord Voldemort treatment in my own home.

"Yes, the one who scored so spectacularly low on his final exam, who went from a B minus to failing in sixty minutes."

"And people wonder where I get my capacity for sass from." I smiled.

"Well, you know what they say about fire magi." My mother chuckled.

"Our burns are sick?"

We ended up in a knock-down drag-out laugh-fest. Minutes later, we leaned on the counter, gasping for air and holding our sides. It felt like both of us needed a good laugh, or really, all three of us. Ember was in the same state on the countertop, curled around the fruit basket for support.

I opened the fridge, produced a pitcher of lemonade, and poured us two glasses. I even splashed some into a small bowl for Ember, who lapped it up, then smacked her lips and stuck her tongue out like a toddler eating a Sour Patch kid. After that, I gave her water in another dish and we drank together, eventually recovering from the laugh-in.

"So, tell me about this new student." I poured more lemonade. "Why the transfer?"

"He bonded with a familiar during his last week at his old school. Unexpectedly, but that happens sometimes. His family reached out and asked if it was possible for him to attend Hawthorn."

"Oh?" I tried to hide the intensity of my curiosity. I had a million questions about the mysterious new student but wouldn't be able to ask them all. "Why did they call you?"

"I went to middle school with his mother."

"So he's from Providence?" I blinked. "Was he at Trout?" Trout Academy was a prep school for magi and changelings down in Rhode Island.

"No." Mom took a deep breath. "The Academy."

"The what now?" I almost dropped my glass, lemonade and all. The Academy was practically juvie, despite its pricey tuition and fancy branding as a place for young extrahumans to learn self-discipline.

"You heard me. Since you're both on disciplinary probation next

15

year, I'm sure you'll run into him more than you might expect. There are study requirements you'll have in common."

"I thought Familiar Bonding was just for first-years."

"He'll need that since he's new to familiars. Second-years on probation have a mandatory study hall, one they spend with the previous year's top student as a mentor."

"Oh? The top student?" I shake my head. "Hal's in the infirmary half the time, so he's got no time to mentor anyone."

"The top student last year wasn't Hal Hawkins. It was Logan Pierce."

"What?" I blinked. "Wow. I'm proud of him, but I had no idea."

"That's the other reason I wanted to talk to you. I was just about to call the Pierces, speak with Logan, and inform him about the extra responsibility next year. But from what you and Bubbe have told me, his home life is complex."

"You could say that." I wasn't sure how much off-record information Mom had about Logan's dysfunctional family. Between my friendship with him and Noah's with his older sister Elanor, Bubbe knew just about everything.

"Maybe you could join the call with me. It might help for Logan to see a familiar face. We're dropping an unexpected change on him, after all."

"I think you're right, Mom," I said, nodding. She knew about Logan's accommodations at school. He wasn't a typical learner and had unconventional strategies to deal with it. "Sure. It'll be nice to see him, even if it's only on a screen."

Logan Pierce had been one of my best friends at school last year. We got so close, people made bets on when we'd date. We decided to stay platonic like I am with Izzy or Cadence, a relief for both of us.

Mom went into her office. I let her have privacy for the information she handled. It wasn't easy, especially not after what she did last summer.

Mom had secretly gone down to Providence, testifying on official record against her own brother without telling any of us, not even Dad. We didn't find out until Passover, when she brought the news clipping as her symbol of liberation. She'd freed herself from the toxic half of her family finally and totally with that act.

Could she be hiding something personal in her office among work stuff that everyone steered clear of for legal reasons? Yes. Would she? Again, yes. It wasn't easy to deal with the idea that your mother had survived childhood by using judicious dishonesty, especially not while I was still trying to figure out who I wanted to be.

I was lucky at the same time because each person in my immediate family gave me different examples. Some of my other friends had it worse, and sharing our problems gave us all more perspective.

Mom opened the door again, letting me into her office. She had her video conferencing computer pointed at the bookcase behind her, which was mostly for show. She did sometimes use a few of those books but kept it tidy. This would be an asset when calling the Pierces.

Logan's parents were all about how things looked, though not in a professional or stodgy sort of way. They were a showbiz family, so fixated and focused on being flashy that all of Logan's academic and other achievements didn't matter to them. They disparaged his artwork and his grades, saying they'd never look good on stage.

Mom pulled up a chair for me to sit beside her in the camera's range. We waited through the chimes as the conference call software made its connection. It was early in the morning in Las Vegas, which was where Logan's family lived, but the call was part of a calendar agenda displayed on Mom's screen, with invitations given and accepted. Apparently, they'd agreed to it.

When someone answered, the camera turned on so we could see the other end of the call. I hadn't formally met Logan's parents, just seen them in passing at Parents' Night last fall. They'd largely ignored Logan, lavishing most of their attention on his sister Elanor. But today, the entire family hadn't shown up. Only one of them answered the call.

"Good morning Mrs. Pierce." Mom's tone was cool and professional, designed to keep things calm.

"What's this about then?" Mrs. Pierce stretched, stifling a yawn.

"You can't possibly want to talk to Logan." She gave me a side-eye Izzy would have envied.

"As a matter of fact, I do." My mother gave a slight nod. "Headmaster Hawkins asked me to inform him about a special assignment starting this fall."

"Then why isn't the headmaster calling?" She closed her eyes. "Unless this isn't an assignment. He screwed up again. I knew he couldn't handle things at Hawthorn, not with his disability."

I sat blinking, my mouth wide open. Logan told me about how his parents made him feel lesser and not good enough. I thought it was only about performance art, which Logan only did under duress. But there she was, dragging his name through the dirt, and he wasn't even there to defend himself.

Mom's face stayed neutral, almost stony. Clearly, she'd heard this sort of thing before from parents. The fact that it was all too common from her perspective turned my stomach.

"Mrs. Pierce, your son had the highest grade point average in his year. That's why he's being asked to mentor a transfer student this fall."

"That's impossible." She clicked her tongue against the top of her mouth. "Not that he couldn't make grades with enough outside help." She glanced at me. "But he's been to your house, so you know what I'm saying. Logan can't do this. He's not normal. Can't even look people in the eye when they talk to him. My son's no mentor."

"He helped plenty of us last year, you know." I couldn't keep my mouth shut any longer. "Logan's got some of the best study tips we've ever heard. I even use them."

"Yes. Aliyah, right?" She raised an eyebrow. "I hear *you're* on probation."

"Not academically." I grinned. "In large part, thanks to my good friend Logan."

"Is that Aliyah?" Logan's voice was muffled, coming from the other side of a closed door behind Mrs. Pierce. "Can I talk to her?"

"Part of the purpose of this call is to discuss this with Logan. I'd appreciate his presence." My mother nodded.

"I'm not sure I'll permit him to do this."

"Mrs. Pierce, your son will be seventeen this summer."

"Well, yes, but that doesn't mean he's an adult."

"In the Massachusetts Magical Academics Department, it does. He can make certain decisions about his schooling the year before he's a legal adult. Your permission is not required."

"Well, I never." She shook her head. "He's still sixteen for another two months, and this is Nevada. Nothing here says I have to let him talk to you."

"That's true." My mother nodded. "I'll simply send him a certified letter instead. You can expect that next week. Or you can allow us to have this chat, and you won't be bothered in the future."

"I think you ought to send the letter, Mrs. Morgenstern." She stifled a yawn again, but this time it looked different, as though she'd faked one of them. I couldn't figure out which. "The difference between our time zones is inconvenient. My son shouldn't make decisions without a proper night's sleep. He had a very late night, rehearsing for our new show. I'm sure you understand."

"Perfectly." My mother's smile could have cut diamonds. "I'll send the letter then. Remember, it requires his matching signature, which I have on file."

"I know what certified mail is." She waved as if she sat on a parade float instead of a tufted chair. "Good day."

The screen went blank. I didn't even get a chance to talk to my friend. It occurred to me I could have begged a few moments on account of my birthday, but it was too late for that. I needed to think more quickly in the future.

"Mom, are the other parents always like this?" I shook my head. "How do you deal with it?"

"I have a unique blend of perspective and experience when it comes to these issues." She shut down the software. "It's unfortunate, but we always do what's best for the student. At least the laws in our state allow for that."

"Is this why you chose Hawthorn? For the academic program?"

"To help people like me, yes." She looked up at me, eyes rimmed with the red of unshed tears—the angry kind. "I got my wish. To be the person I needed at that age."

"They're lucky to have you, Mom." I stood up. I would have offered her a hug, but sometimes when Mom got like this, she needed the distraction of work. "Can I get you anything? More lemonade?"

"No, I've got to print that letter and get it to the post office as soon as possible." Mom made a few clicks with her mouse, doing exactly that. "But when I get back, how about we go get a coffee? Something fancy over at the Witch's Brew. It's your birthday, after all."

"Sounds great, Mom."

I got out of her way, and less than twenty minutes later, we sat in the coffee house, having a nice afternoon together. I wished Logan the same, no matter how unlikely he was to get it in the near future.

CHAPTER THREE

It was hotter inside than outside, typical for August. The house at 10 1/2 Hawthorne Street didn't have central air, a fact my father lamented in the kitchen that morning. Bubbe's office did, but we didn't have a compressor for the top two floors. There was nothing we could do about it in the immediate future, either. Not unless one of us befriended an ice magus.

"I'm going out!" I hollered to my parents as I grabbed my knapsack off the floor near the front door.

"Where?" Mom's voice from the office.

"Dunno, someplace cool." I had the front door open but didn't want to leave until getting the go-ahead.

"Have fun!"

With that permission, I headed out the door and down the front stairs, not bothering to lock up behind me as I jogged down the driveway. At the end, I stopped, already wiping sweat off my brow.

"Peep?" Ember circled my head, waiting for me to pick up the pace.

"It's hot out here for me." I chuckled. "Must be perfect for you, though."

My dragonet's element was fire. She breathed it, so a day with high temperatures wouldn't bug her. She didn't land on my shoulder, probably because it was too slippery from the humidity and the insta-sweat that went along with it on dog days like this. I'd taken a shower ten minutes earlier, too.

"Peep!" Ember pointed her nose directly at Izzy's house, which was in front of mine.

"Yeah, that was the plan." I turned the corner and headed up to the door, ringing the bell at the apartment, not the divination parlor. Isabella Mendez, my best friend, was also from a family that lived and worked in the same building, except their spaces were side by side instead of stacked, and her family were clairvoyant psychics instead of magi.

The door opened, revealing my friend. She was shorter than me, like most girls I know, and practically everything about her appearance was opposite. Her hair and skin were dark while mine were fair, and she favored buns and braids on the sides of her head instead of up top or in back. We both wore messy buns that day because nobody needed hair sticking to sweaty faces.

"Oh, no way." Izzy crossed her arms over her chest and shook her head. "I'm not going to the Willows. The Tanks are down there."

"So what?" I shook the bag of leftover Arcade tokens. The Tanks were the local shifter gang and Izzy was not a fan, a point of contention between her and Cadence. "It's boiling, and we want the beach."

"Can't we go to Hawthorn and swim in the baths?" She sighed. "Messing doesn't have anything like a pool. And besides, they're closed all summer."

" Last time I tried to stop by, the headmaster said I can't come in. Probation sucks." I shrugged. "I can only go on campus if he approves it and I've got an escort."

"Oh. Sorry." Izzy stared at her flip-flop-clad feet. "I still can't believe it's this big a deal after all this time."

"Well, lying about being an extramagus is a pretty colossal mistake to make at my school."

"Magi." Izzy looked back up, shaking her head and clucking her tongue. "So uptight. It's no big deal at Messing if someone's psychic and a vampire or whatever. I can't understand why it's even a thing."

"Because psychics don't end up with a case of mixed nuts from having extra...extrahumanness, I guess." I shrugged. "But we're boiling out here. Literally." I indicated the sweat beading on my forehead.

"Okay, I get it. Let's go."

"But where?"

"How about tracking down our literal breath of fresh air?" Izzy waggled her eyebrows, then stuck her tongue out like we were still seven.

She meant Dylan, of course. If it were Cadence making that face and suggestion, I'd get angry at her for being crass about a guy who's in a relationship. But Izzy was probably just making a dad joke.

"I think he's working, anyway." I shrugged the jest off. "That boy's middle name should be workaholic."

"So, let's go to Walgreens and get a soda or something." Izzy beckoned. "It's air-conditioned."

We headed to the sidewalk, turning toward Derby Street and the drugstore. Besides Dylan, Brianna worked there. She was a goblin changeling who went to Gallows Hill with Cadence.

Salem was one of those towns where you could do everything or nothing almost any day of the year. It was magical, literally and figuratively, but also mundane, especially in summer. Nobody thought much about witches riding on brooms, jack-o'-lanterns, or tumbling particolored leaves during the dog days of August. Not even the signs declaring this the witch city could fight thermometers screaming one hundred degrees Fahrenheit.

The blacktop parking lot and glass veneer of Walgreens focused the heat. I imagined this was how a bug felt under a magnifying glass in the sun, wielded by some sociopathic little tyke. My mind dreamed up a kindergarten-aged version of Alex Onassis.

"Ugh." I shook my head and wrinkled my nose, wishing I hadn't thought of him. Maybe Izzy was right to stay unentangled romantically. Breaking up had side effects, apparently.

"Yeah, I know." Izzy pointed at the door. "If you can't take the heat, get into the Walgreens."

"Peep!"

Ember soared toward the door, dipping and weaving through the air in front of it. There was nothing quite like worrying about my familiar crashing headlong into a plate-glass window to motivate me, so I opened the door and let her fly through, following close behind.

The welcome blast of cold air blew my hair away from my forehead. When walking into a warm building after being outside in frigid temperatures, people exhale. But opposite conditions were opposite, so I breathed in as much of the artificial coolness as possible. Then I tripped over my own feet and landed flat on my face on the doormat.

"Oh, no!" Hurried footsteps chased the exclamation.

The set of hands helping me up was also nice and cold, but they didn't belong to Dylan Khan. My rescuer was Brianna Collins, and it was awfully nice of her. Nobody was obliged to pick a klutz up off the floor, so I appreciated it.

"Thanks, Brianna." My face was red and flushed, but I still hoped everyone in the store thought it was just because of the ungodly heat outside. "Flip-flops conspired against me just then. Sorry."

"Aliyah, seriously?" Brianna shook her head. Was her face a bit ruddy, too? "No need to apologize. I'm sorry."

"Sorry." I brushed off my hands, besmirched by the welcome mat. Or maybe the unwelcome mat, all things considered.

"Jeez, this is getting old, and you've only been doing it all summer." Izzy pulled a bottle of Sprite out of a cooler nearby, then handed it to me. "You just apologized after being told you don't need to apologize. Somebody's Canadian." Izzy's forehead wrinkled as she patted her satchel of tarot cards. "Like, for real. Someone in here."

"Did somebody call for aid from the Great North?" A grinning face peeked out from behind a Hallmark display. "Hi!"

Grace Dubois waved, a card in her hand. She gulped before lowering it, and I saw a pastel floral illustration on the cover. A streak of gray rounding the corner on the floor distracted me. Lune was here too, and clearly happy to see Ember. The dragonet landed, and they hopped around on the floor together.

"So, the Ambersmiths let you go out today?"

"Yeah, it's a supply run." Grace sauntered from behind the shelf, pushing a collapsible shopping cart piled high with snacks. "Everyone down at the shop is hungry, thirsty, and tired, so they sent me out."

"I've barely seen you since my birthday back in June. They must be working you hard. We missed you." The silence that followed that statement was less than comfortable, but I wasn't sure why.

"Yeah, I get it." She chuckled, glancing over her shoulder. Her knuckles whitened around her grip on the cart's handle. "Anyway, I should check out and get going."

"I'll help." Izzy stepped up, grabbing an arm full of assorted sodas from the cooler and walking them up to the counter. An apologetic wince twisted her expression. "Gives us time to chat."

"Thanks. I hadn't gotten the drinks yet." Grace nodded once. "I appreciate it."

"Right. It's almost like I'm a mind reader or something." Izzy chuckled. And just like that, the tension between my friends broke.

Everybody laughed. Izzy had that effect on people, getting them to laugh with her instead of at her. And if there was one thing Grace loved in this world—besides Lune—it was a good laugh.

As Brianna rang up Grace's purchases and they did the whole transaction, we chattered away about the heat. I couldn't believe we only talked about the stupid weather. Something still felt wrong, like my friends were avoiding some subject. I figured it couldn't hurt to mention someone we all had in common.

"So, how's Dylan?"

Everybody shut up. I just stood there blinking like an idiot, because I would never have guessed he was the forbidden topic.

Your circus, your monkeys.

"Was he fired or something?" Could Dylan Khan, the hardest-working teenager I knew next to Grace, have lost his job? It was the only reason I could think of for all the awkwardness.

"No, nothing like that." Brianna let out a nervous laugh. "Maybe he's working at Hawthorn."

"I was wondering about campus, actually." I picked up a pack of gum and twirled it in my hands, trying to find something to help me feel less awkward. "Izzy mentioned having a swim in the baths to cool off, but I can't go because of probation. Do you think the headmaster would give me permission? And would you be our escort?"

Brianna blinked because she knew almost nothing about Hawthorn's policies, but Grace shook her head.

"I've no idea. I haven't been to campus all summer."

"Oh. Okay." I tried to keep my expression neutral. Grace had a bad habit of bottling things up, to the point where last year she'd had a mental health crisis. Her counselor was Headmaster Hawkins, so I worried but didn't say anything about it in front of the others.

"I'm still having meetings about school stuff." Grace elbowed my arm. "But at the shop after hours, not on campus. Sorry, I can't help you."

"Well, what about Lee being your escort? He'd do it for Izzy."

I nearly jumped out of my skin because I didn't expect to hear a voice right behind me. But at least it was familiar, so I settled down quickly.

"For crying out loud, Cadence." Izzy snorted. "I don't want to date anyone."

"I'm not saying you do. But he's on campus." Cadence shrugged, her red-orange hair cascading over one shoulder. "Sorry about listening in, but I love swimming, and Lee's cool. We haven't been out since Aliyah's birthday."

"I guess you have a point." Izzy sighed so much she practically deflated. "Sorry I haven't been around."

"Me too." Grace shrugged.

"Yeah, sorry." I grinned, predicting the response.

"Aliyah, stop apologizing!" Izzy stomped her foot. Something had her more on edge than a spinning coin.

There's only one thing to do about that.

"What's your problem today, Iz?" I leaned against the counter.

"Peep?" Ember perched on my head, which probably made me look ridiculous at a serious moment.

"Fine. I'm pissed off. Yeah, I'm being a bitch. Said I was sorry already."

"So talk about it." Grace put a bag of snacks into the cart, sighing. "I mean, you can't ignore all your problems. It's not healthy."

"This isn't the place." Izzy shook her head. "But yeah, I need to talk about next year. Probably we all should. As many of us as possible."

"Even me?" Brianna's eyes widened.

"Yeah, I guess." Izzy flipped a tarot card on the counter between them, then swept it away before I saw anything besides the Cups suit.

"I work until six." She glanced at the register. "If that's too late, I understand."

"It's not. That's good for dinner at Engine House." I pointed diagonally across the street at my favorite pizza place. "Let's meet there later. It's air-conditioned."

"I have to go back to work, but I'll see you later. And I'm bringing Dylan." Grace didn't smile, but she waved and headed out, pushing the cart.

CHAPTER FOUR

Cadence, Izzy, and I headed down Derby Street, making our way toward Winter Island Park. We loved the Willows, but Winter Island had the best swimming area within walking distance.

Tourists blanketed the sand, towel-covered spaces headed up with umbrellas and beach chairs. That never bothered us. As locals, we weren't shy about using our town's resources. Ember got excited as soon as she saw the ocean. She loved swimming.

We dropped our towels and the clothes we wore over our swimsuits, then headed for the water to jump right in. It was cold, briny, and exactly what we needed on a day where the temperature flirted with one hundred degrees even without the heat index. Cadence swam circles around us because she's a mermaid, which meant she'd turned her legs into a finned and scaled tail.

She splashed water in my face and I laughed. From behind us, I heard a chorus of delighted squeals and gasps. On the beach stood a gaggle of kids about middle-school age. The redhead pointed and the jet-haired girl beside her jumped up and down. The olive-complected boy with them tilted his head, blinking for all the world like a cat who'd just woken up from a nap. The fourth, a pallid younger boy, dropped the book he held. He shrugged at something the other boy said, then retrieved the tome, shaking sand off its pages.

I got the impression the kids were extrahumans. Probably shifters, though the boy with the book could have been a magus or a psychic. Cadence waved, smiling at them and flipping her tail out of the water. Whenever kids noticed her, she always put on a good show. Before the Reveal, she wouldn't have been allowed to swim in public, so I never got on her case for showing off mermaid-style.

"We're just trying to swim. Why do we have to show off for tourists all the time?" Izzy rolled her eyes. "Do they think this is Tahiti?"

"Come on, Izzy, they're kids. Salem's a magical place." Cadence grinned. "If you'd never seen the tail before, you'd react the same way."

"She definitely did the first time she saw it," I said, splashing at my friends.

"Yeah, okay. You got me there." Izzy rolled over on her back, floating. She gazed up at the brassy blue sky.

The cold water lifted our spirits, and so did Ember. Her swimming antics were hilarious. At times she swam like a duck, wings folded over her back, her peeping reminding me of baby mallards at the end of spring. Sometimes she dived, waving her serpentine tail in the air. At one point she came up with a mouthful of seaweed, spitting and spluttering because that was not part of a fire dragonet's balanced diet.

I laughed so hard I got a cramp and had to leave the water. As a mermaid, Cadence didn't have that problem. Izzy was in a solemn mood, limiting her laughter to chuckles.

I was wringing my hair out at the line the water made with the sand when the two girls who'd been watching Cadence ran up to me.

"Ask her, Hope," the brunette whispered.

"You ask her, Saya." Hope shrugged.

"I can't." Saya blinked.

"Hi, girls." I gave them my friendliest smile. "What can I do for you?"

"I don't know." The brunette's shoulders shook. She mumbled something else.

"My friend just wanted to know if that's really a dragonet," Hope asked, smiling.

"She sure is. Her name's Ember, do you want to meet her?" My familiar loved people, especially kids.

The brunette only nodded. I whistled, and Ember took off from the surface of the water. She landed on the sand between the girls and me and hopped toward them.

"Peep?" She swayed her head up and down, a serpentine nod.

"Wow." Hope held her hand down. She knew something about magical creatures, then. Saya copied her. I got the impression they'd known each other for years.

Ember hopped up and down, capering and carrying on playfully.

"Cool." The catlike boy sauntered over, grinning from ear to ear. "That's not something we see every day in Newport."

"You're sure we won't get in trouble, Cosmo?" Saya glanced over her shoulder.

"Relax. Your bro's cool. Um, not literally." The boy tried to put his hands in his pockets, but his swim trunks didn't have any. He blushed.

"You guys." The smaller boy tilted his head as though listening to someone who wasn't there. It reminded me of Izzy's grandfather, who was a medium. "Bob says we gotta go. Sandwiches are almost gone."

"Fewmets." Cosmo glanced over his shoulder. "Race ya!"

Both the boys ran back up the beach toward an umbrella about halfway up.

"Thanks, Miss." The little brunette gave me an actual curtsy. "Ember's adorable."

"You're welcome." I wasn't sure how to curtsy, so I bowed instead.

"Bye, Ember!" Hope waved, then grabbed Saya's hand and ran after the boys.

"Hey, Aliyah!" someone called. I turned to see who it was. Waving from under an umbrella was my friend from school, Faith Fairbanks.

We hadn't always been friendly. Last fall, we got into plenty of arguments, but we were past that by winter break last year. That was a good thing since we'd leaned on each other pretty heavily last spring. I headed over to say hello.

She sat with her boyfriend, Hal Hawkins. He looked better than the last time I'd seen him, but that was not saying much. He had a debilitating chronic illness with no cure, but at least he felt well enough to be at the beach that day.

"How are you guys? I've barely seen you all summer."

"Not too bad," Hal said, "The doctors down in Boston have helped a bit. I'll probably go into town every other weekend after school starts to keep up with the treatments."

"So, your mom hasn't been giving you any trouble?" I raised an eyebrow. Hal's mother used to be in charge of his health care, but that had changed recently in family court.

"Nothing that affected my treatment." He grinned. "More of a puzzle. But I'm dealing with it."

"You're going too easy on her." Faith patted Seth, the small critter in her lap. He was a sha, a canine species with undeath magic, affiliated with magi since ancient Egypt. "She screamed at us this morning. Nin hasn't come out of my beach tote all afternoon."

The hibiscus-printed bag leaning against the umbrella pole quivered slightly. Ember peeped softly at it. A few little squeaks came from its open top, but Hal's familiar didn't emerge. Nin was a Pharaoh's rat, something like a cross between a mongoose and a ferret with space magic.

"Fair point." Hal gestured at an insulated bag between them. "Would you like an apple?"

Hal looked younger than the rest of us, in part because of his illness, but he acted more like an adult, probably for the same reason. And suddenly, despite the salt air and all the swimming earlier, I wasn't hungry. But the offer of food reminded me of something.

"We're going to Engine House for dinner like around six o'clock. If you guys are still in town, do you want to come?"

"That sounds great." Faith smiled, a rare expression for her even on a good day. "My train back to New York doesn't leave from Boston until ten."

"Sounds great. See you then." I waved, then headed back down the beach and toward Izzy and Cadence, who were still in the water.

I didn't know that dinner would be more awkward than awesome.

I got to Engine House first, so I went straight to the back toward the largest table. This one had a booth along the back wall with tables and then chairs on the other side. We'd need as many seats as possible. Instead of perching, Ember swooped through the air, making figure eights. Other patrons at the restaurant watched the show she put on.

"You must be excited, huh?" I smiled at my dragonet.

"Peep!"

"It's been a while since you've seen Gale, I totally get it." I didn't need to go into detail about how I missed her friend's magus, which was inappropriate. Dylan was with Grace, so only Ember knew about my feelings for him. And my brother Noah, who'd guessed it last year and hadn't mentioned the matter since.

Not that I had any idea what to do about them besides keep my mouth shut. My dating experience included a discussion with Logan where we agreed to stay platonic and a dating-by-default situation with Alex the mega-jerk.

I'd ended things with Alex by asserting myself. Izzy and Cadence had helped me realize what was wrong with that relationship. To say Alex hadn't been happy would be a massive understatement. He'd practically vowed revenge at the end of last year. My friends and I, even the ones from town, had to watch our backs.

They'd be on campus for extramurals between all three of our schools, a simultaneously exciting and scary prospect. Most of my friends from school and town got along, but Izzy and Grace hadn't stopped competing all summer. Cadence had just adopted a blasé attitude toward everything except boys.

Maybe that was the point of this dinner, part of the reason Grace recommended we sit down and talk. Hal and Faith might inject some solidarity into the group. They had been good at that last year. I'd do everything I could to help us avoid trouble once school started. My friends deserved no less.

One good thing about my seat in the back was visibility. I could see all the windows from here, and saw when Brianna approached the restaurant, tucking her Walgreens apron into the satchel over her shoulder. She pushed through the door, ducking slightly. She didn't need to since the door was tall enough, but I understood. She was self-conscious about being tall and lanky.

"Hey, Aliyah!" She scooted into the booth to sit beside me. "I know I'm early, but that's when they let me out, so here I am." Her grin seemed real, but the little laugh sounded nervous.

We'd hung out during breaks from school last year. She was not quite this awkward then, but maybe the impending extramurals had her on edge. School wasn't easy for Brianna. She'd mentioned getting flack about being a goblin changeling before.

"Hey, yourself." I smiled back. "I already ordered a pizza mountain and two pitchers of soda, but if you want something else, you can add it to the tab. My grandma just paid me for helping out in her office."

"No, I'm good, thanks." Brianna folded her hands on the table, looking down at them. "Anyway, before everyone else gets here, I was wondering—"

She didn't complete her sentence because Izzy showed up. She sat directly across from me in the chair by the window. Right away, she looked over her shoulder, jerking her thumb at the door.

"Cadence is here, but she's outside talking to some bruiser." Izzy rolled her eyes.

"Oh, that's Bar." Brianna jerked a thumb at the door, where Cadence chattered animatedly at a tall, wide, and solidly built fellow with a thick steel bar piercing his septum. "I bet you can see why they call him that."

"Yeah, I get it." I wondered where I'd seen that guy before. "He looks familiar."

"He was at the concert on Halloween with Cadence and Crow." She raised her eyebrows at me, then glanced at Izzy. Whatever she was trying to convey nonverbally fell short of my comprehension.

"Right." I nodded. "I remember now. Bar's a troll changeling and Crow's some sort of bird shifter. Cadence said they don't work at the Gallows Hill newspaper with her. "

"Exactly. Crow said he'd help this year. She talked him into it."

"Mermaid, magic voice, duh." Izzy rolled her eyes but smiled.

"What's the holdup?" I asked.

"She's trying to convince him to hang with us." Izzy shrugged. "I don't think it'll happen."

"Why?" I blinked.

"Troll changelings are hardheaded in more ways than one." Izzy rapped her knuckles on the side of her head.

"Yeah, her mermaid stuff doesn't work on them." Brianna smiled.

"Maybe it's a good thing." Izzy gestured at the remaining seats. "We won't have room with everybody else we invited."

"Normally I'd say the more the merrier, but you've got a point, Iz." I nodded.

"Cadence would rather have Crow here than Bar." Brianna repeated her mysterious eyebrow raise.

"What's this all about then?" Izzy narrowed her eyes.

"She's got a crush, but what else is new?" Brianna let out that nervous laugh again.

"Yeah, what else is new?" Izzy shrugged. "Tons, apparently, that she hasn't told me. Or her parents, probably. But enough about Cadence. What are you up to?"

"Just working, mostly." Brianna fiddled with the empty cup in front of her. "Trying not to freak out about playing Bishop's Row at extra-murals this year."

"Am I the only one who isn't bothered by any of this?" I blinked. "It'll be fun."

"You told us an influential new first-year is a magisupremacist, and you're not worried?" Izzy raised her eyebrow.

"Well, crap." I winced.

Cadence walked through the door, shaking her head as she strode briskly toward us. She took the seat on the other side of Brianna.

"What now?" Cadence asked.

"I'm a little more worried about next year than I was previously." I grimaced. "Thanks to our psychic friend."

Izzy lifted her hand, giving us all a little golf wave and a parade-float smile.

"Better nervous and prepared than confident without a clue. At least that's what my parents say." Cadence rolled her eyes. " But won't it be fun? A little danger's exciting sometimes."

"Okay." I blinked. "You know how most of us feel about that kind of thing, Cadence. Danger bad."

"Life is danger, friends. You either sink or swim." Cadence's smile had never reminded me of a shark's until that day. "Lucky for you, I'm an expert, and I've been coaching Grace. She's got a plan for this year."

"Yeah, you're a daredevil." Izzy nodded. "The two of us have vetoed all your dangerous ideas since forever. Of course you're going into next year like it's the nineties and we're in the X-games."

I waved at the door, probably more frantically than I had to.

"Look, there's Lee." I had to change the subject or Izzy and Cadence would drag on each other for another ten minutes. Thankfully, my classmate's arrival stopped that before it began.

"Hello." Lee grinned and sat beside Izzy. When she glanced at him, the corners of her mouth turned up, and her previously tense shoulders eased down a notch.

"I've got your Sprite and your Coke here." The pitchers of soda settled themselves on the tabletop because the waiter was a psychic, the telekinetic kind. "Root beer's coming with your pizza in just a few minutes. How many plates do you need?"

"Nine, I think," I answered.

"Better make that ten. I ran into Azrael on the way here." Lee added.

"Great." Izzy leaned back to drag another chair from the table behind us. "Exactly what I needed."

"I don't think he'll bug you much anymore, Iz." Cadence leaned her elbows on the table, folded her hands, and set her chin on them.

"Oh?" Izzy blinked. "What happened?"

"Rumor has it he's moved on." Cadence studied her pearl-pink fingernails.

"Rumor?" Izzy side-eyed the mermaid. "You're not even at school with him. Haven't been for months."

"You think just because I'm not on campus, it means there's no gossip to follow?" Cadence snorted. "I'm good at my job."

The bell over the door jingled as Hal walked in with Faith.

"Guys, we're here, but there's a problem." Faith approached the table, Hal straggling behind her. She jerked her thumb at the window to my right.

We all looked outside to see an unfolding scene that could have come straight out of a teen movie.

CHAPTER FIVE

Dylan and Grace stood outside the window, light from inside spilling shadows long and stark on the sidewalk and into the street next to the Engine House. The window framed them, letting us see more than we probably should have.

Grace had her arms crossed over her chest, her posture as straight and defiant as if she were facing down a monster. And maybe one lurked out there in the street that night, some awful presence between the two—a monster they couldn't agree whether to capture or slay.

Dylan stood with one hand out, shoulders shaking, head down. I knew he dared to look in her eyes because he faced me. He pleaded with her, begging for something she couldn't or wouldn't give.

I'd never seen him like this, not even on the day he and Logan had experienced the strain and drama of bonding with familiars they thought were wrong for them. Dylan Khan had accused me last year of wearing my heart on my sleeve, but he'd always seemed opposite: able to hide his feelings behind a six-foot hedge of quirkiness.

Whatever he said to Grace that night, it left her unmoved. Their discussion was a mystery to us, even after she shook her head and walked past him toward the restaurant's door. He followed her, head down, with one shaky hand reaching up to fling tears from his eyes.

Neither spoke about the scene outside, but Cadence patted the seat beside her, glancing up at Grace. And Hal and Faith moved down so Dylan could sit between them and Lee instead of across from her.

Our pizzas came out then, floating over from behind the counter to settle on the table at evenly spaced intervals. The psychic waiter used his powers to bring us our order, including the root beer. As amusing as this usually was, it didn't cheer me up, because my friends carried the burden of whatever had passed between them on the street.

Dylan's nickname at school was "the bottomless pit." His dragonet, Gale, usually snapped up any scraps he left behind, but that night, Gale stayed tucked around his neck, sleeping. Dylan barely managed one slice of pizza, leaving sauce and cheese along with the crust and a few stray slivers of mushroom on the plate. Grace wolfed down almost half a pie on her own, chasing it with so much root beer we had to order another pitcher.

When Azrael Ambersmith walked in the door, Dylan excused himself, leaving his nearly full paper plate, a half-glass of Sprite, and bewildered friends. Azrael didn't take the vacated seat, instead squeezing into the booth beside Grace. He raised an eyebrow at the crumb-filled plate in front of her, then glanced at me.

"What do I owe you?"

"Nothing." I fidgeted, wishing I could go after Dylan before he got to campus because I couldn't follow him there until school started. "Bubbe technically paid, so thank her next time you see her."

"What was that?" Izzy raised her eyebrow.

"Um, don't you know?" I wanted to keep Grace out of Izzy's hot seat. "Psychic friend?"

"Yeah." She shrugged, then for the first time in over a year, Izzy did emotional triage. "But we're here for a reason. Stuff to hash out before school starts."

"I'll check on him." Hal tried standing but fell back in his seat and rolled his eyes. "I guess not. Stupid body. They just don't make them like they used to in my family."

"Not funny." Faith shook her head. "But I get it. I'll go."

Faith nodded to me as she stood, pushing the chair in behind her. I watched Nin scuttle out of her tote to Hal's shoulders, Seth peeking out to yip goodbye as she left the restaurant.

"Let's do this already." Grace snagged another slice of pizza. "You know, the talking about the tension stuff."

"Okay, Grace." Izzy leaned on the table, hands flat against its wooden surface. "We get stuck in moments, which is a good thing in life-threatening crises. But if we can't move forward, we end up with patterns, like unwanted rivalry." She glanced at me. "And default relationships."

"She's right." Hal nodded. "I watched it happen last year. I couldn't do much to help, either."

"Okay, Iz," I said, blushing, "What do we do about it?"

"I wish I knew." Izzy shook her head. "I'm just seventeen like the rest of you, remember?"

"I have this elective I take with other changelings at Gallows Hill." Brianna leaned back against the padded seat of the booth. "It's supposed to be on maintaining glamour, but it's more like a class in emotional adulting."

"Yeah." Azrael nodded. "I'm in that too. It's self-care, like putting on mental armor."

"Sounds like some folks at our school could use that," Grace mumbled around a mouthful of pizza. "Including me."

"It sounds too personal." Izzy shook her head. "I'm not sure I'd want to be talking about my feelings for a grade. A for everybody."

"It's not like that." Brianna shook her head. "We do yoga, free-writing, and guided meditation. One time we were all tired right after team tryouts, and we took a nap in class like it was kindergarten or something."

"I didn't fall asleep." Azrael tilted his head. "But it was nice to lie down for a minute."

"I think that was the point. We got to stop that day after all the going we did." She sighed. "But anyway, I have a whole book of notes. I could get a copy for you guys. Maybe you can read it in study hall or whatever folks at Hawthorn do during free time."

"Wow, thanks, Brianna." I grinned. "I know that'd help me."

"We still need to talk. I spent most of the summer butting heads with my friends. The point of school break is blowing off steam, a detox before the next year, but it didn't happen for me." Izzy gazed at her hands on the table, letting her fingers curl for a moment. But they flattened again, tips paling.

"Look, I'll go first." I sat up, jostling Ember on my shoulder. She made a sleepy peep before opening her eyes. "This summer I've seen you guys around, but I haven't *seen* you. Our time together felt shallow."

"You've got something there." Cadence nodded. "At school I floundered, but this summer, I waded ankle-deep, like I was scared to get real with my friends."

"I've been so tired." Hal shook his head. "The trips to Boston, the treatments. They helped, but just enough to go to and from them. Even sitting on the beach sapped me. I went to bed to get enough energy to come out for pizza."

"And I can't talk." Izzy stared at the table. "Not about what really bothers me. That place; it's just bizarre. I know we're all extrahumans, the opposite of mundane. But the school stuff you guys talk about?" She shook her head. "Messing's on another planet."

"Oh, Iz, I had no idea." I reached out and put my hand over hers. "I'm sorry."

"You're not a mind reader, Aliyah." Grace dusted crumbs off her hands. "A lifesaver, yeah, because you react fast when it matters. But nobody can know what's in someone else's head, no matter how close they are."

"Hey, that's my line." Izzy gave Grace a wan smile. "I didn't expect it from you, but thanks anyway."

"It's like we were all wrong." I glanced at Cadence then Izzy. "Like we got replaced by body-snatchers all summer."

"You know what?" Azrael leaned around the pitcher so we could see his face. "I felt like that for the last two years before we started our prep schools. I couldn't be the real me. In the group, I mean."

"That was my fault." Izzy shook her head. "I'm sorry. I didn't know how bad that could feel. Like being replaced."

"How could you feel replaced?" Grace blinked.

"Every weekend, Aliyah went on about her awesome roommate, Grace." Izzy looked her in the eye. "That's how. It's not your fault, you're just being yourself. But after Messing, I feel like a friend by proxy, and all last year, you got to have that with her." Lee patted her shoulder.

"You guys are all awesome." I insisted. "None of you are replaceable, including our absent friends."

Nobody said anything after that for a while. Everyone had a bite of pizza or a sip of soda and digested things, both physically and emotionally.

After conversation resumed, the topics changed back to speculation mostly, talking over the activities we'd do once school started. I thought we were out of the woods, at least those of us still sitting at the table.

Faith and Dylan both needed to be looped in on this, and whatever argument Grace had gotten into with him, they'd need to make sure nothing festered. I wasn't sure what had happened, and I didn't find out until a week later because an entirely different can of worms opened for me on the way home.

CHAPTER SIX

"Sorry you missed Gale, girl."

"Peep."

Ember sat on my shoulder, resting her head on top of mine in a fit of what I could only imagine was ennui. I didn't blame her, though. I felt more uneasy than anything else. I wanted to spend more time with Dylan, and not just because he was my friend. He couldn't possibly be okay after whatever had happened outside Engine House. I had no idea how he'd been all summer because he barely left campus except to go to work at Walgreens.

Come to think of it, no one had really seen him outside work besides Hal and Lee. Hawthorn Academy was a big place square-footage wise, despite its few students. Maybe they hadn't spent much time with him either.

I wished I could talk to Logan about Dylan, and wondered what he'd say. As roommates, they'd had each other's backs. But Logan remained on the other side of the country.

"Aliyah, wait up!"

"I'm hearing things." I shook my head, agitating Ember, who turned on my shoulder to look behind me.

"Peep!" She sounded annoyed, not alarmed.

"Yeah, okay, I'm sorry." I kept walking. If someone had followed us, that was all for the best.

Ember let out an honest to goodness roar and flapped her wings, letting go of me to fly back along the way we'd walked.

I'd never seen her angry enough to fly away like that before. I turned to discover what might have set her off.

"Logan?" I froze in place, blinking.

"Yeah, sorry." He shrugged, bags bouncing on his shoulders. The streetlight he stood under was a bluish LED, so his face looked more purple than red under it.

"Meow?" The cat at his feet shimmered in the light. His mercat Doris had glistening silver-gray fur that looked perpetually damp, mottled with charcoal markings.

"Don't apologize, just tell me why you're here." I stepped toward him.

"Well, your grandmother said if I ever needed somewhere to stay," he began, struggling with two rolling suitcases large enough to make my brother Noah jealous.

"Did your parents kick you out?" I gazed at all the luggage, wondering how in the world he'd brought it so far from the train station on his own. That walk was almost ten blocks and uphill half the way.

"Well, no, not exactly. I think I kicked myself out. Maybe." He sighed as one suitcase toppled over on its side. "It's hard to explain."

"That part can wait." I reached down and righted the bag, dragging it beside me. "For now, let's just go talk to Bubbe, okay?"

He nodded. "Sounds like a plan."

I peered at him, counting. He had two messenger bags, one knapsack, and a large rectangular duffel slung over his shoulders. I reached out and snagged the duffel and the knapsack, sharing his burden.

"Where's Ember?" I looked around for my dragonet, then whistled for her.

"Um, here." Logan lifted one of his arms. Ember's little face peeked out from his side.

"Peep?" She blinked, then made puppy dog eyes at me.

"Okay, you can ride on Logan if it's okay with him."

"Yeah, that's fine, Ember. Just hang on, okay?"

"I guess she missed you."

"I missed all this." Logan jerked his chin, indicating the streets of Salem. "And our friends, of course."

"Listen, I'm almost a hundred percent sure Bubbe will let you stay, but you might be downstairs in the animal hospital."

"No problem for me. Dr. Doolittle, remember?" He grinned, but the expression didn't touch his eyes.

"Yeah, I remember." Logan had a special talent for communicating with magical critters. I wasn't sure how it worked, but he'd stopped a gym full of panicked animals from stampeding last year. I'd never seen anything like it.

I wanted to ask him a million questions but didn't. He'd only need to repeat it to Bubbe and probably my parents, so for now, we'd be better off in silence. At least the remaining distance was short.

As we turned the corner into the driveway between my house and Izzy's, she peered out her living room window. Lee joined her momentarily. The two of them waved at us, then Izzy held up a finger. I stopped walking, motioning for Logan to do the same.

"Izzy wants to say hi. Is that okay?"

"That's okay."

As I got up to her house, I noticed Lee's familiar Scratch loping behind them. The two seemed comfortable with each other, which made sense. Izzy wasn't shy around magical critters, having grown up in front of a veterinary office.

"Logan, I wasn't expecting to see you until school started." Lee held out his hand for a shake. "What's up?"

"It's a long story, and I'm tired. Thanks for saying hi. I'm glad to see you guys."

"Do you need anything?" Izzy glanced at all his luggage. "Probably not, but I figured I'd ask."

"You know what?" Logan nodded. "Yeah. There's one thing. Would you mind not telling Dylan I'm here until I'm ready? I'm just too exhausted for now. It'll be at least a couple of days before I'm rested."

"Oh, no problem. I get it; long flights take so much out of people." Lee grinned. "But I bet Dylan will be happy you're here too."

"Thanks." Logan sighed.

"Rough summer?" Izzy raised her eyebrow.

"Like sandpaper." Logan's yawn went on longer than the words that came before it. "Sorry."

"I better take him in. He's still got to talk to Bubbe."

We said goodbye, then walked up the driveway where I rang the bell at the veterinary office. I rarely did that, but it was after hours, and I wanted to let my grandma know someone was here besides family. She answered the door faster than I thought she would.

"Bissel, why did you ring the bell?" Bubbe glanced past me at Logan. "Oh. Hello, Logan. Let me help you with your things."

She didn't ask why he was here but had known he'd show up to accept an offer given nearly a year earlier. I wasn't surprised. My family's kind of big on helping.

I followed them in through the waiting room behind the counter and then past the door to the back. Doris padded behind Logan, keeping close to his heels. Across from the kitchen, Bubbe stopped. She opened a door, one I'd never seen her use in my presence.

"Isn't that the controlled substances closet?" I blinked.

"In a manner of speaking." Bubbe gave us a half-grin. "It's controlled, and there are substances inside, but it's not for medication. Have a look."

We peered through the doorway. The room shouldn't have fit in the hallway between the two examination rooms on either side, but it was bigger on the inside, like Hawthorn Academy's campus. Even so, it was a relatively small space.

"It's a bedroom?" I gave Bubbe a sidelong glance. "But why?"

"Bissel, you knew our house was built at the same time as your school. They're connected in many ways."

"Whatever the reason, I'm glad." Logan seemed to deflate, as though he were far more exhausted than he'd let on earlier.

48

"You can stay here for as long as you need."

"Thanks. Not too long, though. School will start soon." Logan shuffled through the open door, dragging the one suitcase Bubbe left him with behind him, then he set it aside. "I'll see about staying on campus for school breaks."

Bubbe cleared her throat. "It costs extra, and in the past, students in your *situation* have run into resistance on that front."

"I understand." Logan turned, glancing back at us. I passed him the duffel bag, and he took it but shook his head. "For now, I just need to rest."

"Of course." Bubbe nodded as she passed him another bag. "The kitchen's across the hall. If you're hungry or thirsty in the night, help yourself to snacks. Use the paper plates and the utensils with them; that way everything's kosher. The bathroom is next door to the kitchen."

"You're a lifesaver." Logan took the luggage I'd carried, heaping it in a pile near the door on his side.

"I'll wake you for breakfast tomorrow morning, okay?"

"Meow." Doris head-butted my shin, then walked past Logan into the room.

"If it's okay with Doris, it's okay with me. See you tomorrow, Aliyah. And thanks again, Dr. Morgenstern."

He closed the door, leaving us in the hall. I glanced at my grand-mother, wondering what she'd meant by students in the past in Logan's situation. Mom had stayed here over a summer while at Hawthorn, but I assumed she'd been the only one. I opened my mouth to ask for more details, but Bubbe shook her head.

"Yeah, I know. It's late, and he needs rest. I just want to help."

"That breakfast invitation was a good start. It's waffle day, right?"

"Right." I turned toward the back stairs that led up to our apart-ment on the second and third floors of the building. "Thanks, Bubbe. I love you."

"I love you too."

I headed up the stairs, remembering how last year when my solar magic started coming in, I'd despaired at the top of them. This time around, my concern was for someone else. It was a different sort of burden, so I expected it to feel lighter, but it didn't.

Logan Pierce was in serious trouble. Nobody could have guessed how much, either.

CHAPTER SEVEN

"Waffles!" I hollered down the stairs because Ember kept tugging on my shirt, trying to keep me from leaving the kitchen. I wanted to fetch Logan, but she had berries on the brain. "Waffles up here! Get them while they last!"

"Fat chance." Noah slapped his hand over his mouth because he said them *to* me instead of *at* me.

My brother held grudges like superglue. I turned, trying to counter his pessimism about the availability of delicious waffle-y goodness, but discovered the truth. The waffle batter was almost all gone.

"No way! Waffles!" Logan nearly knocked me over, dashing through the door. He was a picky eater, but I knew from Sunday breakfasts on campus that this was one of his favorite foods.

I let Ember continue pulling me away from the door for safety's sake. Good thing, too. Doris was hard on Logan's heels and would have tripped me in an unfortunate direction if I hadn't moved in time.

I lived in an almost literal zoo, but I wouldn't have had it any other way.

Logan dashed around the counter, skidding to a stop in front of the waffle iron and the bowl beside it. He opened it and ladled batter onto the iron. He closed it, flipping after it buzzed, then got his waffle out just as it turned golden brown.

"I think I can get another half out of this." He held up the bowl, tilting it to scrape the bottom with the ladle. Sure enough, Logan was right.

It was only then that I noticed Noah snickering, and not in a kind way, either.

"What's so funny?" I turned, putting my hands on my hips and glaring like a basilisk.

Noah gazed straight past me, of course, still ignoring me. His attention was focused on Logan Pierce.

"It's just," Noah put his hand over his mouth, lifting his pinky, face turning red, "your shirt."

"Oh, no." Logan hung his head, staring down at the picture and caption emblazoned on his t-shirt.

I blinked, shaking my head so hard anybody watching might have thought I had water in my ear. But I didn't. I was just that surprised.

"Gray Fullbuster is my husbando?" Noah raised his eyebrow. "Not the attire I expected from you."

"It's Elanor's." Logan shook his head again. "Sort of. It was her gag gift last Christmas. I didn't realize it was with my pajamas. She must've snuck it in there before...I mean, I don't know."

"Oh, my God." Noah whipped out his phone. "This is too funny. We've got to take a selfie and send it right now. She'll laugh her ass off."

"You'll do no such thing, Noah." Mom stood in her office doorway, arms crossed over her chest. "Ease off, and no contacting Elanor beyond social media likes until I say so. Especially not about her brother."

"Okay?" Noah blinked.

Mom didn't usually forbid him from anything. Most of the time, I was the one she got strict with. That rarity gave her words more impact, so he listened and put the phone back in his pocket.

"Thanks, Mrs. Morgenstern." Logan set the ladle and bowl back on the counter. "I'm trying to keep my head down."

"It'd be best for you to stay away from campus too, then." Mom crossed her arms over her chest. "At least for the time being. Stick to this building and the backyard. I know that sounds boring but better safe than sorry. And keep our guest's presence a secret. Am I clear here, Noah? Aliyah?"

"Yeah, Mom." I nodded.

"Crystal." Noah sighed. "He's 007 or whatever until you say so."

That's when I noticed Logan had trembled so much he'd dripped the last few drops of batter on the floor, and the half-section inside the iron had gone uncooked. I couldn't get on Noah's case since he'd done nothing wrong, but I needed an outlet for all the tension, so I went to work tidying up.

After snagging a paper towel, I closed the waffle iron before wiping the floor so Logan wouldn't slip. The iron buzzed, and I flipped it for him. I retrieved the bowl and ladle, bringing them to the sink. Finally, I tossed the dirty paper towel into the trash under the counter.

"No need to bang around, Aliyah, geez." Noah rolled his eyes.

"So, now you're talking to me? Because you don't like how I cleaned the kitchen?" I rinsed my hands briskly. "After ribbing my friend over a t-shirt."

My face heated, the anger I'd tried to channel rising again. So did my hands in the water running over them. I checked the faucet. Cold. That meant my temper was about to cause a magical outburst. Not a good look.

"Settle down, Aliyah." Logan got his half-waffle out of the iron, placing it on the plate with the other one. "I'm okay. Got my big boy pants on."

"Okay. As long as you're all right." I took a deep breath and let it out slowly, then one more for good measure.

"I'm fracking sorry, okay?" Noah turned his back and sauntered toward the living room with his half-eaten plate of berry- and syrup-drizzled waffles.

"Peep." Ember landed on my shoulder, nuzzling my face. That

meant she smeared it with strawberries, of course. She'd been sneaking them again.

"I look like I've been snogging a vampire now, don't I?" I sighed.

"You're not wrong." Logan grabbed the fork and knife from the cup next to the stack of plates on the counter. "Hey, where's the syrup?"

"Hold on, I'll get it." I reached into the cabinet to grab the bottle. Once I held it out to Logan, I realized my mistake.

"I don't think so." He shook his head at the bottle of ketchup.

We had a laugh at that, thank goodness. The tension had to break somehow. I wondered about his issues with his parents and the reason he'd left, but there was only one way to find out why.

"So, tell me about that shirt. It looks like anime. What's it from?" I pulled a chair out at the table in the dining room, nodding at it.

"It's from an anime called *Fairy Tail*. We binged it together at the beginning of the summer." Logan took the seat I offered, setting his plate down.

"Sounds cool. Who's the character?" I sat beside him, spooning strawberries on my waffles.

"So, this guy." Logan gestured at the shirt with his fork, "Gray Fullbuster, does ice magic. And this girl with water magic gets a totally insane crush on him. Because I'm a water magus and Elanor ships just about everything in the universe—" He took a huge bite of waffle.

"I get it." I grinned. "Her OTP for you is with a fictional ice magus."

"Right." He nodded, pushing pieces of waffle through the syrup on his plate. "Because she's Elanor." He shrugged.

"Which means?" I raised my eyebrow.

"She relates everything to herself, and she's queer." Logan stared at his food. "So naturally, all her shipping is gay."

"Makes sense."

We enjoyed our waffles, talking about silly things Doris and Ember had done over the summer. Some were little habits they'd formed or tricks they'd learned. Since Doris was a mercat, some of those were the opposite of what most people would expect from a feline.

"She stopped sleeping in the kitchen sink after that."

"I didn't even know you could put garbage disposals on timers." I giggled. "But I'm seventeen, and this isn't a smart home. What do I know?"

"Yeah, I guess." Logan shrugged, changing the subject. "I avoid the kitchen too most of the time. We've got a conservatory, like an indoor greenhouse. I used to take care of all the plants in there until Hawthorn. I missed my philodendron all last year if you can believe it."

"Totally." I nodded. "I bet they'd let you have a plant on campus. The lights are solar, so it would do okay in there, right?"

"I should've thought of that." He dragged his fork through dregs of syrup on his plate. "But I'm not sure how I would've brought Benny on the plane, anyway."

He named his plant Benny? How adorable.

Of course, the Evil Inside Voice would pick one of Logan's glum moments to insult something endearing. I finished the last of my strawberries, trying to think of some safe topic to break the silence. Logan managed on his own.

"I wonder how Zeke handles being on campus if all the lights are solar? He's a vampire, but he lives there. How do you think that works?"

"I'm not sure how vampires work physiologically, but I do know a thing or two about solar magic." I held my hand out, palm up. "I'm going to conjure some solar energy right now. Check it out. Once I get it going, hold your hand over it and tell me how it feels."

I focused, calling the magic I'd tried banning myself from the year before. Bubbe had practiced with me three days a week all summer, and it showed. My hand filled with light as I kept a picture in my head, an idea of how that type of sunlight felt.

"It's soft somehow." Logan grinned. "Like an easy afternoon stroll."

"Right." I gave him a smile with my nod. "Because I'm calling it while relaxed. And it's solar energy, not real sunlight. Bubbe explained it as something we conjure from feelings of what sunlight means to us."

"So, vampires who were solar magi could conjure their magic

still?"

"Possibly? For the older ones, it's probably not easy to think kindly of the sun."

"Would they get burned?" Logan studied the side of his index finger and the small scar from the fire in our first lab last year.

"I don't know. Bubbe says vampiric magi get hungry after conjuring. But anyway, that's why vampires can go to the Seelie side of the Under. There's solar energy there, but it's the Sidhe Queen's magic, not the sun. Does that make any sense?"

"Sort of." Logan leaned back in his chair. "I have a million more questions about it, though."

"Better ask at the library once school starts. I just told you everything I know."

"That's fair." He nodded.

"I was wondering something too." I watched him spoon strawberries on his plate, then mix them with the syrup.

"Hmm?" Logan glanced up. The expression he wore reminded me of how he'd looked in Creatives, thinking of something to draw.

"When do you think you'll talk to your family?" The misty quality on his face evaporated like lifting fog.

"Never." He stared back at his plate. "My parents said I'm not one of them anymore, so I guess we can't talk. I'm out. If it wasn't for Bubbe and the nice lady at the airport who changed my ticket, I'd be on the streets in Vegas alone." He dropped his fork against the edge of the ceramic, all interest in the fruit gone. "Why did you ask that?"

"Because things come up." I closed my eyes, imagining my mother down in Providence, testifying against her own brother. "Does it have to be your whole family? What about Elanor?"

"That's up to her, but I'm not holding my breath." Logan's deep sigh reinforced his declaration. "She'll probably just cut me off. They do an awful lot for her."

"So, you don't think this can be fixed?"

"I've tried all my life to fix it." Logan stared into my eyes. Usually, he was thoughtful and caring, a quietly sensitive soul, but this time, his gaze was pure adamantine. "They have to take the first step, and even then." His jaw tightened. "Even if they come with an apology, I still might say no."

"Why?" I blinked, unable to imagine not forgiving anyone in my family. But no two families were the same, a lesson I'd seen demonstrated outside the classrooms over and over at Hawthorn Academy.

"Because I have to pick something, Aliyah. Choose a way to handle this." Logan's eyes clouded like a storm rolling over the bay. "I'm never what they want, and every time I get close, they change the rules on me."

"I don't understand?" I reached across the table, taking Logan's hand. "But I want to."

"It's always been that way." He shook off my grip. "Being a Pierce is conditional, like living in a maze of 'if-onlies.' If only you were a triple-threat like Elanor. If only you were a showman like your father. If only you were like the telekinetic kid in that other family's act."

"That stuff doesn't matter, Logan." I turned my hand over, placing it flat on the table. "Not to your friends. We think you're awesome. And grades don't lie. You're top of the class."

"My parents didn't get the memo." He snorted. "My heart can't take any more. They either love me or they don't. Nobody turns out the way their parents expect. Going to school with all of you last year taught me that much."

"You're right." I nodded. "Just don't be surprised if you have to face them again. There's a reason 'absence makes the heart grow fonder' is an old adage. And some people's ideas about fondness aren't all sunshine and roses."

"You sound like somebody's grandma."

"Thanks." I reached out again, offering my hand instead this time. Logan eyed it for a moment, then took it. "Even though I talk like an old babushka, I'm your friend. And I'm not going anywhere, no matter how many plants you've got in your dorm room, husbando shirts you wear, or mercats you adopt off the streets."

Logan didn't say anything, but he didn't have to. Neither of us did. That's the way friendship is. And for about a week, things went smoothly for him.

CHAPTER EIGHT

Six days after he arrived, Mom invited us into her office to read a message for Logan.

"It seems your transfer student arrives today." Mom lifted the privacy screen on her monitor so Logan could see it. "Headmaster Hawkins has requested your presence on campus to help him with housing orientation."

"Housing orientation?" I asked, "Is the new guy a fire magus or something? Why would anyone need orientation to inhabit a dorm room?"

"I don't know." Logan bent to peer at the screen. "I guess I'll find out. Or rather, *we* will." He grinned, then pointed at the message.

"Oh!" I blinked. "Headmaster Hawkins let you have a plus one?"

"Looks like it," he said. "So you get to visit campus before the school year starts after all."

"Peep!" Ember leaped off my shoulder, soaring through the air. I felt her excitement since magi with a familiar bond often shared emotions with our critters.

"They're letting me move in, so I'll tell Bubbe I don't need the room anymore." Logan straightened. "I'll go pack my stuff."

Mom tilted her head, gazing at him. "Remember, you can stay here on breaks or weekends if you need to get off-campus."

"Okay." He nodded and his eyes brightened, expression dreamy.

I knew him well enough to guess he didn't think he'd need it. For better or worse, optimism remained part of Logan's mental landscape, despite the crap his parents had heaped on him all summer.

"There's more information here for you, Logan. From the head-master." Mom turned toward the printer, pulling the freshly ejected sheet from its tray. "Let's have a look."

"Thanks, Mrs. Morgenstern."

Since my friend was in good hands, I headed upstairs, packing one of my suitcases with things I wouldn't need until school started. I could put them in the room I'd share with Grace a week later. I glanced at the trusty old communication orb, my lifeline on the offline campus to Izzy and Cadence. At Hawthorn, it was forbidden and had gotten me in serious trouble last year. Should I bring it and risk more probation, or leave it behind?

Getting caught with a contraband magipsychic device might get me suspended or even expelled. I'd start this year on disciplinary probation. But the orb saved two lives last year, maybe three, I wasn't sure. Leaving it behind would be nerve-wracking.

I'd been all but promised more trouble on campus by the outgoing mean girl, who'd enlisted her younger sister and my ex to continue harassing me. I knew but had no proof that she'd been behind a magisupremacist hate crime. Said trouble would extend to my friends from town.

In October, the Hawthorn Academy campus would see the most diverse group of students in its entire history during extramurals. Our school's bylaws excluded much, including vampire students, a ban Messing Academy and Gallows Hill didn't share. Would I be putting this diverse group of extrahumans at risk if I didn't bring the orb?

But Izzy and Cadence were on their school's teams, so they'd be on campus with me. We could work together to make another orb in an emergency, possibly with faculty permission. One of the events was a magipsych fair, during which students could make devices like the orb. Maybe the risk was less than I imagined. I packed more mundane tools for protesting hate instead.

The Vamp Lives Matter t-shirt I'd stolen from Noah last year went into the suitcase, and another with the Night Creatures' latest album art on it. I threw in an Ultimate Shifter League shirt and one bearing the logo for Monarch Motion Pictures, a faerie-run indie film company. If I wanted to fight back against discrimination, I'd do it wholeheartedly. And with style, I thought as I added the houndstooth leggings that looked particularly cute with the first shirt.

Headmaster Hawkins shared my sentiments, but I wasn't as sure about the rest of the faculty, so I surrounded the bundle with menstrual supplies, underwear, bras, and cozy socks. A box of Auntie's Anti-cramp tea rounded out the packing. Even if somebody checked it, which could happen to students on probation, they'd only see comfort items. Some folks were still squeamish about looking through stuff like that.

The next order of business was adding accessories, fussy little things like necklaces and scarves I rarely bothered with in town. Noah wouldn't pick them out for me this year. He hadn't spoken to me since that accidental instance on waffle morning. I figured he wasn't likely to any time soon.

"How do people even figure this stuff out?" I shook my hands, one of which held a blue choker and the other an orange teardrop pendant.

"Peep?" Ember tilted her head to the left and then the right. She blinked a few times, stared at the tunics I had hanging on the closet door, then back at the necklaces. "Peep peep."

My dragonet swooped down, snagged the orange teardrop pendant from my hand, and dropped it in the suitcase. People weren't necessary to make fashion choices, apparently.

"Hopefully, you've got good taste in jewelry." I shrugged, placing the choker back in the box on my dresser.

"Want help?" Logan stood in the doorway, Doris brushing past his legs and into the room. She leaped into my suitcase, turned in a circle, and made herself comfortable on top of the lingerie bag. "Picking outfits is something I did to get out of more performing."

"Yeah, sure." I shrugged, smiling at the purring mercat.

"Doris does that to me all the time, gets in the bags I'm packing as if I'd forget to bring her." Logan chuckled. "Where's that string of freshwater pearls? The ones you wore with the pink dress on Valentine's Day?"

"You think I'll need those?"

"Yeah. You can wear them with all those dresses." He waved his hand at the garment bag on my bed, which contained the mint green dress I'd worn to parents' night last year along with a sample from Ambersmith Fashions Grace had dropped off for me last month.

"Okay. What about scarves?"

"No clue." Logan shrugged. "Nobody wears them in Vegas unless they're hiding a hangover. Let's not get drunk at any ragers while on probation, okay?"

We laughed.

"Guess I'll just bring the most comfortable ones."

I grabbed a yellow and white floral chiffon, then a silky emerald green. On top of that, I added a knobbly woolen one for when it got colder. My gloves and coat went in on top since, while I wouldn't need them in September, I would want to be warm on the way home on weekends in November.

"Oh, no." Logan sighed. "I left my winter stuff in Vegas."

"Maybe Elanor will bring it."

"I don't know." He leaned against the doorframe.

"You messaged her about Benny though, right?"

"No. Not yet." Logan looked at his feet, then at Doris in the suitcase. "After I've moved in on campus, I'll send her a message from the headmaster's office. It's safer if they don't know I'm here."

"Safer?" I blinked.

From his parents, of course.

"Come on, Queen Doris." Logan didn't answer. "Time to get out of there."

The mercat stood up, stretching each limb one at a time. Eventually, she stepped out of the suitcase, but she took her sweet time. I didn't mind; it gave me space to breathe. For whatever reason, I'd gotten nervous about going to campus.

You should be. Your friend's gone renegade from his influential family. Do you honestly think they'll let it lie? What was on that paper your mother didn't let you see?

"Hey, Logan?"

"Hmm?" He already looked exhausted.

"Are you meeting this new student on the way in?" Ember perched on my headboard, shuffling from side to side with her wings partly out like a canary in a room full of cats.

"Yeah, I am." He shrugged. "Why?"

"Do you want to bring Izzy with us, just for the walk to find the door?" I kept my eyes on my dragonet. The suggestion had a profound effect on her behavior. The shuffling stopped, and she folded her wings.

"Are you getting a funny feeling?"

"Yes." Ember echoed my answer with a peep.

"Okay, then."

I grabbed the suitcase and the garment bag. Once we said goodbye to my parents, I headed down the back stairs with Logan and we got his luggage from the hallway in Bubbe's office. In the waiting room on our way out, we ran into Eston, one of our classmates.

"Logan?" Eston blinked. "What are you doing here?"

"Just heading to campus. I'm mentoring the new student in our year."

"I mean, *here*." Eston waved his hand, indicating Bubbe's office. "At the Morgenstern's."

"Why are *you* here?" Logan pulled his suitcase along behind him, heading toward the exit.

He's trying to change the subject. Failing miserably at it, too.

"Familiar license. I'm from New Hampshire, so it's just a medium drive for me. But you, you're—"

"In town early. I know." Logan's laugh came out flatter than usual. "Funny, running into you here."

Coincidental, perhaps.

"They've been looking all over for you, man. Watch out."

"Okay." Logan pushed the door open, beckoning to me with his chin. "Gotta go."

"Aliyah, watch out for him. This isn't good."

Get more information.

"How? What do you mean?" I tried stammering out more questions because it's rare that I agree with the Evil Inside Voice. But outside the door, I heard Logan calling to Izzy in the driveway. "Oops, gotta go, Eston. Sorry."

"Just be careful." Eston headed toward the door Bubbe held open for him, then looked back over his shoulder. "See you next week."

"Yeah, see you." The door closed behind me.

CHAPTER NINE

Out in the driveway, it was almost too bright. The sun beat down on us, without even a single wispy cloud in the sky to dim its rays. Of all the times to forget my sunglasses. I squinted, shuffling along the gravel and hoping I wouldn't trip.

I didn't, which was a good thing because Izzy stood at the end of the driveway. She had a bungee cord with her, which confused me until she took two bags off of Logan's shoulders and set them on top of his rolling suitcase, securing them with the stretchy cord.

"How did you know I needed that?" Logan scratched his head.

"Psychic. But really, I watched you come up the driveway last week, remember? Shoulder injuries are not a good look."

"Thanks." Logan grinned as Doris headbutted Izzy's shin. "We're all nervous and wondering if there's anything to it."

"I hear you." Izzy nodded, reaching into the satchel she always wore slung on one hip. It contained her tarot cards, the ones she'd use to get a little extra information about whatever situation arose.

She pulled out a card, then frowned.

Trouble, of course.

"Who are you fighting with, Logan?" She turned the Two of Wands around.

"Um. My parents? Maybe my whole family."

"Would they call the police on you for any reason?"

"I'm not sure? It happened once when I was ten, but I never understood why."

"Maybe we should go through the fence behind my house." On Hawthorne Street behind Logan, I saw a police cruiser drive past more slowly than usual. "Come on up the driveway now."

"Peep!" Ember swooped behind Logan, diving at him until he headed back in the direction I'd indicated.

We squeezed past my parents' car, heading toward the gate in the fence. I opened it and we hustled through, Izzy closing it behind us. We had to lift the suitcases instead of rolling them because the path was a series of stepping stones with gravel between them. All the way in the back right corner of the yard, a large jasmine bush stood sentry in front of the hole in the fence. Noah and I had thought it our secret for ages, but a few years ago, after my brother bonded with Lotan, we realized Bubbe knew.

Lotan tried to go exploring, which was how we discovered unaccompanied critters couldn't get through. A magical ward banning lone animals covered the hole in the fence. Bubbe exercised some of her boarders and patients recovering from various injuries out here, so that made sense. I knew how to take it down because we'd practiced wards in Lab last year. All I needed was to match and banish the element making the magic barrier.

As I conjured my solar magic, Logan spoke.

"What did Eston say? After I left?"

"He said to be careful, and I'm taking his warning seriously." I snapped my fingers, banishing the fire and shutting off the ward. "But it's also that card, the Two of Wands. It's meant the police before in Izzy's readings, and I just saw a squad car drive down Hawthorne Street."

"I don't get it." Logan shook his head, ducking under the shrubbery I held aside for him. "They told me to leave. I'm almost an adult already. And they didn't know where I went."

"Hold on." Izzy drew another card, the Page of Wands reversed. "Half the time, this card signifies Noah. Maybe he ratted you out."

I'm too ashamed to repeat the string of words that came out of my mouth right then, but the Evil Inside Voice had a good long laugh at them. I was angry enough that some flowers on the jasmine bush wilted.

"Chill out! We're in the middle of a big getaway, remember?" Izzy patted my shoulder, helping me focus enough to turn down the wattage on my solar magic.

Once we got to the other side of the fence, I put the wards back up. We headed down the walkway beside the Peabody Essex Museum. Since the rest of our route traversed pedestrian-only terrain, I relaxed. Cars couldn't go on Essex Street, and conventional technology didn't work there. Most of the Salem PD didn't have access to magipsychic tech at that point, and only one officer was an extrahuman.

Oh, look, it's Pirate Day. Lovely.

The Evil Inside Voice's commentary wasn't welcome, but it wasn't wrong either. A banner hung from poles set up beside the Peabody Essex Museum, bearing an old-timey message: Ye Olde Salem Pirate Festival, 8-8 today!

Immediately after making the turn, we dodged clusters of puffy-shirted people and began scanning the buildings for Hawthorn Academy's migrating entrance. Its location varied every twenty-four hours as part of campus security, and it figured that on the day we were in a hurry, we didn't find it on the first few tries.

"What's the rush, you guys?" Azrael Ambersmith jogged to keep up with us.

Logan panted. "Just trying to get to school."

"It's way down there by the Italian restaurant." He pointed past a gaggle of pirates. Yes, people in pirate garb walked down, along, across, and around Essex Street. "Are you avoiding someone? Do you need help?"

"Yeah, help would be good." Izzy nodded. "Can you throw a glamour on our pal Logan here? He needs to blend in."

"Okay." Azrael cracked his knuckles. "What do you want, pirate garb?"

"Um, I don't know?" Logan shrugged, blinking owlishly. The crowd and the chaos were getting to him, then. He needed help.

I glanced at the festive folk, noticing that most of them wore garb more akin to Renaissance Faire attire than Pirates of the Caribbean. This meant plenty of enormous face-concealing hats instead of bandannas and eyepatches.

"Yeah, pirate." I nodded. "Go for it."

"Sure." Azrael concentrated, then tapped Logan on the shoulder the way he had when we were kids playing tag.

A moment later, Logan's clothes sort of fluffed out. His shirt grew long, frilly sleeves, and his Bermuda shorts became pantaloons. A flick of Az's wrist added a leather vest and a sword belt to the imaginary ensemble. The glamour did nothing to mask his features, but the feather-bedecked tricorn hat perched on his head helped with that.

"Nice timing, Az." Izzy jerked her thumb. "Check it out." A police officer on a bicycle pedaled slowly past us down Essex Street as we made it to the restaurant he'd mentioned earlier.

"Oh no, I did not just help you evade the cops." Az paled, eyes widening in horror. "I'm gonna get in so much trouble if my dad ever finds out."

"It's okay." She pulled a card but didn't show us. "It's a bogus reason. We won't tell your dad."

"Yeah, Logan's a good kid, I promise." I patted Azrael's shoulder. "He was the valedictorian last year. All we have to do is get him on campus, and everything will be fine."

Logan blushed, shuffling his feet and staring at his boat shoes, which looked like tall leather boots now. Something hit him in the back of the head, knocking the glamoured tricorn hat right off it.

"That shouldn't happen!" Azrael stepped back, blinking and holding his hands up. He wasn't surprised, but scared. "It's glamour."

"Gryphon beats glamour, my fine unfeathered changeling friend." The guy talking was short, slight, and dressed all in black except for the navy blue Hawthorn Academy blazer, to which he'd somehow added silver piping on the seams. His jet-black hair was parted on one side, where a stark white streak covered one of his eyes. "What is this, Dress Like a Pirate Day?"

"Excuse me, who are you?" Izzy crossed her arms over her chest, tapping her foot and glaring at the newcomer.

"Door." He smirked, pointing at himself and then at the thing we sought. "But that's not my name. It's Dorian Spanos. I'm the new guy."

"Why did a gryphon hit me?" Logan rubbed the back of his head. "I kind of need that hat right now."

"Might as well ask why snow falls down instead of up." Dorian sighed, ironically. "So, what are these reasons of yours?"

Before anyone could answer him, the bicycling police officer screeched to a stop beside the group. Azrael froze, except for his hands, which visibly trembled. His face went white as a sheet.

"Logan Pierce?" The officer put down the kickstand and got off the bike. "Show me your ID slowly."

"Oh, no way." Dorian's smile was broad, showing a set of even white teeth.

"Yeah, I'm Logan Pierce. My ID is in my back pocket here. I'm just going to reach for it."

The police officer waited, then checked the piece of plastic Logan handed over. She peered at it, tilting it in the light and watching the sun play on the hologram Nevada put on its state IDs. Apparently, Logan didn't have a driver's license.

"Looks like the real deal." The officer tossed her head, the ponytail under her bike helmet shining ruddily in the sunlight. "You're coming with me, though, Logan. Your parents want you escorted to the airport."

"He's not going to the airport." Headmaster Hawkins strode through the door to Hawthorn Academy, heading directly for our group. "Mr. Pierce is expected at school today. His tuition is paid in full for the year, and he's got work to do here."

"I'm sorry, Headmaster, but his parents reported him missing and said they had reason to believe he'd be in Salem."

"His parents are mistaken." Headmaster Hawkins held out a piece of paper, handing it to the officer. "I've got an agreement he signed to mentor a student at my school, beginning today."

"Oh?" The police officer raised her eyebrow, stepping back so sharply her ponytail bobbed. She glanced back at the ID. "He's seventeen. They didn't tell us that."

"Have a look." He smiled mildly. "It's notarized and everything."

I blinked because notarization requires all signatories to be present in the room with the Notary Public. As far as I remembered, Logan had signed his document in Nevada after receiving it via certified mail.

I managed to catch a glimpse of the paper as he passed it and noticed its date was last week and the notary my father.

"It seems to be in order, but I'll have to show it to my lieutenant. Hang on a moment." She got out her phone and tried taking a picture, then shrugged and laughed at herself. It didn't work because this was Essex Street.

I looked for Azrael since he might know some way to take and convey a picture to the police station, but he'd faded into the crowd.

"Let's make this easier." Headmaster Hawkins said. "Why don't I bring the document to the station? If your lieutenant thinks it's not in order, we'll rectify it together."

"That works." She nodded. "Assuming there's supervision for the students on campus while you're away."

"Several of the faculty and staff are here preparing for the start of classes. Mr. Pierce's professor is one of them. Will that do?"

"Yes." She nodded. "Once the students enter the school, we can go."

We said goodbye to Izzy, then Logan and I headed through the entrance, along with Dorian, whose mischievous gryphon was perched on his shoulder. Once the door closed behind us, the new transfer student leaned against it and laughed so hard I thought he'd fall over.

"Holy shit." Dorian grinned at Logan, wheezing in a breath between clenched teeth. "You're not what I expected at all. This is gonna be awesome. Mentored by a student who fought the law. And won."

"Some people think that's a bad thing." Logan blinked.

"Not me. Didn't they tell you I'm a transfer from the Academy?" Dorian waggled his eyebrows. "I'm starting on probation."

"No. They did not tell me that." Logan's voice was deadpan. He'd been caught off-guard and out of his element.

I had his back. "Yeah, we're a couple of miscreants, for sure." I elbowed Logan in the ribs. "I'm on probation too."

"Sick." Dorian nodded. "When do we get food in this place?"

"Next time's lunch, in half an hour. What room are you in? We can put your stuff away."

"I just have this bag." Dorian peered at all the luggage. "You look like you overpacked, man. You too, fellow probationary student."

"Yeah, it's a bad habit." I shook my head. Of all the times to pack more like Noah than me. "What can you do?"

"Anyway, I'm on the third floor. I guess everyone in our year is, right?"

"Yup." I pulled the suitcase behind me toward the stairs. "It's voice-activated, like an escalator except magical."

"Aliyah, what are you doing?" Logan leaned toward my ear, whispering as we walked.

"Speaking miscreant, I guess." I shrugged. "Just come up one step." I beckoned to the new guy.

"Right." Once he got on, I spoke the words "third floor," and the staircase started moving.

On the way up, Logan gripped my elbow tightly, like a lifeline over the side of the boat in stormy seas. I'm not sure what had him so ill at ease. The headmaster had solved the police problem. But if his parents had called to report him missing when they'd actually kicked him out, things were not okay.

I couldn't miss the way my friend kept staring at the new student. Maybe he found Dorian intimidating. Or maybe he worried that his parents had been right all along, and he shouldn't have accepted the offer to be a student mentor. That he was out of his depth here.

Or it's something else. You certainly don't know everything.

I shrugged off the snark from the Evil Inside Voice. Either way, he'd need help. Too-cool-for-school Dorian Spanos was a wild card. I'd had enough trouble with one of those last year, and now one of my friends had to deal with the 2.0 version. Grace would need a heads-up. She'd texted the day before about having a plan for the year ready to go.

As it turned out, an entirely different set of difficulties loomed on the horizon for our group.

CHAPTER TEN

We escorted Dorian down the hall toward the room he'd share with Eston. Even though Alex remained at Hawthorn Academy, he'd room with one of the first-years. I had no idea how Eston felt about any of that. Usually, he reserved his thoughts and opinions for his girlfriend Kitty. Eston was the quiet type.

"Are you going to unpack that?" Logan pointed at the still-closed duffel bag on the floor.

"Nah. I'll save that for later." Dorian laughed as he sauntered back out the door. His gryphon tilted her head, blinking at us with a soft caw. "I'll hang with you guys while you stow your stuff, then we can get some grub."

"Okay, I guess." Logan shrugged.

"Is that cool with your girlfriend here?" Dorian waggled his eyebrows.

"Friend who happens to be a girl."

"That's fine." I snorted, imagining Izzy and all her protestations about boys.

"Cool-cool." Dorian nodded, his smirk blossoming into a genuine smile.

"Let's drop your stuff off first, Logan." I offered. "You shouldn't have to lug all those bags to my room and back."

"Peep!" Ember crept out from under my hair, shaking herself free. After that, she stretched her wings, yawning. I kept walking toward the room I shared with Grace.

"Oh, no way!" Dorian smiled. "You've got a dragonet?"

"Yup, one of two here." I shrugged. Ember trilled playfully.

Logan nodded. "My roommate has the other one."

"Will we see him today?" Dorian picked up his pace. It wasn't always easy for my shorter friends to match my stride, and the new kid was no exception.

"I'm not sure," Logan said. "Dylan's a workaholic with two jobs, so he might not be around."

"Oh, Logan. I meant to tell you something about Dylan." I glanced at Dorian. "Maybe it's personal."

"How's something maybe personal?" Dorian blinked. "Either it is or it isn't, right?"

"Things can be totally complicated around here. You get used to it." I gave Dorian a half-smile, then headed back into the hall, closing the door behind me.

"Oh, boy." He rolled his eyes. "Drama llama ding-dong."

"You can say that again," Logan muttered.

"Meow." Doris glared up at Dorian as though daring him to repeat himself. Sometimes, the mercat reminded me of the reference librarian at the Salem Public Library.

"I won't. Are we cool, Doris?" Dorian leaned forward, peering at the feline as he walked. His gryphon leaned forward too, head bobbing. "Mercy's sorry about the hat earlier. She didn't know she'd cause such a ruckus."

"Yeah, I think she's okay with you now." Logan shrugged. "The two of us are kind of on the serious side. And here we are."

Logan put his hand on the flat wooden panel beside the door to his room. The lock clicked and he opened it, pushing his way inside. The lights came on as Dorian and I followed Logan in. He helped, lifting the largest suitcase to the top of Logan's bed, but he winced a little while doing it, like something twinged or pinched.

"At least it's obvious which one is yours." Dorian jerked his thumb at Dylan's unmade bed. A beat-up acoustic guitar sat there, partially draped by a sheet. "For a workaholic, his housekeeping's kinda sloppy."

"Not usually." I closed the door behind me. The last thing I wanted was Dylan to walk in on us talking about him. "I hope he's okay. He had some kind of argument with Grace outside Engine House last week. He came in and sat for maybe five minutes, but I haven't seen him since."

"Really?" Logan dropped his knapsack, then headed toward Dylan's side of the room. He peered at the desk and into the trash can and looked beside the door. "Well, he's been here today. And he's wearing his work shoes now, so he must be on a shift at one job or the other."

Dorian raised his eyebrows, watching Logan intently, and said nothing. I wondered what he thought about all this. Pretty much all the students in our year erred on the side of kindness, and I wasn't sure yet whether Dorian would be on board with it. Time would tell.

"Well, I'll get Doris's stuff out, then we can go to the cafeteria." Logan opened his knapsack, producing a plethora of cat accessories.

Hawthorn Academy supplied food and water for the magical critters, but anything else had come from the students. Despite Logan's parental issues, Doris had been taken care of, at least. But I expected nothing less from Logan. For all I knew, he raided the feline accessories from his family's show.

"All set." Logan brushed his hands off, then headed toward the door to open it. "Everybody out."

"I'm just gonna drop this off in my room, no need to unpack." I stopped two doors down from Logan's.

When I opened the door, Dorian stopped to hold it open. I collapsed the handle on the suitcase, then pushed it under the bed. After that, I turned to find him staring at the wall over Grace's bed, which was adorned with the usual Hawthorn Academy wooden carvings but partially covered by her posters.

"Your roommate's into K-Pop?"

"Yup." Ember added a peep of her own. She liked Grace's music.

"I'm sorry."

Something about Dorian threw me off. It seemed like he was hiding something or trying too hard, or both, but Logan had to help him. Mentorship was part of everything else he'd have to deal with, and his plate was already piled high. I'd have to get along with Dorian somehow, but I also had to stand up for my friend.

"I'm not." I put my hands on my hips, planting my feet. "That's a snobby thing to say."

"Yeah, it was. I shouldn't have said it. Bad inside voice, no biscuit."

Don't get any ideas about talking to me like that, miss.

"I know a little something about unruly inside voices." I snorted. "But be careful. Our year is pretty chill. The third-years, not so much, and I've got no idea what the first-years will be like."

"That's not true." Logan sighed. "We kind of expect a bit of trouble."

"Trouble?" Dorian cracked his knuckles. "What kind?"

Most of my friends would've blinked, stepped back, or otherwise expressed alarm. Not Dorian Spanos. He seemed more intense than chaotic, so I wondered whether he was a daredevil or had a death wish. Either could throw an enormous monkey wrench into practically every social dynamic we'd built last year.

"Mean girl stuff." I shrugged. "There's a downright awful one coming next week. Don't worry, my K-Pop-loving roommate has a plan."

"We should probably tell him about Alex."

"In a while." I headed toward the doorway. "Maybe off-campus, okay?"

"Oh, come on. Now I'm curious." Dorian's voice cracked on the last syllable.

"Don't worry, you'll hear about it." Logan put a hand on his shoulder to escort him away from the door. "Just not here."

"Oh, it's like that, is it?" Dorian tensed, eyes widening until Logan dropped his hand. He swallowed before continuing, "You guys are lucky you can leave campus. The Academy didn't let us do that."

What was all that about, I wonder?

I kept my lips zipped. The silence as we walked down the hallway felt like one of the enormous, wobbly bubbles Cadence had insisted on making all through grade school. They floated along almost impossibly before popping. Anyone in direct proximity got soap in their eyes. I knew better than to tamper with the social equivalent.

"First floor." I activated the staircase as soon as we reached it.

I didn't want to continue the conversation about The Academy. I'd overheard just enough about it through the door of Mom's office. Dorian must've picked up on that because he changed the subject.

"What kind of food do they have here?"

"Just about everything." Logan smiled. "Not every day, but the selection is good, and they rotate things. They're also good with allergies and special diets, that kind of thing."

"The stuff we got over at the Academy was crap." When the stairs stopped, Dorian paced ahead of us, turning around and walking backward. "Sometimes I thought it was dog food."

"Ugh." Logan wrinkled his nose.

"Exactly."

"Look, they have panini." I pointed at the board.

"I'm surprised they're even open." Logan shook his head. "I mean, almost nobody's on campus."

"The headmaster said Luciano and Nurse Smith are." I shrugged. "Those two would mutiny without a decent meal."

"Makes sense," Dorian said, laughing. "So, profs eat the same stuff we do?"

"Yeah, why wouldn't they?" Logan blinked.

"You've probably never been stuck at a crappy school, either of you."

"I've been to them." I sighed. "My mom works in extrahuman education."

"Well, you're right about me." Logan shrugged. "All the schools I went to, the food at least looked good."

"I care more about how it tastes." Dorian stepped up to the counter. "I'm starving."

I got my usual turkey on pumpernickel with avocado, while Logan got ham and Swiss. Dorian ordered two sandwiches, one Italian with provolone and the other roast beef with cheddar. The sandwiches came out so fast they might have been made in the future. Maybe they were. The cafeteria employed Penelope, whose familiar could warp time.

We took our trays to the beverage station, where I got iced tea. Logan went with his usual Sprite. Dorian got a cup and went along the line, putting a little of everything cold in his cup, and I mean everything. He added all the sodas, juice, and even the iced tea.

"What's that?" Logan blinked.

"Beverage roulette." Dorian took a sip, then wrinkled his nose. "You never know if it's going to be good or like this." He took another sip, longer this time.

"Why not dump it out and try again?" Logan asked.

"I made it, now I have to drink it." He shrugged, then headed toward the tables. "Them's the rules."

"Let's sit here." I put my tray at the booth we used last year.

We ate in silence for a few minutes. Dorian must have been hungry because he finished his entire first sandwich. I only managed a quarter of mine.

Something moved, so I turned my head to see what it was, but nothing was there. Logan did the same thing, but Dorian laughed.

"It's just my familiar." He pointed to where I'd seen the movement. "Look up at the light fixture. Mercy likes those."

I made out a shape on the light. It reminded me of how a hawk used the sun for cover, so the prey wouldn't see it before the final dive-bomb. Sure enough, a moment later, Mercy the gryphon plummeted through the air, dipping into the trash can and coming up with a sandwich crust. She fluttered over, perching on the edge of the table with her prize.

Lovely. A trash gryphon. What will young Headmaster Hawkins allow on campus next? Ah, yes. The extrahuman riffraff, including your town friends.

"I'd better read up on gryphons." I stared down my sandwich, nostrils flaring as I resisted snapping back at the Evil Inside Voice. "It's one of the few critters I know little about. They rarely partner with magi."

"Oh, yeah, nobody expected it," Dorian said. "I'm already the odd magus in the family. My familiar was just the latest straw. Hopefully, the fact that Mercy's unconventional won't be the last."

"Are you in trouble with them?" Logan asked flatly.

"Nah, my folks are good people. They just don't know what to do with me. They're psychic. I'd think I was adopted, but I look just like them. Except for this." He indicated the white streak in his hair. "It came in with my magic."

"I know how you feel. I'm the lone introvert in a showbiz family. They love getting in front of people and making spectacles out of themselves. I'd rather sit in a corner and draw."

"Right on." Dorian nodded. "And yet here you are at the school they sent you to."

"They're not happy about me being in Salem now." Logan closed his eyes. "But the tuition's non-refundable at this point."

"Yeah, about that." Dorian leaned on his hand, reminding me of Cadence. "Did they really call the police on you?"

"I guess." Logan shrugged. "News to me. Unpleasant, but that's not exactly new. Tell him, Aliyah."

Dorian blinked and said nothing. He glanced at me, eyes widening.

"He was staying with my grandma because they kicked him out of the house last week." I made a fist against the table. "She offered him a place last year because they didn't want him bonding with Doris. She's apparently not fancy enough for them."

Doris chose that moment to turn on the charm, leaping up on the back of the booth behind Logan and pacing back and forth like the world's glossiest feline tightrope walker. She stared at Dorian the entire time as if daring him to share in the Pierce Family consensus.

"No way." Dorian watched her. "Totally gorgeous."

"Thanks." Logan's face was almost as red as the tomato garnish beside his sandwich.

"So, someone expected their shenanigans." Dorian glanced at my curled hand and then back up again, but at Logan, not me. "What kind of parents call the cops when they gave you the boot?"

Go on and tell the boy his parents are toxic. Evil, even. Make him cry right here in front of his mentee, who already makes him feel awkward.

I closed my eyes and swallowed the fiery diatribe against the entire Pierce family, excluding Logan. This was his story to tell.

"They always treated my sister better than me." Logan cut the crust from his sandwich and tossed it to Mercy, who gobbled it down in moments. "But is that normal? I've got no idea."

"It's not." Dorian and I startled each other by speaking at the same time.

"Jinx, you owe me beverage roulette." Dorian laughed and slapped the table.

"After I finish my sandwich, okay?" I grinned.

"Thanks, guys." Logan stared down at his ham and Swiss, then picked it up and finally took a bite.

Sometimes a well-placed laugh is just as important as a shoulder and an open ear.

A moment later, Lee headed toward us, sauntering over from the food line. He had tomato soup and a side of sweet potato fries on his tray.

"Is this seat taken?" he asked.

"There's always room for another friend." Logan waved his hand, and Dorian scooted over. "Dorian, this is Lee. He's in our year, too."

"Hey." Dorian bobbed his head. "What's up besides the crazy solar light fixtures?"

"The ceiling." Lee grinned. "Anyway, good to meet you."

We went about the business of lunch, the conversation turning academic. Since Dorian was in Professor Luciano's section with Logan and me, we answered most of his questions. If that bothered Lee, he didn't show it. He barely spoke until after we finished our food.

"So, I've been wandering the halls, helping Scratch exercise. And I heard something."

"Couldn't have been ghosts, right?" Dorian glanced around.

"No. Campus is between worlds, so ghosts can't come here." Lee shook his head. "It's music. Apparently, Dylan has a new hobby."

"You mean my roommate?" Logan blinked. "Okay."

"After the umpteenth time I walked past his room, he came out and asked if I'd go see him at the open mic night."

"Oh, yeah." I nodded. "The Witch's Brew has one every Sunday. It's at seven."

"Yeah, that's tonight." Lee twirled the spoon in his empty bowl. "He might appreciate more people rooting for him than little old me."

"I'll be there." I nodded. "With friends from town, hopefully."

"Oh." Logan gazed at the crumbs on his plate. "I probably shouldn't go off-campus. Not unless Headmaster Hawkins says it's safe."

"Huh?" Lee peered at Logan. "Why not?"

"He's avoiding the cops." Dorian grinned. "You should have seen it. They almost arrested him in the middle of Essex Street."

"Even if I can't make it, go with Lee. You'll meet a ton of cool people, Dorian. Including Dylan." Logan got up, snagging his tray. "I should unpack and track down the headmaster. See you all later."

"Wait." I got up. "I can't be on campus without you until school starts, remember?"

"Oh, sorry." Logan paused, his back toward our friends at the table. "I'll walk you out."

"See you guys later!" I waved at Lee and Dorian.

We walked together in silence, dropping off our trays at the dish-washing window. He didn't speak until we got into the vestibule between the lobby and the exit.

"Sorry this is so hard." I reached out and patted his shoulder. Ember landed on mine, then craned her neck toward my friend, peeping softly at him.

"I didn't expect it to be easy, but the police?" He hung his head. Doris trotted over, rubbing her body against his legs. He opened his arms, and she jumped into them.

"Listen, if you need me, send a message out with Lee or Dylan. I'll stop by."

"Thanks." Logan cuddled Doris, who put her paw on his cheek. "I wish I could look on the bright side, but I'm not sure there is one."

"It got Dorian on your side, at least. He seems like a rebel, but now maybe he'll take advice from you?"

"We'll see." He shrugged. "I'll ask the headmaster if you can come to the library this week. I'm bringing Dorian there, so maybe Hawkins will—"

"Maybe I'll what?"

Last year, we would have jumped out of our shoes at the sudden interruption, but we'd gotten used to the headmaster's habit of randomly and suddenly appearing on campus.

"Allow Aliyah to come and go freely to campus. To help Dorian." Logan peered at him. "Just so he knows more about his classmates."

"That's difficult." The headmaster frowned. "I'd need a fully detailed academic agenda, which you haven't learned how to make yet. You can try, but I doubt you'll make a qualifying one before school starts." He reached for the door to the lobby.

"Headmaster?" I stopped him. "Can Logan come out into town tonight? It's for a friend's event."

The headmaster's shoulders drooped. He answered my question but addressed it to Logan instead of me.

"I'd advise against your leaving campus until further notice, Mr. Pierce." He shook his head. "I'm sorry if that means you miss out socially, but you'll be safest here."

"I trust your judgment, sir." Logan bent his head, letting Doris rub cheeks with him.

Just like that, Headmaster Hawkins let go of the doorknob and vanished.

"Maybe we can record Dylan's performance for you," I offered.

"Nah, it's Essex Street." Logan shrugged. "See you, Aliyah."

I didn't leave campus until the lobby door closed behind Logan. The entire walk home was spent hoping his situation might improve. Maybe I should have prayed instead.

CHAPTER ELEVEN

Open Mind Night
Dylan

On any other day, I loved the aroma of coffee and cookies—weird for a kid raised on tea and biscuits. But it was night, the kind with microphones at the Witch's Brew.

They'd packed the place to the rafters. Instead of five or six patrons rattling around like the last handful of peas in the tin, at least thirty people milled about.

I never minded being the center of attention. That was why I'd thought writing a spoken word piece and setting it against the backdrop of every power chord I could muster was a good idea. But the prose that came out wasn't my usual fare. Nothing humorous or even eye-rollingly corny visited my mind. Emo was more like it. Ugh.

Apparently, music magic was a thing. I couldn't use it, but once I saw the sizeable crowd, I thought maybe I should've tried learning it anyway. I hadn't bothered doing the research, and I'd called myself an overachiever back in London. So much for local coffee shop stardom. I'd flop, I knew it. Nothing felt more sure at that point in my life, less than a week after Grace Dubois had dumped me outside the Engine House, then sat there with our friends like the world hadn't ended.

There'd been no way to argue with her. I wanted to be with her, and I cared about her more than anyone I'd been with. She wanted to take things to the next level, and I'd kept her waiting on that for over six months.

Something about the idea of sex with Grace didn't feel right. Mum always said that when Dad kissed her, the world went away. Nothing close to that ever happened when Grace kissed me. I told her I just wasn't ready, but the truth was, I might never be, and I didn't know why.

I'd avoided everyone since then except for Lee Young. He was the chillest person at Hawthorn, so it was nearly impossible to feel awkward around him. He'd never been particularly good friends with Grace either, unlike the rest of my school chums.

I glanced down at the sign-up sheet. Fortunately, two people had signed up before me, so I wouldn't have to open, at least. I wouldn't have to perform at all if I didn't want to. I still hadn't taken the essential leap—inking my name on the paper. Without that last action, I'd be off the hook.

I almost walked away. None of the locals or tourists in this place cared if this particular air magus got on the stage. I wasn't famous, though some of my regular customers from Walgreens nodded and smiled in greeting.

That was it, then. I set the pen down and almost let it go. Maybe I could practice for another week. Perhaps I'd even manage to write a piece with at least one pun for the following Sunday. Nobody would know or care, I thought. I was wrong.

Gale, my dragonet, snored on the coat rack. Maybe he had the right idea—sleep this impulse and my misery off. But before the pen contacted the table's surface, I glanced up. Big mistake. I couldn't walk away since most of my friends had shown up.

Lee Young held the door open and Aliyah Morgenstern walked through it, leading the usual crew. She hadn't just brought Izzy and Cadence, either. Oh, no, practically everyone followed her in, kids from town and Hawthorn Academy and one I didn't recognize, a goth guy only slightly taller than Hal Hawkins.

There was one blessed absence from the usual crew, however. Grace Dubois was nowhere to be seen. If I'd spotted her, I would have done my best to look invisible and beat feet out the back door. I'd rather get up in front of Parliament in my skivvies than perform in a coffee shop with her in the audience.

Don't get me wrong. There's nothing horrible about Grace. It wasn't her fault my heart was broken. But the last thing I wanted was for her to hear these words I'd written about her. Her absence gave me strength.

I twirled the pen in my fingers, pointed the business end of it at the paper, and wrote my name on the third line. After that, I took a deep breath and carried my guitar over to the ordering line. A nice cold drink was a requirement at that point.

In the UK, I would've snuck a flask of whisky from Dad's study. But crossing the ocean was impossible, so I settled for red zinger tea on ice, extra honey. As I waited in line, something tugged at my elbow.

I looked down to find Ember, Aliyah's familiar, clutching my sleeve and peeping up a storm. She peered at the area around my neck and even tried looking down my shirt. Clearly, she hoped to see Gale. Our familiars were all friends, too.

"Peep?" She tapped my nose with her snout, then pulled her head back, blinking.

"He's over there, Ember." I jerked my chin at the coat rack beside the stained glass clock.

"Peep!" Ember took off, sweeping up toward the perch to meet her friend. He woke instantly and they jumped up and down, greeting each other and waving their tails. If only I was that happy to see my friends, but their presence only made me more nervous than I'd expected.

When the barista handed me my tea, I took it in a trembling hand but remembered to tip. I'd worked food service long enough to appreciate how much work she'd done. The glass was slippery and I worried about dropping it, even though I was one of the best athletes at school. I'd never been clumsy—an asset, I guess, with all the jobs I needed just to afford Hawthorn Academy.

I had a scholarship for tuition, but supplies and the mundane aspects of living were more expensive than most kids my age understood. You needed personal care items and clothes, basic stuff almost all of my classmates took for granted. That brought me back to why I'd ended up in a relationship with Grace: she knew that struggle firsthand. I closed my eyes, wishing I was back in my dorm practicing. At least that had felt something like solace.

Making a spectacle out of myself wasn't an issue until my feelings got involved. Not just feelings. I'd had those all my life and expressed them, but up until this summer, they'd been overwhelmingly positive. What bothered me was expressing the other side. I thought nobody would tolerate negativity. The things you learn in school, right?

"You mind if I come do this with you next week?"

I turned, finding the unfamiliar Hawthorn student behind me. As it turned out, he was slightly more punk than goth, though almost equal parts of both. A familiar perched on his shoulder, a white gryphon with the head of some sort of seabird.

"For open mic? No, I don't mind." I shrugged. "But I don't know why you'd need me around."

"Because if I'm not a complete idiot, you're Logan Pierce's roommate from Hawthorn Academy. I'm Dorian Spanos, your new classmate." He held out his hand. The gryphon tilted its head, cawing softly. "And this is Mercy."

"Dylan Khan. My familiar is Gale, the blue guy on the coat rack." I went to shake his hand, but he pulled back quickly.

"Too slow." Dorian grinned. "Seriously, man, thanks. Your roommate talked about you for like an hour today. He thinks you rock harder than diamonds."

"Logan?" I blinked. "He's here?"

"No, he had to stay on campus, but he asked me to say hi. He's mentoring me because I transferred from the Academy." Dorian snorted. "Lucky me, I get to start school on probation."

"Isn't that a task for the best student in the class?" I was surprised because my roommate couldn't have the top grades. He had a learning disability. More than one, with accommodations and everything. "Logan's—"

"Yeah, I know, right?" Dorian threw back his head and laughed. "Definitely doesn't seem like the brand of straight-laced on most eggheads, but there you go."

"Okay." I wasn't sure what Dorian meant by that. Logan took practically everything seriously. Had he changed? I didn't want to know, at least not during a bout of stage fright. "You're a poet, then?"

"Oh, no way." Dorian glanced at the barista waving at him. "You'll see sometime. Later, dude, my order's up."

"Later."

I scanned the room for an empty seat, someplace I could take a load off while waiting for my turn at the mic, but I saw nothing nearby. The only empty tables were over by the entrance, and I didn't want to walk all that way once they called me. Fortunately, there was a counter with plain wooden stools where I could set my drink down and lean for a while, so I took that option.

"Heard you were coming." I turned, finding Aliyah's brother Noah behind me. "Overheard a couple of other things too. Sorry about Grace."

"Oh, thanks, Noah," I said and nodded. "I didn't expect to see you at open mic night."

"I'm usually here in the summer. Just not last week." He glanced at my glass of tea, where my hand gripped it. "Nervous? It's okay if you are. Elanor gets butterflies every single time she sees the light that means they're recording. Calls it red-light fever, and she's been in front of a camera since birth, practically."

"I'm not usually nervous. It's just that tonight, the piece I'm doing is personal." I glanced at the crowd. "I thought it'd be totally dead in here."

"Well, that's the way the cookie crumbles." Noah elbowed my arm. "At least you've got a whole table of people rooting for you."

"Why don't you go sit with them?"

"They're all Aliyah's friends. And yours. Not mine."

"I'd like to think we all could get along."

"That's easier said than done in my experience." Noah turned his hand, curling his fingers to study his nails. "Things get complicated, especially when certain relationships end."

I didn't have much to say to that. Not anything I wanted to hear come out of my mouth, anyway, so I nodded. Even if I only partially agreed with Noah, his feelings were valid. He'd been through a bad breakup too.

The first act went on, a guy who introduced himself as Ethan. It was the telekinetic psychic who worked at the Engine House. He waited tables and ran the register there, using his powers to aid in his work. At times I envied him.

Levitating food and beverages to customers would have made my food service job on campus so much easier. But we are what we are, and I was an air magus, not a telekinetic psychic. Maybe someday I'd have enough control of my element to create that effect.

Ethan had music playing during his act but didn't utter a sound the entire time. His whole performance was telekinetic, done while standing almost perfectly still. He turned himself into something like the eye of a storm using various stuff from a bag he had on stage with him plus random things patrons brought up. They stepped forward one at a time, adding to the whirling collection around him.

The items from his bag all gave off light somehow. Some of them were glow sticks, the kind kids carried on Halloween while trick or treating. Others were flashlights, which he flipped on their axes to make strobing patterns. Napkins, stirrers, lids, and even cups joined them. He made patterns with the items, moving them back and forth around over and under each other. When he finished, he set everything down simultaneously in a semi-circle behind him on the small platform that served as a stage.

I was glad I wasn't second. I pulled the sheet of paper with my poem on it out of my pocket, glancing down at it. I felt like maybe it wouldn't be enough. Ethan's would be a hard act to follow.

The next performer didn't seem to mind, though. She looked

familiar in a vague way, like she was related to someone I knew. Her hair was reddish-orange and riotously curly like the Disney princess who accidentally turned her mother into a bear, but this woman was decades past thirteen. She wore a green t-shirt that said Redheads Have More Fun and carried a block of clay with her.

I blinked, shaking my head, wondering what kind of performance she could possibly do with that grayish cube of earth.

"That's Wanda Ambersmith, Azrael's cousin. She's a sculptor." Noah jerked his chin at the clay.

"That's not performance art." I blinked.

"Just watch her." His smirk was like a dare.

Noah was right. Without using her hands, Wanda shaped the clay before our eyes in a process reminiscent of time-lapse photography. She worked faster than any mundane sculptor I'd heard of, and more neatly too. In Creatives at school, some of us worked clay, but nobody in my year was an earth magus like Wanda. Time wasn't the only thing she didn't waste. All the clay became something, no excess cut off or moved aside.

At the end of her performance, she lifted a small statue off the table in front of her, holding it up for the entire crowd to see. My heart sank more spectacularly than the *Titanic* because it was a moon hare—Grace's moon hare, Lune. It even had the scar on his flank. My ex must've spent all her time with the Ambersmiths that summer. Must still be spending time with them.

Instead of the usual rounds of applause, spectators came up to have a look at the sculpture. That gave me time to run away. I grabbed at the paper with my poem, but it wasn't on the counter anymore. I glared at Noah, who held it up, lips moving as he read the words silently.

"I'm getting out of here," I snarled. "Give that back."

"You'll do no such thing." Noah held the paper over his head. "Your poem's amazing and needs to be spoken aloud. It's a little raw but totally moving. I understand why you don't want to do it here, not with this crowd, but you will get up there and play. I'll read this so you don't have to. Lord knows it's no foreign sentiment to me."

"What?" I blinked.

"Open your ears and your mind." Noah held the paper between us. "You heard me. I'll let you go if you're really not okay with this, but you'll owe me a favor later."

"No." I looked Noah in the eye, surprised at finding an unexpected ally, one who'd been through something quite similar the year before. "No need for that. Yeah, you can read it. And if anyone asks who wrote it, we don't answer."

"You're an odd duck, Dylan Khan, but not from a bad egg." Noah grinned when the MC called my name. "Let's go."

Noah sauntered toward the platform, stepping on top without breaking his stride. I followed, staying behind him. I used to play MMOs, the kind of video game where you team up with your mates and slay Internet dragons. In those teams, one player got in front of the others, took all the hits, and kept the boss occupied while the rest of the team laid out heaping piles of damage. We called them "The Tank."

Even though this open mic idea was all mine and I'd written the words, Noah Morgerstern stepped into the spotlight for me. He tanked that behemoth of a crowd, keeping their attention. If it wasn't for his decision to help, all the misery racing through my subconscious would have stayed under the surface, festering.

He waited until I'd strummed a few bars of the cobbled-together chords before speaking my words.

"An Open Mind

You said we'd always be open.
Arms, hearts, minds.
But I can't find
Any good reason
In this smolder season
Why I'm left behind.

All the things you were

And I wasn't.
What mattered to you but
Doesn't
Sit on my shoulders
Well, we're older
So smolder away
And away from me

Not close, you said, but
Closed like an airless
Space station
Separatist nation
Glottal vibration
I got tossed
So get lost
In someone new

Does it matter to you
How I can't breathe
Friends smile, try being cool
While I see the
Heartbroken
Unspoken word

I could find
An open mind
On every street corner.

And that might be what I need.
It's not what I want.

An open heart's more my speed."

Instead of just applause, cheers, whistles, and even a few howls sounded from all over the room. I'd only expected a response from my friends. Maybe Noah was right; maybe I had a talent besides manual labor and Bishop's Row.

But if so, I'd keep it on the down-low for the time being. Nobody had to know that poem was mine. Insisting on reading my words up there was Noah's way of telling me I wasn't alone. The territory I stood at the edge of was more well-traveled than expected, and someone who had no particular bias in my favor considered my feelings valid.

That made all the difference.

CHAPTER TWELVE

Aliyah

Noah went to Hawthorn Academy on his own the Sunday before classes started. He didn't even want Mom and Dad walking with him. I'm not sure what he was up to, but I definitely cared. He'd been quieter than usual since the open mic night. If that poem had anything to do with the state of his heart, I felt for him.

I had a sneaking suspicion that poem wasn't Noah's, even if it sounded like familiar fare from him. It could have been Dylan's. I wondered why neither of them claimed the credit. Had they collaborated? I tried asking Cadence and Izzy what they thought.

Cadence just shook her head, saying she felt bad for both of them. Izzy had nothing but disdain for the subject matter.

"Of all the things to write about, honestly. Romance." She snorted. "Dreadful way to ruin amazing friendships."

I'd left it at that. Izzy might never care much about romantic love, and that was okay, even if her opinion differed quite a bit from mine. As far as Cadence was concerned, Izzy's ideas could have come from another planet.

"It's okay if you don't believe in love, Iz." Cadence sighed. "I believe in it enough for both of us."

Izzy harrumphed and turned her back. The two of them said nothing more about the subject. I hoped they could keep from arguing about it while I was at Hawthorn. Izzy clung to opinions like a sloth to a tree and Cadence quoted everyone, from characters in books and movies to real-life people. The last thing I wanted was to come home from school one random weekend to find they'd stopped speaking to each other.

In any event, I wouldn't have walked straight over to Hawthorn. I'd promised Grace I'd meet her in front of the Ambersmiths' dress shop on Washington Street. She said she needed help with her things, and since I'd brought most of mine to campus the day Dorian arrived, I had plenty of hands.

"Wow, Grace!" I stopped on the curb and blinked at my roommate. "You look amazing."

"Thanks!" Her smile reminded me of a crescent moon. "I made this myself, and a whole wardrobe worth of other stuff." She gestured at the pile of garment and duffel bags on the sidewalk beside her.

This was the only time I'd seen Grace wear anything with a skirt outside of the formal dances last year. They looked good on her in general, but the one she had on now was particularly flattering. It had pleats and navy-blue piping that matched the school blazer perfectly. If that wasn't enough, the fabric she'd fashioned it from had a color-changing effect.

It wasn't iridescent, or anything like the mood rings Mom and Dad laughed about in the touristy trinket shops on Essex Street. In a way, it reminded me of the hypercolored shirts Bubbe showed me in pictures of Dad when he was my age, but the fabric on Grace's skirt wasn't anything so mundane. I could tell she'd used Umbral magic and something else mixed together on the fabric. It moved when she did, apparently activated kinetically.

"What did you do to that?"

"My own magic mostly, with a little changeling glamour. Azrael spent a couple of weeks in the dress shop with me, but his cousin told him to get lost after that. Fortunately, we worked on enough fabric together to make an entire wardrobe like this in my size."

Grace pulled aside her blazer to show me the shirt she'd paired with her outfit. Instead of the threadbare and utilitarian flannels of last year, her blouse rivaled the ones in designer shops on Newbury Street in Boston, and once again, this was a magical garment. It fit her like it had been sewn on, with no hint of mundane fasteners like buttons, zippers, or ties.

"You're going to be the best-dressed student this year." I hefted a bag, slinging it over my shoulder.

"Then my plan for school domination will go off without a hitch." Grace winked. "Somebody's got to give Temperance Fairbanks a run for her money. I've got plans, but first impressions matter, so clothes are important."

"Why you, though? I mean, it sounds like a lot of work and not much fun."

"Faith shouldn't have to deal with any more sibling rivalry. She deserves to just be contented with Hal all year." Grace sighed.

"Sounds like a good idea." I nodded, slinging on another bag to balance the weight. Hal's illness was terminal, so I agreed. He and Faith shouldn't have to waste any of their time together.

"Thank goodness I overheard Alex and Charity last year with you." Grace arranged the rest of her luggage on and across her body. "Their plan was to rule the school and sway public opinion against all the other extrahumans. I'm going to stop them, no matter what it takes."

"Can I help?"

"I'm not sure with what just yet, but definitely." Grace nodded. "Probably, you'll spend a lot of time looking otherworldly and vaguely threatening. Easy for you."

"I'm not sure any of us can really out-mean the mean girl, though."

"Yeah, nope. I'm going to out-cool the mean girl, then use niceness to get her into orbit." Grace snorted. "I'm Canadian, remember?"

We laughed our way across the street and around the corner to turn down Essex. Once there, we looked from side to side, searching for the magical migrating door. We found it next door to the Witch's Brew. As I reached to pull it open, Grace stopped me.

"I want a coffee before heading in there." Grace sighed, gazing down at her shoes. "I'd go to the café on campus, but that'll be awkward."

"Okay." I changed direction, heading into the coffee shop instead. We got in line, where I shuffled my feet before asking the million-dollar question.

"Hey, did you want to talk? About you and Dylan, I mean."

"There's not too much to talk about, at least not stuff I want to say in a crowded coffee shop. But things were kind of weird between us for a while."

It was our turn, so we ordered our drinks. Nothing fancy for me, just coffee with a splash of soymilk. Grace went all out and got a chocolate cherry mocha with extra whipped cream.

"You think he'll be okay?" I sprinkled cinnamon in my coffee.

"I'm not sure." Grace stuck a straw through the whipped cream. "I feel bad, but we didn't want the same things from each other. It's all private stuff."

We took our coffees and headed back out again. This time we marched straight through the door into the vestibule, then into the lobby at Hawthorn Academy.

Last year when I arrived, everything was strange, exciting, and far more awkward than expected. This year was totally different, thanks to Kitty, who'd arrived with her family shortly before us.

"Mama, Mom!" Kitty jumped up and down, squealing. "These are the friends I told you about, Grace and Aliyah. Girls, this is Mama, and that's Mom."

The trio of women smiled and waved. Kitty looked almost exactly like her mama, who was pale with ruddy hair and freckles. Her mom had curly dark hair, bronze skin, and a pair of golden wire-rimmed spectacles perched on her nose.

"It's so good to meet you." I held out a hand toward the women. "I got one of your makeup kits for Hanukkah last year, and it's been awesome."

"I'm so glad to hear that." Mom shook my hand. "And you were worried." She dropped a wink at Kitty's mama.

"Not anymore." Mama smiled.

"You came an awful long way to drop Kitty off at school." Grace grinned.

"It's on the way, actually." Mom adjusted her glasses. "We've got a health and beauty convention to attend in Boston later this week."

"Cool." Grace nodded.

"If you don't mind my asking, who's your designer?" Mama gave Grace's outfit an appraising glance. "Obviously, the blazer is the school's, but the rest of your ensemble is quite remarkable."

"I made them myself." Grace slipped her blazer off and turned in a slow circle, showing off her handiwork. "I spent the summer in an internship at Ambersmith Fashions, and this is what I did with my spare time."

"This is interesting. We've heard of Ambersmith, but many of their designs seem geared toward an older clientele."

"That's one reason I wanted to work with them." Grace nodded. "They could use a fresh perspective, I thought."

"Well, it's clear you're doing amazing things, Grace."

"Thanks so much. I appreciate it." Grace's cheeks reddened and she bowed her head, reminding me of the day she'd made first defense on the Bishop's Row team last year.

"Hey, Grace, Aliyah." Logan waved from the stairs. I watched him descend, with Dorian following.

Kitty's parents made their goodbyes and headed toward the door, while Kitty dragged her luggage toward the staircase, heading up after Logan and Dorian stepped off. I saw that while Logan wore a simple t-shirt and jeans with his blazer, Dorian's outfit would have looked at home in a Shrine of Hollywood catalog. Grace didn't match his goth theme, but the quality and care he'd put into his attire were on par with hers.

"Who's this, then?" Grace put on an enormous smile.

"This is Dorian Spanos from Rhode Island." Logan put on the good old Pierce family manners. "Dorian, this is Grace Dubois."

"Right, Aliyah's roommate." Dori took the hand she offered and shook it firmly. "The one who loves K-Pop, right?"

"Well, you're an enormous improvement over Alex Onassis." Grace wrinkled her nose. "Actually, that's not as nice as it sounded. Anything's an improvement over Alex."

"What's wrong with him?" Dorian raised an eyebrow.

"He's literally toxic. Poison magus, used to date my roommate. He flunked finals last year, so he's been held back. You're taking his spot."

"Oh, yeah, the bigot." Dorian nodded. "Logan told me a few things about that guy."

"Really?" I glanced at Logan.

"Only a little, I swear." Logan winced. "I figured somebody had to warn him."

"I'll catch him up the rest of the way." Grace snagged Dorian's arm, lacing hers through the crook of his elbow. "Let's have lunch. I bet we'll have loads to talk about."

As Grace escorted Dorian to the cafeteria, Logan and I stood there blinking. He scratched his head, and I shrugged.

"What just happened there?" I tilted my head.

"I'm not sure." Logan shook his head. "Dating's confusing."

"I cornered the market on that," I said, smiling. "I guess maybe you did too."

"I might be imagining this, but I think Grace grew up an awful lot over the summer."

"No, I agree with you. This new Grace has got a purpose, too."

I sauntered toward the café with Logan, filling him in about my roommate's plans. We stopped at the end of the line, where upper-classmen stood waiting to order coffee from none other than Dylan Khan. One of them turned, revealing a familiar face.

"I'm not judging, Aliyah, but aren't you caffeinating a bit too much?"

"No, Darren, I'm good." Noah still avoided his ex-boyfriend, but he wasn't my enemy. "Just waiting with Logan. He could use a latte or three, don't you think?"

"Perhaps." Darren nodded. "He's been working hard."

"Yeah, Dorian's a handful," Logan replied. "He's had me running around with him all over campus this past week."

"If you ask me, it's that gryphon of his." Darren jerked his chin at Dorian's familiar, who'd perched on the edge of the garbage can between the café and the cafeteria. "That critter seems to be all over the place."

"That's pretty typical of the species." I shrugged. "My grandma says she requires a security deposit for boarding them. What can you do?"

"Make sure he's in Familiar Bonding for one thing." Logan sighed. "Looks like I'll be back there again this year if only to help Dorian through it. I think his familiar needs it more."

"Maybe I'll go too." I grinned. "Second-years on probation can opt-in."

"You hardly need that. I mean, look at the two of you." Darren nodded at Ember, who'd been sleeping on my shoulder half the morning. "Thicker than thieves."

"Maybe I want to keep my friend company and meet some new people." I sighed. "Also, I'm still on probation. Any good deed will help me in that department."

"If you ask me, they came down too hard with your punishment." Darren turned toward the counter and ordered a pot of tea from Kayleigh, the café's manager. She beckoned him toward the other end of the counter. "Anyway, I'm sure I'll see you two around the lounge."

"See you later, Darren." I waved.

We finally got to the counter, where Dylan stared at the doorway to the cafeteria. On weekdays, it was closed, but on weekends and during school breaks, it was open. It perfectly framed Grace sitting with Dorian, the two of them laughing at a booth over sandwiches and beverage roulette.

"You okay, man?" Logan leaned on the counter.

"I'll deal." Dylan's voice sounded unusually flat. I didn't like it. "What are you ordering?

"Nothing, just saying hi." Logan blinked.

"Well, hi. There's a line behind you. They kind of pay me to help them, and once I'm through this one, I'm off-shift."

"No, wait," I added. "Get Logan a triple latte. I think he needs it." I jerked a thumb at Logan's puffy eyes.

"Okay." Dylan busied himself with the espresso machine, pouring the shots into a cup and adding frothed milk. "Here you go."

"Dylan, do you want to hang out at the welcome party?"

"Maybe, but I'm leaving at the first possible minute. Totally worn out. You don't want me around. I'm a stick-in-the-mud lately."

I blinked, unsure what to say to that, but luckily, Logan had an answer.

"That's okay, I don't want to watch Elanor parade around either. After they introduce the first-years, I'm out too."

"Thanks, bro." The tension in Dylan's shoulders eased. "I'll appreciate the company. Next!"

We got out of the way so Dylan could finish helping the line. I knew his manager would get back to the counter soon, but for now, we had to let him do his job.

"What's next for you, Aliyah?"

"I guess I'm taking Grace's luggage upstairs." I pointed at the suitcase and bag she'd left sitting beside the staircase, then at the ones I still carried.

"I'll help."

He grabbed some luggage with me and we stepped on the first stair, calling out the third floor. Once we got to my room, Logan left the cases, saying he'd better check on Dorian.

If Grace was enlisting him in her quest for cool, Logan and I might end up doing a lot of behind-the-scenes work for them. Maybe I'd like to be in the background for a change. During last year's first two days at Hawthorn Academy, I had been the center of disaster and unwanted attention.

As it turned out, I was wrong about all of that.

"We just didn't want the same things from a relationship, Aliyah." Grace held a blouse with mother-of-pearl buttons between her and the mirror. "He's amazing, smart, funny, and athletic, but what can you do?"

"Not break up?" I slipped one of my spare school blazers on a hanger. "I don't understand, maybe because I didn't even really like Alex. But what do you mean, the same things?"

"Oh." Grace's face in the mirror reddened. "Aliyah, I'm talking about sex."

"Like, he pressured you?" I blinked, unable to imagine Dylan Khan leering and looming like boys in movies.

"Yeah, no." Grace shook her head. "More like the other way around."

"Um." My fingers fumbled, the tunic I held dropping back into the suitcase.

"I stopped, of course." Grace sighed. "He wasn't comfortable, I could tell. The first time was that night you walked in on us. I asked him if he was ready and he said no but that he loved me, so I waited. Over the summer, I asked again. Same thing. I realized it just wouldn't work."

"Oh, Grace. I'm sorry."

You're not and you know it. March out of here this instant and ask that boy on a date. See what happens.

"No." Grace said it, not me. My jaw dropped because for a moment, I thought she'd heard the Evil Inside Voice. "There's nothing to be sorry about. Some people just aren't compatible, no matter how much they care about each other."

"Are you okay?"

"I'll live." Grace snorted. "I've got outfits to rock, mean girls to outdo. Having something to keep me busy helps. And that you're not walking on eggshells around me."

"What do you mean?"

"Logan's giving me the cold shoulder." She sighed. "Can't blame him after I dumped his roommate."

"I'm not sure that's just about Dylan, though."

"What do you mean?"

"His life's a mess," I said, and I told her all about the last couple of weeks.

"Leaping Luna." Grace whistled. "I understand now why the headmaster's confining him to campus, but it sucks. What's he going to do on Parents' Night? They showed up last time."

"I don't know." I moved to the dresser with a stack of leggings. "I haven't asked him yet."

"There's time, I guess." Grace put the rest of her clothes away in the wardrobe, then opened another bag and started stowing pairs of shoes under her bed. They all looked new.

"Did you make those over the summer, too?" Last year, she'd only had one pair of sneakers.

"No, Az did. He ended up doing a good job at his uncle's shop. Definitely cobbler material, that guy."

"That's a pretty significant gift, Grace."

"Not really." She shrugged. "I'm the one who convinced his uncle to give him a chance there. At least, that was what Azrael said when he gave these to me."

"Well, he's always been a good kid."

"Izzy disagrees." Grace raised an eyebrow. "Says he's obsessive. I didn't get that impression."

"She's hands-off in the displays of affection department. Really, they're different from each other." I glanced down at the row of shoes. "We all are. That's what you were saying earlier, right?"

"Yeah, Aliyah." Grace stood, holding her arms out. "And sometimes, exactly the same."

We hugged, then left the rest of our unpacking for later so we'd make the welcome assembly on time.

CHAPTER THIRTEEN

I sat in the front row again like last September. Other repeats included Headmaster Hawkins appearing out of nowhere and Grace sitting with me, but this time, the rest of our year joined us. We took up all the seats in front of the podium, baffling the students in Noah's year, who stuck to the back.

"Stealing the scene. I like it." Hal peered around Faith and me, grinning at Grace.

"Good." Faith clutched his hand and nodded at me. "Because here comes trouble."

Grace stared placidly ahead at the headmaster, posture straight enough to balance a stack of books on her head. She'd said earlier that I was supposed to look otherworldly and vaguely threatening, so that's what I kept in mind when I turned to see what Faith meant. Or rather who.

Even without my ex escorting her, I would have recognized the girl walking across the room as Temperance Fairbanks. For one thing, she was built along the same lines as her sisters, despite her darker hair. For another, hard laughter dropped from her lips like diamonds into a lead-crystal vase.

I narrowed my eyes, nostrils flaring. Ember stood up on my shoulder, wings out and hissing softly.

Good, you sense that power, then. She's got more than the other two. Possibly even you.

"What's her element?" I murmured to Faith.

"Water," she whispered back.

I considered the implications. The other water magi I knew were deep, a bit quiet, and generally pleasant people. In our studies last year, Professor Luciano had taught that water was a sympathetic element, able to comprehend and conform temporarily while retaining its essential nature. Logan exemplified that, so how could Temperance Fairbanks be as horrible as Faith implied?

Because she understands of course, foolish girl.

That made no sense, so I tuned the Evil Inside Voice out and watched Alex bow slightly while waving her toward a seat in the center aisle across from Grace and one row back. They sat right behind Kitty and Eston, whom Alex greeted despite the chilly reception Kitty gave him. Eston stared at his shoes, mumbling something about a long drive.

"It's not like you think." Faith murmured. "Her water magic, I mean."

I'd ask her what that meant later because Headmaster Hawkins took that moment to begin his speech.

"Welcome, students." This year, Headmaster Hawkins didn't smile, and I couldn't fault him for it. His son sat in the same row with me, after all, and he looked ashy and thinner than he should have. Hal hadn't even had a growth spurt.

"Summer is over, and it's time to settle in for the new school year. Since brevity served me well last year, I'd like to rely on it again. However, that's not in the cards this time."

Ah, yes, the chaos to come.

I sighed and tried to tune out the Evil Inside Voice. The assembly information had to be important.

"Your rooming assignments come from the pneumatic tubes to my left. Your class schedules should already be in your rooms; check the desks. First Years will report back here for their campus tour after lunch." Headmaster Hawkins cleared his throat. "I want every student to make as much effort as possible to get into the routine this first month because in October, extramurals will begin."

"You'll be hosts and ambassadors to students from Gallows Hill School and Wolf Messing Preparatory. I expect you to treat them with care and respect, as you'd wish to be treated if they hosted us on their campuses. Even though we'll be competing in many events against our guests, some projects will require your collaboration with a diverse group of extrahuman peers and their teachers."

Like last year, Headmaster Hawkins stopped his speech to make eye contact with each student in the room. When our eyes met, I felt a sense of welcome, which eased the tension in my shoulders. Even Ember settled down, but that feeling was short-lived. As his gaze shifted to the next row, I watched his knuckles pale as he gripped the sides of the podium tighter. His Adam's apple bobbed as he swallowed nothing.

I looked over my shoulder. He'd locked gazes with Temperance, and from the way her eyes narrowed and his widened, he didn't like what he'd seen. He moved along to the next student but took less time with each of them than last year.

"You see?" Faith whispered.

"Yeah." I nodded.

"You're all dismissed. The welcoming party will commence in this very room after dinner this evening."

Students rose from their seats or leaned forward, chatting with each other. Our group did the same. Grace and Dorian stood at the head of the room, smiling brightly even though their words to us were anything but.

"Read any good essays this summer, Hal?" Grace asked, raising her eyebrow.

"No." Hal sighed. "I mean, I read some, but most weren't good."

"Give us the bad news first." Dorian tilted his head.

"Sorry about your sister, Dorian."

"Oh." He shook his head, cheeks red. "Well, that's not the bad news I meant."

"You did it again, Hal." Grace sighed, shaking her head.

"Give him a break, he's due at the infirmary in a half-hour." Faith stood up.

"Why not talk about this there?" I offered. "Hal won't be late for Nurse Smith, and it's bound to be more private than the lobby."

Nobody said anything, but most of my classmates clearly agreed. Grace, Dorian, Logan, Kitty, and Eston followed Hal and Faith toward the infirmary. I started to bring up the rear when Lee Young stopped me.

"What's up?"

"More like down and who." Lee tilted his head toward the other side of the lobby.

"Dylan." I nodded. "I'll go over and talk to him."

"Wait," Lee said. "I know you get distracted sometimes, but try and remember to keep an eye out for him. He's not doing so great, and everything I've tried isn't helping much."

"Then why are you asking me?" I blinked. "You're the one who notices this stuff. It's kind of like your superpower."

"You're kidding, right?" Lee blinked back.

"No."

"If my superpower is noticing, then yours is helping. Whatever you try, when it's for someone else, it works." He grinned, fist-bumping my shoulder. Before I could make any reply, he headed toward the stairs with Scratch bouncing behind him. That was how I ended up alone, staring across the room at the wall Dylan leaned against.

It was almost the same spot I'd stood in the year before, despairing about fitting in or even making it through the first week of school. Someone I cared about had gotten himself stuck in the same position, which nearly broke my heart.

You had it bad. Why shouldn't he suffer alone as you did?

"Why should he, when I could help?"

Indeed. So why are you standing around?

So, this particular bout of negativity in my heart and mind didn't come from the Evil Inside Voice. Instead, it was garden-variety self-doubt telling me Dylan Khan wouldn't want any sympathy from me. I almost turned my back on him, but someone wouldn't let me.

"Peep?" Ember craned her neck, twisting it until her eyes were level with mine. Then, she tapped me on the top of the head with her tail. "Peep. Peep!"

After that, she launched off my shoulder, sailing toward Dylan with the enthusiasm and speed she usually reserved for me. She left me little choice but to follow her. I wasn't sure what to say, so I just leaned against the wall beside him.

We stood in silence, neither daring to break it. Ember and Gale swooped back and forth in front of us. I turned my head to look at Dylan and saw that he stared straight ahead, watching the dragonets. Finally, he spoke.

"What's he like?"

"Hmm?"

"The new kid." Dylan swallowed. "The one she's spending so much time with."

"Oh." I turned, putting my right shoulder against the wall instead of my back so I could face my friend. "Dorian reminds me of Cadence, but not a girl, and monochrome instead of rainbow."

"Cadence is good, right? I mean, she wouldn't, um, hurt anyone?" The extra sheen over Dylan's eyes meant he needed an answer.

"Not on purpose, no." I shook my head, even though he wasn't looking at me. "I think they're just being friendly, for what it's worth."

"I'd say that's worth about pocket lint." Dylan closed his eyes. "You're clueless about that stuff, Aliyah."

"That's fair."

"And honestly, who wouldn't like Grace DuBois? She's awesome." All the air went out of him. His breath hitched as he took one to speak again. "Lee came up to the counter this morning. Talked at me about some kind of 'this too shall pass' stuff."

"He's not wrong." I sighed. "But getting through the time before stuff passes? That's harder than it should be."

"You don't really understand." He finally turned his head. The corners of his eyes held teardrops like cut glass. "I'm alone in this."

"Nah. Saw you with Noah at the Open Mic. He gets it."

"Yeah." Dylan's gaze softened. "He said I can talk to him any time, but I don't want to."

"So, what do you want?" After uttering those words, I could barely breathe. I didn't know why.

"To be with my friends and forget about her for a little while, but that feels impossible. They all went off with her like she's Miss Salem or something." The tear staining his cheek gave my voice back.

"I'm still here."

"Thanks for that, Aliyah." Dylan turned, mirroring my stance against his section of the wall. "So, can you tell me why?"

I blinked, unsure what he asked for until he continued.

"What's with the Fashion Week wardrobe? Why are they following her like a pack of coyotes? And why did she choose Dorian to hang all over?"

"Dorian's got the charisma to pull weight in a power couple. Because she's trying to rival Te—"

"And here we have the mad pyromaniac and the class clown." Alex's voice sounded far too close to my back.

"Funny," a sweet-toned feminine voice said. "But looks aren't everything."

I stood up straight and turned. This put my eyes almost on a level with Alex's, so I gave him my best glare. My anger kept my vision to a tight focus, so for the time being, I ignored the girl at his side.

"Poison the air someplace else, Onassis," I hissed.

Alex snorted. "Discriminate much?"

"Relax, Alexander." The feminine voice spoke again. "It's the lobby. Anyone can be here. And if Miss Disciplinary Probation Morgenstern makes trouble, I'll take it to the headmaster."

I turned to face the speaker, and the first thing I noticed was that her hair wasn't the same close up as it had seemed from afar. It reminded me of water in a creek, brown with deep undertones. She'd bleached out the underneath and dyed it dark green. I soon saw why.

A pair of tentacles the same hue slid along the right shoulder of the girl's blazer. A moment later, a head moved out from behind her neck, eyes shining at me from under her earlobe. I'd seen one of these before.

"Grundylow." I blinked, everything I'd read about them coming out of my mouth before I could stop it. "Spawn of Grendel, loves brackish water and drowning things. Associates with water magi."

"Told you she was a total nerd about critters." Alex rolled his eyes and tugged her sleeve. "You saw she-who-shall-not-be-named and one of her charity cases, Tempe. Let's go do something else."

"Wait, which is this one?" She flicked her pinkie at Dylan. "The orphan?"

"Nah." Alex shook his head. "He's the over-caffeinated clown."

"Could have fooled me." She shrugged and turned her back on us, linking her arm through Alex's and sauntering away.

As Temperance Fairbanks walked away, the grundylow parted her hair and stared at me. Its grin curved, matching the angle of the knobby horns on its head, which reminded me of the brambles that grow in seaside swamps.

"So, I guess we've met the new mean girl."

"Definitely not the same as the old one." I jerked my chin at the eerie critter. "We'll have to watch out."

We didn't know the half of it.

CHAPTER FOURTEEN

During the welcome party later that night, I acted as a shuttle between Dylan and the rest of our friends. I refused to abandon him, but I needed to back Grace up from time to time. Mostly, though, she had a good handle on her new circumstances. By that, I mean the altitude she'd gained in the popularity stratosphere.

Elanor Pierce stopped to chat with Grace more than once. Last year, Elanor didn't give the kids in our year the time of day. Temperance and Alex had a gaggle of new students hovering around them, but not for long. By the time the magipsychic slideshow showcasing the new first-years began, several of them had approached Grace and Dorian to see what all the fuss over them was about. Two even stuck around.

I needed a break from the constant churn of social activity and ended up leaning against the wall with Dylan to catch my breath. Ember perched on the chandelier with Gale.

"Looks like she's getting on." Dylan stared across the room, letting his eyes wander amongst the people in Grace's orbit.

"Check out her competition, Dylan." I jerked my thumb at the smaller throng of kids in the corner with Temperance Fairbanks. "If you can call it that."

"And we thought Charity knew what she was doing, sending Temperance to be the new It Girl." He snorted. "That stumble's worse than Logan out on the Bishop's Row court."

"Be nice." I elbowed Dylan's shoulder. "Nobody's good at everything, and he needs all the help he can get lately."

"It's just a basis for comparison. I didn't mean to insult my mate." Dylan sighed. "It seems like everything I do is all wrong."

"I get it."

"Yeah. Thanks for understanding, Aliyah." He waved his hand, dismissing the crowd. "Being here in the corner."

"There's no way I'd leave a friend all alone." I swallowed, praying I wouldn't blush.

"Right. Being nice, it's punk as fu—" Dylan put his hand over his mouth, eyes wide "I can't believe that almost slipped out, sorry."

"Awkwardness sort of compounds on itself, like interest on a bad loan." My face felt flushed, though he wasn't looking at me anymore. "But it gets better, Dylan."

"You're being summoned again." Dylan nodded toward the throng of people around our friends. This time it wasn't Grace beckoning me over but Hal Hawkins.

"Will you be okay for a few minutes?" I raised my eyebrow, awaiting his response.

Dylan gave me a grin rarer than diamonds. "Yeah, I'm okay."

I patted his shoulder before heading toward Hal. Ember swooped down, peeping over her shoulder at Gale as she perched on my shoulder. Crossing the room wasn't as difficult as it might have been for Hal with his energy-sapping illness. I stood behind him and Faith, whose arm he clung to.

"What's up?"

"As soon as they show the last student, I'm out. Let's bring Dylan with us." Hal took a few short, shallow breaths before continuing, "Faith's staying, but I need help navigating a room this packed."

"No problem." I glanced at Faith Fairbanks. "You sure you don't want to go with Hal and leave the socializing to me?"

"Oh, you can't always get what you want." She sighed. "I need to keep an eye on them." She jerked her chin at Temperance and Alex.

"All the more reason for us to switch tasks." I raised an eyebrow. "Or do you think I can't handle him like I did last year?"

"I know you can, but I'm the one who knows Tempe's tells. Anyway, you're a sledgehammer, and this is a scalpel job. I've got Alex covered; got a new preventive tactic."

"Okay?" I blinked. "Care to elaborate?"

"Meet me for a swim tomorrow night and we'll talk about it."

"Sure." I nodded. Faith and I hadn't worked together magically. Our skills weren't compatible, more like oil and water, but teamwork might be the key to surviving this year. However, something might throw a monkey wrench into our swimming plans.

"Don't we have to worry about Tempe invading the public bathroom?"

"She's on the second floor and lazy. There's no way she'd come all the way to the third floor to use ours."

"It's starting, look."

The magipsychic display lit up. A series of faces with familiars and names flashed across it, simultaneously announced over speakers in the chandeliers. The first was one I recognized, an Ambersmith, not a sibling of Azrael's but one of his cousins. Her name was Giselle, and she had a raven familiar, which didn't surprise me. I remembered her as insatiably curious and secretive, so a raven fit perfectly. She was one of the first-years hanging with Grace.

Next was Temperance, her grundylow grinning eerily at the screen. His eyes seemed to meet mine, making me shiver. A blond boy with a buzz cut followed her. He wore horn-rimmed glasses and held a cat familiar in his arms. His name escaped me.

My heart almost stopped when the next student showed up, partly because at first glance, his last name looked like Morgenstern. I blinked and shook my head and read Magnuson, Arick. He had the same initials, but the uncanny coincidences ended there. Arick had tousled shoulder-length light-brown hair with a pair of small plaits behind each ear, Nordic style. He stood near Dorian and had no familiar. I guess we'd see him in Familiar Bonding, then.

Alex Onassis flashed up on the screen. I turned away. If only I could ignore him for the entire school year. But that would be impossible. I needed to help my friends counter Temperance's machinations, and he was firmly and clearly on her team. We'd confront each other sooner or later. I might be the only person he feared on this campus.

I'd lost count of the number, but the next student I noted in the slideshow was the last one. Michelina Zanelli had brassy blonde hair and tanned olive skin. Like Arick, she had no familiar, but she stood alone behind the refreshment table like I had last year.

"And we're out." Hal rested a hand on my arm.

"I'll make sure he gets upstairs safely, Faith."

"Thanks."

I escorted Hal Hawkins across the room, locking eyes with Dylan as we got closer to his section of the wall, I felt Ember tug my hair, so I helped Hal lean against the wooden surface and turned.

"Hi." A boy stood behind me, extending his hand for a shake. "I'm—"

"Arick Magnuson, I saw." I nodded. "It's nice to meet you, but I'm kind of busy right now."

"I just wanted to ask how you got your dragonet." He glanced at Hal, his brow wrinkling. "Are you okay?"

"Hal's not feeling too well." I shook his hand. "Stop by my table at breakfast or dinner and we'll talk."

"Oh." When the handshake ended, he turned his hand palm up and stared at it like he'd just met a celebrity.

Oh, no. It seems you've got a fan club. Infamy is greater than fame.

Hal leaned more heavily on my arm, nearly throwing me off-balance.

"Come on, Hal, let's get you upstairs." Dylan came to support him on the other side. "See you later, Magnuson."

"Yeah, later."

We didn't speak again until I asked the stairs for the third floor.

The only sound on the way up was Dylan's yawn. Once we reached the top, Hal finally said something.

"You're someone's role model already." Hal grinned, lips pale and eyes sleepy. "Good going."

"Maybe." I shook my head. "But what could he know except that I'm an extramagus? The last person who considered that awesome was Alex."

"It's probably Ember." Dylan raised his eyebrow. "Dragonets attract loads of attention. I mean, I know from personal experience and everything."

"Thanks, Dylan." I sighed. "I hope you're right."

"It can't be that bad, surely?" Dylan shook his head. "I've never seen Alex go for someone who wasn't attractive. I mean, look at Darren."

Hal sighed. "I'm sure all his interest in her came from the extramagus thing. He must have asked me a hundred questions about her powers after Valentine's Day last year."

I felt like I'd been frozen in a block of ice because this wasn't something I expected other people to understand, let alone point out. I stopped walking in the middle of the hall.

"Thanks, Captain Obvious." Dylan blinked. "You broke Aliyah."

"Sorry." Hal's forehead wrinkled, making him look just like his father for a moment. "I didn't mean to upset you. I just don't feel like I have time to mince words."

"I knew all this, but I didn't expect anyone else to notice." I took a deep breath and continued on our way toward his room. "At least you unleashed that now instead of mid-crisis or something."

"Yeah." Dylan nodded. "As much as I'd like to laugh and say what crisis, I worry we'll have more than one this year."

As we waited for Hal to palm the plate next to his door and go inside, I realized Dylan was on to something. Fewmets would hit the fan eventually, probably several times once extramurals started. If I'd had a djinn's lamp, I would've wished for him to be wrong, but even magical wishes might not equalize the social battles ahead.

CHAPTER FIFTEEN

The first-day lecture should have felt like a review. Professor Luciano talked about a subject most extrahumans had been hearing about since early childhood: coincidence.

"The idea of fate is as old as humanity." As he spoke, an illustration of three women at a loom appeared on the chalkboard. "Extrahumans know more about it because of our connection with the Under, and by association, with changelings and their faerie parents. Destiny is not as simple as the idea that your path was decided before birth. It works in patterns, cycles that could be either followed or broken. We call that coincidence."

Luciano's take was extremely old-school, likely a product of his education at the oldest extrahuman universities in the world. Or perhaps because of his Italian citizenship and heritage. The cradle of magus society was the Mediterranean.

"As adult magi, you'll need to know how to recognize, research, and track coincidental patterns. Your third-year studies will largely focus on that. For now, I want you to begin paying attention. Anything that looks like a pattern should be noted and discussed with your peers during library time. At the end of the year, you'll turn in a brief personal essay about what you noticed."

Everyone furiously scribbled notes, even Logan, who always got a transcript of the lecture as part of his IEP accommodations. Everyone must have found this idea and the assignment interesting. It gave me a strange feeling, like part of my brain had floated up to the ceiling.

Maybe that's why I went through the motions for the rest of the day until Gym, which shook me out of the odd funk.

"Listen up, kiddos, because I'm only telling you once!" Coach Pickman clapped her hands to get our attention. "You might be second-years, but you're still twerps to me. If you want to make the extramural Bishop's Row team, you'll work your hinies off, starting this minute."

She stopped in front of Dorian, who stood with his hand in the air, a tactic that had worked wonders on Professor Luciano that morning. It flew about as adeptly as a waterlogged pigeon with Coach Pickman.

"Spanos. What's your problem?"

"I'm just checking. You got the note from Nurse Smith, right?"

"Necessary medical device, boo-fricking-hoo. You're still running laps. Everyone new to me does. I made Hawkins do it last year with his note, and you're no different."

"But, Coach!"

"No buts in my gym unless they're on the court running laps. Snap to it, Spanos!" She clapped her hands so close to his nose I thought she'd pinch it.

She turned her back on Dorian, which was a good thing under the circumstances. He dropped his jaw, then narrowed his eyes as he snapped it shut. The look my classmate gave the coach was like a hail of arrows on a battlefield. As I sauntered toward the starting line marked on the track around the court, I slowed my pace to walk beside Dorian.

"Dude, she's harsh but fair most of the time. It'll be okay. Just run the laps. Look at it this way; you can't be any slower than Logan. He's practically a turtle."

"Easy for you to say. He said you're the fastest kid in our year." Dorian hung his head, tugging on the section of shirt covering his chest. It clung oddly like he wore something under it. "This is going to hurt."

"I'm sorry. She's only tough at the beginning. If you have any problems today, she'll find something else for you to do."

"Maybe your psychic friend can give me a reading about gym class." Dorian rolled his eyes. "Thanks for checking on me, from one delinquent to another."

"Lee Young says giving a damn is my superpower." I shrugged. "Who am I to argue with that?"

Coach Pickman's whistle cut off our conversation. Like last year, the simplicity of running lulled me into a sense of calm, which was a tough state to attain at school. Gym was one of my only escapes from feeling like a misfit on this campus. If I were perfect, I'd love it here, but I'd learned last year that nobody was.

You could be, with a little work in the right direction.

"No." I disguised my response to the Evil Inside Voice in measured breathing as I paced my run. Last year, it had wanted me to give in to my temper and live up to my mother's notorious Hopewell heritage. Instead, I'd decided to do everything I could to stay good.

I glanced over my shoulder and saw Logan and Dorian at the back of the pack, though Dorian's face was red and he was sweating far more than I'd expected. Maybe he had mundane asthma or something. I hoped it wasn't an awful magical malady like Hal's.

Without Alex Onassis in our class this year, I pretty much had no competition on the track. Faith paced herself well and was the next fastest, but she still ate my dust. I hoped to get on the extramural team this year, but it was a long shot even with my speed.

Elanor Pierce was the star player at our school, and my brother Noah was a close second in ability and skill. In our year, Dylan and Grace were both better athletes than me. Lee and I would probably compete for the last slot on that team, with one of us on reserve. If we got that far. There were three other students in Noah's year who'd give us a run for our money.

I watched Hal press the button on the stopwatch as I passed the finish line, then I leaned forward with my hands on my knees, just breathing. When Faith pulled up after me, we both sat on the bench near him.

"Sorry, Aliyah." She shook her head. "I'm not much of a challenge in here."

"That's okay, I can take it easy for now. Lab's next, are you ready?"

"As long as Luciano doesn't start with the hardest experiment again, I am."

"I promise to put out any fires, whether I start them or not." I put my right hand on the left side of my chest.

"No more fires." Bailey, the next classmate to finish laps, managed those three words through her athletically-induced huffing and puffing.

"It wasn't my fault, Bailey."

"Not the second time." She rolled her eyes, then sighed. "Give your sob story to my sister."

"Hmmm?" I blinked. What in the world was Bailey talking about?

"I'm never switching to Team Dubois." She snorted.

"Whatever." Faith narrowed her eyes. "Why bother talking to us then, Bailey?"

"Hit the locker rooms, kiddos!" Coach Pickman jerked her thumb at the doorway.

"We're not trying on any gear?" Logan blinked.

"No." Coach Pickman crossed her arms over her chest shaking her head. "There's only two of you with any chance of making the team. Next time, we're focusing on mundane sports. Remedial, but hopefully fun. Catch my drift?"

"We're too early for Lab." Hal set the stopwatch aside, along with the notepad he'd used to record times. "What should we do?"

"Report back here after you're cleaned up and in your regular clothes. I've got something to show you."

We all headed to the locker room as she'd instructed, even Hal, who hadn't done anything besides change into his uniform. Our locker rooms had one common area with benches and hooks for bags and blazers, with sauna access, a steam room, and a first-aid station.

The middle doorway led to a smaller gender-neutral locker room, the one on the left was just girls and just boys on the right.

Even though it hadn't been a challenge, I'd exerted myself, so I went to the girl's side and rinsed off in the shower before changing. When I emerged, Dorian still sat in his gym uniform, ridiculous purple shorts and all. It looked like he was waiting for something, although everyone else was dressed and gathering their school blazers.

"You okay, Dorian?" I stopped and sat on the bench next to him.

"Yeah." He took a few deep ones. "I can change fast. Don't worry."

"It wasn't about changing, it's the health stuff. After that run, are you all right?"

"Yeah. Hal said you were one of the first to notice something was up with him. I get it, but I'm okay. It's physical, but I can deal."

"Okay." I nodded, standing up. "If you need anything, you know where to find me."

"You're the nicest miscreant I've ever met." Dorian chuckled. "And that's saying a lot. The Academy's full of them."

"Thanks, I guess. See you out there."

Dorian must've been the master of fast changes because, by the time I'd found a spot on the bleachers, he emerged from the locker room in his regular clothes. I gave him a quick smile as he walked across the court.

"Morgenstern, Fairbanks. You can goof off because I want you both at tryouts for Bishop's Row. The rest of you pay attention." Coach Pickman pointed her whistle at the ceiling. The scoreboard descended.

I should say it served as the scoreboard on every other occasion I'd seen it. This time, it looked like the screen out in the lobby, and there weren't any scores on it. Instead, it displayed a PowerPoint presentation.

I didn't goof off, but I didn't study the subject raptly either. I'd seen something like it before from Cadence. Coach Pickman was telling the class about cheer squads. She recited words off the slides in a monotone, giving the impression she'd had nothing to do with its creation.

"Coach Chen is organizing a cheer squad. If you have questions or want to join, talk to him." Coach Pickman put her whistle to her mouth and gave it three sharp blasts. "Dismissed!"

We filed out of the gym, entering the hallway in one group. The doors were wide enough to allow for that, and it let me get a look at Logan's face. His eyes were alight, like the day he'd met Doris. I hadn't seen him this excited for a long time.

"So, cheer squad, huh?" I smiled.

"Yeah, looks like it." He grinned. "I bet I'll see Kitty there, and Eston too."

"Maybe me if I don't make the team. Which seems likely."

"You'll make it." Dorian elbowed my shoulder. "Grace isn't going out for Bishop's Row this year."

"Oh?" I blinked.

"Yeah, says she wants to leave it for Dylan. He loves it, and it's not her favorite thing."

"I still have to worry about all the third-years, plus Faith, Lee, and my brother." I shrugged. "Not to mention that part of my probation came from an incident at Bishop's Row last year, so I might not even be eligible."

"You are." Hal held the door to magipsychic lab for Faith and stood there keeping it open for the rest of us. "My dad said he's letting everybody try out."

"Even Alex?" I raised an eyebrow.

"Yes."

"Bummer." Dorian snorted. "I can't stand that guy."

"You haven't even met him."

"I met Noah last night, who mentioned your ex a few times. His reputation precedes him."

"So does mine."

"Yours is like a patchwork quilt, while his is all one color." Dorian shook his head.

I shrugged. "Still, it's better to form your own opinion, don't you think?"

"Didn't he put a poison whammy on you?" Dorian blinked. "Why defend someone like that?"

"I don't know." I stared at my hands.

You do—first kiss and all. But you won't tell Mr. Spanos that.

"Maybe because I don't want to tell you what to think about someone else." I squared my shoulders, looking Dorian in the eye. "You can find out for yourself."

"Facts are facts, Miss Morgenstern." Professor Luciano did his usual butting in, which was his right in his classroom, after all. "The most salient fact at present is that Lab starts now, and you haven't chosen a bench or a partner."

He was right. I looked around the room, noticing that Hal and Faith sat together this time. Bailey was with Logan, which made sense now that everybody knew he had been at the top of the class in our year.

"Morgenstern, I choose you!" Dorian pointed at me, then the bench in front closest to the door.

"Peep?" Ember perched on the edge of the lab bench, blinking at us.

"Caw!" Mercy dive-bombed Ember, knocking her off the table. The critters soared up to tussle overhead. I knew it was playful since I could sense Ember's mood and Dorian smiled at their antics.

"Get your familiars under control and into the designated area, please."

As if in response to the professor, Seth barked at the pair of airborne playmates three times in rapid succession. Ember broke free, circling Mercy once before swooping down to rest on top of the little carpet-covered doghouse Seth hung out in during lab.

Mercy took a spin around the garbage can, which was empty, to her dismay. After that, she followed Ember, settling on the perch above her. It was almost like a pecking order, except the critter with the most authority was on the ground floor.

"Before we begin, I've got an announcement from Nurse Smith." The professor held a slip of paper up, reading from it. "Due to a delayed shipment of supplies, Familiar Bonding will begin tomorrow. Apologies for the late start."

"Saved by the USPS?" Dorian nudged me, winking.

"Ears open, mouths closed. This year's labs will expand on the themes we learned last year." Professor Luciano leaned his hands on the teacher's bench at the front of the room. A moment later, the cubbies under our benches opened, revealing the vintage 1980s trapper keepers that held our lab manuals. I ended up with the same unicorn as last year. Dorian's had a yin and yang symbol on it.

"Don't worry, class, we're starting with the basics this year. Safety!"

"Thank goodness," Logan muttered under his breath behind me.

"It's not all boring regulations and tours around the room." Professor Luciano grinned. "I'm also handing out a list of projects for the extramural lab collaboration exercises. Constructing these devices will require you to team up with students from the other two schools. If you try to do any of them with just magi, you will fail spectacularly."

"Is he always this gung-ho in here?" Dorian blinked. "I mean, in lecture, he's kinda blah."

"He loves the lab." I giggled behind my hand. "Maybe a little too much."

The tour was uneventful, as was the demonstration Professor Luciano did with all the safety equipment. It was a good thing, though. Either there had been additions to the equipment closets, or I'd forgotten some of what I learned last year. Maybe a little of both.

The list of collaborative projects was ten pages long. Each had a one-paragraph description, along with the recommended group makeup by extrahuman type. One was for making communication orbs, like the one I had smuggled onto the campus last year to communicate with Izzy and Cadence. This one could record and had a scrying feature. I tapped it with my finger, searching for my pencil with the other hand to circle it.

"Found your project?"

"Maybe. Depends. It says here we don't get teams assignments until October after the other schools send their groups over."

"You'll work with your friends from town, right?"

"Maybe, but a faculty member has to approve and supervise each group, and I like meeting new people." I blinked then put my hand over my mouth.

"Self-discovery is a pretty amazing thing," Dorian said that like he'd been around that block a time or five.

"Totally."

As it turned out, I discovered more than that in the month between the first day of lab and the beginning of extramurals. Not all of it was so hopeful, either.

CHAPTER SIXTEEN

The breakfast crowd could be intimidating, but at dinner, most of us sat in the lounge with takeout bags. Since Grace and Dorian stuck to the cafeteria that day, I was out there with Dylan and Eston, who wasn't a huge fan of crowds. Dylan wanted to avoid Grace, and I liked going over the day's notes in relative quiet.

Arick Magnuson approached me then and stood, shifting his weight from one foot to the other.

"Hi, Arick Magnuson." I grinned. "Have a seat."

"Thanks?" He sat on the edge of an ottoman none of us was using. "So, I heard a number of things about you yesterday, and I have a question."

"Yeah, she's really an extramagus. No, she's not evil. And unfortunately for her, she's Alex Onassis's ex-girlfriend. Did I cover everything?" Dylan's nostrils flared. "Enough to take back to Tempe?"

"No." Arick blinked, then turned away from Dylan to look at me. "You found a dragonet to bond with, and Elanor Pierce said you helped her brother and his roommate find their familiars. Since I don't have one, I was hoping— "

Arick hung his head to hide his reddening face, which was a lost cause. I tried to remember being this out of sorts. It felt like ages since

127

then. Maybe I didn't need a point of reference. Bubbe said empathy could work without that. It seemed like a good time to try.

"As far as Ember goes, she found me. I didn't go looking, and anyway, there's no wrong or right way to meet the right critter. Familiar Bonding will help. I'm taking it as an elective, so I'll see you there."

"Really?"

Eston's big black dog circled Arick. The canine was dour and fiercely protective of his magus. The new kid froze in place. Once his critter finished his appraisal, Eston looked up, catching Arick's gaze and staring into his eyes. After a moment, he spoke.

"Nobody in your family does familiar magic, so why are you at Hawthorn Academy?" Eston tilted his head, adjusting his glasses. He didn't blink.

"I've been reading about them my whole life. They're the only thing I ever wanted to study. Nothing else back home in Bergen felt right to me."

"That'll do." Eston nodded, then gazed at my page of lecture notes. He was with Dylan in Professor DeBeers' class, and part of what we did over lounge dinners was look over each other's coursework.

"I still don't know about this kid." Dylan crossed his arms over his chest. Even Gale peeked out from behind his head to give Arick a withering glare. "If he's carrying tales, I'll find out."

"Go easy." I shook my head. "He's a first-year, and not even from this country. Like you, Dylan."

"And Alex last year. I think caution's wise." Unfortunately, Dylan made sense.

"I'm giving him a chance. If you guys don't want to, that's your decision." I shrugged. "Don't try to stop me from helping."

Dylan dropped his arms, and Gale eased his stance.

"Thanks." Arick exhaled. "You don't know how much of a relief it is to hear that."

"You should get some food before they close the caf." I jerked my chin at the doorway.

"Yeah. Right." Arick looked everywhere but at our faces. "Maybe tomorrow, I can get takeout like you guys?"

"Hang on, this is my duty as a food services employee." Dylan tore a section of brown paper from his own bag and pulled a pen out of his pocket. He sketched a quick though sloppy map. "That's how you get to the takeaway window. Ask for Penelope."

Arick nodded, saying nothing else. He stood and tucked the makeshift map in his back pocket before hurrying away. I noticed a series of four small and jagged tears in the tail of his blazer. Had he been in a fight? If so, why hadn't he mentioned it?

"That might come back to bite you." Eston shook his head.

"He doesn't seem evil." I raised my eyebrow.

"It's not him. The damage on his blazer means Tempe's singled him out." Eston pointed at his dog's nose. "Grundylow claws."

"It's Grace's deal to navigate popularity oceans. She's like a captain." I shrugged. "We don't have to look popular."

"What's our job, then?" Eston tilted his head.

"We're the brute squad." I leaned back in my comfy chair. "I'm the scary extramagus. Don't make me lose my temper."

"Yeah. They won't like Aliyah when she's angry." Dylan smirked. "Good thing you're not always angry."

I laughed, relieved to hear him crack a joke. Last year he was the class clown, after all.

"That's fine and well." Eston nodded. "You're athletes, the closest thing we have to jocks. But I'm kind of not that."

"I'm the brawn, like John Luther." Dylan leaned forward, elbows on his knees. "But you're like Sherlock Holmes, making sense of everything."

"Ah. The brain." Eston nodded, adjusting his glasses.

"Bingo."

"Speaking of brains, we should go over this list of projects." I tapped the stapled packet of papers. "Work out a strategy."

"Shouldn't we have Logan's help with that?"

"Help with what now?" Logan leaned in the doorway.

"This list. We've got to narrow it down." I flipped to the second page. "This orb device looks like a challenge, but one we can handle for sure."

"Because of your friends in town?"

"That's right. I'm going to see Izzy and Cadence this weekend and talk to them about potential teammates from their schools."

"This project requires changelings." Eston adjusted his glasses.

"I know two, Azrael Ambersmith and Brianna Collins. They're both goblins."

"Good." Eston nodded. "Goblins are masters of illusion, perfect for a visual display. But we've only got one Umbral Magus in our year. That's Grace."

"What's a good stand-in?" Dylan flipped to the last page, a list of extrahuman subtypes. "Not solar, right?"

"Undeath." Logan nodded without even looking at the paper. "Faith can do it if Grace isn't on the orb team. And fire will help, so either Kitty or Aliyah."

"This is college-level magical theory stuff, Logan. Have you been studying all summer?" Eston blinked.

"Pretty much. Mrs. Morgenstern loaned me a couple of books."

"Wow." He grinned. "We should hang sometime and talk theory. I love this stuff, and my folks don't get it."

"I'd like that." Logan smiled.

Dylan got preoccupied all of a sudden with a patch of dry scales on Gale's neck. I couldn't blame him. The look on his face reminded me of how I'd felt last year when Noah focused on his school friends and left me behind. Back then, I'd needed a friend, so it was time to be one.

"The Magipsych Fair isn't all we've got to worry about." I elbowed him. "We should do some extra practice before Bishop's Row tryouts. Together."

"We're going to have company, though." Dylan gazed at his shoes. "I asked Lee to practice with me already and he said yes."

"That's cool."

It's not, and you know it. You wanted time alone with Dylan. Tell him it's not okay.

"Hey, are you going to eat that?" Dylan pointed at my side of coleslaw.

"Down the bottomless pit it goes, I guess." I handed it to him, glad to see his appetite coming back.

The Evil Inside Voice was right. I wasn't happy about sharing my time with Dylan, but it couldn't be helped. Maybe it was better for him to have more friends around than just me anyway.

Dylan Khan was not okay, no matter what he said. Maybe branching out would help him get better.

I did a full sweep of the third-floor bathroom despite being tired. Eight was the hour I usually started winding down before bed at Hawthorn Academy, not ideal for swimming, but Faith wanted to meet, and I'd agreed. I had to make sure none of the first-years lurked in a stall or the changing rooms first.

The bathrooms at Hawthorn Academy were enormous, outfitted with the usual sinks, toilets, and showers. They had a couple of old-fashioned clawfoot tubs as well, but the main feature was the Roman Bath, which was like a swimming pool, deep and long enough to swim laps in.

The campus between worlds had unlimited space when it was built, and everything classical in an ancient sense had been in style back then. While attendance had been low since the Reveal, the Hawkins family hadn't decreased the campus's size from the old days.

Faith Fairbanks took full advantage of that. Swimming was her preferred sport. Growing up in Salem meant I'd become adept at it too. It wasn't my favorite physical activity, but I could keep up with her.

I'd gone into a stall to put on my bathing suit. When I emerged, Faith was already at the side of the bath. Ember swooped down from her perch, landing beside Seth. He pranced and capered, letting out a series of short happy barks in response to her peeps. It was nice to see them relax and play together.

Faith sat at the edge of the pool, her legs in the water. I joined her.

"So, what's this about Alex?" I stuck my tongue out and blew a raspberry. "Sorry. Thinking about him brings out my inner sixth-grader."

"No need to apologize. He sucks." Faith snorted. "But I think I can keep him from being too much trouble."

"What's the idea?"

"For you, distraction. My plan is to zap him from time to time with a little undeath energy. He'll get sluggish. Since he always plays up that cold-blooded snake vibe, acting like he's not a threat, no one should notice, but just in case—"

"You need me to light things up?" I shook my head, chuckling. "Fire didn't work out so well for me last year."

"You've got way more control now, Aliyah." Faith kicked a foot, splashing. "Anyway, you can choose which shiny magic to use. Solar's less flammable, right?"

"Yeah, it's safer." I grinned.

"Bonus points if they think it was Noah." Faith turned her head, looking me in the eye. "Everybody knows he still hates Alex because of the whole Darren thing last year."

"I didn't even think of that." I sighed. "Some schemer I am, huh?"

"You are definitely not evil overlord material, but I've got it covered."

"Because you're evil?" I blinked. "You, the doting girlfriend?"

"I had the upbringing for it, which doesn't miraculously vanish just because I decided to reject it." She looked up, eyes as limpid as the pool, and colder. "I'm using everything I learned at home for good now."

"Heaven help Hal's Mom, then." I eased off the topic of Faith's family.

"You don't know the half of it. She is going to be in deep shit once it hits the fan."

"I thought the custody hearing happened already?"

"There's one more in May. Anyway, the last one opened a can of worms, for Mrs. Hawkins, anyway." Faith sighed. "I'm all for escaping your toxic family, but once you hurt the family you choose, all bets are off."

"What do you mean?" I raised an eyebrow.

"She married, had a kid. That's her family now, and she screwed them over. That hearing only hinted that she's a dhampyr, but her family will find her sooner or later." She crossed her arms, rubbing them with her hands. "They're probably horrible people."

"Are you sure?"

"No, but it's logical." She closed her eyes. "Now we have to worry about them showing up out of the blue."

"If she'd been honest with the doctors, medical privacy would have protected her and Hal. There wouldn't have been any stories in the paper.

"Karma isn't real, but coincidence is, and even more of a bitch."

"They're Hal's family too." I reached out, patted her shoulder. "Maybe he takes after them, and there's nothing to be afraid of."

"I'm not scared of vampires. I told Hal to let them come and catch these hands." She held them up, palms out toward the water, staring at the backs of them.

Usually, Faith would grin or snort to indicate sarcasm, but her statement carried no humor. This was deadly serious to her. She'd risk death to protect Hal. It reminded me of how devoted my parents were to each other.

"Neither am I. Fire hands, remember? But nothing says they have to be monstrous."

"Stephanie's age makes it likelier. Her parents had her before the Reveal, and with pre-reveal vamps, you never know. That isn't just shitty Fairbanks family philosophy, either. Remember the turning spree that generation did back in the day?"

"I do. I'm a Night Creatures fan." I sighed. "And I'm half-Hopewell. Nothing like finding out your uncle tried to take over two worlds to give you a perspective on twisted family trees. I'll keep hoping they're outliers and decent folk. I mean, Hal's one of the best people we know, right?"

"I'd hope right along with you, but Mrs. Hawkins is way too fearful. I watched her face throughout the hearing."

"Sometimes, I think you've seen way more than anyone our age should have."

"Whatever." She pushed off from the edge of the pool into the water. "Enough gloom and doom. Let's swim."

We spent the next hour doing exactly that. The water couldn't wash away the sins of our families, but it helped us forget them for a little while.

CHAPTER SEVENTEEN

Familiar Bonding was in the infirmary, which was the closest thing Hawthorn Academy had to a basement. Along with the ramp leading down from the main floor, the infirmary also had no windows. This was good because one of the infirmary staff, my favorite, was a vampire.

Ezekiel Brown greeted me with a grin and a slight nod. I hadn't seen him since last year, so I smiled back.

"Hi, Zeke!"

"Miss Morgenstern, what brings you here at this time of day?"

"Familiar Bonding."

"You hardly need it this year."

"I kind of think it's fun." I indicated Ember, who let out a loud snore from my shoulder. "Anyway, Logan's bringing Dorian Spanos because he's new to familiars. He's got an unruly gryphon. Maybe I can help."

"Those are sound reasons." Ezekiel nodded. "Although I had assumed you dropped by to visit with young Master Hawkins and Miss Fairbanks."

"Oh, they're here?" I clapped, waking Ember.

"Yes. Just a moment, and I'll see how amenable they are to a brief visit."

"Thanks, Zeke."

While waiting, I paced the room. This area of the infirmary included Nurse Smith's varnished pine desk, a line of chairs, and Ezekiel's antique roll-top writing desk, which stood beside the first aid cabinet. Ember fluttered to her favorite perch from last year atop the cabinet, but she'd grown and didn't fit anymore. The formerly cozy nook was now a tight and unpleasant squeeze.

"Peep." Ember flew back down to my shoulder, tucking herself around the back of my neck and slumping down. I sensed her disappointment

"It's okay, girl. Everybody grows." I shrugged. "Kind of a fact of life."

"You take the good, you take the bad." Dorian Spanos sauntered through the door. Mercy swooped in behind him, soaring in a figure-eight overhead.

"What?" I blinked.

"I guess I'm the only one at Hawthorn obsessed with eighties sitcoms." He sighed as Mercy took off from his shoulder to fly around the room. "At least tell me you've seen the *Golden Girls*."

"Only because of Noah." I shrugged. "Though that was a few years back."

"I think he needs to re-watch it." Dorian shook his head. "Your brother isn't the kind of person I'd thank for being a friend."

"Is he giving you crap?" I put my hands on my hips. "If so, I'll have words with him. Totally not cool to grief the new kid."

"Nope. Just plain old snobbery." Dorian shrugged.

"Yep, sounds like my brother."

"Crap on a crap cracker." Dorian stared at the ceiling, blinking and stepping backward. "Look out below!"

I craned my neck up, just barely making out the winged shape above the chandelier's orbs of light. It was Mercy, of course, and she had something lumpy and rank-smelling that rustled in her talons. Doris, who'd just walked through the door, looked up at the gryphon and hissed.

I didn't run, dodge, or duck and cover. Maybe I should have. Dorian's familiar wasn't up there for her health. Oh, no, nothing as simple as a playful romp or one-sided game of tag for Mercy the trash gryphon. I heard a tearing sound. Doris turned tail and fled, caterwauling down the hall.

She's been in the waste bin. That's the trash bag.

"Eww, gross!" I tried to fend off the garbage raining down on my head. Fortunately, Mercy hadn't explored the biohazard container or the one with sharps, but I did not appreciate having a musty banana peel for a hair accessory.

"Peep!" Ember untangled herself from my shoulders and leaped into the air, snagging the fruity refuse off my head. She deposited it in the nearest trash receptacle, which didn't have a bag anymore. The remnants of that hung from Mercy's talons in long plastic shreds.

The entire floor of the infirmary's front room was a minefield of refuse. I glanced at the side of the trash can and noticed the extra bag hanging over its side. After stepping over a few pieces of debris, I snatched it and began collecting bits and bobs from the floor. Dorian rushed to help, but he didn't look where he was going and ended up slipping in something orange.

"Whoa!" He managed to keep his balance, a good thing because if he'd fallen, he would've ended up with a partially full container of yogurt on his backside.

"What's going on in here?" Nurse Smith tapped his foot in the doorway.

"Just reporting for Familiar Bonding. I guess we need it." I glanced up, dropping a handful of odorous crumb-coated plastic wrap into the trash bag.

"There's no way Ember's responsible for this mess." Nurse Smith put his hands on his hips, glaring at Dorian. "Hup!"

Dorian's demeanor changed like lightning, and he stood at attention. He looked like someone auditioning for a role in *A Few Good Men*, a far cry from his smirking nonchalance in class and whiny defiance at Gym.

"It's Mercy's fault, Sir."

"Caw!" Mercy swooped down, dive-bombing Nurse Smith's desk. She landed beside the placard with his name on it, peering at the shiny surface with curiosity blazing in her eyes.

"Don't you dare." Dorian snapped at his familiar, hands still and straight at his sides. "This is our last chance." He looked right through me, his lower lip trembling.

Somebody wasn't supposed to spill those particular beans.

"I care about the health and safety of everyone on this campus." Nurse Smith dropped his arms. "Working with a familiar takes practice, and you're a year behind. Bonus points for bonding with a gryphon. They're a handful but not the worst. That honor belongs to the karkinos." He patted the pocket on his scrub top. "That's why I run Familiar Bonding. Take it one day at a time. Messes can be cleaned up, and most faculty and staff here accept apologies. Unlike the school you came from."

"Thank you, sir." Dorian cleared his throat. "Did you go to the Academy?"

"Let's just say I'm in the know." Nurse Smith shook his head. "If you have trouble with your gryphon again, come straight to me. Understand, Spanos?"

"Yes, Nurse Smith."

"Good. Now help clean this up. We've got first-years without familiars on their way."

Dorian nodded, then moved to help me. After we finished getting the trash laden bag into the can, we moved to the sink in the corner and washed our hands.

"Your hair still has banana in it." He reached up and plucked a string from the peel off my head, washing it down the sink. "Sorry about that."

"The day I met Ember, she got stuck in my updo, so I've had worse critter-related insults to my hair. I'm fine."

He nodded, opening his mouth. Before Dorian could speak, Ezekiel emerged from the treatment room. He shook his head, placing one finger over his lips.

"They've fallen asleep. Since there's time before the dinner hour, I'll let them rest."

"Good choice." Nurse Smith nodded. "Please get the other room ready. I'm off to fetch the guest critters."

As the infirmary staff went about their business, Dorian and I found seats. Mercy perched on his arm and he shook his head at her, reaching down to stroke the feathers under her chin.

"What's gotten into you, girl?" He sighed. "Not enough open sky?"

"Gryphons are pretty adaptable, Dorian. There's enough room for airborne critters to stretch their wings here. Maybe she's not used to so many other animals around. You said you found her alone, right?"

"It was weird." Dorian shook his head. "Random. Not anything that's ever happened at the Academy before. The campus has wards to keep magical animals out, so—"

Logan interrupted by stepping through the doorway.

"Hey, are you okay?" He put his hand on Dorian's shoulder. "Doris told me about the trash."

"I'm still a little meh." Dorian gazed up at Logan, who blushed and looked away, dropping his hand. "But I will be okay in a few minutes."

"Am I interrupting something?"

I looked up to see Arick Magnuson standing in the doorway. His hair was wet enough to drip and he was missing his blazer, which reminded me of my misadventures last year.

"No, but what about you?" I gestured at him. "You look, um, rumpled."

"I'm okay now, I guess. It's been a rough day." He looked at his shoes. "Nothing like what the other kids in my year say about yours, though. No fires."

"One of those was my fault." Logan shook his head. "Lab accident. But yeah, we had an incendiary start last year."

"Where did you hear that, anyway?" Dorian crossed his arms over his chest. "Alex Onassis, by any chance?"

"No way." Arick shook his head. "He barely talks to anyone unless Temperance tells him to."

"You only answered one of my questions, kid." Dorian gave Arick so much side-eye he could have been a fish.

"Don't be so hard on him, Dorian." I shook my head. "We don't need to know the rumor mill's exact details."

"Just trying to cover all the angles." Dorian shrugged. "Don't want to assume."

"Someone's got to be a skeptic, I guess," said Logan.

"I'm not trying to tell you the earth is flat or anything." Arick blinked. "Anyway, I'm sorry. Repeating rumors isn't nice, and you guys are stuck with me for a month. Sorry."

The looks we shot at each other after Arick's self-deprecating statement could have come from the OK Corral. Maybe I relied on too much hyperbole, but the agitation level was supercharged. They barely noticed when the other first-year with no familiar, Michelina Zanelli, took the seat nearest to the door. She sat with her head down over folded hands. I couldn't see her face from behind the thick sheet of hair.

It all defused when Nurse Smith returned, pushing the cart with the unbound critters, just as he had last year. We stood up and followed him as he wheeled it into the larger treatment room.

He didn't give any explanations. Logan handed around his battered notebook from last year, which they flipped through avidly. As for me, everything from Familiar Bonding was second nature after growing up in a house over an extraveterinary office.

When Nurse Smith let the critters out, they ambled around, checking each of us out. I held my hand down for each of them in turn, setting an example of how to behave around unfamiliar animals.

Logan followed suit because he had at least as much experience with meeting new critters as I did. Despite our drastically different sources, some knowledge was common between showbiz and medicine. Dorian left the notebook to the others and kept trying unsuccessfully to coax Mercy down from the chandelier.

Last year, Dylan and Logan had been reluctant to interact with the unbonded animals at Familiar Bonding. Arick was totally the opposite. If anything, he was too eager. Even the friendly poodle seemed wary of his attention. Michelina sat still and let them come to her.

Eventually, a possum with golden fur and a yellow tail climbed into her lap, though she only patted its back a few times hesitantly.

I tried to keep my observation of the quiet girl covert, but that didn't work so well. The main thing I noticed about Michelina Zanelli was how careful she was, like she thought the whole world watched her. I realized Elanor Pierce had this same trait, but the difference was, Elanor loved an audience. Michelina dreaded it.

"Hi, I'm Aliyah," I said after moving to the seat beside her.

"Lena." She didn't look up.

"The possum likes you, Lena."

"Okay." Her voice cracked, and she covered her face with her hands.

I didn't know what to think about that, let alone do. I looked up, hoping for help from my fellow students, but Logan was busy explaining something to Arick while Dorian played tug-of-war with Mercy, who'd finally alighted on the floor. Fortunately, they were using a pull toy from the box in the corner instead of medical supplies.

"Hmm. Class is over for now, though I've got a few words for you all." Nurse Smith looked up from the notes on his clipboard. "This year, we'll do a selection of worksheets. At the very least, it will reinforce some of your lessons from the lectures."

"Are you saying we won't get to play with the animals tomorrow?" Arick stared at Nurse Smith like a disappointed puppy.

"I'm saying both you and Mr. Spanos need more information than you have about magical animals. Most of the families who send their children here have familiars in the house. With Mr. Spanos, most of his relatives are psychic and unable to bond with a familiar. But you, Mr. Magnuson?" Nurse Smith tapped his pen on the paper. "You're an enigma."

"Sorry." He winced. "My dad said something like that last week."

"Nothing to apologize for, as long as you're willing to do the work."

"I understand." He nodded. "And I am."

"What about Lena?" I asked, determined to speak up for the shy girl. Nurse Smith didn't get to answer.

CHAPTER EIGHTEEN

"Help!"

A clatter of footsteps sounded in the hall before the speaker turned the corner, arms full of fluffy canine—his poodle familiar, Clementine.

"Darren?" I blinked.

His critter was in big trouble. Nurse Smith cleared his throat, raising his voice.

"Move! I've got an emergency here and need space."

We moved aside, Arick running out of the room and up the hall. Dorian stepped backward until he disappeared through the doorway. Logan and I remained front and center, in full view of the drama unfolding on the cot in front of us. The rest of the unbound critters crowded at our feet, herded beside us by Doris and Ember.

"Her pulse is high, too thready." The nurse looked up. "Did you find her like this?"

"She just collapsed after dropping a cup in the trash for me." Darren's voice quavered. "I don't know what did it. She hasn't been sick."

"Ezekiel!"

The vampire stepped through the door. He took one look at the dog on the cot, then leaned forward, wafting air toward his face and inhaling through his nose.

"She's been poisoned. Neurotoxin."

Behind me, Lena gasped and sniffled.

"Neurotoxin?" My nostrils flared, red tinting the edges of my vision. I knew a magus on campus who wielded that substance: Alex Onassis. My throat choked with anger, and I could say nothing more. The air around me began heating rapidly.

That's right. Get fired up and then find him. Make him pay.

I almost gave in because familiar-based magi had a code. Familiars were off-limits, always. Attacking someone's critter was a heinous act, like harming an infant. I lifted my foot and switched my breathing pattern to suit a sprint, but before I could take off, cold fingers interlaced with my blazing ones.

I looked to my left, expecting to see Dorian. He was an ice magus, after all, and had been nearby last time I checked. But it wasn't the new kid holding my hand. It wasn't even Logan, who'd used his water magic to counter my fire before.

"Chill. You've got to cool it, Aliyah."

"Dylan?" Logan named my savior. He stared down at our hands, blinking. When I copied him, everything looked normal.

"Yeah. It happened in the café. I followed Darren."

I shivered because Dylan's grip on my hand was colder than his air magic, which usually mirrored ambient temperature. The involuntary movement shook me out of my anger, and Dylan's grasp too.

"Administering antidote." Nurse Smith snagged the syringe off a tray Ezekiel held out toward him. "Darren, you have to keep calm. Hold her down."

"Okay."

But he couldn't. Darren trembled, his grip too loose. He paled and doubled over, holding his stomach. Was he picking up on her symptoms? Clementine flailed, nearly bucking off the cot in the grip of a seizure.

I rushed around to the other side of the dog, Ember swooping down in tandem. She dived to the opposite side of the cot, leaning against the poodle's hindquarters before she could fall off. I reached out, grabbing Clementine by the scruff of the neck with one hand and blocking her back with my other shoulder. After that, I locked an arm around her, pinning her to the cot on her side.

"Antidote incoming." Nurse Smith worked quickly, taking the dog's front paw in his hand and giving the injection with a grace I hadn't imagined he possessed.

She whined, crying and straining against my grasp. Darren, now definitely affected by his familiar's dire state, reached toward her face. Her teeth clicked together, jaw clenching and eyes rolling. He pulled back just in time. The impact of this entire ordeal felled him, and he collapsed into the nearest chair, slumping over and dry-heaving.

Dylan, always quick to respond to rogue bodily functions due to his time in food service, placed a wastebasket under the ailing magus.

"Will she be okay?" Dorian asked.

"I don't know." Nurse Smith shook his head, his forehead a tangle of furrows. "She's not improving as expected."

"This antidote is supposed to react with great alacrity." Ezekiel shook his head. "In magi. But neither of us are experts in extraveterinary medicine."

"Call my grandma."

"The headmaster's already on it." Dylan nodded. "He saw the whole thing upstairs. We just have to wait for her to get here."

Bubbe showed up with one of her levitating animal crates that transported heavier critters too sick to walk. When she was ready to leave, Darren followed, shakily leaning on her arm. Headmaster Hawkins stood by and waited for them to depart.

"I'll want a statement from you, Mr. Kahn, including a list of everyone in the café leading up to this incident."

"I'll talk to my boss. She was manning the counter too." Dylan nodded. "I should get back up there to finish my shift."

"No, I've closed the café down for now." The headmaster sighed. "It shall remain out of commission until it's been swept for evidence and thoroughly sanitized."

"You don't think it was something in the food or drink?" Nurse Smith asked.

"I've yet to rule that out." He sighed again. "But I hope not."

"Mr. Brown said it's a neurotoxin." I raised an eyebrow, taking a deep breath as I went ahead, damned the torpedoes, and stood up to the headmaster. "I hope accidental contamination isn't all you're ruling out, sir."

"My investigation's details are on a need-to-know basis. You, Miss Morgenstern, do not need to know."

"What about me?" Hal stood in the doorway, clinging to Faith's arm.

"No."

"You're the headmaster." Hal narrowed his eyes. "Sir."

I wondered what that exchange was about, but didn't get a chance to ask.

"Everybody out of my infirmary." Nurse Smith waved his hands in a shooing gesture that didn't include Hal's father.

Even Zeke filed into the hallway with us, heading up the ramp and into the lobby. He turned down the corridor beside the stairs toward the takeout window. The vampire CNA was friends with Penelope but didn't much like mingling with the rest of the students. I couldn't blame him, with anti-vampire sentiment rampant on campus.

When I turned, I noticed Dorian was nowhere to be found. He'd either faded into the crowd of students milling about socializing or had headed up the stairs without saying goodbye. I asked where he went, but Dylan and Logan didn't know. Lena stood nearby, back pressed against the wall, shrugging.

"Dinner?" I jerked my thumb at the cafeteria, including the shy girl in my question. She shook her head and made a beeline for the stairs.

"I'm not hungry after all that." Logan sighed. "I'm going upstairs to hit the books, and maybe the showers. See you tomorrow."

"I'm not hungry either, but I could use a cuppa." Dylan beckoned, sauntering toward the cafeteria. "Come on."

Once we were seated with tea and toast, which I insisted Dylan include, I asked him the million-dollar question.

"What's with the super-chilled air?"

"I don't know, but I'm worried it's the good old E-word."

"You need to do something about that right away." I picked up my tea to keep from fidgeting. The idea that Dylan might also be an extra-magus had me on edge for reasons I couldn't define. "If last year taught me anything, it was to ask for help. The headmaster said I should have gone to Luciano about it."

And you're still not telling anyone about me, or asking your crush whether he's got a devil on his shoulder. How interesting.

"Don't worry, I'll learn from your mistake. Watch."

He pulled out his notebook from the lecture, the one that transcribed everything off the magical blackboards. These worked two ways, letting us ask teachers questions outside class by writing them in the book.

"Do you have a pen?"

"Sure." I pulled one from behind my ear and set it on the table. I didn't want our hands touching again, especially not when he could see my face.

"Thanks."

I watched him print out words requesting a meeting with Professor DeBeer immediately. The words faded, typical when the recipient saw the message. A new one appeared briefly, instructing him to report to her office in twenty minutes. At least he'd have time to finish his toast and tea.

"I'm going to nip this in the bud." He grinned. "No secrets, no lies."

"Good." I held the teacup in front of half my face, hoping to hide any awkward expression that might cross it. "Make sure you say the E-word right away. That was my mistake, not telling anybody."

"Well, you've got Luciano, so I can barely blame you. He's not an approachable fellow."

"You'd be surprised if you were in his class. He looks and sounds stodgy, but underneath it all, he's a big softie."

"How?" Dylan's eyes narrowed. "He's a poison magus. Don't you suspect him? You know, about Clementine?"

"No way." I shook my head. "He taught for decades overseas in very exclusive schools. If he were the type of guy to do stuff like that, his career would've ended ages ago."

"Fair enough." Dylan chewed on a triangle of toast. "But he was in the café right before it happened."

"That doesn't mean anything. Darren mentioned the trash can. I'm surprised the headmaster only asked for a list of people. Familiars have their own powers, and some are natural enemies. Bubbe uses herbs and light or sound to soothe them, but I haven't seen anything like that outside of the academic wing and the cafeteria. That's one reason we have Familiar Bonding, right?"

"Yeah. To make sure their bonds with magi tempers their instincts. I hadn't thought of that."

"Another thing. Those ties go both ways. Our critters influence us, too."

"I just can't imagine any familiar so bad they turn their magus evil. Gale keeps me company and helps just by being here. He's vain as a peacock but kind when it counts."

"Some people might use their familiar's instinct as an excuse for bad behavior. Or lean on their critters so much the bond goes sour."

"I know what you mean. Logan's family is a case in point." Dylan shook his head. "He lived with you for a week, so you know about their dysfunction. They're awful. I'd hoped they were the exception."

"According to Bubbe, they are. She says very few magi with familiars get as close as the Pierces to outright exploitation."

"I want to ask Logan how he's doing. His parents tossing him out, then calling the cops is madness. But I don't think he's ready to talk."

"It hasn't been that long. Just give him time." I shrugged, mostly at myself. Because there I sat, unable to take my own advice.

"Yeah." Dylan swallowed, then looked at me. "I'm sorry."

"Why?" I blinked.

"Because I feel like a whingy bastard." He stared at the dregs of his tea. "I'm supposed to make grades, become a doctor, and then make money, not talk about feelings. Or start writing poems and playing guitar badly. Noah didn't write that piece at Open Mic, I did."

"How many people love art, music, and books? It's all because of how those things make us feel. You went out on a limb, catching feelings and showing the world. That takes bravery, chutzpah. Don't put that guitar down just yet. You're not whiny, you just have a heart. I'm sorry for not reaching out sooner."

"I'll stop apologizing when you do."

"Something tells me the devil's throne will get encased in ice before that happens with either of you."

"Butt out, Spanos," Dylan snarled.

"I need to talk to Aliyah about—"

"Sod off!"

I blinked and shook my head, shocked, but maybe I shouldn't have been. The fuse on the powder keg between Dylan and Dorian had to run out sooner or later.

"Yeah, sure, fine, whatever." Dorian rolled his eyes, removed his hands from our table, and walked away, his back making way too straight a line.

"I can't stand that bloody fop." Dylan wrinkled his nose. "I don't know how you tolerate having him around all the time."

"Mostly for Logan." I shrugged. "He makes people laugh, at least."

"He's witty, I'll give him that. And well-dressed, thanks to wealthy parents. But his defining trait is laziness."

"What do you mean?"

"Dorian Spanos can't be bothered to participate in Gym. Has to have a doctor's note. In Creatives, he sat around the entire time watching Grace bust her ass at the sewing machine. And in the library, he sat in the corner conjuring lewd ice pictures on the wall where the Ashfords couldn't see. He's trouble."

"Well, I think Logan likes him. Likes-likes."

"Bollocks."

"The heart wants what it wants, Dylan." I gazed into my tea.

"Don't I know it." He crumbled the last of his toast into his empty cup, then put his plates together. "But mine's broken. Later, Aliyah."

He knows nothing about your *heart.*

I watched him leave, passing Tempe Fairbanks in the lobby on his way. She smirked at me and tapped her temple, then turned it in a slow circle beside her head. I rolled my eyes. She turned her back and followed Dylan.

So of course I rose from my seat and bolted toward the doorway, but by that time, both Tempe and Dylan had gone.

CHAPTER NINETEEN

Dorian
Gryphon-Egg Problems

I couldn't handle watching the poodle and her magus. I know, I know. I'm a goth who sees beauty in darkness and knows death was change through tragedy. But I am also seventeen, and staring death in the face like this again would be too much, too soon.

That's why I ran away from my problems at Hawthorn Academy for the third time in as many days. I'm a coward, I admit it. I wouldn't be any good to my classmates and the new friends I'd made amongst them if the shit hit the fan courtesy of Temperance Fairbanks or anyone else, for that matter. They didn't know that about me yet, but eventually, they'd figure it out.

Yesterday, I would have told you my secret identity as a scaredy-cat was safe. Until the case of the poisoned poodle, I'd thought Grace was exaggerating, Faith had serious sibling rivalry, and Aliyah was a paranoid extramagus. The only one I trusted on campus was Logan Pierce, but he barely spoke about Tempe in particular or magisu-premacists on campus in general. His main concern was his family, and I didn't blame him.

It's ironic that my own folks accepted me no matter what, not that I didn't need it, all things considered. Ironic and lucky, I guess. I was secretly a unicorn in more ways than one. Anyway, Logan's home life sounded like a horror show, and I was worried about Parent's Night for his sake.

But I digress. That happens to me a lot. I don't know whether it's cowardice or laziness, but I'm all talk and no action. Changing the subject is safest most of the time, but it flies like a hardboiled egg in emergencies. Everyone and Aliyah's actual grandma wanted to act right then, which was why I ran off to find a place to hide.

At the top of the ramp coming up from the infirmary, I saw food service staff with protective aprons, goggles, and gloves on, closing off the café. Even that sadistic Coach Pickman helped. I couldn't hide in there, and I wouldn't want to for fear of neurotoxin contamination, but I needed a place to calm down with Mercy, who I'd tucked under my arm inside my blazer.

The library was closed, and the cafeteria bustled like downtown Providence during WaterFire. I would've gone to my room, but Eston was there with Kitty, plotting their Truncheons and Flagons adventures. Or enjoying some other form of alone-time.

I backed up, trying to remember Logan's descriptions during our campus tour. My brain kept firing blanks, not coming up with anything. Logan liked his quiet time, but probably managed most of it in his room since Dylan worked so much. I couldn't remember him mentioning any safe haven on campus besides the Café de Poison.

I glanced around the lobby, noting that the exit to the outer hallway was blocked by an enormous cleaning cart. Nowhere was left but the academic wing. When I got to the double doors with their stained-glass mural, my plan was foiled. The doors refused to budge when I pushed on them.

"Caw!" Mercy wrangled her way free of my blazer, swooping toward the doors. She wrapped her claws around the handles then flapped, throwing her weight backward.

I shook my head, sighing. "Out of the way, Mercy."

She cawed again and let go of the handle, allowing me to reach out and pull. The door opened, of course.

"Not just a coward, but an idiot too."

I stepped through the doorway to find the hall dark, though it wasn't pitch-black as I'd feared. The magical light fixtures gave off a dim glow, like dark mode on a phone.

I paced the hall, holding my forearm out in front of me to let Mercy perch there. She wasn't nearly as heavy as she looked because a gryphon's bones were hollow. That made them delicate, another reason for my caution since bonding with her. I reached out with my other hand and stroked the top of her head with my finger.

She leaned into my display of affection, as always. While walking, I relaxed into the unexpected quality time with my familiar and thought back to how I'd ended up with this adorably uncouth half-avian in the first place.

The Academy didn't allow pets, magical or not. They had wards to prevent all kinds of animals from congregating, mating, or giving birth on the premises, too. That is why I was stunned to see the large speckled egg in a shoebox outside my window one winter morning.

Calling what they have at the Academy windows was a gross understatement. They were small patches of wired glass, letting through only the dingiest version of sunlight. Sometimes I pretended to be a fish in winter, swimming under a thick layer of ice while I looked out the ersatz window in my dorm room.

Anyway, I had no idea what kind of egg it was, only that no animal had laid it there naturally. That meant a person had put it there, possibly a telekinetic psychic or a winged shifter. Magic didn't work on the interior or exterior walls at that school, including faerie glamour. The Academy was the closest thing extrahumans had to a military school in New England, and it was on near-constant lockdown.

I said my parents accepted me. I might have given the impression they were lenient, but that's been impossible for them over the last few years. I ended up at the Academy because I snuck out of the house after my sister went missing, doing that running thing toward where I thought Cassandra would be.

After a near-brush with a member of the Gitano Family, they sent me to the Academy for my own good. Dad never said it in so many words, but he was an empath, so I felt it. Mom might have had a vision. I wondered whether she saw me finding the egg, too.

No matter how it got to a windowsill on the fifth floor, I watched the egg every day. I knew it was magical after about a minute because I used the skills they taught magi in class and checked. It was blue and white, like my ice element. Maybe that was why I felt a connection, even though it was just this spotty oval on the other side of iron, wards, and glass.

Every morning I'd wake before inspection. Yes, they had that. Staff came in to check that our beds were made properly and the rooms tidy according to regulations. Anyway, before all that, I'd silently greet the egg. It turned into something like a ritual, checking the aura, seeing it pulse and glow brighter, like the baby growing inside it responded to a walking mess of a person like me who didn't know himself yet.

I took to caring about the mysterious egg more readily than any of the discipline exercises they made us do at the Academy. I peeked at it every night also, wishing her sweet dreams. Yes, even then, I knew the baby inside the egg was a girl. She told me, and I trusted without question. If only it was that easy for everyone else.

That year, I needed a friend badly. My roommate got sent to the Academy after putting another guy in the hospital. He called me sissy, a girl, and a whiny bitch, so I kept my head down. No jokes, nothing but deadpan compliance, worn like a mask.

The little life inside the egg made me feel connected, together with somebody in a way I hadn't felt since my sister went missing. She'd been seen with an older man in her sophomore year of college before vanishing. Out of this world, as it turned out.

They found her dead in the Under, aged an impossible number of years in a bargain with a Tsuchigomo—a sacrifice of life-force to the creature, payment to save the son she'd birthed there.

"Caw?" Mercy tilted her head, her inquisitive noises bringing me back to the present.

"What's up?"

She flapped her wings, pointing her beak at a room that turned out to be occupied. I heard muffled voices within. It looked like a classroom, not one for my year or maybe not any other. The academic wing had an awful lot of empty classrooms. I thought maybe listening in on someone else's drama might get my mind off my own problems.

I found myself hiding in the adjacent broom closet, index finger against the wall, using my ice magic to filter sound through the wood to assist in my eavesdropping. I'd learned that at the Academy, too, but spying was a self-taught skill.

"They'll never suspect it was us."

"Who's taking the rap, do you think?"

"Probably the wrong person. They'll question Onassis, of course."

"I'd make that mistake too. I hope you didn't make this puzzle too hard. You're a genius, even if none of them realize it."

"They'll get to it eventually, and then our hurdle will get canned. Probably lose his license, too."

"I still don't know why you have to get rid of him."

"He's a sympathizer, first of all. And second, he's protecting the biggest threats to the long game. Daddy said so."

"I don't get why, though."

"He's one of them, of course. Why else would I have asked you to pull his sealed record?"

"How did you open it?"

"I only peeked, and that's my little secret." The voice sighed. "But I can't show it to anyone else."

"Shouldn't we be trying to prove he's been lying instead of this frame job? A familiar got hurt."

"We can't prove that unless he reverts, which he won't; the conditions aren't likely for a withered old fool like him. Besides, Hawkins must know and just not care. This is better."

"What if you're wrong and he does revert? Won't they go easy on him, as they did on the Morgenstern girl?"

"I have a backup plan: an accusation to make. He'll still be removed from the equation, which will only help with the inferiors invading our campus."

"If Hiram were here, we'd never have to endure this whole degrading ordeal."

"True, but we also wouldn't have the opportunity to teach the inferiors a lesson right here on this campus."

"Point, set, match."

"I love it when you talk sporty to me. Come here."

Okay, so I'm a bit shady. I've listened in on all kinds of back-alley deals and clandestine meetings. I'm from a part of Providence owned by organized criminals. Being in the background of my family's dealings with them gave me a taste for selectively overhearing private matters, but I had zero interest in the carnal activities of a couple of bigots.

That's right, I'd just listened in on a conversation between magisupremacists, which my parents had been assured weren't tolerated on this campus. I removed my finger from the wall like it had suddenly heated to the temperature of boiling oil. After that, I extricated myself from the broom closet as quietly as possible. The last thing I wanted was to get caught by that dastardly duo.

If I'd been Grace Dubois, I would've tried peeking through the window to discover the identity of the couple in the classroom. If I'd been Aliyah Morgenstern, I might have burst into the room, hands ablaze, and confronted them. Logan Pierce would have called in the authorities. But I was Dorian Spanos, consummate coward. I couldn't do any of that, even though Mercy took off from my arm and fluttered in that direction.

"We're out of here, come on," I mouthed. Mercy always understood me, even when I didn't include volume while talking to her. Gryphons have amazing hearing, which explained how she heard me in the egg in the box on the windowsill through that magically warded glass.

She followed me because familiar bonds were stronger than anything in either world. And coincidence, the truth behind the myth of fate, warped and weakened even the most ironclad rules and regulations turned against it. The connections we made with others, when true and from the heart, could overcome almost anything, even a psyche full of fear like mine.

One warm spring morning at the Academy, something was wrong with Mercy's prenatal aura. When I realized she couldn't get out of her egg, I acted immediately. My roommate woke blearily, unwilling or unable to fathom my anguish over an egg on a windowsill.

I reached a hand out and pressed it to the glass, summoning all my strength and focusing on lowering its temperature as much as possible. The wards should've prevented this. They probably would have if I wasn't so desperate and hadn't also felt a fear that mirrored my own from the other side. It pushed my conjuring power to heights I'd never even heard of, let alone felt before.

The egg stopped rocking back and forth, as it had been for the last few minutes while Mercy failed at breaking out of it. I sensed her in there, stilling physically to muster her magic. Her efforts were downright Herculean, heroic in a way I never imagined anyone who cared for me could be.

In that utilitarian cinderblock room, I screamed without thinking, without stopping to adjust my pitch lower first. My voice went full soprano without cracking, but the glass did. That had little to do with the sound coming from my mouth, though. It was mostly ice, a deep arctic freeze.

And then the crack imploded, shards of metal-laced glass flying inward through the window. My hair took on a grainy feeling like I'd laid in sand at the beach, and a patter like hail falling on a frozen pond sounded behind me. My face was wet in spots but with blood, not tears. Coincidence was on our side. Mercy and I were destined to save each other.

I reached through the small opening in the wall. If I'd been thinking I wouldn't have. I would've feared hurting my unhatched friend with my ice-rimed fingers.

But as it happened, the cold was exactly what Mercy needed to escape her egg. She'd been an ice gryphon all along, half-Arctic Fox and half-Arctic Tern. She hatched to the sound of the school's alarms blaring, and the first spoken words she heard outside the egg weren't mine but my horrible roommate's.

"Sissy's got a trash gryphon."

Before I could respond to his indignities, the door burst open. The Academy's brute squad dragged me off to the captain's office. Yes, they called the head of the Academy "the Captain."

They locked me in a room alone with Mercy until my parents showed up. Because they're amazing, that only took half an hour. Rhode Island is a small state, but they lived on the other side of two bridges from the Academy.

They home-schooled me for the last few weeks of that year, then pulled some strings and got me in at Hawthorn Academy on probation, but still an improvement in my academic life. My social one, too. Until the poisoning, anyway.

"Caw!" Mercy kept trying to fly toward the classroom, but I stood at the doors leading to the lobby already. I wasn't going, and my familiar knew it. I reached out and pushed the door, and she sailed through over my head. I would've walked in and mingled with the crowd in the lobby or the caf, but I couldn't yet. The experience alone in the academic wing had me too shaken up for that.

My sister had died because she knew too much and pushed too hard. She got caught up with the wrong guy, and he used her for his own ends. When she stood up to fight, they struck her down forever. I owed it to my parents and Mercy not to end up in the same situation. Maybe this time, instead of cowardice, running was the better part of valor.

I gazed at the stained-glass doors for a moment, trying to compose myself. The mural on them was titled Long Division, depicting a scene straight out of the Under. I couldn't stop the tears. I just couldn't handle it anymore—the stress of being in a new place with magi who had no idea what they might be in for.

My family had already lost enough to shifter crimelords and magisupremacists. Now here I was, trapped on a campus with more than one and no idea whether they were students, staff, or faculty— because I had run away.

I needed to talk to somebody, knowing that instinctively. Who could I trust? Obviously, the people I'd overheard were still in the academic wing. It'd be easy to jump to the conclusion that anyone out in the common areas right now wasn't them. But they couldn't be acting alone.

I wouldn't go to the headmaster because he'd start an investigation. The student handbook said that in cases of serious allegations, accusers couldn't remain anonymous. There was no way to be sure who at Hawthorn Academy was safe to talk to, except for the one person they'd mentioned.

Aliyah Morgenstern.

But when I found her in the cafeteria and tried approaching her, Dylan had nearly bit my head off. I left, heading into the hallway between the lobby and the school's entrance, which wasn't blocked anymore. I leaned against the wall, thinking about requesting to call my parents to ask if I could go home. Chickening out again.

"Caw." Mercy butted her head against my cheek. When she did that, an idea cracked through the heat of my panicked thoughts like an ice cube dropping into a fresh cup of coffee.

I could wait until October when the extramural guests arrived on campus. I'd definitely find allies against organized bigots amongst their ranks. Not all magi were magisupremacists, but all magisupremacists were magi. Other extrahumans could probably be trusted. In October, I could make psychic, shifter, and changeling connections, and then I'd have help with all this.

"I love you, Mercy." I stroked the fur on her hindquarters, and she curled her bushy tail around my wrist. "I don't know what I'd do without you."

CHAPTER TWENTY

Aliyah

At the end of dinner, Dylan headed toward the stairs. I couldn't handle any more socializing, but the café was shut down anyway, along with the lounge beside it. I wasn't sure what to do, so I paced around the lobby, trying to think of somewhere to be alone.

I walked down the hall toward Penelope's window, just to have room to stretch my legs without passersby looking at me. When I reached the end, I turned around and headed back. I thought about checking the gym, seeing if it was open. Maybe I could run some laps. But I remembered Coach Pickman saying it was being cleaned that night.

That left me no choice but to head toward the stairs. Maybe it'd be best to sleep off my bad mood. While dodging through the crowds of chattering groups in the open space, I kept my eyes down to avoid getting sucked into any conversations. That turned out to be a huge mistake.

My shoulder made contact with someone, and I looked up into the face of the last person I wanted to see.

Or maybe you do want to see him. Give him a piece of your mind, why don't you?

I typically didn't heed advice from the voice in my head because that way lay madness, but nothing about this entire day could reasonably be called sane. My mouth opened, spewing thoughts and opinions before I could stop their escape.

"How dare you!" I put my hands on my hips, glaring into Alex Onassis's eyes. "She's in intensive care, you asshole."

"What?" He blinked, taking a step back. His basilisk reared up on his shoulder, mimicking his movements.

"I understand you're no friend of Darren's, but hurting his poor innocent dog? That's beyond the pale, even for you."

"Clementine's in trouble?" His face paled and his jaw dropped. "I wouldn't hurt her in a million years."

"You expect me to believe that?" The right side of my mouth curled up in a sneer. "She was poisoned with neurotoxin, your specialty. I have direct and personal experience with that."

A gaggle of first-years stood transfixed by our confrontation, but I didn't care.

"I didn't!" He held a hand up to his cheek as though he'd been slapped. "I wouldn't poison someone's familiar. What kind of monster would do that?"

"You tried to whammy a sauna full of magi last semester." I snorted. "You wouldn't have stopped if I hadn't gotten in your way, either. I know you wouldn't think twice about it with other extrahumans."

"I'm not evil." He shook his head, the hand he'd held to his face before now trembling in front of it. "Familiars are off-limits. And we shouldn't be talking."

"It's true." Elanor Pierce sauntered over. "Pick your battles wisely, Aliyah. Your bully is showing."

"I'm not a bully." I blinked.

You could've fooled me.

"I'm not." I wrung my hands, focusing on Elanor instead of the voice. "But if you'd been in the infirmary, saw what happened, you might be asking the same questions."

"Not in that tone or in that state." Elanor raised her eyebrow, jerking her chin at my fists.

"Oh." I glanced down, seeing the glow around them. I hadn't set my blazer on fire; this was solar magic. All the same, my lack of self-control disturbed me. "Sorry."

"Is it true about Clementine?" Elanor crossed her arms over her chest, tilting her head. "Was she really poisoned?"

I nodded. "Nurse Smith called my grandmother in and everything."

"I gotta go check on Darren." Elanor dropped her arms. "If you guys have a knock-down drag-out, I'm reporting you both to the headmaster. You're both on probation. Stay civil or get the boot."

I put my hands behind my back, and Alex's shoulders eased. He took a deep breath, then let it out with a sigh, seeming to deflate. There was nothing quite like the threat of imminent expulsion to stop a fight at good old Hawthorn Academy.

"It wasn't me, I swear on all the gods of Olympus." He put his hand over his heart.

"Fine." I took a deep breath, trying to settle my agitation. "I believe you. About this."

"Thank the gods."

We stood in silence as the hushed group of students around us dispersed.

"Don't thank them just yet." I shook my head. "We're on opposite sides at this school. Clementine wasn't your fault, but somebody did this, and I'll find out who eventually. If your poison was involved in any way, even if someone stole it, I'll make sure everybody knows."

"So will I." He nodded. "Nobody steals from me and gets away with it, Aliyah. But I'm not the only poison magus on campus by a long shot."

"I know what you've been planning all summer." I turned my head, giving him side-eye to shame the devil. "I saw you last year, with Charity and that costume."

"What's that supposed to mean?" He stuck his nose in the air. It was a world of difference from how he'd reacted when I accused him of poisoning Clementine, so I knew he lied this time, but pressing further was too risky.

"Whatever." I shook my head. "I've got my eye on you, and Tempe too."

"Go write a Hallmark card or something, Goody Two-Shoes." He snorted. "She's not afraid of you."

"She should be." I turned on my heel and stalked toward the stairs, glancing over my shoulder to gift him with a withering glare. That should have been the end of the conversation, but Alex called after me, words that echoed in my ears, cementing themselves soundly enough to plague my dreams all that night.

"Nice talk." He raised his hand in a golf wave. "Your Uncle Richard would be proud."

My grandmother called on Darren the next day to give him a report about Clementine. She was on her way out while the second-years had lunch. Bubbe stopped by to say hello as I sat at the largest table in the cafeteria with everyone in my year. Even Dylan ate with us that time, though as far away from Dorian as possible.

After greeting my friends, she asked for a moment of my time. I got up, dropping my plates and tray at the dishwashing window before going into the lobby with her. Bubbe and I found seats on a bench near the double doors leading into the entrance hall.

"I'm not supposed to ask this according to the headmaster, but what happened to Clementine, Bubbe?"

"It was neurotoxin like Ezekiel said." She sighed, running a hand through her aquamarine hair. "If you hadn't helped hold her down for the nurse through that seizure, she might still be sick, or worse. I've sent samples to a lab in Boston, but so far, it looks like it had a non-magical vector."

She went on to explain that the poison might have been conjured by magic, but it had been delivered by putting it on a surface Clemen-

tine came into contact with. The lab results would do more to determine if the poison was magical or mundane in origin.

"Who uses poison magic mundanely at a magic school?" I blinked.

"Someone without poison magic, or any magic at all, who wants
poison magi or critters like them to get the blame," she answered. "A
poison magus covering their tracks is another possibility."

"The only person on campus without any magic is Ezekiel." I took
a deep breath, trying to calm myself. "Some anti-vampire jerk could
be trying to get him fired."

"I'm well aware, Bissel, but I won't say more until the lab work
comes back." Bubbe put her hand over mine. "Except that I want you
to be careful. Ember too. Remember that fire magic lets you burn
poison out of yourself. If you have any friends with that element, you
ought to show them how that works."

"So, you think we're not safe?" I blinked.

"I'm saying it's best to be prepared. I'm a medical professional,
and it's something we learn over years of practice. So, perhaps
mention it to your friend with the Sphinx, and Elanor Pierce as
well."

"I'll do that, Bubbe. Thanks for the advice."

"Don't be a stranger this weekend, Bissel. I'll see you soon."

The rest of the week went by with little incident. Familiar Bonding
continued with worksheets and magipsychic presentations given by
Nurse Smith. The only interaction the first-years got with critters
came from Doris and Ember making friends with Lena and Arick. She
let Doris curl up in her lap while he practiced keeping his hands away
from animal's faces and taking a few calming breaths before
approaching them. I thought that by the next week, they'd both be
able to continue the course as intended.

Lena seemed likely to find a magical companion, something
sedate, but I wasn't sure Arick would ever bond with a familiar. He
might be one of those rare students at Hawthorn Academy who ended

up on the educational track like my mom. That would be a shame since he clearly loved animals with a passion.

Darren vanished from any social activity. We had a high tea, a study group, and a movie night that first week, but he attended none of those. The only time I saw him was on the way in and out of the cafeteria, and he rebuffed all my efforts at checking on him. I did see him whispering with Elanor in the hall between classes, so at least he talked to someone.

I decided to take Bubbe's advice and help my fire magus friends learn to counter poison. Kitty was easy to find, so I started with her. She ran her weekly Truncheons and Flagons game on Wednesdays, so I dropped by her room after it let out and Faith was on her way to the baths for her swim.

"I never tried burning poison out. Is there anything on the subject at the library?" she asked.

"Yes. I found descriptions in this book about Bishop's Row." I jotted the title down on a piece of paper for her. "We can practice together if you want. No poison's required for that, thank goodness, but it's easy to run out of energy, so we should have our familiars nearby."

"Can we give it a go now?"

"I guess."

The basic principle was something like having a fever, except induced and controlled by magic. We both conjured fire, and then I showed her how to focus it inward. By the time Faith returned from the baths, we sat flushed and panting at the round table in the middle of the room, our familiars snoring on the table between us.

"That was like a hot yoga workout." Kitty laughed. "Whew!"

"What was?" Faith raised an eyebrow.

"Some fire magic stuff." I yawned, too tired to think about anything but sleep. We said goodbye and I left for my own room, letting Kitty explain the exercise.

I tried to look forward to the weekend. I'd go home on Saturday and meet with Izzy and Cadence to chill out from all the school stress. Plenty of my classmates needed a break, and I tried encouraging them to join in. It wasn't easy, considering nobody seemed inclined to come into town with me.

Dylan insisted on sticking around campus with his guitar. I said we wouldn't mind if he brought it along, but apparently, he wanted to practice with some other folks. My momentary flash of jealousy cooled when he explained Elanor was looking for a guitarist to join a musical act in the extramural talent show.

Faith and Hal were heading into Boston for a visit with his doctor. They'd leave on Friday during Familiar Bonding, so I couldn't even see them off. Grace planned to spend all weekend in Creatives, working on a project she insisted on keeping secret. And Dorian had to do homework and help Nurse Smith clean the infirmary, an ongoing task since Mercy had trashed the place that first afternoon in Familiar Bonding.

Finally, I tried to coax Logan into town, asking him if he'd visit Bubbe at least, but he said he wanted to help Dorian catch up on last year's critter-specific material. I couldn't argue with his insistence on encouraging good study habits.

Logan's academic strategies had propelled him to top of the class last year, so who was I to criticize? He was probably still worried about his parents, too, so I gave up. On Friday night, I hung out with Grace. Over chips and salsa, the subject of Logan's crush on Dorian came up. She wasn't surprised.

"Maybe they'll get together someday." She grinned at my blink. "You know Dorian's bi, right?" Grace shrugged at my dropped jaw. "We discussed it on the first day. We're only together for show, temporarily. He gets to skip the whole newcomer garbage and I get to look strong, keeping the rebellious guy in check. Exponential cool factor that makes up for no longer dating the athletic class clown."

"Oh." I looked away, avoiding giving voice to the first thought that popped into my head. "Why temporarily?"

"Because Dorian's helping me cement popularity with Hawthorn students. He won't go over well with psychics, shifters, and changelings, though, so I'll need to be single and eligible in October when the competing students get here. Then I'll play the field."

"Everybody in town loves Dylan, though. Cadence and Izzy do, and they're popular at their schools already."

"Why didn't I just stay with Dylan then?" She sighed. "Isn't that what you want to know?"

"You told me already. Too much emotion, right?"

"Not from him." She rolled her eyes, chagrin morphing to anger. "How can you be in love and not have sex?"

"That makes no sense." My face felt nearly feverish. I'd always imagined true love not requiring all the messy-seeming naked body stuff, or only exploring once you had a long history of devotion and trust. I couldn't imagine what it felt like, desire for the sake of it, but she took my words differently than I'd intended them.

"Right!" Grace's nod was as emphatic as applause. "I'd rather get stuck being celibate with someone I don't want to bang all the time."

I didn't contradict her because we'd end up in an argument about a subject I found utterly baffling. I had no time or energy for that. Instead, I got ready for bed. Spending the weekend coordinating events with Izzy and Cadence might end up as an exercise in cat-herding anyway.

CHAPTER TWENTY-ONE

"We got the same list of projects." Izzy nodded. " I singled that one out too. Mostly because of you, Cadence."

"Me?" Cadence batted her eyelids, smiling. "Oh, you shouldn't have, Iz."

"You know practically everyone at Gallows Hill. Who's going to help most with this experiment? And will they be participating in extramurals?"

"Let's see. What kind of shifters do you need again?" Cadence raised her eyebrow.

"You can't tell by looking at this description?" Izzy tapped the paper, her eyes widening. "Have you been asleep in class?"

"Don't get on my case. I do a lot of work at school. And I've always been a little scatterbrained, you know that." I didn't like how strident Cadence's voice sounded while she was defending herself.

"I can always invite Azrael over and ask him." I shook my head. "Or we could just tell Cadence what we're looking for. Let's all chill out. We've got this."

"I don't need a lecture, Aliyah." Izzy's jaw clenched, eyes too shiny.

"Sorry, I didn't mean it to come across that way." I reached out, putting my hand over hers. "Are you okay?"

"I might not even have a spot on the extramural team." Izzy's lower lip trembled. "After I worked so hard last year."

"What happened?"

"Everyone at Messing is fickle. It's hard to describe, so I won't. I'll just give you a name." She took a deep breath, steadying her hands and her voice. "Jonah Arnold."

The name meant nothing to me, but it did to Cadence. She gaped like a, well, fish.

"No. Way. How did he get into your school? He's a vampire."

"Messing Academy admits psychic vampires as long as their years of existence total eighteen or less. Jonah's clairvoyant just like me, uses tarot cards and everything. Anyway, Dean Adelphi said he was automatically on the extramural team. That means I'm not going to make it."

"Doesn't Adelphi understand how much prejudice there is at Hawthorn against vampires?" I blinked. "Having him there is dangerous."

"That's why she's doing it." Izzy sighed. "Messing's its own counter-culture. Also, it's basic strategy. They're keeping redundancy to a minimum, like we're a Swiss Army Knife instead of a team."

"But aren't you, like, super-popular?" Cadence asked. "Isn't leadership important to Dean Adelphi's selection process?"

Izzy and I shook our heads at the same time. She jerked her chin at me, so I explained as best I could.

"Do you remember how Hal Hawkins was on my Bishop's Row team last year, just because he was the only space magus?"

"So it's nepotism?" Cadence narrowed her eyes. "Is Jonah related to the dean? Could you cry foul?"

"No and no."

"Is there any way you'd both be sure to go?" I tapped my pencil on the packet of experiments. "Magipsychic lab projects are a big deal, but that and Bishop's Row aren't all we've got going on."

"Maybe. Nobody's said anything official. I just overheard the dean talking to a teacher. She said he's our biggest asset." She patted the bag she always wore at her side to carry her cards.

"Got a weird feeling right after that, but didn't have time to do a draw."

"That tears it." I grinned. "The weird feeling could have been about Dean Adelphi's next hair appointment, for all we know. Let's make sure you're not redundant."

"Maybe."

"What extracurriculars are you doing?" Cadence flipped open a notebook and produced a pen with a downy black puff at the top. "If they're different from Jonah's, that'll help."

"We both play Bishop's Row." She shook her head. "He's a vampire. His reflexes and speed will get him on the team, no problem."

"What else?" Cadence wrote Bishop's Row, then moved her pen.

"Okay, fine. I'm in the chess club." Izzy rolled her eyes. "But he's the president."

"Okay." Cadence didn't bother writing that one down. "What else?"

"Ballroom dancing, which he got trophies for back in Chicago where he's from."

"So have you, in Boston!" Cadence dropped her pen and pad, clapping her hands and squealing. "Partner up with him for the talent show and boom, you're essential too."

"Cadence, you're a genius." Izzy leaned over and hugged her.

"You just told me I needed to study more." She giggled.

"Genius isn't just academics." I smiled, then rubbed my growling stomach. "I think it's pizza time, ladies. Let's head out and celebrate this stroke of brilliance at the Engine House."

My friends agreed, so we packed up our papers and notebooks, then headed into the early autumn day together.

***

"Bubbe?" I knocked on the rear door of her office, the one at the bottom of the back stairs. I'd just gotten back from my day out with Cadence and Izzy, and I'd promised to visit her this weekend.

"Just a moment, Bissel!" I heard her voice call from down the hall.

Her footsteps sounded solid and reassuring on the other side of the door as she approached and opened it. We smiled and hugged, then I followed her down the hall. She paused outside the entrance to the kitchen and turned to face me.

"Your friends are here, Harold Hawkins and Faith Fairbanks. They brought something I think you ought to see."

"Oh?" I blinked but nodded. "Okay."

She opened the door and I walked in, then sat across the table from Hal and Faith. Bubbe set an empty mug in front of me and poured red zinger tea from a pot. After that, she took her half-full beverage from the table and headed into the hall to do rounds for her boarders and patients. Mine was the only mug with steam rising from it, so they'd been there for a while.

"Hi, you guys." I wrapped my hands around the warm cup. "What's up?"

"Remember last year, before you righteously dumped the poisonous bastard?" Faith studied her nails.

"Yes, unfortunately." I nodded.

"You asked if his mother could look into Hal's family. Well, she did, but he waited until now to tell us about it. Anyway, he gave us this."

Faith pushed the piece of paper across the table toward me. I didn't look at it, at least not yet.

"Why are you showing me?"

"We thought you might have some idea what this means." Hal tapped a line at the bottom of the paper. "You're fanatical about the folks down at Providence Paranormal College."

"Oh. I'll help, I just didn't want to go poking around in your private stuff. Not after all the mistakes I made in that area last year."

"The mistakes turned out to be an advantage, though." Hal sighed. "Alex came through, but I can't get my brain around why."

"He sent it to us by way of Arick Magnuson, who positively quaked in his boat shoes." Faith rolled her eyes. "At least we've got one ally among the first-years. You made quite the impression on him in Familiar Bonding."

"I hope you're right." I sighed.

"The document seems to be in order, anyway." Hal tapped it again.

"But this bothers me. Something about it feels almost too familiar. Uncanny, even coincidental."

"All right, all right. I'm looking."

I held the paper up, reading the words printed on it. The document was brief, mostly a list of names with relationships to Hal's father.

"Gamila Haddad Hawkins is my grandmother. She made the stained glass mural on the doors to the academic wing." He shook his head. "I never met her, though. She's fae and went away for some reason. Business with a monarch, maybe?"

"I don't know. I only remember your dad saying his mother made that artwork."

"Let's stay focused on Stephanie's side of the family." Faith sniffed. "What there is of it."

"There's nothing here about her except that your mother's maiden name was Kiln." I tapped my temple, trying to remember. "And you're right, it rings a bell. Reminds me of something I heard, but it's off somehow."

"Absolutely." Hal nodded. "It's unique because everything on Dad's side is a birth or baptismal record, but hers is a GED record at North Shore Community College. She covered up being a dhampyr, but that can't be all."

"That name must be an alias." Faith said. "It makes sense, but if you're hiding your status, why do it with a name so odd it draws attention?"

"Because you aren't sure what your name is?" I shrugged. "Her kind were victims for ages, moved from one place to another and fed from. Maybe Kiln was the only name she could think of that wouldn't hurt anyone."

"My mom never had much empathy," Hal said, "And she's the opposite of genuine under the masks she wears in public. No, Aliyah. I can't afford to entertain the idea that she's somehow secretly sad. You never met her, so I don't blame you for misjudging her."

"Parents screw up." Faith put her arm around him, leaning his head on her shoulder. "They're flawed, they make mistakes. The really bad ones do horrifying shit on purpose, like sell their kids to the highest bidder, which is my guess about how she ended up here."

I couldn't say anything. My own folks were as close to perfect as you could get, despite my mom's estranged family. Anything I said would sound trite, so I looked at the paper again, trying to think of an alternate path to discovering Stephanie's true identity. My brain kept going back to Logan's parents and how they'd put out an Amber Alert to the police. That gave me an idea.

"Have you thought about missing person records? Cold cases?"

"No." Hal blinked. "I hadn't."

"I had." Faith sighed. "It takes a lot of in-person legwork all over New England. We'd have to hire someone for that. A private investigator."

"How much do you think it would cost?" Hal raised an eyebrow.

"No clue." I shrugged. "I don't know whether minors like us can legally hire them anyway, but it's something to look into."

"I'll check on it." Hal gave me a wan grin. "Thanks for brainstorming with us, Aliyah."

"I'd hardly call that a brainstorm, but you're welcome. I was wondering, what brought you here?"

"More vitamins for Nin and a checkup. Can you believe it's been almost six months since the last time?"

"Wow." I shook my head. "So much has happened since then."

"How's Dylan holding up, by the way?" Faith asked. "We've barely seen him since the beginning of the year."

"He's not doing so great. Feels left out of everything, mostly." I sighed. "At least he's got guitar."

"It must be even worse with the café closed. I heard about you confronting Alex the night it happened. Good job getting information out of him. Maybe that's why he finally gave the report to us."

"That's not why I did it. Total knee-jerk reaction. I'm kind of embarrassed." I let out a deflated little sigh. "At least I didn't light up the lobby in a bad way."

"I don't blame you one bit." Faith sniffed. "We still need to keep an eye on him. You know how Grace has our entire social structure planned out? You can be sure Tempe's got something similar going on, and if I were her, I'd counter you with Alex. You might have caught him off-guard that time, but be careful."

"I'm sorry, Faith." Hal shook his head. "You should be the one leading our crowd. You were born for this, but instead, you're stuck ushering me around."

"I wouldn't be anywhere but with you, and Grace is doing just fine." Faith squeezed his hand. "That girl has an uncanny knack for managing any task she puts her mind to. Besides, I like using my powers for good." She grinned.

"What did Grace say the first day? We're going to nice them to death?"

"It might not be that simple, but that's the idea, and I'm sticking to it." Hal nodded. "What did you say last year? Kindness is punk AF?"

We all laughed at that. Bubbe returned with Nin's vitamins to a room full of mirthful teenagers. I followed as we escorted Faith and Hal out the front door. After they left, I turned to my grandmother and hugged her.

"Bubbe, thank you."

"What for?"

"For being so kind to my friends. Helping us all. Going above and beyond. I appreciate it."

"Bissel, it's the least I can do. After we get to be a certain age, many adults think back to the teenage years, remember it as some golden age, but then we get even older and remember the rest. How hard it all was at the same time."

"There's something Logan says in Creatives: that it's almost impossible for something bright to stand out unless the background's darker. He's talking about art, I know, but isn't art like life?"

"And the other way around." She sighed, but the corners of her mouth turned up instead of down. "I know I already did my rounds, but would you like to have a look at our current guests?"

Of course I would. I followed my grandmother down the hall, filling the rest of my Saturday with the familiar but still fascinating task of helping around her office.

CHAPTER TWENTY-TWO

Much like the previous year, the weeks went by in routine. Bubbe returned Clementine to campus on Monday at dinner time. I saw it happen; we had our take-out dinners adjacent to Darren. The lounge was cramped because only part of it had opened before the café, which remained closed.

Familiar Bonding proceeded, and we discovered Lena's element was poison. That shocked me. Shyness wasn't usually a personality trait amongst poison magi, and possums tended to avoid them, but she ended up bonding with the little marsupial despite all that.

Arick was a wood magus like Lee Young. He didn't find his familiar among the ones Nurse Smith presented, either. He bonded with one in the library, but not before he completely lost hope. I only saw it because I offered to return a book for Ezekiel.

"It's not going to happen, Mr. Ashford." Arick put his head down on the counter, something I'd never seen a student do in the library. "Is Academic as boring as they say?"

"Why not have a look at the introductory text, Arick?"

He pulled a large battered volume out from under the counter and set it beside the boy's head. It made a faint booming sound, but hollower than I would have expected from a tome that size. Arick stood up immediately, staring at the cover, which shook slightly before bouncing up and down.

"Oh, dear." Mr. Ashford took a step backward. "Cover your faces, students!"

As if in demonstration, he held his palms over his mouth and nose, like the masks carpenters wear to keep out wood shavings. Moments later, I copied him, rushing to Arick's side to encourage him to do the same. I knew what was coming.

The book's cover flipped open, letting out a voluminous cloud of papery dust. I squinted, wanting to see the critter emerge. I'd never watched one hatch before.

The pointy head looked more canine than reptilian, but that was because bookwyrms were chimera. It shook its mane out, sending up more dust, then yawned, revealing its froglike tongue. When it tried to climb out of the now-hollow tome its egg had been laid in, the poor creature succeeded but ended up falling headfirst off the counter.

"I got you!" Arick dropped to his knees, catching the critter in his hands.

Mr. Ashford lowered his hands, holding them to his heart and smiling. My mouth dropped open as I watched Arick stare into the bookwyrm's eyes. It let out a dusty croak.

"You're welcome, Skinner." He stood up absently, totally enthralled with the wingless critter perched in his hands.

"Your bookwyrm's name is Skinner?" I grinned. "Like the psychologist?"

"He hatched from an education textbook, so that makes sense," Mr. Ashford said.

"Well, it looks like you've got yourself a familiar, Arick." I grinned.

After that, he was all smiles. He waited with me as I returned the book, and I had the privilege of going with him to tell Nurse Smith the good news. Our remaining time in Familiar Bonding was spent on critter training and care, much to Dorian's relief. He and Mercy still needed practice.

Faith and Hal ended up asking Nurse Smith to conduct lessons in the same room as his infusions, mostly so they had company. He seemed slightly better, which was no small relief, especially with the specter of Parents' Night spooking Logan. He talked about it at breakfast one day.

"I don't know what to do, Aliyah." Logan shook his head, then gazed into his glass of juice. "They're going to show up. It's Elanor's last year. What if they try to take me home?"

"It's Massachusetts, and my mom knows all the laws, which are in your favor. She'll be here with Bubbe. They'll stick up for you."

"I can't shake the feeling that they're going to do something awful." He shuddered, almost knocking over his glass.

"I understand, mate." Dylan patted his shoulder. "This year has sucked so far, but once we're past Parents' Night, it's all fun stuff. Extramurals. Remember that? Maybe there's some good on the horizon."

"I guess so." Logan shrugged. "It's just, nobody else had their parents toss them out, then call the cops on them."

"You might be wrong about that." I waved a hand at the bustling cafeteria, thinking about my mom. "Maybe nobody here has been through that, but somewhere in the world, it probably happened before."

"I'm still scared. Can't help the feeling it'll go sideways no matter what I do. I know what you say about assumptions, so I guess I'm an ass."

"At least you're a smart ass, Logan." Dorian sauntered by with a tray full of empty plates. "I wouldn't be managing if it weren't for you, so at any rate, I'm glad you're here."

Logan stared at Dorian like he was a cooler full of ice-cold soda on a hundred-degree day at the beach. He strode by, seemingly oblivious to the attention.

"If I could only find a girl who looked at me the way you do at the Goth." Elanor appeared from somewhere behind me, shaking her head. "You've got it bad."

"No, I don't." Logan jerked his arm so hard he knocked over his juice.

It spilled across the table, splashing the remains of my breakfast sandwich in the process. I managed to avoid any of it dripping on me, thanks to Ember. She swooped down, flapping her wings to keep it from falling off the side like an orange waterfall. I tossed a stack of napkins on the liquid to soak up the deluge.

"Just say something to him already." Elanor sighed. "Do what you can about the stuff you have control over."

"Yeah, unlike your parents." Dylan rolled his eyes. "If you're going to give him sisterly advice, better to reassure him about that elephant in the room."

"I can't." She gazed at her shoes. "I'm not an insurance company, and they're practically acts of God. I'll distract them as much as I can." Elanor looked back up at Logan. "I wish they weren't giving you so much grief."

"Thanks, Elanor."

"For nothing." I finished mopping up the orange juice, dropping the sodden napkin on my tray.

"Whatever, Miss Healthy Normal Family." With that, Elanor flounced away.

"What did she just call me?" I blinked.

"It's several steps up from the crap Charity said about you last year." Dylan shrugged, then placed his hands on the table. The tips of his fingers paled slightly. "Anyway."

Something about his fingernails must've caught his attention because he studied them. He cleared his throat, opened his mouth, then closed it again. After another moment, he leaned back and shook his head. Whatever he was going to tell us remained a mystery.

"Aliyah, I wanted to ask." Logan started bussing the trays. "Will you go to the dance with me? As friends again, I mean. I just don't want to be there by myself, you know."

"Sure, Logan. At least none of us has to go with Alex Onassis."

We all laughed, Dylan somewhat flatly. It broke the tension enough to get us through that day, at least.

As the week wore on, I noticed Hal wasn't as late to class as he'd been at the end of last year. He came in just after the bell, a vast improvement. We partnered up in lab again while Faith headed Bailey off, leaving Dorian with Logan, who was responsible for him academically anyway. Matchmaking had everything to do with it since Faith and Hal noticed Logan's crush.

"You look way better." I waved a hand at his improved color and posture. "Is it the new treatments in Boston?"

"Partly, but Faith's been helping between classes. We meet at that stained glass mural and do the therapies Bubbe gave us last year." He recorded an observation about the fluid in the flask in front of us.

"Well, I'm glad that's working and that the doctors allow it."

"Me too. Who'd have thought the fact that she's an undeath magus would be so serendipitous."

"Coincidence." I smiled at my friend. "You guys are destined."

"I won't wager against you on that." He nodded back.

Neither of us said the obvious: that she was literally saving his life. I think he worried, wondered whether things between them were one-sided. From where I sat, it went both ways. Her family was so toxic it could give Alex's poison a run for its money.

I pondered my ex-boyfriend. Last year, he'd given Charity a vow to help with some heinous effort, but so far, he'd only denied poisoning Clementine and sent genealogy records to Hal. I couldn't allow his baffling behavior too much real estate in my mind. Faith was right; his mere presence could foil me by distraction if I wasn't careful.

Temperance was the definitive force in the social scene for first-years, and Alex was almost always on her arm. So far, it hadn't extended to us. Bailey hung out with the third-years. Elanor Pierce was their It Girl, and dating Alex had backfired because Noah hated him. Most of the third-years snubbed Tempe.

That left her with no choice but to set up a stationary orbit around Elanor's group in hopes of catching defectors before they switched allegiance to Grace. That vindicated her social strategy enough for my classmates to accept Dylan's misery as collateral damage.

Every Wednesday, the school cafeteria had high tea after Familiar Bonding. The crowd around Grace grew, while Temperance's dwindled.

Arick Magnuson brought Giselle Ambersmith, who was his lab partner, to hang out the first week and introduced others each Wednesday. I kept my eye on the rest of the first-years every time because Alex had been sneaky last year, and I had no reason to think he'd changed.

If only I had more information. Bubbe was my only source, and she remained mum about the lab results. The headmaster continued working on the mystery. He'd sent a memo requesting staff and faculty to come forward with information but had let nothing else slip where Hal could hear or see it. Nurse Smith kept his lips zipped so tightly on the matter that he'd excluded Ezekiel.

The week before Parents' Night, Grace declared she needed me for some rounds through the dorm. She had me drag a canvas-covered wheeled rack up the stairs from Creatives and then along the third-floor hall. At first, I wasn't sure what she was up to, but after we knocked on Kitty's and Faith's door, I realized this was the result of her secret project.

Grace hadn't spent all summer just making clothes for herself. She'd made outfits for everyone in our year except Dorian, who she couldn't have planned for.

"Are you sure you don't have changelings in your family, Grace?" Kitty winked. "Because there's this total fairy godmother vibe going on right now."

"Nope." She shook her head. "A little dragon shifter way back on Mom's side is all. Otherwise, just magi. Anyway, do you like it?"

"It's so awesome, I can't even find words." Kitty held the red and orange dress up against her body. It looked like it was made of fire, flickering in the lights like a garment of flames.

"I never would've chosen something like this for myself, but I would've been wrong." Faith shook her head, holding the draped and flowing lavender gown with pale green and gold accents at arm's length and staring at it. "It's beautiful, a real work of art."

"Thanks." Grace blinked. She wasn't unaccustomed to praise, but Faith gave it so rarely even I was surprised. "Come on, Aliyah. If we want to get this done before lights out, we've got to head to the next room."

"Can I go?" Faith asked. "It's Lee and Hal next, right?

"Sure." Grace nodded.

Kitty went back in their room, and the three of us made our way down the hall to the next one. Lee answered the door when we knocked, then nodded and invited us in.

"You didn't have to, Grace." Hal shook his head, gazing down at the ensemble he'd laid out on his bed. The jacket and pants were black damask with a very subtle ram's head pattern, but the tie and vest matched Faith's color scheme.

"I wanted to."

"All the same, send me an invoice." He grinned. "Dad budgeted for my event attire this year, and if you don't, he'll head into town and buy something I don't like nearly as much."

"Me too." Lee stood in front of his mirror, holding his outfit up with the hanger under his chin. His suit was a deep earthy brown with a pine-green cravat that featured a glittering pin matching his signature purple bangs. He looked over his shoulder and grinned. "I was just going to wear my blazer. This is awesome."

"Do you have a date this year, Lee?" Faith raised her eyebrow.

"Maybe I'll bring someone, but only with the headmaster's permission."

"He'll say yes," Hal stated.

Before I could ask who Lee's mysterious date was, we headed out of the room and down the hall once again. This time, we stopped at Eston's and Dorian's room. Grace didn't have anything for Dorian because she hadn't met him until school started, but Eston was overjoyed to see the retro-styled powder-blue suit with its black cummerbund and bow tie. His shirt was ruffled and a darker blue like lapis lazuli, which matched his glasses.

Hailey and Bailey were utterly surprised to see us with the garment rack. Hailey's excitement was palpable, though her sister kept shooting the three of us suspicious glances. The garments weren't anywhere near identical, despite the twins having the same build and coloring.

"I look like a unicorn!" Hailey giggled. Her dress was cocktail length, fun and cute with a kicky circle skirt in iridescent pink fabric. The entire dress had an ombre effect that reminded me of the sky at sunrise. Bailey's dress was a bias-cut maxi with a mermaid skirt. White rosettes that looked like cirrus clouds ran along the spaghetti straps, crisscrossing at the waist in front and trailing down the back of the sky blue gown.

Finally, we got to Dylan's and Logan's room, where Grace first produced a navy-blue suit with gold buttons and seafoam accessories. Logan oohed and ahhed over it while Dylan sat at his desk, emphatically jotting words down in his class notebook.

"Come away from that homework and check out your new duds."

"Really?" He turned his head and raised an eyebrow, his lip curling into a sneer. "You shouldn't have."

"I did for everybody else in our year. Last time I checked, you're still one of us." She shook her head. "Or maybe Aliyah wants to open hers next."

I peered at the rack. Sure enough, two garment bags still hung there. I reached out for the more voluminous one, figuring it had a dress inside instead of a suit. And I was right.

Last year I'd worn something from a mundane shop in Salem, and on Valentine's Day, Bubbe had lent me something magical from her days at Hawthorn. Both of them reminded me more of my fire magic than anything else. Grace had gone the other way with her creation for me.

As I unzipped the bag, hues of gold and pale yellow met my eyes. I'd never worn anything this shiny or light before, and it matched Great-Uncle Noah's necklace because the gold fabric had a sort of red iridescence to it as I tilted the dress on its hanger.

"You've really outdone yourself with this one, Grace." I took it from the rack and held it up under my chin.

"Whoa." Dylan dropped his pen. "You leveled up in sewing, Grace."

"So, are you going to open yours?" Grace tapped her foot. "It's almost lights out."

"I guess." Dylan paced across the room, stopping almost too short of the rack. But his arms made the distance. He snatched the garment bag off it, then went back across the room to stand in front of the mirror on his wardrobe.

Dylan's suit was off-white, bluish instead of beige. Like my dress, it was made from a fabric that changed color depending on how the light hit it. Pale blue flashed in the light, but on his suit, it made a pattern like clouds, or maybe white dunes. I couldn't quite decipher what she meant with the color choices. Everyone else's had something to do with their magical elements, but Dylan's didn't entirely remind me of air.

Does she know he's an extramagus? What's the latest news on that, anyway? He hardly seems like he's gotten help.

I didn't say anything. He'd scheduled that meeting with Professor DeBeer weeks ago, but there hadn't been an announcement or any other information publicly outing him like they had for me. Then again, I didn't know the standard school procedure for voluntarily reporting extramagi. I certainly hadn't followed it last year.

I wasn't in his class and had no idea what might have changed in there, but life on campus seemed harder for him instead of easier, as he'd hoped the day he'd told me about the ice magic. He had no obligation to include me, but it still didn't sit well. Izzy would definitely have flipped cards at that point, but she wasn't there, and I had no way to contact her until after Parents' Night.

Maybe the style choices did make sense without the extra information. Art was objective, so perhaps Grace's interpretation of air wasn't the same as mine. We were from different countries and cultures. Surely that explained it.

Or maybe not. Maybe your "good friend" Grace isn't what she seems.

I rolled my eyes at the Evil Inside Voice, but nobody noticed. They were all too caught up in the drama of Grace giving her ex-boyfriend attire for a dance she'd be attending with somebody else. I couldn't blame them.

As we walked back toward our rooms, Faith and Grace chattered about selecting makeup and jewelry after class during the week. I nodded, smiled, and contributed my opinions, but the strange encounter with Dylan stayed on my mind for most of the week, which made me feel like a bad friend. I should've paid more attention to Logan.

CHAPTER TWENTY-THREE

We had Bishop's Row tryouts the week before Parents' Night, too. I had so much on my mind, it felt like I was on autopilot through the exercises and trials. On Friday when I walked into the gym to read the list, I was shocked to find myself on the team playing mid with Dylan. Faith was on reserves with Lee. Noah stood at the board, smiling at the list.

"Alex didn't make it?" I blinked, taking a step back and bumping into someone behind me. We went down in a tangle of limbs on the floor, and when I partially recovered, I realized it was Faith.

"It's a good thing, too. Neither of us wants to be on any kind of Team Alex. He sucks."

"Not even all that well, according to rumor." Noah reached down, giving Faith a hand up. He left me on the floor, which I expected.

"Gross, Noah. So, are we talking again?" I stood up and straightened my blazer, crossing my arms over my chest. "We're both on the team."

"Only about Bishop's Row." Noah rolled his eyes.

"Fine." I dropped my arms to my sides and peered at the rest of the list. "But no more squicky locker room talk, okay?"

"Whatever. I'm surprised Grace isn't on here." Noah tapped the paper, which listed him as first defense. "She's better than you."

"Grace told Coach Pickman she didn't want to be on the team." I flipped a lock of hair over my shoulder. "Something about letting Dylan do what he's best at, and they still can't get along."

"They're exes, so things are going to be awkward." Noah rolled his eyes, then turned and began to saunter away. "Anyway, see you at practice, kids."

"Is he always like this?" Faith shook her head. "I wish they'd hurry up and chill out. Tempe's been way too quiet this month, and I don't like it. We'll want all hands on deck before extramurals."

"Agreed." I nodded. "Have you talked to him? I know you and Grace spent a lot of time together, but Dylan...well, you saw him with the suit. I'm not sure when he's going to get over it."

"Maybe Hal can ask." She sighed. "Not everyone gets past stuff by talking. I think he needs an outlet, like that open mic night but bigger. The extramural talent show might be the ticket, but it's months out."

"You're probably right." I sighed. "He mentioned practicing with Elanor once but never again after that. If only I knew someone else who was into performance art."

"You do." Faith's grin twisted into the shape I recognized is ironic. "But he's only agreed to talk about sports."

"Crap on a crap cracker." I closed my eyes. "Leave it to you to remind me about my own brother's passion for music."

"Well, it can't hurt to ask Elanor about Dylan." Faith tilted her head, her grin softening. "And you've got every excuse to meet with her, considering she's our team captain. I'll work on Noah."

That was the plan, but since Parents' Night loomed on the horizon the very next day, we didn't get a chance to have our chats before the big event.

Elanor was right. Her parents spent the entire school tour snubbing Logan in favor of her, so Bubbe let Logan escort her around, showing her the second-year set up in the lab, including the row of plants he had growing in the window there. Elanor hadn't brought Benny the philodendron, but Professor Luciano had gotten him a clipping from somewhere, along with rarer seeds, and encouraged him to turn the lab's window into a greenhouse. His entire face lit up, showing that off.

In Creatives, Grace beckoned us all over. She and Logan spent over ten minutes showing my grandmother the outfit sketches they'd designed together for Hawthorn Academy's cheer squad. They weren't as flashy as Cadence's at Gallows Hill, but the getups were stylish and flattering.

"What are you working on, Aliyah?" Dad asked.

"Mostly pottery, but here's something I'm carving from wood. Lee's giving me tips." I opened the cabinet where I stored my projects, producing the oblong chunk of wood I'd been working with. "It's really nothing much."

"I think I see it." Dad nodded sagely, taking the piece of wood for my hands. "There's the head, right? Is this Ember?"

"No, Dad, it's Gale." The clueless expression on his face prompted me to add more. "Dylan's dragonet. You know, my friend, the air magus?"

"Ah, yes. How's he been?"

"You ought to ask him yourself. His parents didn't show up again, and he's way more upset about it than he was last year."

Dad craned his neck, scanning the room. Once he spotted Dylan, he waved and smiled, then made a beeline toward the table where he sat with the guitar the library had loaned him long-term.

"It's nice of your parents, making rounds like that." Faith sniffed behind me.

I turned to see her dabbing the corner of one eye, then removing her hand in a flash before smudging her eye makeup. She blinked a few times, trying to let her expression fall back into resting neutral face without much success.

"Maybe because my mom had a hard time when she was here."

"You don't have to rub it in, Aliyah." She sniffed again, the redness of stifled tears fading from the tip of her nose.

"I'm not, and I'm sorry if it seemed that way." I wrung my hands, frustrated and unable to comfort her. "Anyway, where's Hal?"

"In the infirmary. With his father."

"Okay, then." I nodded, then offered her my arm. "Let's go find our critters and get ready for dancing."

"Together?" She blinked.

"Of course."

"You must have more important things to do."

"Friendship's important, so let's go." I grinned.

She gave me a lopsided one back, and we sauntered across the room. Faith might've showboated a bit, and I couldn't blame her. Her parents glanced up from where they sat with Temperance, examining some jewelry she'd made. They promptly turned their noses in the air and looked away. I understood how Faith might feel, even though my experience in being snubbed by family was limited to Noah. Dealing with one aloof brother had to be easier on the heart than an entire household.

When we found Ember and Seth, they'd been hanging around together. But Ember had dozed off, leaving Seth to prance back and forth in front of her whining, the nails on his paws clicking on the floor.

"Oh, Seth, honestly." Faith gave her familiar a soft smile. "Where do you get all your energy?"

I knew better than to try rousing Ember, so I scooped her up to drape her over my shoulders. She curled more tightly around them in her sleep, a habit she'd gotten into since this strange lethargic growth spurt had started.

"When will she get back to her lively self?" Faith raised an eyebrow.

"Bubbe says by November, most likely." I shrugged. "I miss her peeping at everything, but in a way, I'm glad she's been this drowsy while Mercy makes all the mischief."

We glanced across the room, spotting Dorian and his folks. They cooed over every little thing that had his name on it. He didn't bother introducing them to Grace, either. For her part, she kept her distance, and I hardly blamed her. She wasn't comfortable around parental figures on a good day, and she couldn't be happy about the lack of introductions. She seemed suspicious of how much Dorian's doted on him.

"Such a shame how his older sister died," Faith murmured.

"Really?" My footsteps paused. "I had no idea."

"I'm surprised, with the way you carried on last year about Providence Paranormal."

"I don't remember any ice magi in their pack."

"His sister was precognitive. Remember, he said they're all psychics in his family except for him. Anyway, her name was Cassandra, and she wasn't part of that aluminum foil group anyway."

"Tinfoil. And I remember now. She's the one the mob boss abducted." I winced. "How did you know?"

"Hal read his entrance essay, of course."

"Oh." I shook my head. "You know, I almost forgot he did that with all of us last year."

"A good thing, too. Everything might have gone sideways if he hadn't."

"Good point." I sighed. "And thanks for telling me about Dorian. The last thing I want to do is accidentally upset him by blathering on about my uncle."

"Don't mention it. It's all just part of our mutual crown-straightening society." Faith grinned.

Like last year, we made an entrance for the dance on Parents' Night in one big group. Hailey and Bailey even joined us this time, as well as Kitty and Eston, who hadn't before. Hailey had a surprise guest: Arick Magnuson.

"Temperance won't treat you kindly for this." Faith raised her eyebrow, looking at the shirt and tie he'd matched with his school blazer. "Honestly, asking someone in our year to the dance was a bad idea, Magnuson."

"He doesn't care, Faith." Hailey rolled her eyes. "Anyway, I asked him."

"Right." Arick nodded, smiling at Hailey. Skinner stuck his head out of Arick's pocket, crossing his eyes and sticking his tongue out.

"Whatever floats your boat, I guess." Faith said, clasping Hal's hand.

"First floor," Dorian called at the stairs.

A crowd of parents watched as the staircase moved us down. Expressions ranged from smiles to snorts of disdain, though most were neutral, which made sense. The majority of the parental figures here had nothing to do with us, after all.

Somehow, we were the first students down the stairs. We hadn't planned on that. In fact, Logan had wanted to avoid it. Without Elanor to run interference, his parents made a beeline for us. I escorted him toward my family, hoping the conflicting attitudes would cancel each other out, but of course, we got intercepted.

The Pierce boy can't avoid his family forever. You should know better.

"Good evening Mrs. Pierce." I put on my best smile, ignoring the Evil Inside Voice while extending my hand toward Logan's baffling mother. I'd had no interaction with her besides the strange video call at the beginning of summer. Her attitude and behavior had only confused me since then.

"You clean up more nicely than I expected, Miss Morgenstern." She tilted her head, giving me a once-over. "If only your parents would discipline you properly."

"I suppose the fact that I'm on probation isn't ideal. To you, anyway." I shrugged, allowing the Evil Inside Voice to come out for once. I figured its sass might counter her backhanded compliments better than I could on my own.

"Perhaps you'll be expelled, and my son can find more appropriate company to keep."

"You mean, like me?" Dylan sauntered over, hands in his pockets. Gale stood on his shoulder, glaring daggers at Mrs. Pierce.

"Ah, yes, the work-study kid." She sniffed. "Are you employed under the table somehow this year? It's the only way I can imagine you'd afford an outfit like that."

"Actually, our extremely talented classmate Grace Dubois spent the summer making attire for everyone in our year." I grinned, letting Logan raise his arm to turn me in a slow spin, the better to show off Grace's creation.

"Peep!" Ember swooped down from wherever she'd been stretching her wings, making as if to divebomb Mrs. Pierce before banking abruptly and landing on Logan's shoulder. She rubbed cheeks with him, then hopped over to perch on me.

"So, this is Logan's mother." The familiar voice came from behind me.

"Izzy?" I turned my head to find my psychic friend on the arm of Lee Young, which I would never have expected because Izzy shunned romance like some people avoid musical theater. Maybe she'd come with Lee platonically like I had with Logan. He'd mentioned bringing a friend, not a date.

"Hi." She smiled, but it didn't touch her eyes. I recognized that look. Mrs. Pierce was about to hear some inconvenient truths.

"Izzy, don't."

"Sorry, not sorry." Izzy reached into her beaded cross-body bag and pulled out one of her well-worn tarot cards. She held it up with the back to Mrs. Pierce, snorting before she flipped it around for everyone to see. "Ten of Pentacles reversed. Inauspicious to the max."

"I know what it means, you little charlatan." Mrs. Pierce narrowed her eyes. "I'm in total control of my life and need none of your nonsense."

"I flipped it for Logan." Izzy held her head high, basking in the disdainful gaze. "And thanks to you, he's not."

"This is the reason I didn't want him returning to Hawthorn Academy this year." Mrs. Pierce shook her head. "And why he'll be leaving with me at the end of the evening."

"I'm not going, Mom." Logan planted his feet, clinging to my arm. "I'm staying in school."

"Good luck staying on this campus all year." She stifled what I suspected was a fake yawn. "The moment you step off it, you're coming home."

"This is Massachusetts." The hand he had on my arm went clammy and cold. His voice cracked, but he managed one more defiant statement. "I know my rights."

"Then you'll spend the rest of *this* year here, languishing with misfits and miscreants. But *we're* not paying your tuition next year." Her smile reminded me of a steel trap. "You'll have to drop out."

"I can't believe what I'm hearing." Professor Luciano stunned us all by stepping forward. He snapped his fingers, and his strix familiar took off from his shoulder, silently gliding away. "My best student will have all the help he needs to complete his education. His GPA alone qualifies him for a scholarship I manage, to say nothing of all the volunteer tutoring he's been doing."

"My son *will* fail academically at some point. His grades *always* drop out, and eventually, so will he." She sniffed. "If he thinks otherwise, he must be as mad as that extramagus on his arm."

"If you can't discontinue abusing my students, I will ask Headmaster Hawkins to have you removed from campus."

"That's outrageous." Her smile reminded me of a barracuda's, but the figure that suddenly appeared beside her was a much bigger fish. "*My* husband's on the Board of Trustees."

"But you aren't." The headmaster approached. "Tone it down, or you'll be asked to leave campus for the remainder of the evening."

Her eyes widened, and her hands opened and closed rapidly. She said no more, just turned on her heel and marched back toward the stairs, where she waited for Elanor to descend. The headmaster nodded at Professor Luciano, then headed toward Hal.

"You shouldn't have challenged her, Professor." Logan stared at his shoes. "She'll find a way to get back at you, and you have enough to worry about."

"Nothing's more important than my students." Professor Luciano reached out, patting Logan's shoulder.

"What about your family?" Logan finally looked up, eyes too shiny.

"I'm an old man, Logan, and I never married. You students are the closest thing I've had to family in ages."

I noticed that the scene Mrs. Pierce had made had managed a feat

Grace might not have achieved on her own that evening. It had distracted all the guests from Temperance's entrance with the other first-years. Elanor didn't make much of a spectacle on her way down the stairs, but that was clearly intentional.

The music started, the first song *Darkening of the Light* by Concrete Blonde. It was a throwback for sure, one of my dad's favorites from right before the Reveal. He said he found it oddly prophetic, a sentiment shared and often remarked on by Izzy's dad.

Izzy and I had spent a lot of time trying to decipher the meaning of the simple yet intense lyrics. The best we ever came up with was loss of some sort. We weren't sure what, though we always ruled out death. But now, watching Logan go through the process of losing his family, I began to understand, and I didn't blame him one bit for freezing in place as though rooted to the parquet floor.

How very appropriate. Why not just leave him there?

"No way, Logan. Let's show them how it's done." I escorted him to the dance floor, but by the time we got to its edge, his years of training took over, and he was the one leading.

The entire time we danced, he watched Dorian with Grace over my shoulder. I understood because my eyes remained on Dylan, who stood at the side alone, swaying to the music and tapping one long dusky finger on his shimmering jacket in time with the beat.

All of the Bishop's Row practice I'd done, along with Logan's cheer squad work, let us stay out on the floor for over an hour. He lost himself in the music, getting us through each song on autopilot. It reminded me of how I got running laps in the gym. At one point, I asked if he needed to take a break

"No, do you?"

"If you need to dance all night, I'm here for you."

He nodded, swallowing past some emotion I couldn't understand, but you didn't need to experience identical traumas to stand with a friend. I'd watched my parents do it my entire life without realizing it, so following their example came naturally.

Before the event ended, Dylan and Logan headed to the bathroom. I waited around, reluctant to leave them because the Fairbanks and the Onasseses loitered by the punch bowl. I tried not to snicker as I remembered the stunt we'd pulled last year, but it was impossible.

If only Hal Hawkins was strong enough to teleport something as small as a punch bowl upside-down over the heads of bad parents. I was certain about Mr. and Mrs. Fairbanks, but for all I knew, the Onassises weren't terrible people.

Don't be so naïve. What else explains their son's bad behavior?

"I don't know." I zipped my lips. I didn't intend to start answering the Evil Inside Voice aloud again, so I moved toward the wall, hugging it and staying in the shadows as I approached to do a little eaves-dropping.

"Can you believe it? A psychic at Parents' Night." Mr. Onassis snorted.

"They'll be all over the campus next week." Mrs. Fairbanks rolled her eyes. "Psychics aren't entirely objectionable, though inferior, but I shudder to think of our children on campus with undesirables like beasts and bloodsuckers."

I put my hand over my mouth to stop myself from saying anything. It was more important to listen right then, especially with the mystery of Clementine's poisoning still unsolved.

"I'd never have sent my only son here even though he bonded with a familiar if I'd known the extramurals would include subhumans." Mrs. Onassis sniffed, turning her nose up. So much for them not being terrible.

"Perhaps we should transfer our daughters to Trout down in Rhode Island." Mr. Fairbanks raised an eyebrow, tilting his head at his wife. "It would get our middle child away from that crippled boyfriend of hers."

Oh come on, say something already. Make a scene. It's your forte.

"Trout won't admit students with familiars." Mr. Onassis shook his head. "We already tried that with Alex. And besides, they admit even the savage changelings like redcaps and trolls."

"Perhaps with a large enough endowment, we could change their minds and policies."

"We made copious donations here before Hiram's son took over."

Mrs. Onassis sighed. "My appointment as a Trustee was too recent to prevent this extramural nightmare."

"That gives me an idea." Mrs. Fairbanks' eyes glittered. "Let's discuss it over brunch tomorrow in town. The Lyceum, perhaps?"

"Why not discuss it now? I'd like to return to Greece as soon as possible. It's far too chilly in these northern climes for me." Mrs. Onassis pulled her embroidered shawl tightly around her shoulders.

"Too many eyes and ears here." Mr. Fairbanks made a show of looking bored, but he twisted a signet ring on his index finger, a nervous habit Faith shared.

"What's this?" Grace nudged me in the ribs.

"They're plotting something," I murmured.

"What now?"

"They're vague. We need to get off campus tomorrow to learn more."

"Understood."

The parents exchanged nods and smiles, then sauntered off. In their wake, Grace and I discussed our plan to discover theirs. Moments later, the boys returned from the restroom, and we gathered up at the base of the stairs, waiting for the rest of our friends.

I watched Lee escort Izzy to the exit, where they high-fived each other. Platonic, I thought, but Lee's gaze wasn't just on her face as he held the door for her. Izzy threw a wave over her head at the rest of us as she walked out, glancing over her shoulder at him one last time, smiling mischievously. Nobody else seemed to notice because they didn't know her as well as I did. It baffled me. If there was anything to it, Izzy would tell me in her own time.

We headed up the stairs together, some of us leaning on each other as we let the steps do the work for us. Everyone was tired from the stress of putting on a show for our parents and peers. At least one of our professors was on our side, and we'd managed to come together as a year, classmates working together for a common goal.

A feat we incorrectly thought would be no trouble to manage again.

CHAPTER TWENTY-FOUR

We thought the plan was perfect. Grace, with help from Azrael, would disguise us to look like waitstaff at Lyceum. Dylan would distract management by inquiring about a job. Once there, Grace and I would make a show of bussing tables while eavesdropping.

You know what they say about the best-laid plans.

I tried to shake off the Evil Inside Voice, but it kept nagging me. Azrael and Grace combined Umbral magic and glamour like they'd done it a million times. Considering the amount of fabric they must've enchanted over the summer, that might only be slight hyperbole. Dylan stared into space the entire time, and I didn't blame him. Even I felt awkward watching that, and I hadn't been dumped by one of them.

"This will make us look like whoever a person most expects to see," Grace said after they finished. "But it doesn't affect us because we're in the know."

"Like Doctor Who's psychic paper?" Dylan smiled before he remembered who he was with.

"Dunno, never watched it." Grace shrugged.

"It's like Obfuscate in that vampire game." Azrael elbowed her. "Remember?"

"Oh, yeah, the one your cousin ran." Her cheeks got ruddier. Dylan pressed his lips into a thin straight line.

Control this situation before your plan floats face-down.

"That is like psychic paper, Grace." I rolled my eyes. "Maybe I'll throw a Whovian watch party over winter break. Anyway, we're on a mission, remember?"

We let Dylan go, waiting to walk past the restaurant's large window until he'd been inside for a count of thirty. That part worked, no problem. I thought we'd be fine even though the Evil Inside Voice insisted on reminding me that anything that can go wrong will go wrong, especially at the most upscale dining establishment in Salem.

And it did.

"Why aren't you girls out back prepping settings?" The woman glaring at us had a feral look in her eye, her stance predatory. I recognized her from around town and knew she was a wolf shifter who had run with the Tanks back when I was in elementary school. I couldn't remember her name. Fortunately, she wore a badge.

"I'm sorry, uh, Portia." I ducked my head, going through the motions of submissive body language I had learned about in Professor Luciano's lecture on shifters last week.

"So get back there already, pronto!" She took her hands off her hips and clapped them twice. I scuttled toward the swinging double doors, Grace following me.

"How can we spy from back here?" she whispered.

"We can't." I reached for a napkin, attempting to wrap it around a handful of silverware and failing miserably. "But that might be okay. Peek out the window."

Grace stood on her toes to peer through the round glass in one of the doors.

"Cadence is here?" Grace looked back over her shoulder, blinking at me.

"Yeah, I forgot she comes once a month for mimosas with her mom." I winced.

Grace snorted, padding quietly toward the bin of utensils and stacked napkins. She grabbed a fork, a knife, and a spoon, then raised an eyebrow. "So, we don't have to do any of this crazy crap?"

"You'd better do it five minutes ago." Portia breathed down our necks. "I've got a delivery to sign for. Get those done in that time, or you're out on your asses."

"Yes, ma'am." I reached for the tray of silverware, then nudged Grace with my elbow and jerked my chin at the stack of white linen napkins.

"Okay." She nodded.

We spent the next five minutes wrapping sets of forks knives and spoons in smooth, clean fabric. Neither of us knew what to do, let alone the Lyceum's particular style of silverware preparation, which was why we had to leave before the surly shifter returned.

But we didn't see a way out until Dylan walked by, following the manager. He glanced at us, jerking his thumb at the back entrance and waggling his eyebrows. Before he could elaborate, Dylan turned the corner as the manager explained to him how runners brought food from the refrigerator and stockroom to chefs in the kitchen.

"What should we do?"

"Slip out the back, I guess." I peeked around the corner, checking to see if the coast was clear. Once it was, I beckoned to Grace, and we tiptoed through the hall, scrunching down as we passed the kitchen in hopes no one would see us.

We stopped at the door, then ducked behind a stack of boxes as Portia glared at someone we couldn't see outside the service entrance. I did a few deep-breathing exercises, the kind I used to focus before running or playing Bishop's Row. Grace joined me, which meant this experience even had her rattled.

There's this assumption about umbral magi that somehow they're sneaky or love clandestine and mysterious activities, but my roommate didn't fit that stereotype. She loved socializing, was extroverted, and had trouble keeping secrets unless it was a matter of life and death.

I reached out, hoping to steady her shaking. She nodded, looking in my eyes as we squeezed each other's hands. Finally, she seemed to relax. That was good because the words I heard almost made me freak out.

"You take what we got, or you'll be sleeping with fishes instead of signing for them." The voice was low but harsh like the speaker had been at a concert the night before, screaming their vocal cords raw.

"This seafood isn't up to the restaurant's standards." Portia cleared her throat. "Tell it to your boss."

"Our boss figured you'd say something like that. Remember where you came from, Portia. She'll put you back there if you're not careful, so you take what we got. Understand?"

"Yeah, I get it." I heard a low growl before Portia cut it off to continue, "You tell her this is the last time. I've been out since I graduated, Crow."

"Are you crazy?" I heard a metallic snick. "She's still my boss, and she's killed messengers before."

"You tell her or Crow is on my personal menu, silver switchblade be damned."

This Portia person sounds fun. I wish you could introduce us.

"Just shut up." I put my hand over my mouth immediately, but it was too late. Grace stared at me, eyes wider than saucers and nostrils flaring, on high alert.

"Who was that?" snarled Crow.

"A couple of incompetent bussers." I heard the scratchy sound of a pen on paper. "There, day-old fish accepted. Now get lost, preferably at the bottom of the sea."

"I'd say have a nice day, but that's not happening." The door slammed on the end of Crow's sentence, muffling his last word.

Grace and I hurried back to the relative safety of the silverware station. Portia found us there instead of hiding behind the boxes, but of course, we'd botched the entire napkin-folding assignment and found ourselves immediately and roughly escorted out the service entrance.

The moment the door closed behind us, I whipped out my phone and sent Cadence a text. Hopefully, she'd get it in time and manage to listen in on the scheming parental magi.

I started walking down the alley behind the Lyceum, heading toward Washington Street until Grace stopped me.

"We don't want to go out there looking like this," she said.

"Oh, yeah." I held hands with her and let her banish the Umbral magic holding up Azrael's glamour. Soon the magipsychic illusion dropped away from us, meaning we wouldn't be mistaken for anyone's buddy on the street.

"That was a bust." Grace shook her head. "We got nothing."

"I'm not sure about that." I looked up the side of the building next to us, then whistled for Ember. "A boss of something connected to restaurants, delivering illegal fish to ex-gang members seems like a pretty big deal."

"But it's not relevant. Our problem is this unholy alliance between dangerous families."

"Yeah, that's right, unless us overhearing that instead was a coincidence." I shrugged. "It's hard to tell about that stuff."

"I know." Grace nodded wearily. She perked up a bit when her moon hare Lune came hopping toward her, headbutting her ankle. "Has Professor Luciano taught you guys about coincidence tracking yet?"

"It's next on his syllabus." I sighed. "It would have been last week, but he wanted us to have some knowledge of shifters before the Gallows Hill's extramural contingent came to campus."

"Professor DeBeer stuck to critters that couldn't be familiars for some reason, so I'm in the same boat."

I yawned.

You need a nap.

"Or something else," I answered with my out-loud voice.

"Something else, what now?" Grace blinked.

"Something like a coffee from the Witch's Brew." I rubbed my eyes. "For whatever reason, I'm exhausted. Come on, my treat."

We headed around the corner on Washington Street, pacing toward Essex and our favorite place for coffee drinks.

As we sat with our espresso-based beverages, Cadence got back to me. Her text told us she'd sat on the other side of the restaurant from the shady magi and didn't hear anything they'd said. I showed the message to Grace.

"Back to the drawing board, I guess."

"Oh, well. You can't have everything."

"They have open mic night tomorrow." Grace jerked her thumb at the flier posted on the beam next to us. "Has Dylan been doing those?"

"He hasn't mentioned it. Why not ask him yourself?"

"Because he doesn't seem like he wants to talk yet." She took a sip of her drink. "I'm kind of waiting for him to come to me."

"I don't think that's a good idea, Grace." I shook my head. "He's really busted up, like he thinks you don't even want to be friends."

"Can you tell him that's not true?"

"I have." I sighed. "He's not buying it. It looks like you're leaving him behind from where I sit. Maybe you could apologize?"

"Oh." She held her cup, turning it but not drinking this time. It shook slightly.

"You don't want to be friends with Dylan?" I held my breath, waiting for her answer. A sense of disbelief fell over me, like a blanket fort collapsing.

"I'm saying that in the near future, he might not want to be friends with me." Grace stared at the remnants of foam in her cup.

"Can you fill me in on that?" My voice sounded like soda left out overnight. It must've been worse than even I thought because Ember curled more tightly around my shoulders, lifting her head to rub cheeks with me.

"I'm afraid *you* won't even want to be friends with me."

"Hey, even if something you do makes me angry, Grace, I'm still your friend. You know that, right?" I reached out, placing my hand palm up on the table between us.

"This is kind of a doozie. And a secret, too." She looked around the coffee shop.

I had a glance around too and recognized no one, not even from town. It seemed we'd decided to have our coffee during tourist hour.

"Go ahead, my lips are sealed." I looked her in the eye. "Even if it makes me angry, I promise."

Grace reached out across the table, taking my hand. She clasped it the entire time she told me her plans, including how she expected them to impact the new social dynamic with students from Messing and Gallows Hill on campus.

She was right. You're angry. Why not tell her instead of making a face like a constipated badger?

I kept my emotions to myself because her theories made sense, even if I'd never use her methods in a million years. Everything to do with dating and sex still baffled me.

Grace's entire demeanor changed after she told me her secret, which wouldn't be one for much longer anyway. At least she could be at peace for the rest of today, though I'd have to stay home. I couldn't trust my errant inside voice or my temper to keep quiet around people like Temperance Fairbanks and Alex Onassis. I said goodbye and told her I'd spend the night with my parents.

I stood outside the door to the Witch's Brew, watching her cross Essex Street and enter that day's door to Hawthorne Academy. Then I turned and stared through the window at the clock on the coffee shop's wall, waiting ten minutes.

After that, I hurried through the campus door, checked to see that Grace was in the cafeteria, and grabbed my knapsack with the personal care items I'd want overnight. After that, I went home to call my friends from town.

We met on the playground at our old elementary school.

"I'm sorry, Aliyah." Cadence kicked her feet, disturbing the layer of mulch under the swing she sat on. "If I'd known a half-hour earlier, I could've moved our seats."

"No, it was my fault. I should have remembered mother-daughter mock-mimosa Saturdays. I mean, you've brought us along to enough of them."

"If I never drink another champagne glass full of tonic water and orange juice, it'll be too soon." Izzy snorted. "No offense, but I'm hoping real mimosas are better than the kids' version."

"We'll wait quite a while to find out." Cadence sighed.

"Anyway, I figured today would be a good time for me to give you a heads-up about what you might have to deal with on my campus."

I filled my friends in on all the recent developments, except Grace's secret plan. They'd known of Alex's agreement last spring with Charity Fairbanks to terrorize vamps and other extrahumans, which helped them put all the new stuff in context.

"At least Grace is having some success countering Temperance with her brand of in-crowd. It's a good thing everybody likes Dorian, too." Cadence grinned.

"Everybody does *not* like Dorian." Izzy sucked her teeth. "He's a wild card, and that's the opposite of comforting to plenty of folks. Grace had to fake-date him. Otherwise, he might have been competition."

"Dylan would agree with you, Iz." I nodded. "He fills the margins of his notebooks with stuff like comfort the disturbed and disturb the comfortable. Dylan can barely stand being in the same room with him, and Logan is not himself around Dorian Spanos."

"That's because he likes him, duh." Cadence rolled her eyes. "I mean, come on. It's totally obvious."

"I thought I was the only one who noticed." I blinked. "And Grace, who's around Dorian all the time."

"I did too," Izzy said. "But I'm psychic, so take that with an entire can of salt."

"Did you tell Lee?" I raised an eyebrow.

"Why would I?"

I sat waiting for Cadence to say something, but she didn't.

"He took you to the Parents' Night dance, which is kind of a big deal to Hawthorn students."

"What's this?" Cadence stood up, the swing arcing back and forth behind her. She barely noticed as it smacked into her legs repeatedly. "You went on a date? A real date, like wearing a dress and dancing, the whole nine yards?"

"It wasn't a date." Izzy waved her hand. "We're like partners in crime. Not romantic."

"I know you and Lee hang out alone in your house." Cadence tapped her foot, putting her hands on her hips. "So, what's going on?"

"That's between Lee and me." Izzy gazed steadily into Cadence's eyes. "It's none of your business."

"Okay." She reached behind her, grabbing for the swing, and sat back down. "Anyway, I think I can handle myself on your campus, Aliyah. It should be easy enough to avoid the mean crowd. And don't worry, I've already told everyone on our team who the cool kids are."

"What about you, Izzy?" I leaned an elbow on the picnic table, turning my head to look at my psychic friend.

"Yeah, the Messing folk should go your way for the most part. Jonah is the only one you have to worry about, not that I think the anti-vamp bigots will want anything to do with him."

"Oh, yeah, he's the psychic vampire." Cadence nodded. "What did he say about the ballroom dancing?"

"Yeah, we're teaming up for that. And we both made the Bishop's Row team, too." She sighed. "So your plan worked, Cadence."

"Who plays reverse point?" I wanted to know, so I could compare them to Elanor Pierce. I was prepared to do a little digging to figure out our chances of winning the tournament in the spring.

"Oh, that's me." Izzy looked down, tracing a smiley face carved into the surface of the picnic table.

I had nothing to say to that. Fortunately, any awkwardness Izzy might've noticed went unseen, thanks to Cadence's squeals of glee.

"Oh, my God, I can't believe it!" She clapped her hands. "Azrael's reverse point on our team. What position are you playing again, Aliyah?"

"Mid, with Dylan. Elanor Pierce is reverse point. She's badass, so watch out, Izzy."

"Good." Izzy finally looked up. "Maybe she'll strike Jonah out on the first throw."

"You still don't like the guy." Cadence shook her head. "What gives?"

"It's not that I don't like him." Izzy sighed. "He treats me like I'm his sister."

"Oh." I nodded, understanding. "You've had enough of that to last ten lifetimes."

"True story."

After that, we all stood up, then took a walk around the block. As we went, I filled them in on everything Grace and I had seen and heard in the kitchen. Cadence kept her mouth shut the whole time, which I thought was odd. When we got to Hawthorn Street, I was about to check on her, but Dylan Khan ran up to us and interrupted.

"Aliyah, thanks!" His grin was wider than I'd seen it since before Grace broke up with him outside the Engine House.

"What? Why?" I blinked.

"The Lyceum hired me. Even if the café stays closed all year, I'll make enough money to afford tuition again."

"I've been meaning to ask, Dylan." Cadence tilted her head. "You have to work two jobs just to come to school. Why aren't you on a scholarship?"

The grin faded, and the spark in his eyes dulled.

"Cadence." Izzy elbowed her. "Apologize, jeez."

"No, it's okay." Dylan shook his head. "Because I don't qualify for the need-based ones. My folks don't make a lot of money, but it's too much for financial aid. I got something the first year from a poetry contest, but that was a one-shot deal, and I'll never make grades like Logan."

"Oh." Cadence shook her head. "That's too bad."

"Hey," I tugged Dylan's sleeve, "you just got a job. We should celebrate. I'll get us some pizza, then we can play *Mario Kart* at my place."

"That sounds awesome." His smile returned, not as big as last time, but still, it was a comfort. Like watching Ember flying toward me.

I took up my phone and called the pizza place, making our order for pickup. We got the order and walked back to my house, joking and laughing like we had the summer before freshman year. The next day, all four of us would be in the same school at the same time, though it wasn't easy to forget we'd still be separated into teams. It wouldn't be as simple as before.

You can't deliberately take yourself or your friends back in time to when life was simpler, but sometimes, when you're together, it happens on its own.

CHAPTER TWENTY-FIVE

After breakfast on Sunday, all the Hawthorn students lined the walkway leading from the foyer door to the seating in front of the podium. We waited, watching as students from the Messing and Gallows Hill schools filed past.

The Messing kids kept to themselves, walking with their heads either down or turned toward each other. They didn't fall into a single-file line, but their red-accented gray uniforms gave that impression.

The one exception was Izzy, who kept her head up and locked gazes with everyone she knew from Hawthorn. A freckled redheaded boy walked near her, staring straight ahead. His hazel eyes seemed to look at everything and nothing at the same time, a Mona Lisa smile giving the impression that he knew more than he should about our school. The rest of the psychics reminded me of autumn rain pattering against a bedroom window—uniform, gray, and relentless.

The Gallows Hill students came through the door behind them, their attitude and behavior a night-and-day difference. They were raucous, loud, and vital, like confetti and bullhorns, with one exception.

Brianna Collins brought up the rear, her hands clasped in front of her so tightly her knuckles looked like sun-bleached driftwood. I gave her my best smile, hoping to ease the anxiety I knew she always felt in large crowds. She didn't return the smile but she straightened, walking with more confidence after that.

Cadence glanced over her shoulder, blinking at me and tilting her head in Brianna's direction. I wasn't sure what that meant but figured the mermaid would tell me later.

As instructed, all the Hawthorn students waited for the others to take their assigned seats before choosing our own. It was the first time I ended up closer to the rear for a formal announcement here. I didn't much like it because it wasn't easy to focus on the headmaster's speech. Fortunately, most of it was stuff I already knew about campus.

Headmaster Hawkins tapped the lectern and the magipsychic screen lit up, displaying a map of campus. He pointed out the locations of the cafeteria, the academic wing, including classrooms reopened for guests to use and the infirmary, then moved on to announce that the Gallows Hill students had accommodations on the fourth floor, with Messing's on the fifth.

He introduced the professors and coaches on our faculty, then moved on to the visiting staff from the other schools. Each contingent had an administrator, an academic instructor, an athletic coach, and an artistic mentor. Messing also brought a nurse. When he introduced the administrator from Gallows Hill, his voice cracked.

"It's my mom." Hal murmured from behind me.

"Are you okay?" I didn't dare turn around in my seat but had to ask.

"Yeah. She's here practically by herself, and I've got all my friends with me."

"If she messes with you, give the word, and she's TKO." Faith's voice carried genuine menace, and I could hardly blame her.

After that, we quieted down because Headmaster Hawkins changed the magipsychic display to show us a list of all the extramural competitions running until late next spring.

"Most of you have seen this before. The first of these is Magipsychic Fair, and we've got some special guests to run that for you on campus and in town over the next three weekends." Headmaster Hawkins stepped aside from the podium, then extended his hand.

Two figures emerged from the hallway beside the stairs. I blinked, nearly standing up in my surprise because I recognized them both from the Providence news bulletins the last few years.

"May I introduce Mr. Blaine Harcourt and Miss Kim Ichiro. He's a doctoral candidate at Providence Paranormal College, and she works for the Newport Police Department. You might have noticed the magipsych projects have themes in their areas of expertise. That's because they'll be judging them." He grinned, then glanced at Kim. "You had a few words, Miss Ichiro?"

"Thanks, Headmaster." The young woman grinned, nodding her head. Her nut-brown ponytail bobbed, showing off the nearly blonde hair at the tips. "We're very excited to help with the kickoff event for your extramurals. Your headmaster was right about one thing: it'll be challenging, but you will definitely have a blast. I can't wait to see what you make together!"

It was hard not to look at the Tanuki as she spoke. Her manner was engaging and her voice carried an undercurrent of fun and excitement, but I couldn't help glancing at Blaine Harcourt. He didn't look happy to be here, not one bit. When I noticed his eyes fixed on a spot somewhere behind me, I realized what his problem was.

"Hal, he's scared of Nin."

"But she's harmless."

"Pharaoh's rats are the only natural predators dragon shifters have."

"Crap. How could I forget something like that?"

"Shush." Bailey elbowed me. "They're still talking."

"Sorry."

She was right, but all we had missed was the headmaster dismissing us to mingle in the lobby and that the magipsychic display would introduce each student guest momentarily.

It wasn't easy to pay attention to the displays. I was too busy being pulled around the room between Grace, Izzy, and Cadence, and in all that mess, I had to check on Hal and Dylan. Dorian kept Logan near him most of the time, ushering him into a huddle with Grace, Kitty, and Eston.

I was surprised when a cold hand closed around my wrist. I twisted out of its grasp, turning abruptly and narrowing my eyes at the pale red-haired boy from Messing Academy. His eyes were wide and round, his mouth open like a fish out of water's.

"Who do you think you are?" I put my hands on my hips.

"Peep!" Ember reared up on my shoulder, her wings stretched wide and her breath hot against my cheek.

"Um, Jonah Arnold." He blinked, then composed his expression, but I could tell it was a façade. I'd frightened him. "I know your Izzy. I mean, your friend." He cleared his throat. "Your friend Izzy. We're ballroom dancing partners, and she talks about you all the time."

"So, you thought you could just grab me?" I tapped my foot. "If she talks about me, you know I'm a fire magus, right?"

"Extramagus, actually." He gave me a full smile, including a set of pointy fangs not long enough to signal bloodthirst. "And I'm a vampire, so I guess we are both slightly more dangerous than our peers in a manner of speaking."

"I'd rethink that if I were you." I rubbed my wrist. His grip had been stronger than anything I was used to. "I'm only dangerous to my enemies. Don't make yourself one of them."

"Look, I'm sorry." The smile vanished, replaced by a thin straight line. "I assumed you knew as much about me as I did about you. That we'd meet as friends."

"You didn't pay much attention to what Izzy leaves unspoken, then, and nobody I know is cool with randomly handsy guys."

"I screwed up. I'll apologize more profusely if that helps. It's just, I thought maybe we could talk Bishop's Row. We're both playing on our school teams, after all."

"Maybe later. I've got a lot to do right now." I shook my head, trying to settle my nerves. Jonah had scared me, too. His forwardness reminded me too much of Alex Onassis. "And maybe you're right. I'm slightly dangerous, but mostly harmless."

"I don't buy that for a second." He sighed. "It sounds too much like the kind of thing I'd say about myself. Anyway, for the third time, I make my apologies and invite you to approach me next time. I'll leave you alone unless you do, I promise."

I rolled my eyes and walked away because I wasn't sure how to respond to that. Also, I'd noticed Dylan edging toward the corner again, isolating himself. He shouldn't have to do that, considering Cadence and Izzy were here and nowhere near Grace.

"I just need a minute, Aliyah." He held up a hand, palm out.

"Okay." I glanced over my shoulder. "But Cadence is making a beeline over here. Should I stop her?"

"Head her off for a second if you don't mind." Dylan closed his eyes. "I just need to take a couple of breaths."

"Hey, Cadence." I stepped in front of my friend.

"Hey, yourself." She grinned. "I just wanted to introduce Dylan to a couple of the guys on our Bishop's Row team. Oh, and Brianna wants to see you."

"Okay." I nodded. "He'll be along in a minute. Where's Brianna?" I looked around, not seeing her immediately.

"Trying to find the restroom. For whatever reason, she's gotten super shy all of a sudden."

"Oh." I blinked. I couldn't imagine Brianna Collins, the queen of customer service, being shy. Her trouble with crowds had more to do with ambient noise than people.

"Yeah, I don't get it either." She shrugged. "Anyway, she must have found the restroom because I don't see her anymore."

"Hello, Cadence." Dylan stepped up beside me. "How're things?"

"I could ask you the same."

" I wouldn't answer right now. Maybe later." He jerked his chin at a crowd of Gallows Hill students. "I couldn't help but overhear you want me to meet some people. Shall we?"

"Okay." Cadence jerked her thumb in the direction of the restrooms. "Maybe you want to go in after her, Aliyah?"

"Will do."

Somehow yet another friend needed my help at this gathering. At least Dylan was in good hands. I glanced back over my shoulder at Hal and Faith, entrenched by the door to the lounge, chatting with Darren. They seemed safe enough, but Alex and Temperance stood by the now-empty podium, glaring daggers at Jonah. I couldn't make myself scarce in the ladies' room while a vampire sat alone in a corner with those two around. Fortunately, the perfect person happened to walk right past me. I stopped her with a smile.

"Hey, Elanor, there's someone you should meet."

"Really?" She blinked, then shook her head. "Of course. You have friends all over town, so you know some of these students."

I beckoned her to follow me, then sauntered toward Jonah and made introductions. He knew something about performance art in case they ran out of Bishop's Row topics. I'd done what I could for him. It seemed like the right call, too, since Temperance turned her back and stalked away, Alex in tow.

In the bathroom, Brianna was nowhere to be seen, but one of the stalls was closed, so I figured she was in there. I checked my makeup in the mirror, which wasn't necessary, considering I'd only put on a little lip gloss. After that, just for something to do, I washed my hands. The noise must've alerted her to my presence because a moment later, Brianna emerged from the stall.

Her face was blotchy, her color too high. I saw that in the mirror as she leaned forward to wash her hands, even though she hadn't flushed. So she hadn't been in the stall for its intended purpose. She'd been crying.

"Are you okay?"

"I wish I could say yes." She shrugged.

"Do you want to talk about it?" I leaned against the counter. "I'm here if you do. And our headmaster is also a licensed counselor if you need that."

"It's just, in order to do these extramurals, I had to quit at Walgreens, and I don't know what I'm going to do after that."

"Oh, Brianna. That sucks. Why?"

"I'll be missing most of the holiday season in retail, that's why."

"Dylan didn't say anything about that."

"He quit when he got the Lyceum job. Anyway, we're confined to campus except for school breaks and weekends. That's not enough hours for retail in autumn."

"I had no idea they were doing that."

"Me either, not until after I signed up."

"And you couldn't drop? Or ask for an exception?"

"I tried. Principal Hawkins said no."

"Do you want me to talk to my mom? She might be able to help since she works in extrahuman education."

"It's too late for that. My job's already gone, and next year I'll probably be back in Billerica at the public school."

"Let's not count on that. This is Salem, so there are loads of places you can work."

"I'll have maybe a week and a half after extramurals end."

"Well, you'll have help, don't worry."

"Thanks. You don't know how much that means."

"I'm trying to start a kindness trend. People should help each other."

She blinked, standing perfectly still. She opened her mouth but closed it again, whatever she was going to say lost in the silence between us. After that, Brianna reached for a paper towel, wet it, and wiped her face. Moments later, she strode out the door, shoulders back and head held high.

"I guess our work here is done, girl."

Ember peeped happily from her perch on my shoulder, and we headed out of the bathroom. By that time, the presentation was over and I'd missed my chance to put all the faces together with the names of the visiting students.

I watched as Elanor introduced Jonah to Noah. The two of them acted like bosom buddies. Hopefully, I'd made the right call. I headed toward where Cadence stood with Dylan, Logan, and a couple of familiar characters. I'd seen them before and meant to reintroduce myself but never made it over there.

Grace unleashed her secret plan.

It wasn't as devastating as the scene outside the Engine House, but just as unmistakable to everyone in the room. Dorian Spanos was getting dumped by Grace Dubois. She shook her finger at him, eyes narrowed and color high. He leaned back slightly, arms crossed over his chest, staring down his nose. Mercy perched on his shoulder, cawing at Lune, who turned his back on the gryphon and leaned against Grace's calf.

She rolled her eyes one final time. He shrugged in response. When they parted, the room went silent for almost five seconds. After that, a cacophony of whispers, speculation, and rumor filled the air. Finally, a bell chimed, signaling that the guests' rooms were ready.

I yawned as the visiting students got their room assignments at the pneumatic tubes. I supposed that one upside to the drastically reduced enrollment at Hawthorn was that we had the space for an event like this.

When Grace came to collect me and head back to our room, I was so exhausted I took a nap, something that hadn't happened in years. I didn't wake up until it was time for lunch.

CHAPTER TWENTY-SIX

At lunch, the cafeteria wasn't filled to capacity, even with all the visiting students. The Gallows Hill corner was loud and tight-knit. I wondered what it would've been like if we'd visited their campus instead of the other way around. I laughed, trying to imagine it, which wasn't easy because I'd only ever seen pictures of their athletic facilities.

"Aliyah, hi." Azrael Ambersmith stepped up behind me in the food line. "Can I sit with you guys?"

"Let me guess, you need a break from that noisy crew?" I raised my eyebrow at his classmates, who had pushed several rectangular tables together to make one enormous seating arrangement.

"Bingo!" he exclaimed. "I'm from a big family, but my classmates take the cake. I'm glad you understand. But mostly, I wanted to ask something if it was okay."

"Why wouldn't it be okay? You're my friend."

"There's a little more to it than that."

He glanced toward the row of booths, including the one Hal had staked out for us at the beginning of last year. The kids from our year had taken them over, turning around to chat with each other. The one exception was Grace, who paced in front of them, stopping at each booth to socialize with everybody.

"Wait a minute." I put my hand on his shoulder. "Wait just a minute there, Az. Are you trying to tell me—"

"That I want to ask Grace on a date?"

"Well, no, I thought it was maybe a little bigger and more long term than that."

"She doesn't seem to be very long-term right now." He shook his head. "But do you think she'd say yes?"

"Well, she just broke up with Dorian." I jerked my chin at everyone's favorite goth kid. "But they were only platonic, really."

"Yeah, I saw." Azrael composed his face, speaking flatly. "And plenty of people have deep connections without romance. There's no "only" about it, you know?"

"I don't." I sighed. "I'm probably the worst person to talk to about relationship stuff. Have you tried Cadence?"

"You're Grace's roommate and one of her closest friends, so I figured you're the best person to ask."

"Az, she's not following her heart right now. I don't want either of you to get hurt."

"I know. This last month and the whole situation with Dylan was hard on her."

"Nowhere near as hard as it was for him, though." I blinked.

"No, you're wrong." He shook his head. "I worked with her all summer, so I saw it. She was busted up weeks before they split. It wasn't easy for her."

"She's run everything strategically since then, like a computer." I sighed. "I mean, she talked a little with me, but like it happened last year instead of last month."

"That's Grace, for you." He shrugged. "Keeps anything thorny at arm's length. Anyway, if you think she'll listen, I'll go ask."

"Right now?" I blinked. She'd planned the breakup with Dorian but had said nothing about Azrael. "Are you sure?"

"There's no time like the present." He grinned. "Thanks, Aliyah."

Before I could say anything else, he stepped out of the line and headed toward Grace. I stood there, staring so intently I forgot where I was for a moment.

"It's your turn, already." I glanced over my shoulder to find my brother, rolling his eyes at me.

"Sorry, Noah." I stepped up to the window and made my order, then moved over to wait and let him make his.

"I'll have what she's having," he told the cook.

"So, how are you doing?"

"Not that it's any of your business, but not bad." Noah studied his nails.

"Not bad is pretty good, right?"

"It isn't, but it doesn't totally suck either."

I laughed. I couldn't help it because Noah was just so contrary and perfectly himself right at that moment. Even though I missed how close we used to be, having this exchange with him, however brief, felt precious somehow.

He didn't laugh with me or even at me. I'm not sure he could have mustered anything as free and open as true laughter just then. Noah's biggest flaw might be holding grudges for too long, but the runner-up was taking himself too seriously. I knew that feeling all too well, which was why I felt a momentary surge of euphoria when he smiled.

"Maybe things will be pretty good, you know, eventually." My order came up, so I reached out to move my plate from the counter to my tray.

"Some stuff needs work, but yeah." He nodded, getting his own sandwich from the counter. "I think you're right for once."

He walked away before I did, not even stopping to get a beverage before heading to the biggest round table, where he sat beside Elanor. Jonah immediately defected from the cluster of Messing folk in the far corner to sit on his other side.

"Don't get too comfortable, Morgenstern." Alex tried his best to look down his nose at me.

"You have no say in how I feel about anything."

"This is a warning. Your brother had better watch who he spends time with."

"Your threats suck. I already said I'm not afraid of you."

"A warning, Aliyah." Alex stared into my eyes, unblinking. His were bloodshot and blotchy like Brianna's. "About something. It's not a threat from *me*, and you'd do well to remember that."

He stepped across the way, stopping in front of the DIY sandwich station. He didn't even have a tray, just stuffed some bread and a handful of peanut butter containers into a paper bag and made a beeline out of the cafeteria.

"What was that about, I wonder?" Dorian held a pair of empty tumblers, waggling them at me. "Never mind. Beverage roulette?"

"Sure." I reached out, taking one of the cups and joining him at the soda dispenser.

"Ooh, it's good this time." He grinned at his improvised drink.

I took a sip of my own, then wrinkled my nose. "Too much orange soda."

"You can't win them all." He shrugged, then led the way toward our friends.

We sat with Logan, who'd been by himself at a booth. Hailey joined us, peering at our drinks before inquiring about what they were. Dorian explained beverage roulette, then got up to help her make her own. He seemed unperturbed that Azrael and Grace stood in the corner together, clearly flirting.

"Is he going to be to be okay with that?" Bailey asked from the booth behind us. "Dorian, I mean."

"Doesn't seem to bother him." Logan shrugged, bowing his head, but I noticed his face turning red.

"Goths, am I right?" Bailey snorted, then went back to her food.

I didn't see how the incident started because my back was turned. I'd thought everything was fine, too. So much for all my practice at empathy.

A piercing shriek, the kind that makes rodents in an open field cringe with terror, almost dropped me to the floor. It was so loud and shrill it felt like an ice pick through my inner ear. The edges of my vision wobbled a bit.

Despite the dizziness, I turned and looked around. All I saw was a blur of white and blue circling the two boys in the middle of the dining room.

Dylan's fists were twisted in the lapels of Dorian's blazer. The fabric looked stiff like it had been in the freezer for a week. I couldn't see Dylan's face, but Dorian's face was a rictus of terror.

You can see his breath. Dangerous. Did your ersatz boyfriend ever talk to his professor about being an extramagus, I wonder?

"I said, sorry!"

"Not good enough, Spanos." Dylan growled. Like, actually growled, sounding like a wolf in winter, desperate for prey.

"What are you?" Dorian's eyes bulged, more of the cornea visible than usual. They rolled as he looked around for some way, any way, out of Dylan's grasp.

"Your worst nightmare."

Before their exchange progressed, their familiars plunged down from somewhere near the ceiling. Mercy and Gale were a tangle of wings. Gale's tail lashed through the air, striking the furred part of Mercy's back. I saw why the next moment. Mercy's beak had scratched the scales under Gale's eye, leaving a bloody red welt.

"Peep!"

Ember leaped off my shoulder and rose high, hiding behind the light from the chandelier. I couldn't see her but felt the change in her gravity as she swooped toward the fighting pair.

Just in time, she grabbed them with her talons, pulling up to slow their fall as much as she could. It could've been worse since gryphons are fragile, and breaking a dragonet's fall could severely injure them. Despite Ember making sure Mercy wasn't crushed, their landing was still catastrophic.

"Ow!" Kitty jumped up, cranberry juice splashing all over the front of her blouse. She held one hand to her mouth as the other one dropped the fork she'd been holding.

"Paralysis!"

The voice came from the doorway where Professor DeBeer stood, feet planted. Her lightning bird perched on her shoulders with his wings outstretched. I could see a crackle of energy arcing from his beak to the polished length of wood in her hand.

Wandwork and familiar magic. She must have several advanced degrees.

The effect was immediate, Gale, Mercy, and Ember sprawled across the table, frozen in place, the three of them lying still in the now-ruined victuals. But the Professor hadn't gotten anywhere near the root of the problem.

"He started it." Dorian's eyes went wide, breath pluming like smoke in the space between them.

"You started it when you stole my girlfriend." Dylan's hair seemed to go white in places, while Dorian's blew back from his face.

"You split before I got here."

"Boys, no fighting." Professor Luciano paced from the food line toward my friends, hands outstretched. "You should know better, Mr. Spanos. You're on probation, after all. And Mr. Khan. You've worked so hard to be here. Don't squander it on fighting."

A moment later, he placed his hand on Dylan's shoulder. Luciano's eyes went wide. He stared as though seeing him for the first time, then sighed, eyes going limpid with empathy.

"Enough." Professor DeBeer paced toward Luciano. After that, I couldn't believe my ears or my eyes. "My student, my problem."

She pushed him. Not some elementary schoolyard shove, either. Her hand channeled enough lightning to make me see spots.

Professor Luciano flew across the room, his back crashing against the table where Hal and Faith sat. He struggled to rise but winced and held his back with one hand.

"Professor!" Hal grabbed Luciano's free hand but looked at Faith. "Get Dad."

She sprang to action, leaping off the booth's bench and fleeing the cafeteria.

"You lying, scheming freak!" Professor DeBeer's eyes narrowed, her hands crackling with lightning as she homed in on Dylan. I never imagined she'd ever look this feral or threatening, especially not toward a student. Her temper was higher than Dylan's the moment before, and lightning was one of the most dangerous magics out there.

But I couldn't figure out why Dylan's teacher reacted with alarm. Hadn't he gone to her about his extramagus status the first week of school?

It doesn't matter now. You've got more power than anyone else in this room, even her. Use it unless you want this to get worse.

"No." I broke into a flat sprint, reaching my friends before Professor DeBeer. I stepped into the middle of the cluster, skin humping up into gooseflesh. It felt like the middle of February in a lightning storm, but I wanted to do this mundanely unless my hand got forced somehow.

"Get out of my way, Morgenstern," Professor DeBeer snarled.

"I want to help."

"That's what your kind always say." She turned, stretching one electrified hand toward me. "At least at the beginning. One of you on campus was enough. Two are untenable. See what happens when you lose control? Everyone's in danger, and it's your fault."

Every impulse in my body urged me to step back and drag the boys with me, away from the high-voltage magus, but I held my ground, shaking my head.

"We're kids." I couldn't look into her eyes, afraid I'd find something in them as terrifying to me as a slayer was to a vampire. "We make mistakes. Get in fights."

"Like the one last year when you nearly burned this room down? I've had enough of extramagi and their ruination to last a lifetime." Her eyes went wide, something in them broken. Her gaze turned inward, maybe at some future fear or past horror. "You should have been expelled ages ago."

I had nothing to say to that. Even the Evil Inside Voice stayed silent. I swallowed, unable to get past the lump in my throat, even if I'd had words at the ready.

It's easy to think of something after the fact, a zinger or defiant statement on your right to exist. But when I stood face to face with someone who considered me less than human, my ability to act narrowed. My options got honed down to a single point. I was lucky to just stay put.

So I stood and trembled. My entire body felt wavery, like heat rising off blacktop in the middle of summer. But it was cold, and finally, I had an idea. Simple, maybe too easy, but it'd have to do. I couldn't talk Professor DeBeer down, but she wasn't the only participant in this conflict.

"Dylan, let it go."

Professor Luciano and Hal leaned on each other, looking as unsteady as I felt. Kitty rushed to their rescue, inserting herself between them and getting her shoulders under their arms. The cranberry stain on her silvery gray blouse stood out like a wound.

"He has everything, Aliyah." Dylan's voice stretched almost pleadingly, like he wanted my permission to hurt our classmate. "And he hasn't worked a day in his life for any of it."

"Understood, Mr. Khan." Professor Luciano took a deep breath. "But this situation has more wires than a pipe bomb, and the only way to defuse it is if someone steps down."

"Ask your colleague." Dylan's gaze moved from Dorian to DeBeer. "I thought she was in my corner."

"Isn't that what they hired us to do?" Professor Luciano tilted his head, raising his eyebrow. "Support our students?"

"*He* is the bomb, Lucy." Professor DeBeer shook her head. "Not the situation. Look at him—both ice and air, and bound to do evil and harm."

Dylan's jaw dropped, his face paling as much as it could for someone with his complexion, and his eyes widened. The professor's words hit like a slap, and I knew too well how it felt when someone you trusted weaponized their words.

A moment later, his eyes narrowed. I watched him, wondering because it didn't look like anything I'd felt. Then I remembered the Evil Inside Voice and how it encouraged me to follow impulses. Did Dylan have one in his head?

"You want evil?" Dylan took a deep breath. The air around him got so cold my eyebrows frosted over. "You want harm?"

Across the room, Izzy raised her hand. She held a card up, the Devil reversed. It meant I had to step up and try to take Dylan with me.

"No." I countered. "You're better than this." I stood up straight. "Stand down with me."

"I'm sick of it. Turn the other cheek, be the better man. With grades, with money, and now magic." He turned his head, arctic gaze meeting mine. "But I'll do it for you, Aliyah."

Just like that, the cold vanished. Dylan untangled his hand from Dorian's jacket. Professor DeBeer shut off her lightning, releasing the familiars from their paralysis at the same time. They scuttled across the table. Mercy came up covered in the remains of Kitty's soup, a crouton hanging from her beak.

"Mr. Khan. My office. Now." Headmaster Hawkins' voice boomed through the cafeteria.

"Sir, can I—"

"No, Miss Morgenstern. I'll talk to witnesses later."

"What about my colleague?" Professor Luciano rubbed his back, glaring at Professor DeBeer.

"As I said, later." Headmaster Hawkins looked at Dylan. "I'll listen to Mr. Khan's account of events before doing anything else."

Dylan followed the headmaster, glancing back over his shoulder before exiting the cafeteria. He looked shell-shocked, like he couldn't believe what had just happened.

In the far corner, Temperance Fairbanks held her grundylow and smiled. Alex leaned against the wall near her, gazing at the floor.

"Well, Izzy." I turned to look at my psychic friend, "you wanted to see how magi go to school, right?"

"Not like this." She shook her head, holding up her hand to reveal another card.

It was the Tower reversed, just about the worst card anyone with catastrophic levels of power could get. Dylan Khan, as it turned out, had that in spades.

CHAPTER TWENTY-SEVEN

"Thanks." Dorian caught up with me at the stairs, Mercy cradled in his arms. "For what you did back there, talking Dylan down."

"I didn't do it for you." Ember lifted her head, peering out at him from under my hair, then shot me a withering look. "Sorry. That was mean."

"Help was help, whoever you meant it for." He patted Mercy, sighing over all the condiments and other cafeteria detritus in her feathers and fur. "And this dirty birdie needs a little help from Irish Spring."

"Do you ever take anything seriously?" I stepped onto the moving staircase, and he followed. Izzy caught up, standing a few steps down. "That was a bad scene, Dorian."

"Everybody saw Grace's breakup theater." He leaned against the railing. "And some other guy just asked her out. I couldn't have predicted Dylan would go extramagus on my hiney. And why shouldn't I crack jokes?"

"Was I a goofball back there?" I raised an eyebrow.

"Well, no." He sighed. "But serious isn't my style."

"Bury the hatchet with him. We can't be at each other's throats all year, with Temperance just waiting for us to mess up."

"You have a point, but I can't do it."

"You might have to," Izzy said. "Cards don't lie."

We rode it in silence. At our stop, Izzy ushered us along the third-floor hall.

"So, I have to make nice with Dylan?" Dorian tilted his head at her. "He's the one in trouble."

"I pulled that Tower card for Dylan, but you were the focus of his anger when I did it."

"Would you mind giving me a full reading?" He wrinkled his nose, waving a hand at Mercy. "After she gets cleaned up."

"What?" She blinked.

"Is that so strange?" He asked. "A gryphon having a bath?"

"No, the reading. Usually, magi don't want them."

"My parents are psychics." He shrugged. "For me, it's comforting."

"Well, in that case, sure. My room's on the fifth floor."

"We can use mine." I jerked my thumb down the hall. "Grace is in Creatives, working on a project. I can even give Mercy a bath while you do it." Each room at Hawthorn had a fully stocked grooming station accessible through a panel in the wall.

"Okay, then." Dorian nodded. "Let's go."

I let them into my room, clearing off my desk so Izzy had a surface to work on. After that, I opened the grooming panel, ran water, and added soap. Mercy flew over, ducking and splashing in it like a giant birdbath. At least she liked getting clean.

Anything could happen in Izzy's reading. She'd been precognitive from an early age and had lots of practice, but her abilities had no obligation to follow our social agenda. I hoped Izzy could convince him to make an effort with Dylan.

You can't save all of your friends from his anger. The Ambersmith boy might be his next enemy.

"At least he's not in our class." I put my hand over my mouth, getting suds on my chin.

"I don't know. The headmaster might make him switch with someone." Dorian took my statement in his own context. "Considering what DeBeer said about extramagi back there."

"Oh." I blinked. I hadn't mentioned my inside voice to him, so naturally, he'd thought I'd said something sensible.

"It looks like Dorian's got something." Izzy tapped the card she'd just flipped, the Two of Wands reversed. "He'll have to work with someone he doesn't like in the very near future."

"That could mean a number of people, actually." Dorian sighed. "I'm not sure why Grace installed me in the in-crowd. I'm the least popular third-year guy."

"You have your fans." Izzy tapped another card, the Five of Cups. "Somebody here thinks you're awesome, all shiny and sparkly."

I held my tongue, not mentioning Logan. It was up to him and Dorian to figure that out, and maybe the reading wasn't about romance anyway. Last year, I'd had more friends than expected. Why not Dorian?

"What I really want to know is, will I get expelled?"

"Okay." She nodded, flipping over the four of swords. "That's unlikely. That problem's in the past."

"So, all I have to do is stay out of trouble?" He rolled his eyes. "Not as easy as it looks."

"You've got a student mentor, remember?" I grinned. "Logan's looking out for you."

"Ha." Izzy flipped another card. "Yeah, it looks like you need more support. Logan's a water magus, right, Aliyah?"

"That he is." I nodded. "Why?"

"Check it out." She held up the card. It was the Page of Cups.

"I forget what that one means." I gave Mercy's back a good scrubbing.

"I know it." Dorian sighed. "My sister worked with cards sometimes too."

Neither of them divulged the card's meaning, just exchanged glances that didn't include me. I kept my thoughts to myself, hoping it was positive.

"But that's not enough." Izzy shook her head.

"Okay, okay." Dorian sighed. "Aliyah's right. I have to talk to Dylan."

"Bring a friend." She tapped the next card, the Knight of Swords.

"Dylan used to have a long fuse, but not right now. I had no idea he was an extramagus, either."

I busied myself with changing the soapy water out for fresh. Mercy ducked under the faucet's stream, shaking her feathery little head in the flowing water. Ember peeped from my shoulder, then splashed down to join her.

"Aliyah didn't seem surprised," Dorian said.

"He told me last month. Said he'd talk to Professor DeBeer about it." I close my eyes. "I watched him request a meeting with her that same day, too."

"But tonight, she was the opposite of helpful." Izzy sighed. "Sounds like she's got a hate on for extramagi."

I shook my head. "Enough about that. You're still doing Dorian's reading."

"Almost done." She flipped the last card. "Well, this is frigging great."

Dorian leaned back, his face paling. "The Devil never is unless you're about to go to a party."

"Even then, your fun's gonna be laced with trouble." Izzy shook her head. "This year's a minefield, so we'll have to watch out for each other. Which includes Dylan."

"She's all clean." I wrapped a towel around Mercy, patted her dry, and helped her back to Dorian's shoulder. When I turned, Ember had perched on the edge of the bath, waiting for her own towel and rubbing a patchy spot on her tail. I got her dry and applied some oil.

Izzy cleared her cards away, then helped me put the chairs back. We left the room, heading out to mingle with the other students.

"You want me to what?"

I didn't recognize the voice coming from the newly reopened café, so I peeked around the corner and found Kim Ichiro cornered by her fiancé. She saw me, so I nonchalantly headed to the counter. The manager stood behind it, waiting for someone in the throng of people staring at the menu to order something already.

"I'll have my usual, thanks."

"Caramel latte with soymilk coming up." She busied herself making my drink, giving me the perfect opportunity to listen in on the conversation behind me.

"Bring Cosmo to campus." Blaine Harcourt's voice was at low volume, but nasal and tinny enough for me to hear it.

"Why?"

"Have you seen the boy catch mice? I'll be safer from those homicidal rodents the Hawkins family carries around if he's here."

"Wait a minute." She cleared her throat. "You want a thirteen-year-old boy around all these upperclassmen? In cat form, no less?"

"Exactly." I caught Blaine's nod out of the corner of my eye. "I'm his godfather, and we can protect each other."

"Put on your big dragon pants, Blaine." She poked his chest with her index finger. "Familiars are bonded to their magi. Besides, Hal's a sweetie, and Nin's kind of cute."

"What if an unbonded one comes along?"

"The Headmaster says the only Pharaoh's rats on campus are his and his son's. They're both female, too, so they can't breed."

"I'm not entirely sure I believe that."

The cafe manager handed me my drink. I was about to let them have their conversation and not interfere, but Blaine's face was pale and sweaty, and his hands shook so much that tea sloshed over the rim of his cup. A nervous dragon shifter might vindicate folks who considered shifters too dangerous for campus.

"Excuse me, I couldn't help but overhear. Maybe I can reassure you."

"And you are?" Blaine raised his eyebrow. He also took a step back, allowing Kim to escape the corner and approach.

"She's the Morgenstern girl." She tilted her head, blinking. "Fred Redford said she helped put the fire out at the Night Creatures concert last Halloween."

He shook his head. "I don't see how a student can help in this situation."

"Let her talk, Blaine." I thought Kim might elbow him in the ribs, but she linked her arm through his instead. "Listening can't hurt."

"Okay."

"My grandmother's the extraveterinarian who licenses the familiars here. She keeps a public record of every critter on campus at her office down the street."

"I'm more worried about the off-record ones." Blaine wrinkled his nose. "They could be hiding in secret passages or something."

"There's a book about Hawthorn Academy in the library." I shrugged. "It's got blueprints, maps, and information about all the magical systems in here. It's reassuring."

"Wait a minute." He raised his eyebrow. "Are you a brainiac?"

"No, that's my friend Logan. He had his own concerns about campus security and felt way better after reading it. Maybe it could help you too."

"Come on, Blaine, you love libraries, and we haven't seen the one here yet." Kim did elbow him this time, but gently.

"I suppose it can't hurt. Lead on, Morgenstern."

I brought them to the academic wing, where they both paused at the stained glass windows in the doors. Kim pulled out her phone, asked me to stop, and took pictures before I led them through.

Once we got to the library, I introduced them to the Ashfords, who were busy stamping books. After that, Blaine marched directly toward the index in the middle and flipped through it.

"Wow." He shook his head. "Mr. Waban would have a field day in here."

"Is he the librarian from your old high school?"

"Hardly." Blaine sniffed. "He's the oldest dragon in North America, though he did fill in as librarian at Providence Paranormal for a couple of years."

"I thought your mother was the oldest dragon here?"

"Mr. Waban has at least two centuries on her." He tapped the page under his finger. "Is this it? *Hawthorn Academy: a Study in Between-World Architecture.*"

I nodded. "Yes."

"Smashing." He headed through the stacks, leaving Kim standing beside the index with me.

"I thought he was scared. What happened?" I asked.

"Blaine's a fire dragon, but this is his real element." Her smile carried loads of pride. "If you put him in a library, the rest of the world goes away. Thanks for bringing us here."

"You're guests. It's the least I can do."

"You know, I didn't expect the students here to be helpful. I've heard a thing or three about the Fairbanks family. I'm surprised your school's participating in extramurals."

"It's Hal's dad. Ever since he took over, he's done all sorts of things differently. What do the Fairbanks have to do with it?"

"Mr. Fairbanks holds a seat on the school's Board of Trustees. Didn't you know?"

"Yeah." I winced. "I heard that. Mr. Pierce and Mrs. Onassis have similar views, but that's only three out of seven seats."

"I see." She grinned. "Do you know the headmaster's son? I mean, personally."

"Yes."

"I'd like to meet him if you have time to introduce us."

"He's probably in the infirmary right now. He goes there before breakfast, after lunch, and after dinner every day."

"Oh." The corners of her mouth turned down for the first time since I'd seen her. "Is he okay?"

"I'll let him answer that question." I sighed. "I'm not the gossipy type."

"I understand." She nodded.

"I've got it." Blaine held the book, beaming. "Would you mind terribly if I read it in here?"

"If you don't mind me going to visit with another student." Kim followed him to the table.

"Um." He glanced over his shoulder at the Ashfords, who nodded and smiled. "I suppose you can leave me in the care of these kind librarians for a little while."

"Peep!" Ember blinked sleepily for my shoulder, then crawled down my arm to get a better look at Blaine. "Peep?"

"I get to see your dragonet up close?" He grinned. "I never see them in Newport or even Providence. Mother doesn't like having them around, but there's no accounting for taste."

"Ember's one of two on campus." She flapped her wings, peeping and puffing her chest out proudly.

"She's adorable. I'll keep my eyes peeled for the other." He grinned. "Don't take too long, Kim."

"It'll take as long as it has to." She smiled, then leaned over and planted a kiss on the top of his head. "See you later."

We walked down the hall and out of the academic wing, and I pointed the way to the infirmary. I almost headed down with her when someone behind me cleared their throat.

"I guess I'll see you later too, Miss Morgenstern." Kim winced. "Thanks, and good luck."

Headmaster Hawkins stood behind me. He beckoned, and I followed him to his office. Inside were Professor DeBeer and Dylan, with Logan between them. I stopped in the doorway. The headmaster walked to his desk, sat down behind it, and picked up a pen.

"What's this about?" I asked.

"Mr. Khan tells me you knew he was an extramagus."

"Sort of. He said he was worried he might be one. I told him to talk to his professor, and he wrote a request for a meeting in the two-way notebook right after that."

"Did you see him attend such a meeting?"

"No." I shook my head. Dylan hung his. Gale rubbed against his cheek, chirping softly.

"I see." He wrote something on a paper.

"If you don't mind my asking, why?"

"I do mind, and I won't divulge further details until I've concluded my investigation."

"Oh. So," I said as I jerked my thumb at the door behind me, "I'll just be on my way."

"Have a seat, Miss Morgenstern. I'm not through with you yet."

I pulled up a chair and sat beside Dylan. Ember perched on my shoulder.

"I told you she had nothing to do with this." He protested. "You can't keep her here."

"Mr. Pierce." Headmaster Hawkins ignored Dylan's outburst. "Did you have any inkling that your roommate was an extramagus?"

"No." Doris leaped into Logan's lap, staring at the headmaster.

"It's unlikely." Professor DeBeer shook her head. "I'd expect anyone with his grades to notice something so unnatural."

"I'm still only a student." Logan peered at her. "Where's Professor Luciano? Shouldn't he be here?"

"Good question." The headmaster's face reminded me of a mahogany carving. "Irrelevant for now."

"What about Nurse Smith?" I clasped my hands together as Ember peeped. "He's got that lie-detector flask."

"It hasn't come to that yet. Miss Morgenstern, did you personally escort Mr. Khan to any faculty or staff member the day he told you his suspicions?"

"No. I only recommended meeting with his professor, which was what you said I should've done last year."

"Yes, that was my advice to you with regard to yourself."

I blinked. "You didn't mention other students."

"It's in the handbook, which you will read to me." He pushed a copy across the desk. "Page fifty-eight."

"Any student who witnesses extramagus activity must escort the suspected extramagus to a faculty member within two hours." I looked up after reading. "I'm sorry, I didn't know."

"Ignorance is no excuse, and since you're on probation, I expect you to get informed immediately after this meeting."

"Okay. But even though I didn't escort him, Dylan left the cafeteria, on his way to Professor DeBeer. Did that meeting not happen?"

"Professor, did Dylan Khan meet with you to discuss that he might be an extramagus?"

"No, headmaster. He made an appointment but didn't show."

The pit of my stomach dropped. I couldn't imagine Dylan would lie about that, not to me.

She hates our kind and would just as soon see us all locked up, even if we've done nothing wrong.

"Mr. Khan, for the last time. Did you meet with Professor DeBeer that day?"

"Yes. I went straight to her office. I skipped practice with Coach Pickman, even, and I definitely told her."

"I didn't see him all afternoon." Logan shook his head. "Anyone in our year would say the same thing. Headmaster, there's got to be another explanation."

"Absence is no alibi." The headmaster sighed. "Someone is lying, and the only person with a motive is your roommate. So once more, Miss Morgenstern. Did you witness Mr. Khan approach either of your professors on the day in question?"

"No. He was headed for the academic wing, though." I shook my head. "I saw Temperance Fairbanks walking the same way. Logan's right, there's got to be another explanation. Could somebody have interfered?"

"There are no mind magi on campus. Mental tampering is outside the realm of possibility. For now, I must consider the simplest explanation true. Mr. Khan, you're suspended from extracurricular activities until we test the full scope of your abilities."

"I understand, sir." He closed his eyes.

"You're all dismissed."

Logan and I stood, waiting for Dylan, who was not okay. I couldn't blame him. He already felt like an outsider, and now he couldn't play Bishop's Row until he'd passed whatever test the headmaster had mentioned.

"That includes you, Professor." He stood, placing his hands on the surface of his desk. "I need time alone with my files and thoughts."

"But Headmaster, extracurricular suspension isn't enough. He should be removed from campus."

"Dismissed, Professor. Unless you want to be removed from my office magically."

"Fine." She stood, then sauntered past us, tossing a glare at Dylan as she went. Her lightning bird turned his head, cawing back at us through the door.

We hustled out but gave the professor space. The last thing I wanted was to make the adult magus angrier. In the lobby, Dylan made a beeline for the café, where he went behind the counter and grabbed an apron. He withdrew into serving customers like a turtle into its shell.

Logan and I stared at each other, dumbstruck. His eyes looked shiny, and I knew from the heat at the corners of mine that both of us were about to cry. We awkwardly exchanged goodbyes, and he headed upstairs while I wandered around the lobby like a lost puppy.

CHAPTER TWENTY-EIGHT

"Come lounge in the lounge with us."

Cadence stood over me as I sat on the bench in the lobby. We'd barely spoken since the visiting students had arrived on campus. I felt guilty for spending an hour with Izzy without her, so I went.

Hawthorn Academy students all wore identical blazers over bland yet generally high- quality clothing. Kids from Messing, while quirky, wore green and gray uniforms accessorized and accented in high vintage beatnik style. The Gallows Hill crew was another breed entirely.

The usually sedate and quiet lounge was a riot of bright colors and raucous sounds. Cadence's school didn't do uniforms. I didn't realize that went beyond the clothing on their backs.

The diversity at Gallows Hill made all the difference. I froze in place with my mouth wide open. Even my experience in mundane schools hadn't prepared me for their student body.

They laughed louder, smiled brighter, and shared personal space to a degree I reserved for family and close friends. One glance around the room told me that most of the Hawthorn and Messing students had decided to congregate elsewhere. I could understand how Michelina, Eston, or Logan might find this scene off-putting. I almost left because I'd grown accustomed to quiet here.

I spotted Noah off in the far corner. He sat with Elanor, yukking it up over a game of Uno. I didn't want to be shown up by my big brother, and Cadence was one of those aforementioned close friends, so I stuck around and got punched in the shoulder for my trouble.

"Hey, I remember you," a voice to my right rumbled. Ember looked up without any hint of alarm, so I turned my head toward the speaker.

The guy was tall and way more muscular than most seventeen-year-olds, which made sense. He was a changeling, powerful enough for me to feel the glamour coming off him. I realized where we'd met before.

"The Night Creatures concert, right?" I nodded. "I'm Aliyah."

"Yeah, the veterinarian's kid." He was talking about my father, who worked with mundane animals in a community clinic across town when he wasn't helping Bubbe. "I'm Bar."

"Is that a nickname?"

"Haven't gone by my official name for ages." He grunted, jerking his chin at Ember. "Haven't seen one of those in almost as long."

"Like, literal ages?" I raised an eyebrow. Most changelings grew up in the regular world but some spent time in the Under, where they aged more slowly. Bar might have been around for decades.

"That's personal."

"Okay." I shrugged.

"Be nice." Cadence's voice took on a more lilting tone than usual. "We're all going to get along, have a laugh, sing a song."

I instantly relaxed, like I was alone on the beach in the sun instead of in a crowd of strangers.

"Whatever you say, boss lady." Bar nodded and ambled off, joining a group of what could only be wolf shifters on the big sofa by the wall.

"You didn't just whammy us, Cadence?" I blinked, shaking off the unexpected calm. "We were having a conversation."

"It's officially my job. I'm part of the Safety Squad." She pointed at a pin on her shirt. "The principal picked three of us to keep rowdy students in line. She takes this visit seriously, for good reason."

Cadence looped her arm through my elbow, escorting me to the corner opposite Noah's. Her classmates watched as she smiled and waved like we were on a parade float. Almost all went back to the business of loudly socializing, except for Brianna Collins, who continued watching us.

"Is Brianna on the Safety Squad?"

"Yup, and Azrael, but I don't know where he went off to." She shrugged. "Anyway, the Safety Squad's not why I want to talk. Is Dylan really an extramagus?"

"Yeah, and the worst part is, I've known since our first week back. And now he's in trouble with the headmaster."

"What happened?"

I told her the whole crazy story, including the case of the missing meeting.

"You need Izzy. Find out what she sees for Dylan, if anything."

"What do you mean, 'if anything?'"

"She has a hard time reading for you, didn't you know?"

"I've never seen that happen."

"Not when you're there, silly." Cadence giggled, her voice pitched at a register I knew meant she was nervous. "She can't get an accurate read remotely on you. After you got solar magic, she pulled cards when you weren't there, and they said gobbledygook. She thinks it's because you're an extramagus."

"She might be right." I shook my head. "Maybe Dylan will agree to a reading in person if he ever gets out from behind that counter."

"That sucks. I can't believe his professor." She shook her head. "You watched him ask for a meeting in that notebook. She must be lying."

"That's the thing, Cadence. I'm not sure who to believe."

"Dylan, of course." She clicked her tongue. "Was she hard on him before today?"

"I don't think so, but he's been out of sorts all month."

"Relationship problems do that. He's probably not over Grace. Anyway, I'm on Team Dylan, not Team DeBeer."

"She totally surprised me with her attitude about extramagi." I sighed. "I thought she was a cool professor."

"Maybe there's no such thing as a cool professor." Cadence shrugged. "Teachers aren't here to be our friends. They make sure we learn everything we need and prepare us for life out there." She waved a hand vaguely at the exit hall. "Angels ferrying knowledge up from the inky depths, they are not."

"You have no idea what angels are like for us." I snorted. "In the stories Dad and Bubbe tell, they're terrifying, full of snap judgments and immutable messages. A lot like professors, actually."

"I get it. Your angels are like our demons, diving in to drop nets on our heads."

"Yeah, that's pretty much the vibe."

"Anyway, I met Dorian Spanos earlier. He's interesting."

I sighed. "I wish he and Dylan could just get along. Maybe they'll do it for Logan."

"Oh, yeah, Logan's got it bad," Cadence said, chuckling. "But it looks like someone else is on the sweet romance diabetes train."

She jerked her thumb at the other corner, where Noah now stood, shifting his weight from one foot to the other. I hadn't seen him that nervous since the night middle school put on *Little Shop of Horrors*.

"Whoa." I blinked.

Jonah smiled like a movie star, but with fangs. The way he tilted his head as he spoke made me think he'd asked a question I couldn't hear over the Gallows Hill students. Whatever it was made Elanor clap her hands and bounce in her seat. Noah blushed profusely, nodding.

"Did he just ask him out?" Cadence squeezed my arm. "That's only the cutest thing ever!"

"Not around here. We've got serious vampire haters on this campus, remember?"

"Oh, my God, they're holding hands. Noah doesn't care about any of that."

I watched them leave the lounge, heading toward the lobby. I wondered how Dylan was, hiding behind his work.

Go and find out. You never know what might happen.

"I don't want to know." I put my hand over my mouth. "Sorry, Cadence."

"I'm cool with your inside voice." Cadence relaxed her grip on my arm, patting it. "Sorry, I got a little excited."

"How do you feel about being here? Honesty time."

"It's exciting but stressful. Safety Squad's like herding cats, figuratively. Most of them aren't feline, just the tag-along." She jerked her thumb at a boy I'd seen on the beach before school started.

"Who's that?"

"Cosmo, Blaine Harcourt's godson. He's only here for the Magipsych Fair. At least he behaves himself, unlike other people." She narrowed her eyes, flaring her nostrils at a lanky guy roughhousing with Bar. I'd also seen him before, but mostly, I'd heard his voice while hiding behind a crate with Grace.

"Who's that?" I knew his name but not what Cadence thought of him.

"Oh, Crow? He's nobody, um, important." Her face turned beet-red, and she flipped stray curls of auburn hair over her shoulder. "He and Bar have been friends for ages, kind of like us with Izzy."

"Why do I get the impression you're not telling me the whole story?"

And you're not telling her what you heard Crow doing at the Lyceum. Why is that?

"We've dated. A few times." Her eyes moved from side to side like a nonexistent ping-pong match was happening on my shoulders.

"Wait a minute. Isn't he a bird shifter? Are you telling me a mermaid and a bird have an on-again-off-again relationship?"

"You're taking it way better than my parents did." She shrugged. "Anyway, our relationship status is subject to change."

"Aren't you worried it's too much like oil and vinegar?"

"Oil and vinegar is the stuff of amazing salad dressings," Cadence said, smirking.

I couldn't argue with that, and her nonsensical quip cheered me up. I found myself laughing despite the campus feeling like a powder keg.

"That's the Aliyah Morgenstern I know and love." Cadence patted my shoulder.

"She's been in short supply lately." I sighed. "Thanks, Cadence."

"Any time." She grinned. "Hey, I know you'll be in and out for Yom Kippur this week, but are you going home for Sukkot after that?"

"Yeah, to build the Sukkah, and also for the hour during sunset all that week. They let us off-campus for weekday religious holidays. Did you want to celebrate with us?"

"If it's no trouble, could I have an open invitation?"

"Of course."

After that, she introduced me around. The Gallows Hill wildness wasn't as scary close-up. Instead, it was their version of warmth and welcome and how they communicated with each other and their surroundings. I understood why Cadence loved her classmates enough to take responsibility for them.

Elanor made a quiet exit, and Noah returned with Jonah and a pot of tea. I almost went over to say hello, but they were totally engrossed in each other. I didn't want to interrupt the one nice thing to happen that day.

Yawning reminded me to check the time. There were only twenty minutes before lights out. I made my goodbyes, then headed upstairs to change into pajamas before falling into bed. Grace was asleep when I got there.

CHAPTER TWENTY-NINE

The next afternoon at lunch, the PA system summoned me to the office.

Headmaster Hawkins stood with his back to me in front of his bookcase, hands behind his back. I recognized his posture as a sign of the inner turmoil I'd seen after Hal's diagnosis last spring, but his voice sounded more monotone than it had on that occasion.

"Good afternoon, Miss Morgenstern. You must wonder why you're here."

"Yes, sir, I do." I took a seat in front of his desk beside Professor Luciano, who'd been there when I arrived.

"I've requested your assistance as Dylan Khan's friend and peer." He turned and sat. "We're testing the scope of his abilities tomorrow. You must agree not to discuss this with anyone besides the involved parties and your immediate family."

"Okay, I agree." I folded my hands in my lap, knuckles bone-white. "But why not ask Logan?"

"Mr. Pierce will supervise your classmates while they remain in the library tomorrow during your usual lab period."

"Where will you be, Professor?" I blinked.

"Escorting you and Dylan to the test," Professor Luciano said.

Headmaster Hawkins answered before I could ask my question. "Regulations require an instructor's presence, and Professor DeBeer declined." He bowed his head briefly, revealing the puffiness under his eyes. I heard a noise and felt a rush of air behind me.

"Where are his parents?"

"I'm standing in for them."

"Mom?" I turned, eyes widening as I watched my mother straighten her jacket. The headmaster must have teleported her.

"Extramagus testing is rigorous, unforgiving, and not without safety risks." She sat in the third chair, on the other side of me. "I'm acting as a guardian on his behalf. This form bears his father's signature. "

"This isn't fair." I crossed my arms over my chest. "Why didn't I go through this last year?"

"Last year, we didn't have an unsolved poisoning." Headmaster Hawkins leveled his gaze at me. "If there was unexplained sabotage here last spring, you'd have endured the same process."

"I don't like it."

"Nobody does." Professor Luciano sighed. His strix leaned on his head, pushing his glasses askew. He didn't seem to mind.

"Four of the seven trustees requested further investigation," Headmaster Hawkins said. "It's either this test under my jurisdiction on campus or adding Dylan to the list of suspects on file with Salem PD. They'd detain him for questioning."

"Nurse Smith will be there, right?" I sniffled, blinking rapidly. "Since it's dangerous, I mean."

"Yes, though the risks aren't merely medical. Miss Ichiro and Mr. Harcourt have offered their services in case of an emergency. "

"What good will a dragon and a tanuki do?" I stood, placing my hands palm-down on the desk.

"We haven't covered magical shifters yet, Miss Morgenstern." Professor Luciano patted one of my hands. "Rest assured, those two are uniquely qualified to reduce the risk in this ordeal."

I wasn't reassured, not after he called it an ordeal. I dropped my hands to my sides, but I didn't get back in my seat like a good little student.

"Fine, I'll go. But only for Dylan's sake. If you'll excuse me, I've got to eat something before Bishop's Row practice."

As I paced toward the door, my mother gave me an approving nod. Last year I would've wondered why all day, but I understood her better now. Mom stuck to the rules, but she wasn't afraid to use the system to change unfair ones.

At practice, I stood at mid-court with Lee, where I could get the tension out of my body if not off my mind. Dylan sat on the bench with Faith, watching. He'd been switched to reserves instead of taken off the team entirely, pending his results. Coach Pickman didn't want to replace him. If poison was one of his magical elements, Alex would end up taking his place.

At lunch, he came right out and said so to my face. I'd brushed it off, but the anger festered, so I overdid my next fire orb by a country mile.

"Rein it in, Aliyah!" Elanor hollered behind me. "Let's keep our eyebrows!"

"Sorry." I tried banishing the big fire energy between my hands, which shrank but turned a much hotter blue.

"Time out!" Coach Pickman's whistle cleared the court. "Morgenstern, deep breathing exercises now! The rest of you run laps."

"This sucks." Noah glared as he ran past. Lee jogged behind him, shrugging.

"Said I was sorry." I sat on the court's hardwood floor to begin my breathing exercises. I even closed my eyes but didn't have much success relaxing.

"Come on, you can do this." Elanor made like a good team captain and sat across from me, reaching her hands out to take mine. "We're fire, so it's hard for us to chill. Plus, you're related to Noah, so I expect you to be over the top sometimes."

"Thanks." This time instead of closing my eyes, I stared at our interlaced fingers. A tingle of energy passed between us. "Are you banishing?"

"Uh-huh." She nodded. "After what Logan said you did in Lab last year, I'm surprised you're having trouble banishing over a year later."

"There's too much going on."

"Like there wasn't last year?" She raised an eyebrow. "Charity was a megabitch. Every day feels like vacation since she graduated."

"I'd trade the stuff happening now to deal with her again instead."

"I wouldn't." She shook her head. "She was a powder keg. Tempe is too, but Grace has her checked better socially than I ever managed with Charity. Thank goodness Faith is the black sheep of that family."

"Last year, familiars didn't get hurt. How did you do it?"

"Performance art." She shrugged. "Improv. Guess I'm decent at playing pretend."

"I'm not. I worry about everybody. I need to keep them safe."

"That's not your job description."

"I'm not sure what is." I sighed, finally feeling my fire bank down.

"And you think I do?" One corner of her mouth turned up. "It's not your job to save the world, Morgenstern."

Maybe she wouldn't say that if she knew the whole story.

Coach Pickman blew her whistle again. I managed to get through practice without burning the gym down. I tried to follow Dylan afterward since I wanted to ask him about the next day's testing, but he was nowhere to be found.

Because of the High Holidays, I went to my room, skipping dinner since Yom Kippur meant fasting after sundown. Tired and hungry, I took a bath, got into pajamas, and listened to music to pass the time. I fell asleep before Grace returned to our room.

The next morning I could barely pay attention at Lecture, so I made use of our magical notebooks to keep track. I could always study later, at home after Yom Kippur services and dinner. I found it ironic that

Dylan's test came on my religion's day of atonement. He'd be judged for something he couldn't help, and if he failed, he wouldn't get a chance to make up for it.

When Lecture let out, we left Ember and Gale in the infirmary with Nurse Smith, who put them into the cart that housed unbound critters during Familiar Bonding. They peered at us, Ember peeping incessantly and Gale rattling the wire around the enclosure. Nurse Smith crooned something at them as we walked out.

Professor Luciano led Dylan and me all the way down the hall in the academic wing. The section past the library hadn't been used since long before Noah's first year at Hawthorn. A few classrooms were occupied by Gallows Hill and Messing students. I saw Izzy through one of the windows, eyes wide and eyebrows raised as she watched us file by. I couldn't have told her or Cadence about it anyway.

At the end of the hall stood a set of double doors, fitted with stained glass like the ones in the lobby. I'd never seen these before. Professor Luciano stopped and stared, one hand on the latch, pinned in place like a butterfly to a card, transfixed.

The artwork was striking, no doubt. Red and orange flames flickered above a landscape of purple ice, tinged blue where the firelight touched it. Somehow, the ice and fire together created a heat more intense than the inferno I'd banished last year. It was terrifying and beautiful at the same time, the art even more masterful than the glass on the other door.

That didn't explain why it had so much impact on our professor. He was faculty, so surely he'd seen it before. I almost wished the Evil Inside Voice would chime in and throw me some trivia about this mural, but it was silent about the art.

"*Fire and Ice?*" Dylan read the title, then shook his head. "Impossible."

I died a little inside. Only the Evil Inside Voice noticed.

What did you expect?

"Why do you say that?" I cleared my throat, wishing I hadn't sounded quite so strangled.

"It's by a Morgenstern in 1979. That was before your grandma's time, but after her parents."

"It's by her late brother." Professor Luciano's voice was low-pitched and quavered. "His name was Noah."

"How did you know about my great-uncle?" The professor didn't reply or even bother looking at me, but his strix did.

Her head turned all the way around, and she blinked at me twice. I wondered what that meant until the strix trilled in the voice she used to calm other critters. She pressed her head against my temple and tried to help me understand. It hurt the professor to look at me, but the reason was either lost in translation or a mystery to the professor's familiar.

"Why's the ice purple?" Dylan shook his head. "It looks like poison. Still impossible."

"We are the masters of untold elemental forces, Mr. Khan. More things are possible with love and magic than not, beyond imagining for some, at the edge of memory for unfortunate others."

With that cryptic sentiment, Professor Luciano pulled the door open, holding it as we walked through. I glanced up to see his eyes watery, focused on something far away in either distance or time. Possibly both.

CHAPTER THIRTY

The doors led into an auditorium, where the fresh scents of wood soap and polish permeated the air. The entire place had recently been cleaned, likely for the talent show after Thanksgiving. But while the stage lights were up and the curtains open, only one row of seats stood in the front, with two chairs empty.

That Board of Trustees, no doubt.

We arrived last. None of the seven trustees, my mother, or the headmaster had prior commitments that day. What caught me by surprise was the iron dais on the stage. It wasn't just a platform, though. As we approached, light reflected off the clear sides of an enclosure around it.

Whether it was made of glass, crystal, or something else, I didn't know. Dylan found out, because Nurse Smith led him up to it, opened a panel at the back, and locked him inside. My mother had grossly understated things, calling this process rigorous.

It looked downright draconian. Locking anyone in a cage was wrong, extramagus with unknown powers or not.

You don't know the half of it, my sweet summer child.

The Evil Inside Voice never made a physical sound, but my mind usually perceived it as a drolly sarcastic baritone. Now it seemed throaty and hushed. I couldn't fathom what was different just then, how it could carry more than the vague foreboding sitting in my gut. Wasn't the voice part of my brain? Didn't it come from me, some fragment of personality given autonomy by the extra power flowing across the barrier between my body and Faerie's Under?

"Aliyah, take a seat, please." My mother patted the arm of the chair next to her.

I sat between her and Blaine Harcourt. I couldn't muster happiness at seeing him again or a greeting. His presence was ancillary to Dylan's plight, and all of my mental and emotional energy focused on my friend. That was my charge, my reason for being here: as his peer and witness.

One thing was missing, something I should have realized. Somebody had to administer the test, and though I knew little about it, no individual present had authority with the Extrahuman Registry. Headmaster Hawkins rose from his seat, then turned to face the rest of us with his back to the stage's apron.

"Ladies and gentlemen, to ensure this process follows guidelines set forth by the United States and by extension the International Registry, I invite Director-General Rockport of the New England Regional Extrahuman Registry branch."

I almost turned around to look back through the door I'd come in by. If I had, I would've missed the director's entrance from stage left. He must've waited in the wings all that time, watching everyone arrive.

Instead of addressing us or even acknowledging the existence of an audience, Director-General Rockport paced across the stage with his eyes on Dylan. A charcoal suit covered his tall, rangy body, but it did nothing to diminish the wolfishness of his frame. A fringe of salt-and-pepper hair ringed his otherwise-bald head. His expression was so neutral, I couldn't determine his age. I made a mental note to ask Cadence if he'd ever shown up in the social papers.

Blaine Harcourt tightened his right hand on the arm between our seats. The wood creaked, which made me nervous. If a powerful dragon shifter who could take on a form the size of a football field was scared of this guy, Dylan was in serious trouble, and I couldn't help him. This was a test of his elements and abilities as an extramagus. Interference might force him to repeat the entire process.

"It's okay, Blaine." Kim put her hand over his, but it trembled. After their fingers interlaced, their knuckles went white.

I blinked, unsure what had them on edge. And then I remembered that dragon shifters could see magical energy and tanukis could see the flow of luck. Was it the box that frightened them or Dylan? Or him being inside it? Did Director-General Rockport inspire all that terror?

Be glad you're seated beside your mother.

"I am."

"I will brook no comments from witnesses." The director spoke without turning to face me, but his words hit like a blow to the stomach.

He reached for his interior jacket pocket and produced a pair of metallic spectacles. I sensed they weren't ordinary, but before I got a good look, he put them on, his head obscuring them from view. After that, he put his left hand in his outside pocket. I watched it move under the fabric. The iron and glass box on stage made a noise.

It sounded like the air conditioning compressor outside Bubbe's office. As Dylan's eyes widened with alarm and his hands went up to his neck, I understood. The Director was creating a vacuum in there.

"Use your registered element," he said in an impossibly level monotone. How could any sentient person address another so calmly in a situation this dire? How many times had he done this?

Trust me, you don't want to know.

Dylan set his jaw and responded instead of panicking further. He raised his hands like a mime pressing against an invisible ceiling, then I watched him open his mouth and practically gulp in the air he created around himself. The compressor noise stopped and the director nodded, his hand moving in his pocket again.

"Now, the temperature rises."

This time Dylan nodded, expecting what was coming. I breathed a premature sigh of relief, confident he'd keep cool.

But either he was too unaccustomed to ice magic, or he lacked confidence. It had taken me months to control solar, so I couldn't blame him, especially with how his school year had gone so far. This test was designed to be rigorous, challenging, and exacting. And worse, as it turned out.

Admit it. This is pure cruelty.

I watched as the clear enclosure glowed red. The Director even pulled a handkerchief from somewhere and dabbed his forehead with it. Sweat beaded on Dylan's brow, but finally, he managed the concentration to call on his second element. Rockport nodded again, adjusting whatever control hid in his pocket.

"Additional element ice, confirmed. Now, the temperature drops."

The process repeated with a new element. Did he intend to run him through the entire gamut of magic elements? How could anyone consider this test within humane parameters? Was it new since the Reveal or something that had been in use for ages? How many extra-magi had they done this to? Dylan shivered until his teeth chattered, but nothing happened. Before long, that segment ended.

"Fire element negative. And now, darkness."

I felt numb, detached from everything. Everybody still saw Dylan; nothing looked different to the witnesses. But his eyes went wide and wild, and he wrapped his arms around himself, seeming to shrink in fear from nothing.

Being immersed in impenetrable darkness was a primal fear, one shared by most sentient beings on the planet other than vampires, Umbral Magi, and their kindred critters. But none of us had to endure that terror today, only Dylan.

I glanced down the line of people, four of whom I'd never seen. I recognized Mrs. Onassis, Mr. Pierce, and Mr. Fairbanks. They yawned like Dylan was up there method-acting instead of being punished.

Punishment for being what he is? Horrific.

I'd promised to be his witness, so I couldn't look away. Dylan quaked and quivered in there, terrified but unable to mitigate the absence of light around him. I grasped my mother's hand.

"How long?"

"Another minute." My mother laced her fingers through mine and squeezed. I wished I could get into her lap and curl up there the way I had as a small child, but I was seventeen, and a formal witness for an official Registry test. And an extramagus. No comfort could erase my horror at this cruel procedure. It shouldn't have been an approved global standard for anybody, even Uncle Richard.

"Make it stop." Blaine trembled in his seat, shoulders hunched.

Kim put her arm around him. "Ten seconds."

That small humane act made me feel impossibly guilty. Someone should have been here for him. Not as a witness in a chair, but inside the box beside Dylan, so he wasn't alone. Maybe a shifter or a psychic. Why wasn't that allowed?

"Solar element negative. And now, light."

Who does he think he is, God? Lucifer, more like.

Dylan covered his eyes with his hands, fruitlessly from the way he screamed. This was not a test. It was torture and utterly inhumane. That was why the Registry didn't designate a support extrahuman inside the box.

I'd go through this exact ordeal in less than a year. Everyone with more than one magical element had to, suspicion of crime or not. No wonder Uncle Richard had lied about his abilities.

I'd grown up in Salem and had known the history of witch-trials here for as long as I could remember. Never in my wildest dreams could I have imagined they still existed in an internationally-sanctioned form for any percentage of magi.

"Umbral element negative."

The test progressed, and yes, Director Rockport went through every magical element known to extrahumanity. He ended by testing for the rarest ability in existence, mind magic.

"Now, Mr. Khan, ask to be released without using your voice or body language."

Dylan leaned his forehead against the front of his prison. The tawny skin of his brow was pressed flat and his eyes were closed. Every one of us watched tears pour out, roll down his face, and splash against his already sweat-stained shirt. His hands balled into fists at his sides, and that small act of defiance guillotined my last scrap of composure.

I no longer felt far-off or detached, instead breaking into a series of wet sobs that shook the entire row of chairs, along with my body. My limbs felt stiff and weak all at the same time, my face blazing like the sun, feet as frigid and heavy as blocks of ice.

The seven Trustees at the other end of the row leaned forward to peer at me. One, a very elderly man I didn't know with a thick white beard, sniffled and wiped away a tear. The fox in his lap whined.

Mom had her arm around me, but it did no good. She couldn't offer me any comfort. She could never understand how horrifying this was, watching my friend, already in anguish, endure even more. Knowing I'd be in his place soon enough.

Kim Ichiro got it. Not caring one bit what anybody thought, the tanuki rose from her seat and ushered me out of mine, leading me off to the side and giving me a bear hug I wouldn't have thought possible from someone so short and slight.

"This is the most horrible thing I've ever seen in my life," she whispered in my ear. "My father's a lawyer, and I'm telling him everything. This can't continue."

"Even after Richard Hopewell?" I managed.

"Especially after Richard Hopewell." She patted my back. "He was terrible, but we have to do better than this."

Finally, it was over. In the end, Dylan had aptitude for only the two elements he'd initially admitted to. They could've taken his word for it, but either the system distrusted us or considered us too mentally unstable to give an accurate accounting of our abilities.

Dylan and I might have been born with extra magical power, but the world did its best to make sure we had plenty of other disadvantages.

CHAPTER THIRTY-ONE

We went to Yom Kippur service in Beverly, the same as every year. Crossing the bridge felt different, heavier somehow. On the way there and during the service, I wanted forgiveness more than ever.

At first, I wasn't sure what I'd done wrong, but failure to act hurt others as much as direct harm. I wanted to take a stand and change how extramagi were treated, but it all felt hollow and false because I hadn't spoken out about it.

When the shofar blew, my heart opened along with my mind and cleared away all fear of what my family might think. There was something I could say, maybe even something to do.

The idea couldn't change the past, but it could help tip the balance toward equity for extramagi. I couldn't change the system, but maybe I could expose it.

The ride back over the bridge into Salem felt like hours instead of minutes. When we went upstairs and prepared to break our fast, the last thing on my mind was food despite how good all the dishes looked, how amazing they smelled, how hungry I was. No drop of drink or crumb of food would pass between my lips, not until I told my family about my plan.

"Mom. Dad. Bubbe. I'm taking that test." They paused, hands over chairs, a pitcher poised over the glass in my father's hand—my family, frozen in time. Noah broke the spell.

"What do you mean?" He scratched his head. "Exams aren't until spring, Aliyah."

"Not that." I looked at Mom, pinning her gaze with mine. "You know what I mean. The extramagus test. The one Dylan took today."

"Wait." Noah blinked. "They test extrama—"

"No."

I whirled, startled by Bubbe's voice behind me. The tray of babka in her hand sagged, nearly tipping over. I rushed to her side and set it on the counter, then I put my hands on my hips and planted my feet in front of her.

"No?" My nostrils flared.

"You heard me. There's no way you're taking that test until you have to, Aliyah." Bubbe narrowed her eyes. Her hair, cobalt blue this time, trembled. Was she angry or scared? For what felt like the second worst moment of my life, I realized I didn't care.

That's not true. You care too much. That's always your problem.

"I'm way more dangerous in a wooden school than a boy with ice and air." My voice cracked. "I want Mom to call Director-General Rockport tomorrow, and then I'll take that test."

"What you want is irrelevant, child." Bubbe looked over my head at my parents. "Neither of you will consent to this foolishness. It's out of the question."

I turned slowly, measuring my movement because I didn't want to see what I knew would be there: resignation on both my parents' faces.

"You're right, Mom," Dad agreed reluctantly.

"I'm glad you said that, Aaron." My mother put her hand to her throat, her only tell when frightened. "I'm in total agreement with Bubbe. Minor extramagi need parental consent. That rule's in place for a reason. I won't give mine in a million years. And if you do, Aaron, so help me—"

"I hear you both," Dad said, "but my uncle took it as an adult. The love of his life volunteered just like this when he was younger than

Aliyah is now. In June, she'll have to take it. The test is the only way for extramagi."

"It shouldn't be." I crossed my arms over my chest.

"If that's how you feel, Aliyah, why push?" Noah shuddered. "I don't know jack, but that fucking thing sounds catastrophic."

"Noah, language!" Mom made a zipping motion over her lips. He winced and hung his head.

"It looks like evil to me, and torture is wrong. I want them to test me in public, so everyone knows how bad it is. To make it stop."

"You're not responsible for every extramagi on this Earth." Bubbe stepped forward and put her hand on my shoulder. Her tone softened, but her eyes remained hard and angry. "My brother's powers came in at age twenty, and that test made him suffer every day. What do you think will happen to you?" She sighed. "This isn't revolution, it's self-harm. You're not Moses. You're Jacob, and we're refusing to be Isaac."

"I'm Judah, lighting a lamp." My throat tightened. Ember wrapped around my shoulders, her tail pressed against my cheek. "The test is desecration. If magi have to see it, they'll know we need another way."

"You're still a minor," Bubbe insisted.

"I'm not giving up on this plan."

"You will until you're eighteen and we can't protect you any longer. I was my brother's witness." Bubbe pressed her fingertips to her breastbone. "I sat in your place and saw what you saw, and I've tried to change it all this time because I love you all so much. I failed. What makes you think you'll succeed?"

"Bubbe, I know how hard you can fight." My eyes overflowed. "But you're not an extramagus."

"Is that supposed to mean I don't understand?" Her fingertips paled against her white shirt.

"No, you get it, but you can't speak for a group you're not part of, Bubbe. Not for something like this."

"I only exist because enough gentiles stood up for Jews during the Shoah, Bissel." She sighed. "Like everyone else in this room."

"This test doesn't happen where people can see, but caring for one person is the key to opening your heart. All they know about us is

Richard Hopewell in an orange jumpsuit. I'm asking you to let me be seen."

"She's got that part right." Dad nodded.

"Then go on the news." Noah shrugged. "Do an interview with Cadence's mom. Make a viral video. Mom and Bubbe almost never freak out about the same thing. Maybe they're right."

"Noah has good ideas here. Other ways to raise awareness." Mom put her arm around my brother. I stared, wondering why nobody did the same for me.

They're afraid. You're incandescent.

I looked at my hands. The Evil Inside Voice was right. I glowed with a light too orange for pure solar magic. I'd conjured both elements without realizing it. I'd never hurt my family, but they didn't seem to believe that.

"Peep." Ember craned her neck around to look me in the eye, then reached out with one claw and stroked the bridge of my nose, the way I did with her when she was upset. At least she wasn't afraid.

She's on your side, always.

I turned on my heel and ran upstairs, slamming the door to my room before banging my head on the sloped ceiling. I fell into bed sickened and weeping and curled up around Ember. Even the aroma of Bubbe's chocolate babka turned my stomach.

Eventually, I had to use the bathroom. Outside my door, I found a plate piled with food, a sign of love. Too bad what I needed that day was their support.

CHAPTER THIRTY-TWO

The next day, Dylan replaced Bailey in Professor Luciano's homeroom. Bailey had gone to DeBeer's class with her sister. I waved as he entered the room, pointing at the seat between Logan and me.

Dylan sat in the back, head down over his notebook as the professor gave his lecture. He wasn't alone since Hal came in right after him and took the seat beside him. Faith made her way to the front and sat with us.

I had a hard time concentrating for the second day in a row, for more than one reason. That afternoon we'd be in the magipsychic lab with our teams, working on our projects for the fair. My brain moved a mile a minute on other things besides Axis and Allied magi during the Second World War.

Maybe you're just avoiding uncomfortable subject matter.

I shook my head and activated the book's auto-notes, then doodled in the margins. I'd want to look over more detailed notes later than what I could manage taking now.

"Rumors of shifter and faerie activity during the war became the stuff of foxhole folklore. Magi kept their involvement on more subtle terms. The Allies had magi working in secret as munitions designers, but the Axis magi were more ambitious. If they'd cared more about advancing the mundane Axis cause, Allied forces would have lost the Second World War."

Too close to home for your family.

I couldn't ignore the reactions from my classmates, whose gasps carried through the room. Only Dylan seemed unimpressed, likely because the UK had endured direct attacks on their soil. Although misery loves company, I hoped their stomachs didn't turn as much as mine did. If the Axis had won, I'd never have been born.

Don't go making assumptions now.

"What?"

"Miss Morgenstern, if you're having trouble hearing from the front row, I'm not sure what other accommodation to give you." Professor Luciano turned from his chalk drawing. "However, it is vital that you absorb the lecture from this point forward. It's of extreme importance."

"Sorry about the outburst, Professor."

"Let us continue, then.

"Only the most specialized of educators would be able to tell you that Axis magi were distracted by one specific obsession. I happen to be one of two in the know at this hallowed institution."

Logan put his hand up and spoke after Professor Luciano nodded.

"Who's the other?"

"He's unable to teach here despite holding numerous degrees, but you all know Ezekiel Brown. His knowledge comes first-hand from occupying an Axis magipsychic research base at the end of the war. In a chamber beneath the basement level, he found this."

He completed a chalkboard picture, then stepped aside so we could see it. Instead of troops in uniform, bombers in flight, or a bombed-out countryside, he'd depicted a device I'd never forget after the previous day's events: the glass and iron dais used in the test.

A loud wooden clattering sounded behind me. Dylan had stood, and his chair had toppled behind him. Gale flapped in the air above his head.

"How many?" He pointed at the board. "How many extramagi did they torture? How many died?"

"Nobody counted them. Even today we're not sure, but estimates are in the thousands."

I raised my hand, and he acknowledged it.

"Why isn't this widely known?"

"It's a complex answer. The forces occupying the base couldn't determine what the device was for until much later. They had to keep it secret from their mundane allies. But in the sixties, when it became apparent to our society that a reveal would happen, extrahumans with influence took pains to investigate the Axis records and this device, along with several others in storage. Once we needed a Registry, we had enough magipsychic technology to create our own regulatory organization. The rest is public relations, designed to ensure peace between humans and extrahumans."

"Why didn't they count the extramagi?" Faith asked without raising her hand. "The Axis murdered them just like they did mundanes. Didn't the Allied magi care?"

"I'm afraid they did care, Miss Fairbanks, but for the wrong reasons. The Allies stopped the war, but they were flawed." He looked over our heads. "Do you need a break, Mr. Khan?"

"No." He shook his head, then beckoned to Gale, who landed on his shoulder again. "No, I think I'll be okay hearing this from you, sir."

"Here." Hal righted the seat, and Dylan murmured a word of thanks before sitting back down in it.

The lecture continued, eventually concluding with a list of related books in the library. In Creatives, Dylan immediately got his guitar and sat in the corner, tapping the strings instead of strumming them. I understood he needed to play but didn't want to distract everybody else. All the talk of horrible magipsychic devices had jogged my memory about some of the more beneficial ones.

I got permission and headed down to the library to get something. The Ashfords nodded and smiled, giving me no trouble when I requested the item be checked out under Dylan's name instead of mine. When I returned to Creatives, I headed to him.

"Give these a try." I held the item out to him.

"This guitar's acoustic, so I don't see how headphones will help. Nice thought, though."

"It's magipsychic Bluetooth. Let me show you."

He nodded, so I slipped the headphones over his ears, then took the guitar from him. I held the body to one side and the fretboard to the other while imagining sound moving from the instrument to the headset, then I handed the guitar back to him.

"Give it a try."

He strummed a chord, and his mouth dropped open. He looked up at me, blinking. I smiled.

"Do you like it?"

"How did you know about this miracle?"

"Noah uses something like that at home when he plays bass, but they work with any instrument."

"Wow." He gave me a half-smile. "You're a lifesaver."

"Nah, I just got them from the library."

"It's a huge improvement for practicing. Thanks, Aliyah."

"I'll leave you to it, then." I headed toward the cabinet, intending to do some woodworking, but Hal stopped me.

"He should worship the ground you walk on, you know."

"What?"

"You heard me. Dylan doesn't appreciate you. I know about yesterday. I wasn't there, but sometimes space magic means I see and hear more than I should."

"It was beyond horrible, so I'm going to keep doing random acts of kindness for Dylan Khan if it's all the same to you."

"Are you sure you're okay with pining like Echo after Narcissus?"

"I'll live." I put my hand to my cheek.

He blinked, eyes reddening. Nin poked her head out of his pocket and squeaked, a series of shrill and angry sounds punctuated by an occasional click. Ember hung her head, giving me a reproachful stare.

"I'm sorry," I said, "I want you to live long and prosperously and have, like, ten kids with Faith."

"Me too. You aren't Echo. I just want to see you happy. Loved."

"Not everybody has someone destined for them, Hal. I'm okay with that."

Liar.

I didn't argue anymore with Hal or the Evil Inside Voice, but I didn't have the time or the heart to work on a carving of Dylan's dragonet either. I got a lump of clay and wedged it, preparing it for a piece to work on the next day instead.

In the magipsychic lab, we lucked out in the team department. I worked with Cadence, Izzy, Faith, and Brianna, which meant we could make those communication orbs.

Unfortunately, Professor Luciano wasn't our instructor. Instead, we were supervised by Principal Hawkins, Hal's neglectful mother. I didn't expect much, but she surprised me.

"I love this project." She smiled with genuine excitement. "Communication orbs were one of the first magipsychic items introduced to the mundanes after the Reveal, and they went a long way toward enabling us to integrate our societies."

"Miss, can we please just start?" Izzy had her hand up but didn't wait for an acknowledgment. She was excited, but Principal Hawkins had no idea.

"Part of the extramurals agreement was that we faculty members instruct as well as supervise. I chose this project myself, so I won't drop the ball, so to speak." She smiled, juggling three of the sea glass orbs we'd use in our project. "Don't worry, I know my stuff, and by the time you're done, so will you."

My knees went out from under me and I sat down hard, fortunately in my seat. Stephanie Hawkins' demeanor shocked me because it was nothing like Hal and Faith had described.

Faith sat there, silently wearing her best resting bitch face. I copied her, mostly in solidarity. Izzy joined in too, but Cadence acted like her usual bubbly self.

"I'm going to write some notes on this board here." She picked up a piece of chalk. "You ladies from Hawthorn already know, but I'll mention this for the other students. The booklets on the corner of your table automatically copy everything I put up, so there's no need for you to scribble. Just listen."

I'd learned most of the facts she lectured on by reading about communication orbs ahead of time, but Principal Hawkins was surprisingly entertaining. She gave us mnemonic devices disguised as quips, things we wouldn't soon forget, and when she demonstrated the tools and materials, she used techniques straight out of circus arts, as she had with the orbs.

Stephanie Hawkins was a natural teacher. Although all her extrahuman traits were passive, she understood the material and how we'd use it, and she conveyed it brilliantly. Even shifters were more magical than dhampyr, but nobody else seemed to mind. Especially not Brianna, who knew nothing about her true nature.

You see why Hal's father fell in love with her.

"Whatever." I winced immediately.

"I know, right." Faith elbowed me in the shoulder, briefly jostling Ember, who turned her head and went right back to sleep.

"All right, enough lecture. From now on, you'll have the entire lab period for the remainder of the week to collaborate on your project, write your report, and make your display. As an unassisted group, of course, though I'll be here for safety reasons. I can tell you guys are awesome, so rivals and frenemies might try to spy on you." She giggled. "Think of me more as security than a chaperone."

The work was more intensive than making three orbs with limited capabilities had been last year. This time we'd make six, with visual, audio, and recording capability. Each orb got coated with a mixture of infused solutions we made ourselves. These differences added loads of conjuring work, energy-charging, channeling, and chemical application.

Sorting the ingredients was a persnickety task. Some of the substances and items were nearly identical and stored in similar containers. Fortunately, Brianna had an eye for small details. We put her on the task of categorizing everything.

"I feel like a bull in a china shop here." Brianna stood with her hands behind her back. "It all looks so delicate, like if I sneezed, it'd break."

"Don't worry, we'll need your help with more than sorting." Cadence patted her shoulder. "Glamour is the key magic we'll use to enchant these."

"I'll help you," said Faith. "You point them out, I'll set them aside."

"Aliyah, I could use your help with these." Izzy beckoned me over.

She held a tray of unlabeled vials, all twelve containing white powder. Izzy needed my solar magic to tell them apart because six of them would temporarily turn purple when exposed to UV light. Sorting them must've taken longer than I thought because the bell rang before we knew it.

"See you guys tomorrow." Principal Hawkins opened the door, beaming and waving as we exited.

"Do you think we'll finish by the end of the week?" Brianna shook her head. "It seems impossible to get it done, and we still have Bishop's Row practice three nights a week."

"I'm on my school's team, so I know what you mean." I nodded. "We can totally do it, but we'll be tired."

"How do you think the others are doing?" Faith asked.

None of us knew, at least not until we got to dinner.

CHAPTER THIRTY-THREE

"Why do we have to be teammates, anyway?"

"Settle down." Lee got between Dylan and Dorian. "Professor Luciano picked you. Prove him right since he believes in you."

"You get along with everybody." Dylan snorted. "You've got no reason to be miserable."

"They separated me from my best friend." Lee shrugged. "Anyway, we've got to finish our project, and if we drop the ball, we're letting Grace, Keisha, and Azrael down. So let's get things under control long enough for that."

Dorian nodded. "He has a point."

"Shut your lazy mouth."

"Dylan, can you sit with me?" Logan picked at his thumbnail, one of the habits he couldn't shake in times of stress. "I've got questions about air magic, and the twins keep giggling and saying their ways are mysterious."

"You know everything anyway, but fine." Dylan followed Logan to a booth in the corner.

"He's moody." Izzy shook her head.

"Well, he's still upset over the whole thing."

"Yeah, I know. The breakup. But she's dated and dumped somebody entirely different since then. Is this much trauma normal for romantic people?"

"Well, how would you feel if you and Lee broke up?"

"I told you, we're best friends, not a couple."

"He's behind you."

"Yes, I am." Lee sidestepped to stand next to Izzy. "And she's right. We're not a couple. Anyway, everyone's different."

I couldn't tell them about the extramagus test, so I let them go on about relatively mundane stuff, puzzling things out between friendship and romance. Maybe I shouldn't have, but nobody has hindsight. Even precognitive psychics came by that selectively.

After that argument between Dorian and Dylan, we didn't see any more evidence of unrest from our year, but the first-years were another story. It started that night and got worse over time.

The first thing I noticed was Michelina Zanelli crying in the third-floor bathroom. Faith hadn't been in yet, and I was early for my soak in the clawfoot tub. It was a good thing, too. Michelina sat in one of the shower stalls, water running to wash away her tears as her opossum sat outside, whining miserably.

I waited until she was done and had some time to get dressed before approaching. Since I figured she wouldn't say much, I planned my words carefully.

"Hey, Lena. Welcome to the third-floor bathroom. You're welcome to use it anytime."

"Oh. Thanks, I guess." She pushed the curtain aside and emerged, hair still damp.

"Did you find everything okay? If you didn't, I could give you a little tour."

She nodded, then pointed at the wooden box of bath salts I held in my hand.

"All that stuff's in here."

I led Lena to the other side of the partition, showing her the wall panel where they stored a plethora of toiletries for tub baths. I took my time, explaining everything in my most neutral voice. Maybe she just needed space to calm down after whatever had sent her up here.

If she minded me over-explaining, Lena didn't show it. She followed me around as the toiletry explanation turned into a short tour. By the time we'd finished, she managed a hushed word of thanks before heading out of the bathroom.

Faith held the door for her as she left, then came in with a quizzical look on her face.

"What was that about?"

"I'm not sure. She was crying in there." I jerked my thumb at the shower. "Do you know who her roommate is? Could it be Temperance?"

"I'm not sure. All my sister and I have exchanged this year are dirty looks."

"Okay. Let's find out tomorrow."

"Good idea. Are you swimming tonight?"

"No, I'm too tired. I was just going to soak in one of the small tubs."

We each pursued our individual method of bathing. She was still swimming when I left for bed.

The next day was Friday, and I had to head home for the holiday. My family was preparing for Sukkot. The festival of booths was a lot of fun, even if we got rained out more often than not.

The point of the holiday was spending time with friends and family, so along with Cadence and Izzy, I also invited Dylan and Logan. Logan stayed behind once again, but Dylan left right after class with me, walking down Essex Street away from campus. He needed to escape campus even more than I did.

"Isn't Noah coming?"

"He'll be along later. Said something about extra library research for his group's project."

"Okay. What are we doing once we get there?"

"Mostly making decorations for the sukkah. Paper chains, popcorn on strings, woven fronds for the roof—that kind of thing."

"And then, if it doesn't rain, we have dinner there?"

"That's right."

"My mum would call that 'alfresco.'" He stared at the sidewalk. "Her favorite place to take holidays is in Italy.

"You must miss her."

"Yeah. I haven't seen her in over a year, Aliyah."

"I can't even imagine."

As we walked, I'd edged closer to him, so I dropped my hand beside his.

"I hope it stays that way for you."

He put some distance between us as we turned the corner on Hawthorne Street. We walked the rest of the way in silence, turning up the driveway behind Izzy's house toward 10-1/2. Around the back, we headed through the gate. The corner of the yard with the hole in the fence was currently occupied by a pile of lumber with canvas folded on top.

"That's it." I pointed.

"You only invited me so there'd be another tall person to hold those beams up, right?" He raised an eyebrow, but his eyes brightened.

"That might be among the many reasons, yes." I smiled, covering my hands' shaking. "Mostly I wanted to share a holiday with you. I know that sounds kind of sappy, but it's the truth."

"Right then." He cleared his throat. "How does this thing go together?"

"According to the instructions, of course." My dad stepped out from the back door, waving a piece of paper. "Which I happen to have right here."

Dad spent time with Dylan going over the directions, which weren't complicated. But my father believed in reading the manual. They took long enough that Noah finally showed up. Mom and Bubbe came out to the backyard, bringing a few critters to play in the exercise runs. After that, we all took part in setting up the sukkah.

Once we'd erected the frame, we took a break. Bubbe invited us in for iced tea. I helped her bring the critters back in, and we all stood around in her small kitchen with our beverages. She had a collection of arts and crafts supplies, which Noah, Dylan, and I worked with after the adults left the room with their tea.

"Are your holidays all kind of separated into the adults' table and the kids' table?"

"A little bit," said Noah. "It's more like they leave the fun stuff for us to do."

"Yeah, especially on Sukkot." I grinned, reaching for a container of glitter glue.

"It seems like a lot of work," Dylan said.

"It's a bit of a scramble before sundown, that's true." Noah nodded. "But we don't have to do anything after that besides hang out and eat."

"Will it be like Thanksgiving dinner again?" Dylan glanced over his shoulder at the oven behind him, his stomach growling.

"No, no turkey or any of that." I pointed at the oven. "But if my nose is not mistaken, Bubbe's got challah bread in there. We'll have that, along with some other dinner stuff."

"I wish Logan was here." Dylan sighed. "I feel like I've barely spent any time with him besides sleeping and getting ready for class in the morning."

Like you and Grace, but don't turn him into Gloomy McGloomypants by bringing her up.

"You guys are busy." Noah shrugged. "That happens in the second year. Everything's hectic for you guys, and extramurals are just another time sink."

"I asked Logan, but he doesn't want to leave campus. I think he's scared of his parents." I added a strip of glittery construction paper to a paper chain. "Azrael talked to his aunt. The Salem police won't bother him."

"Yeah, he knows." Dylan nodded. "But he's worried, almost paranoid. He has nightmares about them hiring people to cart him off to the airport."

Noah snorted. "That's ridiculous."

"It seems like that to us." It took a lot of effort not to snap at him. "But Logan's fear is valid. His parents are downright scary."

"Elanor's afraid of them too, but it's still ridiculous." Noah shook his head. "Not his feelings, the situation. I'll talk to him tomorrow. Maybe he'll come over in a large enough group. I know we're just students, but a throng of us can protect him from jerks in a van."

"That's a good idea." Dylan nodded. "This is done." He held up a paper chain. "What else should I make?"

"Whatever you want, I guess." Noah tapped a stack of brown paper. "How about guitars?"

"That's okay?"

"Yeah, we decorate with whatever's important to us that year." I nodded. "Last year, I put up a bunch of paper dragonets. I'd show you one, but they all got ruined in the rain."

He went to work cutting guitar shapes out of brown paper. The stove's timer buzzed, so I got up to take the bread out of the oven.

Moments later, Bubbe shooed us out of her kitchen. We'd finished enough decorations, so we went outside to help Dad put the fronds on top of the sukkah and hang our crafts on the walls inside.

After that, Noah and Dylan went upstairs. Through the window, we heard Noah singing along with Dylan's guitar. They played the same ten bars of music over and over with pauses in between, practicing a song I didn't recognize.

I helped get ready for dinner, but there wasn't much left to do. With most of the preparation done, all that remained was taking things out of ovens and letting them cool. The doorbell rang. Izzy and Cadence had brought Lee along with them.

As the sun set, we gathered in the backyard. Izzy and Cadence had seen all of this before, but Lee and Dylan hadn't.

"What's this one about?" Lee asked.

"We're celebrating how we survived in the wilderness after escaping Egypt," I answered. "This holiday lasts all week."

"Should be forty days since Moses got lost leading us around out there," Noah said.

"That's before he got those ten commandments, right?" Cadence said, "And before Google maps."

"You remembered." Noah grinned.

"So, now what?" asked Dylan.

"Mom and Dad are going to wave the four species, while Bubbe says a prayer."

"Four species? Is that like critters or something?" Lee raised an eyebrow. "How do you wave a mercat?"

"They're plants. We've got palm leaves, myrtle leaves, willow leaves, and citrus fruit."

"And after that, we can eat, I hope?" Dylan's stomach rumbled.

Everybody laughed. His smile reminded me of the ones on his face last year, definitely an improvement in his mood. Maybe music helped him cope or being off campus for a while did him good.

We all helped bring dinner downstairs. I had Bubbe's challah with raisins, dipped in honey. Also kreplach, stuffed dumplings like pierogis but with chicken instead of potatoes.

After dinner, Cadence and Izzy headed back to campus with Lee. Dylan lingered, bringing his guitar out and raising an eyebrow at Noah.

"Yeah, I think I'm ready to show it off." He went back inside and fetched his bass.

"Okay, one two three."

They did *Go Your Own Way* by Fleetwood Mac. Noah sounded like Lindsey Buckingham, too.

"You want to perform that in the talent show," Mom guessed.

"Something like that." Noah grinned. "It's not just us, though. Our band hasn't landed on the right song."

"That's awesome." I smiled.

"At least I'm not suspended from extracurriculars anymore." Dylan shrugged. "Only probation."

"Probation-smobation." Noah snorted.

"You're in the same boat as me." I nodded. "Plain old trouble."

Mom picked up a stack of dirty dishes and started walking toward the house.

"Hey, I wanted to thank you guys for inviting me over. And everything else, too." Dylan stared down at the guitar. "I really needed some time away."

"Did you want to stay over?" asked Bubbe. "If you don't want to sleep out here, I've got space in my office."

"No, thanks. I've got to work before breakfast tomorrow." Dylan sighed. "Can't make my nights too late."

"Do you want me to walk you back?" Noah asked.

"No, I'll be all right. My feet know the way."

He packed the guitar into the library's battered case, and we escorted him through the gate together.

On warm enough nights, Noah and I slept in the sukkah. Because the New England weather was unpredictable, we got our sleeping bags. Mom and Dad said good night to us on our way out, but Bubbe sat outside on one of the folding chairs, staring at the stars.

"I'll get out of your way," she said.

We protested, letting her know she was welcome, but our grandmother must've had other things on her mind. She went inside after bidding us good night. We settled down in the Sukkah, moving the table and chairs and unrolling our sleeping bags in the newly cleared space.

I lay there, holding Great Uncle Noah's *Shema Yisrael* pendant between my fingers. It reminded me of the letters he'd written to his boyfriend, the ones Bubbe said I should share with Noah. I hadn't gotten a chance to look at them.

"Do you think we're in over our heads?" Noah stared at the fronds above his head.

"Absolutely, and we'll drown if we're not careful."

"Why?" He turned his head, so I did likewise to meet his gaze. "Just last week, you seemed the epitome of confident."

"If I tell you something, can you keep it secret? You might talk to Dylan about it, but nobody else."

"It's been ages since you've shared secrets with me, Aliyah. Sure. Go ahead."

I told him in vivid detail about the extramagus test. Probably I shouldn't have because the horror reflected on his face hit me like a sucker punch, but nobody can untell a story.

"So, that's why you fought so hard against Mom and Bubbe on Yom Kippur." He stared.

"Yeah." I closed my eyes, the tears I'd held back finally rolling down my face.

"I don't blame you, not one bit." He wiped them away.

"I'm sorry." I sniffled, opening my eyes.

"Why?" His face was blotchy, eyes bright.

"Neither of us will sleep well."

"Sleep's inevitable once you're tired enough." He sighed, gazing at the roof made of fronds. "I'm glad you told me. That's not the kind of thing to keep bottled up."

"I've learned that's how it is for extramagi—tucking all kinds of horrifying things into neat little boxes so we don't disturb anyone. Meanwhile, they're either jealous of our extra elements or afraid we'll go off the deep end."

"Aliyah, I'll never do the latter, but I'm guilty of the former." A gleaming line formed from the corner of his eye to one of his sideburns.

I couldn't decide how to respond. My brother's honesty wavered when it came to his shortcomings. Offering sympathy in this sukkah that symbolized nights spent in the wilderness was nothing short of miraculous to me.

There was one thing you could always say.

"Nobody's perfect. And thanks, Noah."

I don't know when he fell asleep because it was after I did. When I woke to the sun's first light and birdsong in the mulberry tree, he'd already left.

Before heading back to campus, I grabbed the box with Great-Uncle Noah's letters and tucked them into my backpack. I'd be more likely to read them if they were on campus with me.

CHAPTER THIRTY-FOUR

Our project progressed with little trouble. The others, not so much.

Hal's group worked on a magical toggle, something to turn lights off and on or open and close taps. He just barely managed to lead them via his knack for endearment. Having Bar on the team and backing his leadership helped, but the pair of snooty clairvoyants from Messing wasn't happy with his diminished magical ability. Kitty stuck up for him, but the clairvoyants dismissed her. Izzy said they thought she was "too mainstream," whatever that meant.

Lee, Dylan, Grace, and Azrael had to work with Dorian, who didn't contribute much. If it weren't for Lee and Keisha, the telepath from Messing, they wouldn't have kept the peace long enough to complete their refrigeration unit.

Noah worked with Elanor, Jonah, Crow, and Arick. They got along for the most part, though Crow's aloofness clashed with the otherwise gregarious crew. He also got distracted easily, and none of the others could keep him on task. Their project was one of the most demanding, a full-season carbon-free fuel for a magical space heater.

Logan's team technically had it easy with their magical water wheel, but they had to work with Alex and Temperance. Lena was in his group too, and Logan ended up doing most of the spellwork with her. The bear shifter and the telekinetic psychic on their team spent most of their time looking bewildered and lifting the heavy parts.

As the week drew to a close, we all scrambled. The devices were only one part of the projects. We'd have to compile data, write reports, and make everything in our display fit on top of a six-by-two foot table, so of course, everyone wanted the lab work done by Friday.

I crunched our numbers, and Brianna wrote all the text in the report. She had the best handwriting, like a scientist's. Despite her obvious ability, she had Cadence proofread it on Monday night.

"This is great work!" Cadence smiled.

"Thanks." Brianna grinned back.

"You just need to check the punctuation with someone else, because that's my weak point." She tapped an Oxford comma. "I'm not sure whether this should be here or not."

"I'll bring it to the library." I held my hand out for the notebook.

Brianna handed it over, turning to leave the lounge. Cadence cleared her throat and raised an eyebrow at her.

"Can I go with you?" Brianna asked.

"Sure, why not?"

We headed into the academic wing and down the hall. I was about to push the library doors open, but Brianna put her hand out, stopping me.

"Um, wait a minute." Her face was red and flushed as though we'd been at Bishop's Row practice instead of walking down a hallway.

"All right."

Eventually, she composed herself. Brianna took a deep breath and opened her mouth but closed it again and shook her head. Ember peeped at her from my shoulder.

Where have you seen this before, I wonder?

"Logan. Oops." I winced. "My inside voice jumps out sometimes."

"No, no, I understand. Are you two a thing?"

"We're not. He's got an enormous crush on someone else right now."

"Oh, okay then. Well."

"Well?"

"There's a dance. In December. The December Dance." She cleared her throat. "Do you have a date yet?"

"Oh!" I blinked. "Well, no. But, Bri—"

"So, do you want to go? With me, I mean. I won't be upset if you say no. Not everyone who's queer likes girls."

"I'm not sure if I'm queer, and I like you as a friend, but last time I had an actual date for something, it was a disaster."

"Well, maybe we should organize a stag group."

"Yeah, that'd be awesome. I bet Izzy would be down with that. Lee, too. And if Logan doesn't get his date…"

"Who's he asking?"

"He's probably hoping to get asked. Logan's super-awkward about stuff like that."

"Peep," Ember agreed.

"Me too, Ember." She laughed, her posture and expression more relaxed and easier than I'd seen in a while. "I guess it's library time."

She opened the door and we went inside, where all the grammar and style handbooks we could ever want waited for us.

That night, I walked into the cafeteria intending to chat with Logan and encourage him to ask Dorian to the dance, but he sidetracked me.

"Aliyah, have you heard anything about who poisoned Clementine?"

"What?"

"From Bubbe, I mean."

"No. She hasn't said anything."

"Have you asked her?"

"I haven't." I shook my head, the pit of my stomach dropping as my head got fuzzy and far away. "I feel horrible about it, too."

"You've had other things going on, what with getting pulled out of class and the holiday." He sighed. "But something new happened."

"Oh?"

"Yeah. Lena said she's afraid of getting in trouble about Clementine."

"So that's why she was crying." My hands curled into fists. "She was in the infirmary with us that afternoon. She couldn't have done it."

"Temperance is threatening her anyway. Said she'd get her expelled."

"Where are they?" I stood up.

"Not here." He grabbed my wrist. "Tempe left almost a half-hour ago, but Lena's in the corner with a book."

"I should talk to her." I pulled away and Logan looked past me, a pleading look in his eyes.

"Whoa there, Morgenstern." Dorian shook his head, stepping between me and the rest of the room.

"Sorry, Dorian. Gotta go."

"Not yet." He put a hand on my shoulder, as gentle and soft as the first snowflakes.

"It's important."

"Wait a minute." He sighed. "Please?"

"Okay." I waved at the empty chair beside Logan at the table and got back in my seat. "Step into our office."

Ember fluttered down to the table, peeping softly at Mercy and the gryphon cocked her head, shifting her weight from one foot to the other. Dorian ignored his familiar's discomfort. He turned the chair around and sat down, grinning. Logan nearly melted, but Dorian didn't notice. He stared at me.

Oh, no. Not another inconvenient admirer.

"What are your plans for the December Dance?"

He's smoother than the girl, at least.

Logan stood up and ran out of the cafeteria before I could do or say anything to stop him. Faster than he ever moved on the track in Gym, too.

"Dorian." I groaned. "He likes you, you idiot."

"What?"

"You heard me."

"Impossible. Logan's out of my league."

"Thanks."

"I didn't mean it that way. So, the dance?"

"I'm going stag." I pointed toward the door Logan left by. "Ask *him*!"

"Oh. Right!" Dorian got up and bolted.

I put my head down on my arms, unable to look at Logan's half-empty tray and my nearly full one. I'd clean them up, of course, but I just didn't have the heart at that moment. Ember peeped softly, then climbed on my back and settled against my neck.

"Aliyah Morgenstern?"

"If it's about the December Dance, I'm going stag," I mumbled.

"It's not."

I looked up too far because the person beside the table was almost as short as Hal had been last year. After lowering my gaze, I saw a boy with Dorian's coloring and high cheekbones, but he had a wiry sturdiness my friend did not possess. Then I recognized him.

"Cosmo. From the beach. You're the cat shifter with Blaine Harcourt."

"He wants to see you."

"Really?" I raised my eyebrow, skeptical.

At least it's not about the dance. Blaine's engaged.

"Yeah, really."

"I've got to do something first, though."

"Okay if I tag along?"

"Sure."

I stood up and carried the trays to the dishwashing window, then headed toward Lena with a confused Cosmo in tow. I sat across from her. Cosmo hovered by my elbow.

"Hi there." I let the corners of my mouth turn up but not too much. I didn't want to spook her.

"Hi." She blinked. Her opossum put her paws on the edge of the table and gave me an appraising look. "What is it?"

"I heard Tempe Fairbanks was giving you grief. How can I help?"

"There's nothing you can do since she's my roommate." Lena hung her head. "Why?"

"Because you shouldn't be bullied. You don't deserve that."

"Maybe I do. My element's poison. Clementine was poisoned."

"There's no way you did it."

"Are you sure?" She held the book up, partially obscuring her face. "Because I'm not. Every day she says I did it. That I'm the only person they didn't look at, and it's still unsolved, so it can only be me. Maybe she's right."

"Gaslighting," Cosmo chimed in.

"What?" I blinked.

"Gaslighting. My cousin Tony taught me all about it." He sat beside Lena and put his hand on the table, where she could see it. "The worst kinds of people do gaslighting. They mess with your head, so you don't know what's true."

The opossum sat up in Lena's lap. She leaned over the table, sniffed Cosmo's hand, then looked up at her magus and squeaked. Her fur glowed a faint purple.

"Yeah, Edie," she spoke to her familiar. "You were right."

"Should I have a chat with your roommate?" I asked.

"No." Behind the book, Lena shook her head. "I want out of that room."

"I'll work on that." I cleared my throat. "Also, I'm going stag to the December Dance in a group. You're welcome to join us."

"Really?"

"Yeah. My friends Lee and Izzy will be there. What do you think?"

"Okay."

"Awesome. We'll meet on the third floor by the stairs five minutes before it starts."

We said goodbye, and Cosmo and I left Lena to finish her dinner.

"You're that sure the headmaster will move her room?" he asked.

"Oh, yeah. I'll talk to Hal about it as soon as I've seen Blaine."

"Right, you're friends with his kid." Cosmo nodded. "Makes sense."

"Lead on, then."

Blaine was in the library, which was on extended hours for extramurals. Mrs. Ashford sat behind the desk, looking sleepy. That didn't stop her from giving me a friendly wave as Cosmo brought me to the back corner.

"Mr. Harcourt, you wanted to see me?"

"Yeah." He nodded. "It's about your friend Dorian Spanos."

"What about him?"

"Has he been acting unusual lately?"

"Are you trying to send him back to the Academy? Because if so, I'm leaving."

"No, never." Blaine put his hand over his mouth. "It's a horrible place. Kim still has nightmares about it."

"Okay. I'll do what I can, but he's not my best friend or anything."

"Well, that's sort of the problem."

I blinked.

"He's had trouble with that. Trusting people, I mean."

"Persuading me to buddy up with him won't help."

"It's not about friendship. He overheard something and kept quiet, largely because he doesn't know who to trust here."

"Why you?"

"Kim and I promised to help Dorian and his nephew Cosmo."

"Nephew!" I winced. "Oops."

"Yeah, it's a long and complicated story involving the Under."

"Okay." I nodded. "So, what's this thing Dorian heard?"

"It was about the poor familiar who got poisoned."

"You're telling me because my grandma examined the victim?"

"No. The people he overheard mentioned you."

Lovely.

I must have stayed silent too long for Blaine Harcourt's comfort since he resumed dropping bombs on me.

"Apparently, this duo, or perhaps an entire group, wants to remove all non-magi from campus, which I personally object to. They're willing to kill familiars over it, but first, they want to get rid of all the extramagi."

"All?" I blinked. "There are only two of us."

"The way Dorian put it, there's at least one more—someone with sealed records and influence here. Do you know who it is?"

"No."

"Perhaps Hal Hawkins?"

"Definitely not. He's got a medical condition, pernicious magiglobular anemia. That's the opposite of being an extramagus."

"Hmm." Blaine pulled out a phone that shouldn't have worked in here. Somehow, an app called LORA still functioned. He had a chat window open in seconds through it, with a series of fast replies after he entered what I'd just said. "Lynn says that means his mother's a dhampyr."

"Whoa." I shook my head. "That phone shouldn't work here."

"Yeah, I run with some real geniuses, and this app securely answers a ton of questions. Stuff we've been puzzled about for years."

"Does it have anything to do with why my uncle hasn't been sentenced yet?"

"Your uncle?" He raised an eyebrow.

"You didn't know?" I took a deep breath. "My mom's Richard Hopewell's little sister."

"Had no idea, but it makes sense, magically speaking." He nodded. "Listen, if it's okay with you, I'll tell Dorian to tell you his whole story."

"Go ahead." I nodded. "My grandma won't discuss Clementine, but my friends are trying to stop whoever did it from attacking again."

"We won't be in town much longer." He reached into his pocket, pulled out a card with a phone number on it, and handed it to me. "If you or your friends discover anything, would you mind keeping us informed? I think the connections between Newport and Salem are deeper than we imagined."

"When I'm off campus." I took the card. "I don't have a LORA."

"Right." He nodded. "Take your time, and thanks for meeting with me."

I left, baffled for the rest of the evening by how I could possibly be of any help to a dragon shifter chasing a Ph.D. I wouldn't figure that out until next year.

CHAPTER THIRTY-FIVE

The next day felt like running to stand still. Lecture was an afterthought, but remembering that Dylan was behind on Luciano's topics helped me pay attention for his sake. I shared my notebook with him, focusing enough to take notes. Professor Luciano lectured about the 1920s in Salem.

Bootleggers, rumrunners, and other clandestine operations were part of the local shifter and faerie history, with portals to the Under being used to evade the authorities. Magi stuck to recording the extrahuman secret history. Vampires ministered to patients during the Spanish Flu. A Dr. Brown had saved the most lives during that pandemic.

A few names from liquor-smuggling sounded familiar. Coach Murray's family now owned the Lyceum. The Merlinis and Micellos also rang a bell, but I couldn't place them. I raised my hand.

"Are those last two families still around, Professor?"

"Yes." He nodded. "The Merlinis are more obscure, but the Micellos helped establish Gallows Hill. Bartholomew Micello and Corwin Merlini are on the extramural team from that school."

"Bar and Crow," Dylan murmured. "Huh."

We all tried to blow off steam in Creatives. Dylan went to his corner again with the guitar. He'd gotten good enough that his band had a chance of winning the talent show. I didn't have an inclination toward art, performance or otherwise, but maybe I could help in some other way.

Nobody could see the folks on stage without lights. I jotted a note to Professor Luciano in the notebook about running the lighting booth. Moments later he replied, saying he'd get me in touch with Penelope Andros, the staff member in charge of the stage tech crew.

In Gym, Logan blocked out cheer squad moves with Dorian. Hal took notes and gave critiques. The rest of us practiced Bishop's Row, including orb-conjuring drills. Coach Pickman flat out said she wanted Dylan, Faith, and me to make her proud of the school's team, and Bailey, who was still in our Gym group for some reason, didn't like it. She headed to the showers with her uniform on, sneakers and all.

"What's her problem?" Dorian leaned in the doorway to the gender-neutral section.

"I don't want to know." Faith shook her head.

"You used to be friends," I said.

"I'm still on good terms with Hailey." Faith sighed. "We grew apart, I guess."

The silence felt as awkward as a turtle on its back. I broke it, changing the subject.

"So Dorian, you've got something to tell me?" I put my hands on my hips, hoping he'd talk about what Blaine said he overheard, but he didn't. "What about Logan?"

"What about him?" Dorian raised an eyebrow.

"Did you ask him to the dance?" I tapped my foot.

"Oh my God, tell me you did." Faith put a hand to her cheek. "He's been crushing on you all year."

"I did." Dorian took a deep breath. "He said he'd think about it."

"What?" Faith asked, her head tilting in sync with Seth's. Her familiar seemed as confused as she was.

"I goofed. Asked Aliyah about the dance right in front of him and he ran off." Dorian winced. "Can't blame him."

"I don't know why." I shook my head. "Platonic city over here."

"Grace said I should."

"Honestly?" Faith rolled her eyes. "Follow *your* heart, not Grace's. Is she going with Azrael?"

"No. She hasn't decided yet."

"Huh." Faith narrowed her eyes, probably doing social math in her head. "I could have sworn she had the hots for Az."

"Maybe." I shook my head. "But Grace said she has to date for social reasons, not emotional ones."

"Been there, done that." Dorian pointed at his armpit. "I smell like last week's liverwurst-and-onion sandwich. Better wash up." He walked through the door to the gender-neutral showers.

Faith elbowed me. "We reek almost as much as that. It's shower time."

Bailey cowered in the tiled corner, wrapped in a soaked towel, hair plastered to her face, neck, and shoulders. Her eyes were wide, and she pointed at something hiding in the steam to my right.

"Monster!" Bailey cried. She cradled her waterlogged pigeon familiar, who cowered in the crook of her arm.

I conjured solar magic and looked where she pointed again, expecting to see a spider or insect, but it wasn't anything that benign. Ember reared up, hissing at Temperance's grundylow from my shoulder. It smiled gummily at the bird in Bailey's arms like a frog about to eat a fly.

Seth barked. Faith's nostrils flared.

"Coach Pickman!" I hollered, my hands glowing brighter. "Help!"

I heard the squeak of sneakers on tile, but by the time our coach turned the corner, the grundylow had squeezed himself down the drain.

What it was doing there and why it had terrorized Bailey was beyond me.

You said it—terror. That's the only reason Tempe Fairbanks does anything.

"It's safe, Overton." Coach Pickman clapped her hands. "On your feet."

"I c-can't, coach." She either shuddered or shivered, probably the latter since the water had finally run cold. "It was after Chip." Her familiar cooed, rubbing his head against her cheek. "And he can't even fly."

"Whatever it was, it's gone now. On your feet, Overton. Dry off, tend to your bird. The third-years need the gym in five minutes."

Bailey got up, still shivering. Coach Pickman walked with her to the changing area.

Faith growled as we showered. At first I thought it was Seth, her familiar, expressing her anger, but no. Faith Fairbanks rinsed her hair next to me, sounding like a hellhound.

"I wish I wasn't a Fairbanks anymore." She balled her hands into fists around the towel she'd used to dry tight enough that her knuckles were white. "They do shit like this."

"But why Bailey?" I shut my water off. "And why now?"

"I don't know, but I'm calling her on the carpet. Tonight."

"How can I help?"

"You can't. She's my sister, my responsibility. Maybe I can pin something on her that'll stick. If I don't, she'll only get worse."

"Okay, Faith. Should I tell Hal?"

"I'll do that, but it's Fairbanks territory." She sighed. "Like walking into Mordor. You can't simply walk in."

"At least we got through showering in peace." We got our regular clothes out of the lockers and dressed.

"Yeah. Safer in numbers around water right now." She froze. "Dorian's alone."

We hurried out of the locker room, calling for him.

"Coach Pickman told us what happened and to stick together." Hal stood at the doorway to the gender-neutral area. "I stayed with Dorian."

Faith and I breathed a sigh of relief, then headed into the gym, where Bailey waited with the coach. After hearing her story, the coach wanted us to come with them to the headmaster's office.

We made a formal report, but he said a grundylow's natural habitat included warm, humid places. Unless we could prove Temperance had sent him there with malicious intent, nothing would come of it.

In the lab, we boxed up our gadgets and brought them with our display and the report to the gym. Students hustled to set their tables up. The faculty had assigned our spots, so each project was easily visible. My group finished ahead of the others, but we still had our hurdles.

The delicate communication orbs had to go on stands, or they'd roll off the table. They were made of glass and not magically reinforced, so that was tricky. At least the tables didn't wobble. Once everything was set, I walked around to have a look at the other projects.

On the way, I glanced at a pair by the door. Blaine Harcourt spoke to Hal Hawkins, frowning at Blaine's phone. Blaine tucked the device away and handed Hal a card like the one he'd given me the day before. Blaine went to mingle with the faculty, and Hal left the gym entirely. I stopped at the nearest table.

Only Grace was there. The rest of her group wandered around, up to the same thing I was. She pointed them out, and we waved. I caught her up on my conversation with Blaine and asked about Hal.

"I don't know." She shrugged. "Ask Kitty when you get to their table. Maybe he said something to her. What's got you so curious?"

"Just an impulse to investigate the investigator." I sighed. "Blaine's smart, but he seems out of touch."

"That's a dragon-shifter thing." She nodded. "Why not talk to Dorian?"

"Good idea." I glanced at the cooler on her table. "What did he do for that?"

"It's only ice." Grace sighed. "Literally, that's all. Conjured the cold, but it works. Check it out.

Her group hadn't done as badly as I thought, considering all the arguing. But while the perpetual cooler looked good and worked well, the report on the board had a problem.

"Your pages are out of order."

"No way!" Grace made a little strangled sound. "Dylan and Dorian posted them."

"Here, let's fix it." I took the mixed-up pages down.

Together, we made short work of the problem. After that, we wished each other good luck, and I went on my way.

I spotted Lena hiding behind her group's board with her opossum. Out in front, Alex mumbled something, glancing behind the board at her. I almost walked by and left them to their whispered conversation. But Alex turned his head, and I saw a mark on his neck.

Maybe I shouldn't have cared. Most folks at Hawthorn expected him to have hickeys. He'd been a player before we'd accidentally dated last year, after all. But this looked like a bruise, and he was trying to hide it by popping his collar. That style had been out of fashion for ages. On closer inspection, his futile attempt to cover the mark with makeup was obvious.

"This is good work." I kept my tone neutral, jerking my thumb at the water wheel.

"So what?" He didn't glare as I'd expected. Instead, his eyes scanned the room behind me. "I didn't enchant it."

"The reports look nice. I like the headings, and that font was an awesome choice."

"I had nothing to do with that either."

"Was it Michelina?"

"How do you know her?" He narrowed his eyes, hands on his hips. He met my gaze, but only for a moment. It reminded me of an injured shark I'd seen this summer in the recovery tank at Boston Aquarium.

"Familiar Bonding." Lena peeked out at me, and I gave her a tiny wave. "I spent an entire month with her in there, remember?"

"Stay away from her from now on." The unfriendly expression remained on Alex's face, but his voice lowered to a near whisper. I couldn't figure out why, since Lena was close enough to hear it.

Who's he afraid of? And how can you get him to tell you?

"Are you okay?"

"Why are you talking to me again?" He moved his hands from his hips, crossing them over his chest.

"Everyone's fighting like shas and sphinxes lately. I thought a civil conversation couldn't hurt." I raised an eyebrow, giving him a choice he hadn't bothered offering me the year before. "I'll stop if you can't handle it."

"Get out of here already." He glanced at Lena like he was warning her. She nodded and hid behind the board again.

"All right. Take care of yourself." I walked away, not bothering to look back until I got to the next table over. Lena was entirely hidden from the front, even her feet since the tables all had cloths with skirts.

I didn't want to go over there again, so I just caught her eye, pointed at the project, and gave her a thumbs-up. She grinned. That made the confrontation with Alex worth the trouble.

I stood in front of Noah's table. Their project was a scrying bowl, but they'd gone further than the instructions required. With Noah's solar magic, that made sense. Instead of a crystal bowl with liquid inside, they'd made a liquid crystal screen. Noah's solar magic backlit it so images would show up. It displayed the street outside the Witch's Brew, which bustled with people walking in and out to get coffee during Salem's busiest month.

The images were a step up from black and white but had little in the way of accurate color depiction. It wasn't the type of thing to watch action movies on, but still amazing work for students.

"Wow, Noah. You guys rock."

"Thanks, Aliyah." He grinned. "But I think your orbs will beat our screen."

"How do you figure?"

"We made one device, and somehow you managed six. Three sets of people can communicate on- or off-campus. Or do a conference call. Not too shabby."

"Maybe we went overboard."

"I expected nothing less, with Izzy on your team." He grinned. "She's been overachieving since you two were in diapers."

"I heard Jonah's a lot like that." I grinned back. "He's academically threatening, according to her."

"He says the same thing." Noah shrugged. "I think they're about even."

"Can I tell her you said that?"

"I guess, if that will help her feel better." Noah blushed and studied his fingernails, which were a metallic shade of green. "But I'm biased. I happen to think very highly of Jonah."

"Oh?" I raised my eyebrow.

"You caught me." He looked at the project board instead of my face. "I have a tiny crush. No big deal."

"All right." I nodded, realizing that my brother minimizing anything this much meant it was colossal.

"See you at dinner?"

"Maybe."

"All right." I headed toward my table because the judges would be by soon. For a moment, when I turned, I could hardly believe my eyes.

The floor in the gym seemed to shimmer like someone had covered it with a sheet of glass.

Or water.

"Shut up, you." I put my hand over my mouth. When I blinked, the strange sheen had vanished. Fortunately, so had the Evil Inside Voice. I joined my team without further incident.

We greeted the adults who came by. As the dinner bell rang, we left them to the task of testing and judging our work.

CHAPTER THIRTY-SIX

I waited in line for my pumpernickel sandwich. I already had iced tea because I wasn't in the mood for beverage roulette. Since I had been one of the last people out of the gym, I peered into the crowded dining room, trying to decide where to sit.

One thing I'd never liked about middle school was the segregation into cliques. At Hawthorn, despite the bullying situation, we hadn't had that dynamic last year. Bailey had been the only one who got catty.

This year, it wasn't as easy. With Dylan and Dorian's rivalry, plus Grace spread thinner than too little butter on toast, we'd lost our cohesion. I glanced at the exit, wondering why I hadn't grabbed a dinner bag from Penelope's window.

But I didn't want to be alone. My family was close-knit, and it saddened me to think my friendships at Hawthorn hadn't followed the same pattern.

I wondered again if Bubbe had new information about Clementine, and if she'd tell me. She'd helped last year with Hal's condition, but this time the police were involved. Maybe she couldn't say much.

My order was up, so I put the plate with my sandwich, fries, and pickles on my tray. I decided to sit with Faith and Hal to ask about Blaine.

"He asked about my time in the infirmary." He moved broccoli around on his plate with the fork. "If I'd heard anything about Clementine. And yeah, I know you mentioned magiglobular anemia to him."

"Sorry." Ember snored on my shoulder.

"It's a good thing." Faith patted Seth, who'd poked his head out of her bag to peer at the drowsy dragonet. "Hal shouldn't be ashamed of his illness, and those Tinfoil Hat people are supposed to be geniuses."

"Right." Hal nodded. "Maybe they can help."

"So, what did you tell him?"

"Not much." He shook his head. "Information's locked down. Nurse Smith and Zeke don't talk about it, and Dad's a space magus, so he can hide records in places even I can't find them."

"I'm worried about someone else getting hurt." I sighed, remembering the marks on Alex's neck. Should I tell them?

Would they care? I doubt it. Don't bother.

I blinked, about to defy the Evil Inside Voice. Of course they'd care. Hal spoke up first, and if we weren't all magi at that table, I'd have suspected he was an empath.

"There *is* someone we ought to keep an eye on." Hal glanced at Faith.

"Right." She nodded. "Alex."

"Explain."

"He's the weakest link in Tempe's chain." Hal finally took a bite of broccoli, mostly because Nin kept nudging his fork hand toward it.

"I saw something at the gym." I told them about his odd behavior and the aura of fear around him. And the mark.

"It's worse than I thought." Faith crossed her arms over her chest, her voice quiet and her face pale. "Tonight can't come soon enough."

"I know we talked about this after Gym." Hal put his hand on her arm. "But you shouldn't go alone."

"I'm not bringing anyone." She shook her head. "Her familiar's a horror show, and I won't expose my friends to that kind of danger."

"What about Seth?" I put my hands in the table, leaning forward. "Aren't you worried about him? That grundylow's twice his size."

"I've got to bring him." She shook her head. "Without Seth, I don't have enough magic, not even after all the Bishop's Row practice."

"Ember, will you go with Seth? Be his wingwoman?"

"Peep!" She hopped down from my shoulder, landing on the table to pick her way carefully around the trays. When she reached the other side, she snaked her head under the table and peeped again. Seth answered with a bark and a wagging tail, his blue tongue lolling out of his mouth.

"Yeah, okay. She can come."

"That's better. What about Nin?" Hal asked.

"No." Faith covered Hal's hand with her own. "If it goes sideways, Ember can't carry both of them to safety."

"Do you know a psychic who can scry? I'd feel better with someone watching."

"I have a better idea." I grinned. "If Faith can wait until after the magipsychic fair."

"The communication orbs!" Faith smirked. "Genius!"

"Great. I'll smuggle a set out of the gym later."

We switched to cheerier topics, like the talent show in November and the December Dance. Hal's appetite returned, and he finished enough broccoli for Nin to stop squeaking at him.

Before we knew it, the dinner hour ended, and we headed back to the gym.

On returning to the gym, my stomach churned as if dinner was an entire glass of milk instead of a stomach-settling sandwich. The scene beyond the doors vindicated my rebellious gut immediately.

I'd imagined water all over the floor. Now a giant puddle stretched between the two rows of tables. How had it happened? Had the judges gotten in a fight? No. They had been in the cafeteria for the second half of dinner. The vandal had struck while the gym was empty.

"Our table!" I ran ahead, Faith on my heels. She'd seen the same thing.

The board wasn't damp, it was totally drenched. Ink on the posted report's pages had smudged and smeared, barely legible, but that wasn't all. We'd arranged the orbs in a circle, gleaming softly under the gym's lighting. Only three remained, and one had an enormous crack on its side. Purple-tinted shards littered the floor in front of the table.

"We've been sabotaged." Faith stood with her hands in fists, arms tight against her sides, nostrils flaring. Seth growled nonstop.

"Looks like it." Brianna stepped up beside me, peering at the remains of the orbs on the table. "There's no glamour. This was no changeling or faerie."

"This little mermaid says water magic." Cadence wrinkled her nose. "Ugh, it reeks like a bog."

"Temperance, or her little gremlin." Izzy's teeth squeaked as she ground them.

"It's a grundylow. Gremlins are kind of sweet, actually." I sighed.

"Pure faeries, not familiar material." Brianna nodded. "You really think they're sweet?"

"Nicer than the gnomes I've met," I answered.

"Don't geek out. This is a disaster." Faith glared down at the mess. "I'm getting the headmaster."

She stormed toward where he stood with his mouth wide open. I didn't have time to watch them talk or go listen. Instead, I grabbed a cardboard box and started collecting glass shards with Brianna and Izzy. Cadence refused to touch the water, so she rummaged through her backpack, looking for the rough draft of our report.

"Did anyone take any pictures?" Brianna asked.

I shook my head. "Mundane smartphones are pointless here. We're only allowed to call home in the office."

"Draconian much?" Brianna sighed. "Should've taken a Polaroid, but I was waiting to see if we won something. That won't happen now. Mom's going to cry."

"That sucks, Brianna. I'm sorry."

"Not to worry." We both turned to find Blaine Harcourt walking up behind us. "I took pictures of everything with LORA."

"Who's Laura?" Brianna asked.

"You mean, 'What's LORA,'" He corrected. "It's Kim's magipsychic app that tracks coincidence. I'll send you what I took. Brianna Collins, is it? From Gallows Hill?"

"Yeah, thanks."

"Don't thank me yet. At least one of your professors won't accept snapshots for the written portion. Aliyah needs a copy of your report." Blaine shook his head.

"But Professor Luciano's a good guy." I blinked.

"Are we both seriously talking about Filberto Luciano?" Blaine blinked. "He's an old friend of my mother's, who's not exactly a ray of sunshine. I'm grossly understating here."

"I've heard of Hertha Harcourt." I nodded. "But Luciano's been nothing but kind to me."

"He's got reasons." Blaine studied his fingernails.

"Which are?"

"That's his story to tell." Blaine gave us a golf wave. "I've got to rejoin the other judges. Good luck with old Filberto. I sincerely hope he doesn't make you rewrite your report."

"Maybe you should talk to him now." Brianna jerked her chin at the professor, who'd joined the conversation between the headmaster and Faith. "I'll get the rest of that glass."

"Thanks."

I walked toward them, but the group broke before I got there. Faith met me halfway.

"Are you okay?" She peered at me. "You look like you've seen a ghost."

"No ghosts, but Blaine said he thinks we'll have to rewrite our report."

"What? Why?"

"Apparently, he knows Professor Luciano."

"That's weird."

"Not so much." I shrugged. "Dragons never look the age they are."

"We can ask about the report later." Faith continued toward our wrecked project. "Let's group up before the judges hand out scores." She sighed, hanging her head. The noise she made was somewhere between a laugh and a sob.

"At least they saw it before. Hopefully, they remember it fondly." Azrael initiated a group hug in front of the table.

"I can't believe this happened. We worked so hard," Izzy moaned.

"I know." Cadence sounded like she'd lost a puppy. "This was the best I ever scienced in my entire life, and there's no proof."

"Two orbs still standing, Cadence." Azrael pointed. "That's proof, right?"

"About those orbs, guys." I winced. "I kind of need to borrow them later if that's okay?"

"I guess." Cadence sighed. "Easy come, easy go."

Headmaster Hawkins made his way around the room, pacing past each table. Before he got to us, Coach Pickman hurried over with a sponge but no bucket. Somehow, it absorbed all the water and sat more heavily in her hand.

"Maybe she's born with it, maybe it's magipsych," she muttered, walking toward the locker room with the sponge.

Finally, the headmaster stopped at our table. He sighed, shaking his head.

"This is an awful shame."

"When will we find out how this happened?" Cadence put a hand on her hip, tilting her head to deliver her best fish-eye. "Inquiring minds want to know."

"It might take us some time to answer that question."

"What happens to whoever did this?" Izzy raised an eyebrow. "Will they get expelled?"

"Yes, if it was intentional, but it's possible a familiar did this. In that case, we send the magus and their companion to Familiar Bonding."

"Well, okay." Izzy shrugged. "I guess not every critter is as well-behaved as Ember."

"Izzy, that was rude." I elbowed her. "And Ember's no angel. I trust Headmaster Hawkins to do the right thing."

"Thank you for your vote of confidence, Miss Morgenstern," he said, reaching into the large brown envelope tucked into the crook of his arm, "And I will present you with this." He pulled out a red ribbon and handed it to her.

"We won?" Cadence blinked. "But our project got ruined!"

"It wasn't ruined when we looked at it earlier, and one of the categories was teamwork, which the lot of you amply demonstrated."

"Wow." Brianna pinched herself. "The only time I ever won before was at sports."

"That's second place, Miss Collins." He gestured at another table. "Top honors go to Logan Pierce's group. Their group dynamic was, shall we say, more challenging than yours."

"Thanks, Headmaster." Faith smiled. "It's a relief after all this, you know." She waved a hand at the ruined project

"You're welcome, Miss Fairbanks." He glanced at the two remaining orbs. "You'll have to turn those over to Professor Luciano tomorrow morning. He's responsible for storing all the devices."

"Okay." I nodded, opening my bag and reaching for the orbs. He cleared his throat.

"Since communication orbs are not permitted in the dormitory, they must remain in the gym overnight."

"I understand." I tucked my hands behind my back, crossing my fingers.

In the end, I got help with the orb-smuggling operation. Grace's umbral magic made it almost too easy.

CHAPTER THIRTY-SEVEN

Dog's Night
Faith

I tied my hair back with the elastic Aliyah had lent me. She said it was lucky and I hoped it was true. I'd need that in spades.

"Come on, Seth. We've got work to do."

Placing the orb carefully in the bottom of a frilly oversized tote bag, I thanked the gods its styling hid the glass device inside. Seth went in with it, of course.

Hiding a forbidden activated communication orb with Hal and Aliyah listening at the other end was easy, and getting my sister alone wouldn't be difficult. Confronting her was like throwing rocks at a beehive when you had a severe sting allergy. I knew I'd have to be my own rescue medication someday, which was why I swam every night and busted my ass at Bishop's Row.

My parents sucked. They thought magi should rule the world, and they'd raised my sisters and me to climb the last few rungs of magi high society. They wanted nothing less than our family gaining more prestige than blue-blooded dragon shifters.

Charity was subtle and cautious, passing the buck and blame

whenever possible. For a while, they considered my directness refreshing, but that was before Temperance's first use of water magic in front of our parents. She'd sabotaged Charity's bonding process and scared the baby pricus off. Our sister ended up with a sand cat, which was below parental expectations. Then Temperance had turned around and bonded with Precious, her rare grundylow before I'd even met Seth.

So of course, Tempe became their favorite.

I discovered my blood relations weren't normal, let alone loving when I started at Hawthorn. Hal Hawkins had changed my entire life for the better, giving me a chance at a chosen family. I refused to let my sadistic sister screw that up.

In front of Tempe's room, I made the tightest fist I could and hammered the door. I shocked my knuckles on the solid wood, imagining myself an officer of the law come to bring justice.

"Who is it?"

"Faith. Open the door, Michelina."

Seth added a short, sharp bark, punctuating my request. She opened the door a crack, peering out so I only saw a forelock of mousy brown hair and one amber eye.

"*She* won't like that. What if she's angry? I don't want to be here for that."

"You could go to the library. Just let me in."

"Oh." She blinked, opening the door wider. "Hadn't thought of that."

"Thanks." I held the door, pointing at the pink-nosed critter behind her. "Take your opossum. I don't want either of you in range."

That distracted Lena long enough for Ember to fly into the room and perch on a rafter above the chandelier.

"In range of what?" She gathered the bundle of gray fur into her arms.

"Anything." I stepped aside to let her pass. "Earshot, line of sight, melee. You name it."

"Why?" She paused in the doorway.

"Because I know what she's been doing."

"How?" Lena's eyes widened. She turned, backing away from me into the hall.

"I have my ways." If Michelina wanted to believe I had omniscient psychic friends, I wouldn't contradict her. I had my own hunches anyway, and if I was lucky, Lena might say too much.

"She shouldn't have done it." Lena blinked. "I told her someone would find out."

"You were right. Now, skedaddle already." I waved my hands, shooing her into the hall. She scurried away.

I stepped in and closed the door firmly. Seth poked his nose out of the bag, pointing it at my sister's bed. I sauntered over, sat on it, wriggled a bit, and then reached under the mattress and pulled the hidden item out.

"Too predictable." I rolled my eyes at the journal.

Before I could open the book, it seemed to change shape and I dropped it.

It tumbled from my hands, my fingers suddenly slippery, as though it were made of ice. It bounced once, then vanished in the shadows under Lena's bed.

I peered under to confirm my earlier hunch and saw nothing but a dust bunny. It had to be a magipsychic device, though I couldn't be certain it was the one I most feared.

Temperance could have put together an extra toy on the side during Lab, but my sister couldn't enchant multi-element gadgets without friends, which she'd never make. All the same, I hoped the diary was a first-year-level charm. The alternative, that she'd smuggled a weapon used by war criminals onto our campus, was worse.

Behind me, she cleared her throat.

"The simplest explanation's probably true." I stood, turning the shoulder with the tote on it toward the wall behind me. "Hello, Tempe."

"So, you're not completely stupid. Maybe this won't be boring." My sister stepped out of her wardrobe, brushing a stray scarf off her shoulder. She tittered. "There. I'm out of the closet."

"You're straight, Tempe." Blunt instruments worked best on her.

"At least I'm not attracted to anemic little halfbreeds." She sneered.

"You're with Alex Onassis, and you criticize my taste in men?"

"Your beau won't make it to manhood. Hopefully, he dies before knocking you up and diluting our bloodline."

"Enough about boys. Let's talk about screwed-up magipsychic devices."

"I'm not done with *men* yet." She sniggered. "I'm using Alex, of course, but better than the way Grace used Dorian. He doesn't like how rough I play with him."

"That's abuse. The second I have proof, you're getting expelled."

"Proof of what? He's almost twice my size. Surely, if anyone's abused, it's me."

"You disgust me."

"Same." She laughed. "I hope you're grossed out by good old Grace, too. Power-coupling with a sissy is so last century."

"She dumped him. Copy that part."

"Alex must learn his place. I'll keep him, even though my real boyfriend is a way better smash."

"The imaginary studly boyfriend story again." I rolled my eyes. "Cut the crap. You heard me talking to Lena. I know what you did."

"You're bluffing."

"Prove it."

"I've got a pure element so I don't have to, but nobody trusts an undeath-dealing freak like you. Too bad Mommy didn't leave you in the bath as an infant."

She stepped forward, grinning, hands up. I knew what came next because she'd threatened me with drowning more times than I could count, so I held my hands up, palms out, fingers slightly curled the way Coach Pickman had taught us in Gym. And I conjured.

Seth whined in my bag, lending me strength as I pulled more undeath energy.

I wasn't sure it had worked, not until the water draped down six inches in front of me like a liquid sheet instead of over my nose and mouth. I'd never blocked her before and had spent years subjected to her whims, which generally consisted of "training" me to guard against her attacks.

Temperance only struck when something else hadn't gone her way.

It had felt strange, being an older sister afraid of the younger for so long. In books and movies, abuse came from bigger hands belonging to someone older. None of it looked like my experience, not until Aliyah told me about Alex. Maybe this battle wasn't just about Lena, the ruined project, or the poisoned familiar.

"What in Hades do you think you're doing, Faith?" Temperance snarled.

"Standing up." That was all I could muster through the strain of conjuring.

"I had no particular beef with you until tonight. Why bother?"

"Nobody deserves how you treat them, not even an ambitious twat like Alex."

"I already said I never hurt him." She batted her eyelids, her grin through the water reminding me of a corpse in a pond.

"Who bruised his neck, then? You can't lash out at me like at home, so he's your new scapegoat?"

"You're remembering things wrong." She snorted. "You're bigger than me. You must be crazy, accusing me of that."

"Bullshit." I struggled to take a breath. "I know what you are."

Seth whined again, trembling inside the bag. He was worried, and rightly so. All that talking had cracked my defense. Water splashed through, crashing against my shirt and drenching me from neck to toe.

I took a deep breath, focusing to conjure another orb. This time I spread my hands farther apart, hoping to protect more than just my face. I wouldn't put it past her to attack Seth. She'd almost killed him once.

"Get that mangy mutt, Precious." Temperance jerked a thumb at my familiar.

The grundylow crept out of her hair. She'd hid him in there since the day they bonded. I still couldn't believe she'd watched *Lord of the*

Rings and decided Precious was the perfect name for her familiar. And she called *me* a freak.

Any self-respecting magus or critter would dodge my energy. Grundylows had an affinity for both water and undeath, so he didn't care. Seth knew I couldn't hold both Temperance and her familiar off.

He leaped from the bag, glancing at the ceiling as he went. Seth was smart and knew I had to keep the orb intact. As fearful as he was at times, that sha was a fighter. He'd endured Tempe for years beside me, and this time, he had backup.

"Mount-Doom his slimy ass," I managed.

Our familiars circled each other, exchanging blows just once before Ember made her move. She swooped down, scooping Seth off the floor. Precious gibbered below, shaking one webbed fist at them. She alighted with him on top of Lena's wardrobe, where he sat growling down at the grundylow, whose hands were too slick to climb the varnished surface.

"You could just admit you're crazy and leave." Temperance glanced at the door and smiled at me. "I'd let you go."

"No. You're gonna stop."

"What? I did nothing wrong. You made Lena let you into *my* room and brought that flappy lizard inside."

"Everything. You'll stop now before anyone else gets hurt." I shook my head. "You can fool everyone else, but not me. I know what you're capable of. You're not allowed to terrorize this campus. I was here first."

"Charity was here first and gave *me* her blessing, not you. Because you're weak, freak." She snickered. "But for laughs, let's hear your deluded demands. Go on."

It amazed me how effortless it was for her, not lying but conjuring so much water. It exhausted me, defending myself and the truth, but I got a reprieve. She banished her water and put her hands in her pockets, tapping her foot like I was a joke. Or worse, an inconvenience.

"Dump Alex. Confess to wrecking the magipsych project, and don't mess with any living thing on this campus. That includes your roommate and all the familiars."

"He won't let me dump him, I had nothing to do with it, and I don't mess with people."

"Here's an example. You brought that illegal gadget in here, didn't you?"

"What gadget?" She snorted.

"The one from our basement."

"I never saw anything like that."

"You were with me when I found it."

"More delusions."

And just like that, I wasn't sure. It was years ago when we were in elementary school. Maybe I remembered it wrong, but I couldn't let Tempe use this tactic. I'd seen her skewer Charity with it.

I chose another weapon: decency on someone else's behalf.

"Lena's terrified of you. Stop scaring her."

"It's not my fault she's afraid to live with someone powerful."

"Our parents are loaded. Apply for a single. Leave her in peace, and break up with Alex. Smash your real boyfriend instead or whatever."

"If I dumped Alex, he'd kill himself." She giggled. I ignored how sick that was.

"You expect me to believe that?" I snorted. But if I was right and she had the device, she might be telling the truth. What if it did mind magic?

"He'll do anything I say." Her smile resembled a bleached skull. "Unlike the hot messes you keep around. They barely do things your way."

I couldn't take any more of my toxic sister. Charity had teased Aliyah last year because her uncle was evil. Tempe was at least as bad, maybe worse. If subtle, scheming Charity hadn't noticed, nobody else in my family would see it either.

"They're friends, not a Burger King franchise." I sneered. "Coincidence will catch up with you, and nobody will be on your side when it does."

"Get out of my room."

I raised my arms, and Ember swooped down to place Seth into them. She perched on my shoulder as I tucked him back into my bag.

In the doorway, I turned my head and looked over my shoulder at Tempe.

"Last chance. Cut the crap."

"I was right. You know nothing." She gave me a golf wave. "Talk, talk, least of my sisters."

She slammed the door behind me. Ember peeped on my shoulder, shifting her weight from one foot to the other. I didn't know much about dragonets, so I couldn't decipher her behavior, but Seth whimpered.

"What's wrong?" I got on the stairs and called out my floor, then checked on him.

His tongue lolled out of his mouth, its usual light blue color a darker shade. It looked swollen, too. He kept sticking it out, opening and closing his mouth, and his breath came fast and ragged, like chiffon shredding under a set of claws.

"I'll take care of you." I got off the stairs, prepared to head for Aliyah's room, but she was already in the hall, running like she knew I had an emergency. Because of the orb, I thought.

"Faith, we've got to get Seth to Bubbe's right now."

"Why?"

"Because I know those symptoms. He's been poisoned."

"It's past curfew, and the headmaster won't let us leave." I whispered, "And the orb, probation. You could get expelled."

"I don't care." Aliyah grabbed my hand, leading me toward the stairs. We got on for the first floor, but she kept walking, pulling me with her.

As we reached the hall that led to the street, Headmaster Hawkins appeared in front of us with a pop that would have startled me last year. Now I was used to space magic.

"Where are you going?"

"It's an emergency, Seth needs a vet right away."

"Let me see."

I held my familiar up for the headmaster. He took one look at my sha and opened the door for me, but he stopped Aliyah.

"Miss Morgenstern, you're staying on campus."

"Okay. Sorry, Faith. Remember, you're never alone."

I couldn't figure out why she'd said that or given in so easily until I remembered the orb in my bag. She and Hal would be with me all the way to her grandmother's. I hurried down Essex Street toward the extraveterinary office.

Doctor Morgenstern answered the door as I rang a second time. Her pastel-green hair stood up a little on one side. I'd almost forgotten about those random whimsical color choices. She held a cotton swab and a plastic vial in one hand.

"Did the headmaster tell you?"

"Yes." She rubbed the swab against Seth's muzzle, picking up some green foam, then put it in the vial. "Go straight back to the first room on the left."

I followed her orders immediately—a side effect of growing up in an unpredictably cruel family, I guess. I might have reacted quickly, regardless. Seth's life was on the line.

In the exam room, I set the bag on the table with Seth still inside. He'd been sick in there, and his fur was slippery with it. I turned, looking around for something to help get him out of the bag. Doctor Morgenstern had everything under control. She handed me a flannel blanket. I swaddled Seth and placed him on the table. He laid down on his side, panting heavily, more green foam around his mouth.

I stayed beside Seth, stroking his back, hoping these weren't his last moments. The doctor set the vial on the counter, the liquid inside turning purple. After washing her hands, she reached into a refrigerator under the counter, producing a syringe and a vial of medicine. Doctor Morgenstern unwrapped the syringe, stuck the needle in, and drew up a dose.

I watched, not nearly as fascinated as Aliyah might be. I used to consider medical practice squicky and bedside manner a display of weakness. My time with Hal as he managed his illness made me understand it took strength to seek help and to give it kindly. Everything good in my life would never have happened without Seth. Our bond was my first experience with love and care. I couldn't lose him now.

"Don't worry, Faith." Doctor Morgenstern put her hand on Seth's head behind his ear, which drooped instead of sitting straight up like usual. "It's the same poison that made Clementine sick, and this is the antidote. He'll make a full recovery, but I need you to hold him while I administer it."

I nodded, leaning over Seth and wrapping my arms around him. He kicked his feet, all four of them, struggling against the toxin. When the needle went in he whimpered, jerking a few times before lying still. I looked up at Doctor Morgenstern, sniffling.

"Is he okay?"

"Seth's okay. Listen to his breathing."

She was right. His body had stilled, but Seth's breathing had become even and measured, though slower than usual. He rolled his eye to meet my gaze and gave one more whimper, then wagged his long tail under the blanket. I kissed the top of his head. He licked my hand and closed his eyes. A series of snores made me hope he'd be okay.

"Thanks, Dr. Morgenstern."

"Any time."

"This is my fault." I stood, staring at my increasingly blurry hands. "I shouldn't have got into it with Tempe."

"Would you mind discussing that with me?"

"If it'd help Seth." I sniffled, embarrassed by the waterworks.

"I think so."

"Can I use your bathroom first?"

"Of course." She nodded. "I'll clean Seth up, make tea, and meet you in the kitchen."

"I'd rather have it here."

"Understood. I'll see you in a few minutes."

The little washroom was spartan and tidy. I'd gotten some of Seth's vomit and foam on me, so I washed my hands, arms, face, and even a section of my hair. Paper towels and soap took care of the spots on my shirt, which would go directly into the laundry as soon as I returned to campus.

But should I go back there? Shouldn't I insist on staying here? I knew Aliyah's grandma had a spare room, but I didn't want to ask for too much.

I headed back. Seth was clean, dry, and wrapped in a fresh blanket. She'd set up a folding table. The tea tray sat atop it, bearing a pot with a yellow cozy, two cups with saucers, and all the fixings.

I'd expected all of that, but not Doctor Morgenstern holding the communication orb. My bag was upside down in the exam room sink, still damp but dripping dry. That explained how she'd found it.

I froze in the doorway, wondering if she'd tell the headmaster. I'd get suspended, or worse, get Aliyah expelled.

"I thought it was bad, but not like this." She gazed at the device. Shapes moved across its surface, distorted from my side. I stepped beside her, trying to get a better look.

"That's my sister." I blinked. "But how?"

"Someone set it to record." She set it on the end of the table with Seth, who was nestled in extra blankets.

"Too bad it erases on replay. My Magipsych Fair group won second place with that orb. And I didn't toggle record." I glanced at the wall, lying to protect Hal and Aliyah. "I'm not sure who did."

"Seth's smart enough for that." She set the orb down in a nest of blankets. "You need to talk to someone, Faith."

"Tempe's the one who needs a shrink."

"She'll never admit that because she can't be honest. Do you know what gaslighting is?"

"Yes." I rolled my eyes. "Seriously, Doc. I'm seventeen, not seven."

"Nice sarcasm you've got there." She raised an eyebrow. "But this is serious. Temperance will continue making you doubt. That's why you need help."

"I don't need therapy."

"It's more than that." Dr. Morgenstern poured tea for herself, then held the pot over my cup and paused.

"Yes, please." I didn't want to have this conversation, but she'd saved Seth's life. The least I could do was listen.

"You need a record, corroborated by someone who believes you. I'm not talking about Hal either. Have you told him about Temperance?"

"I toned it down." I stared down at my tea, reluctant to sweeten it like maybe I didn't deserve it. "Didn't want to scare him away."

"You're standing by your boyfriend through a debilitating illness. Do you think a toxic family will scare him off?" She leaned back, holding her cup between tented fingers.

"Okay, you've got a point. But if his dad finds out, he might make us break up."

"Why do you think that?"

"Don't all parents keep the 'wrong sort' away from their kids?"

"There's no one way parents act. Most teach their children how to avoid harm, but yours didn't, and you don't seem to think they'll change. You need an adult to confide in."

"Headmaster Hawkins is the only therapist at school."

"Talk to me, then." She sipped tea. "I've got a license."

"If Mom and Dad find out I'm talking to a counselor—" I couldn't finish the sentence.

"Make appointments for Seth." She nodded in his direction. "He'll need regular checkups after this."

"Where'd the poison come from, anyway? I mean, you saw Seth tangle with Precious. Are grundylows poisonous all of a sudden?"

"No. All I can say is that this poison originates from a mountain town in northern Italy."

"Oh." I blinked. "Like Michelina. And Professor Luciano. Do you think they know each other?"

"Your sister's roommate?"

I nodded.

"I didn't know where she was from." She sighed. "My work on this case is limited by how much information the authorities give me, which isn't much. So thank you."

"My help backfires like I'm Hurricane Faith."

"I've felt like Hurricane Mildred before. Chaos is part of life. Feelings are always valid since they belong to you. How you act on them is your choice. I told Aliyah as much last year."

"Did it help her?"

"I'd like to think so, but I only give advice. It's up to the listener to take it or leave it."

"Can I bring Seth back on campus tonight?"

"He needs more care and observation. I discussed it with the headmaster when he told me you were coming."

"I don't want to leave him alone."

"I'll stay with him."

"That seems impossibly kind."

"Kindness is never impossible, but I think you know that."

"Maybe." I sniffled, the tears returning because she was right.

I made a second trip to the bathroom and washed my face, unashamed this time. Doctor Morgenstern acted like crying was the most natural thing in the world, and maybe it was.

She didn't want me walking home alone, so she called Aliyah's father down from upstairs, and he accompanied me back to campus. As I headed inside and up the stairs with the orb hidden in my still damp bag, I realized something.

My parents were wrong about practically everything, but I didn't have to follow in their footsteps. The most profound lesson for me at Hawthorn was rediscovering hope. It had become a dusty artifact locked away in the battered Seward chest in my mind.

Remembering where I came from was important, but understanding I could move beyond it was even more so.

It was after lights out when I knocked on Aliyah's door to give the orb back. She snuck out of the room with Grace, using Umbral magic to put it back in the gym. I didn't go, even though they offered. I'd had more than enough danger that night.

Back in my room, Kitty was already asleep with her sphinx curled up on the pillow beside her. I thought I'd have trouble sleeping without Seth, but exhaustion blessed me with thankfully dreamless sleep.

CHAPTER THIRTY-EIGHT

Aliyah

I was relieved to see Faith return to campus, but not because of the orbs or even that utterly brutal fight with Tempe. It was all about how magi shared their lives with familiars.

When Ember's wing was injured, I'd been a mess, and I hadn't even officially bonded with her yet. I couldn't imagine how it was for Faith, who'd had Seth for years before school started. Grace understood that well.

"I'll check on her tomorrow before breakfast." Grace turned down her bed. "Are you in?"

"Absolutely." I helped a sleepy Ember off my shoulder.

"Was it Temperance? Who poisoned Clementine, I mean."

"I can't imagine how." I got in my bed. "But she had to be involved."

"How do you figure?" She kicked off her new slippers. Bunnies, of course. Lune shook his ears at them until Grace helped him up to the foot of her bed.

"Seth got poisoned in her room. Remember how Charity never got her hands dirty? Maybe Tempe's using a similar strategy. It fits Blaine's theory, too."

"Blaine Harcourt?" She sat.

"He thinks there's more than one person involved here." I filled Grace in on my conversation with Blaine in the library.

"That's messed up." She shook her head. "And yeah, she has access to other powers, but we can't do much to find out how. Faith shouldn't go this alone."

"So we help like you guys did last year when I went solar on the Bishop's Row court."

"Yeah. And last winter, how you stuck with me. You're a good friend."

"So are you, Grace."

"That's a topic for another time. Goodnight, Aliyah."

Before I dropped off to sleep, I said a small silent prayer that Seth would recover quickly.

The next morning, we waited outside Faith's room until she emerged for breakfast. We stuck to her like glue for the rest of the day. In Lecture, I sat in the middle row with her instead of in front. At lunch, Bubbe walked Seth in on a leash. She took it off his collar and he bounded straight to Faith, hopping into her lap to sniff her plate. She gave him some scraps, thanking Bubbe.

In Creatives, everybody talked about the talent show, which was the next extramural event. Over a month would go by since it happened after Thanksgiving, but that didn't dampen our excitement.

Dylan practiced the song he'd done with Noah at Sukkot, along with other songs by Fleetwood Mac, Noah's most recent retro music binge-fest. His skill improved every time I heard him play.

Grace sketched another entire set of outfits, slated for the crafts fair at the end of the year. She sat with Faith, asking her opinion on colors.

"It's a shame you can't make dresses on stage." Faith pointed at one design, a purple ombre suit with a peplum jacket and pencil skirt. "This one's super-sophisticated."

"What about a fashion show?" Logan asked.

"That's not a valid act for this contest." She sighed. "So what if I'm not performing anything? I'm busy enough."

"I'm doing everyone's makeup." Kitty grinned. "Maybe you can help in the dressing room or something."

"What about you, Aliyah?" Logan asked.

"The lights," I said, "Someone's got to make sure everyone sees you."

"Well, I won't be standing in them," Logan deadpanned. "I'm a recovering performance artist, remember?" He grinned as everyone laughed.

"More room for me then, my dude." Dorian peered at the sketch on Logan's easel. "I'm doing a standup routine."

"But you're not funny." Logan peered up, blinking slowly. Yeah, he was milking it, but we all laughed again anyway.

"You should really do the act with me, Logan, although I'm not sure I can call you a straight man."

My mouth dropped open. In all the drama over the Magicpsych Fair and Faith's misadventures, I had forgotten all about Dorian's plight with the December Dance.

"Are you guys going to the December Dance together?" Kitty clasped her hands together.

"If I'm lucky," Dorian replied.

"I don't know." Logan turned his easel, but not before I caught him blushing. "Still thinking about it."

Dorian moped, so Kitty left them alone about it. "What about you, Aliyah?"

"I'm going stag in a group."

"Sounds fun! Better tell Lee. He'd be all over that."

"He is. So's Izzy."

We all got back to our projects except for Dorian, who hung around nearby, pointedly not whittling the piece of wood he held.

"What's up, Dorian?"

"Do you think he'll forgive me?"

"I don't know."

"Well, can you put in a good word? I mean, you *are* his best friend."

That was interesting.

"He said that?"

"Says. All the time." Dorian sighed. "Please? I'd owe you big time."

"Maybe. Dorian, can you tell me what you overheard the day Clementine got poisoned?"

"Scaly Spice told me you might ask about that."

"Ha!" I put my hand over my mouth. "You seriously call him that?"

"Not to his face. Anyway, yeah. I'll talk to you about that day. In private."

"That's fine." I nodded. "Now, why not actually carve something?"

I showed Dorian the whittling tools, demonstrating what I'd learned while working on my misshapen figurine until the bell rang.

Lab was an uneventful observation of the botanical experiment from the day before. The tiny seedling hadn't grown much either, which meant tomorrow would be more of the same. I almost wished Professor Luciano hadn't taken it easy on us after the Magicpsych Fair, but I couldn't blame him. We'd all worked extremely hard and done excellent work, according to his comments on our reports.

During the rest of the week, Dylan haunted the café. He hung around the place way too much, considering he barely worked there anymore. Maybe he missed it, but every time I asked about it, he talked about the Lyceum instead.

Portia was still there, managing everything. Dylan said she was a total taskmistress, but it was good money. I asked if he'd seen Crow, but the bird shifter hadn't been to the restaurant during Dylan's shifts.

He never discussed the extramagus test, and neither did I. It hung unspoken between us like a floral wreath from a long-forgotten funeral service. Our conversations weren't easy anymore, though he'd dropped his grudge against Dorian. Neither of us seemed able to find the right words, and I wasn't even sure what I wanted him to know.

That you're into him, of course.

The Evil Inside Voice was right, but I couldn't say something like that. Dylan kept getting knocked down, like a small craft in a stormy sea. Confessing my feelings could be another wave, one that might capsize him.

The weeks stretched on like the now-bare branches reaching for gray November skies outside. There was a full Thanksgiving dinner being served on campus because of extramurals, but I invited all my friends to drop by my house for dessert if they wanted to.

On the holiday, Dylan, Logan, and Grace showed up. Izzy, Lee, and Cadence arrived after dinner at her house. When we finished dessert, the doorbell rang. Faith and Hal told us Kitty was up in New Hampshire at Eston's house. Dorian brought Cosmo over from the Hawthorne Hotel, where they'd had restaurant turkey with Blaine and Kim.

After sunset, Hailey walked in with Arick Magnuson on her arm. Bailey arrived with Brianna, Elanor, and Jonah, who gave Noah a big smile before sauntering into the living room.

You don't have to invite vampires in. The threshold thing was a myth. Besides the need to drink blood, which they could buy in cartons at stores and order in glasses at restaurants, they weren't much different from the rest of us.

Having so many visitors for dessert and coffee was nice. We even repeated last year's outing with Bubbe's babka and plastic mugs of hot chocolate, but this time, we hung around in the backyard, watching the boarded critters that were outside for exercise.

"I can't believe you grew up with all these magical animals."

Jonah had spoken to Noah. The two leaned together against the rail on our small back porch. The closeness of their hands mesmerized me. Was I about to learn some fundamental secret about how romance started?

Cadence elbowed me, then tilted her eyes to her right. I looked in that direction to see Dylan wearing a scowl, which wasn't remarkable lately, but Cadence rolled her eyes, tugging my sleeve and jerking her chin at the gate from the driveway. Her face fell like a rock off a cliff into the sea as Bar walked through and closed the gate behind him.

"What's wrong? Thought you'd be happy to see a friend from Gallows Hill."

She pouted. "He's just not the one I wanted to see."

"Why do you keep breaking up with Crow if you want him around?"

"He and I are too different, Aliyah." She shook her head. "You wouldn't understand."

"Maybe I do." I put my arm around my friend's shoulder, giving her a brief side hug before dropping it again. "But if you're not compatible, why bother?"

"I can't help it." She sighed. "There's just something about him, the way he walks. And how he smells. And that body. He usually hides it, but damn, he's sexy under that trench coat."

Troll changelings must have amazing hearing because Bar leaned against the fence beside the gate as though he'd been sucker-punched. He'd come over here on his own, probably to see Cadence, and found her obsessing about someone else.

That was something I understood, so I left Cadence chatting with Grace and got up to greet him. Maybe we could avoid the awkwardness of unrequited crush-clashes.

"Hey, how are you doing?" I held out my hand to Bar. "Welcome to my backyard."

"Thanks. Did you really know Cadence her whole life?"

"Almost. We met in kindergarten."

"Take a little walk with me?" Bar jerked his chin at the mulberry tree.

I nodded. We stopped by the enclosure, where some mercats frolicked in a small pond. Bar was massive, over six feet tall and built like a boulder. He leaned forward but not against the fence. I couldn't blame him. Cats with fishes' tails were mesmerizing, but the look in his eyes didn't match how I normally felt watching them.

"So, what's up?"

"This might sound weird, but the friend I usually talk to about this stuff has a serious conflict of interest." He took a deep breath and closed his eyes before continuing in a lower voice, "Do you think she likes grand gestures? When guys ask her out, I mean."

"Cadence?" I blinked. "She's a romantic, but not like that. She prefers making her own splashes. But Bar, I think you ought to know..."

"Yeah, I already do. She's got it bad for another guy. Conflict of interest, remember?"

"Oh." Bar's situation felt all too familiar. I wanted to help, but I couldn't even solve my own crush problems. "Well, does she know how you feel?"

"No. We don't talk about feelings. Usually, we just act."

"Why?"

He turned his head, and we stared into each other's eyes for seconds that felt like eons.

"I guess magi are different." He shook his head. "Trolls aren't big talkers."

"It's not much better for me. I can't tell the person I like, either. It's hard."

"Didn't used to be. Not until I started having so many more feelings, you know?"

"Maybe caring too much freezes people up like deer in headlights. It's okay if you don't agree, but I get it."

"Nah, you walk the walk. Must've been crazy, realizing you're an extramagus."

"It sucked. My friend's going through the same thing now, but I was lucky. It's been way harder for him. His family's overseas."

"Well, at least he's got you."

"I guess." Bar was right, but all I could think about was Hal saying Dylan didn't know I was alive. I changed the subject.

"Why don't you just ask Cadence to the dance? You've got to start somewhere, and technically, that's just one date."

"Yeah, I just don't know how to say it." He shook his head. "She's a mermaid."

"I don't either, and my crush is a magus like me." I glanced at Dylan, who'd taken out his guitar. As he strummed, Noah turned and started humming along.

"Oh, it's like that."

"Yup. Been that way for a while. I have a hard time with dating stuff."

"Hey, I got an idea."

"Oh?"

"Yeah. We count to three. I go ask her, you go ask him. Just say the first thing we think of."

"I would, but I told everyone I'm going stag in a group of friends. I don't want to let the people I already included down."

"That's easier." He grinned. "We ask them to do your friends thing?"

"You're pretty smart, Bar."

"Nah, just random genius flashes. So, what do you say?"

"Let's do it."

Cadence and Dylan both loved the idea, and Dylan said yes immediately. Cadence insisted we invite Crow. Bar nodded, so I agreed to it. It wasn't the ideal outcome, but better than nothing.

When we went back to school on Monday, we spent most of our time preparing for the talent show. There was a dress rehearsal, during which I discovered Alex was across the aisle from me in the sound booth. At least there'd be two walls and ten feet between us.

But there wasn't much time to worry about him. I worked hard, modifying lights in response to the shinier costumes. Everyone looked amazing, too. Grace had found an entire closet of forgotten costumes from Bubbe's school days and managed to alter them to fit everyone in record time.

I lingered in the cafeteria all through dinner, but Crow was conspicuously absent, along with Grace. I got a strange feeling in the pit of my stomach. Was this how Izzy felt when she had a premonition? Grace had never mentioned a date for the dance. I asked all our mutual friends, but they were clueless.

When I finally got the chance to ask, Grace said she hadn't decided yet.

CHAPTER THIRTY-NINE

I read through some of Great Uncle Noah's letters in my free time. Almost all of them were love letters addressed to his boyfriend, a guy named Bert. They were cozily romantic, something I hadn't seen in fact or fiction before. My great uncle's love story was sweet and emotional, without any mention of sex. For some strange reason, it gave me hope that I might live my own someday.

I haunted the cafeteria and the lounge by the café, still trying to make good on my promise about Crow. Dorian dragged me away on Thursday night, insisting now was the time to tell his story. When I walked toward the empty academic wing, he paled.

"Anywhere but there."

"Okay." I steered him toward the stairs. "Why?"

"You'll know soon enough."

He knocked on his own door, which puzzled me at first, but when Eston emerged with Kitty, I understood. They giggled, and Eston's glasses were a little foggy.

"Hmm." Kitty glanced at us, then giggled again. "We have good timing."

"Oh yeah, we do." Eston grinned, pushing the door open wider and stepping into the hall so we could get through. "Have fun."

"Thanks." Dorian caught the door. "But we're studying, hardly fun."

The pair laughed, leaning on each other as they headed down the hall. Kitty looked back at my empty hands and called, "Don't forget your books, then!"

"It's not like that." I hung my head, hiding in my hair.

"Maybe we shouldn't go in there." Dorian sighed. "We don't want to start rumors."

"Too late. You already said we're studying, and this conversation is long overdue." I stepped across the threshold. "Anyway, you're courting Logan. Maybe they think this is for advice or a pep talk."

"Maybe."

He closed the door, waited for me to have a seat, and told me everything he'd overheard. When he finished, he sat. I got up and paced.

"So, there's good news and bad news, Dorian."

"Good first."

"We know who one of those people was."

"What's the bad news?"

"Confronting her won't work. She's a chronic liar, and you can't believe a word she says."

"Who is she?" Dorian shrugged. "I've got nothing."

"Temperance Fairbanks."

"How do you know?"

"Something she said to Faith about having a secret boyfriend, who she, um, likes better than Alex."

"That part fits." Dorian nodded. "And the guy wasn't Alex because everyone talked about how you fought in the lobby that day."

"It has to be a Bishop's Row player," I said. "Because of the point-set-match thing."

"Yeah, and a magus because of all the bigotry. So, how do we find him?"

"Process of elimination, and maybe a little research. He's a jock and he's straight, so it isn't Noah, but more than half the school tried out for our team. How do we narrow it down more without Tempe noticing?"

"Coach Pickman has me on filing duty because of my medical thing." Dorian grinned. "I could peek at the student files."

I stopped my pacing, turning to face him. He tugged on his collar and cleared his throat. Was he paler than usual? Bonier? More tired?

"You haven't mentioned that for a while. Are you okay? You look pale."

"Uh, it's only life-threatening without treatment. Basically, I have to wear, um, things that make it harder to do sports."

"That doesn't sound good. Can I help?"

"You already do every day." He let out a robotic-sounding laugh and tugged his collar again. "I'm only pale from skipping my veggies."

Go on. Ask again. Pry like he's an oyster.

I didn't. This was Dorian's circus and his monkeys. I'd give him the same respect I'd given Hal and let him talk about it when and if he wanted to.

"Thanks for the chat and the help, Dorian."

"Don't mention it. Literally." His shoulders eased. "And now I'm exhausted."

"See you tomorrow, then."

"Yeah. See you."

I left and headed toward my room to get ready for bed, refocusing my mind on finding Temperance's secret boyfriend. But I still said a prayer for Dorian Spanos, hoping he didn't have a debilitating condition like Hal's. He'd seen enough tragedy in his life.

I had the best seat in the house for the talent show, an unexpected benefit of the light booth. Everybody was amazing. I could hardly believe those were my friends and family. Yes, I said family because of Noah's band, Piercing Whispers.

The first act was Dorian's stand-up comedy. His routine lampooned ice, snow, and made popular culture references. I giggled through the entire thing, but not because the jokes were particularly innovative. Dorian had amazing comedic timing, and his delivery was spot on.

Next the curtain opened on Bar and Crow, dressed in garb that would fit right in at King Richard's Faire. Their stage combat routine had the audience gasping, whistling, and applauding. Bar threw glamour in there, but only to make sparks when their weapons clashed. I didn't know much about that particular performance art, but the routine made me want to give it a try.

After that came Izzy's and Jonah's ballroom dance routine. I expected a cha-cha, or maybe merengue, Izzy's favorite. Instead, they walked out dressed like Gomez and Morticia Adams and danced to *Vampire Club* by Voltaire, a Boston local musician who'd performed in Goth clubs and fan conventions since before I was born.

The fourth act was Piercing Whispers. I knew every one of the band's members. Elanor played keyboards and shared vocals with Noah, who played bass. Dylan rocked out on a brand new guitar in his favorite color, blue.

Where did he get the money for that? Even the Lyceum can't pay that well.

Behind them at the drum set sat the last person I expected. Arick Magnuson. His bookwyrm Skinner was coiled on his head like a beanie that bounced to the beat.

The other familiars all had some part in the performance. Gale swooped back and forth over the band, dropping glittering bits of ice. Elanor's phoenix FiFi backlit them. Noah's serpent Lotan sat atop Elanor's keyboard, swaying like a metronome. They played one of my favorite classic rock songs ever.

I'm talking about *The Chain* by Fleetwood Mac. Its music and lyrics had always hooked me because it reminded me of those moments right before disaster, like when a plate tilts against the edge of the table and you move to grab it. Will you catch it in time? Will it break to bits on the floor?

It had played in my room the summer before middle school when Cadence almost ran away from home. She came to me first, insisting I had to help her get to Boston Harbor. She planned to catch a transatlantic liner so she could jump off in open water and meet the undersea family her parents had left behind.

I called Izzy immediately and we'd talked her out of it, promising to stay friends forever. Since then, *The Chain* reminded me that our connections had real power. We could make a difference to the people in our lives and keep them from shattering on the floor just by loving them before they fell.

It doesn't make a difference to Dylan.

"I didn't ask you." I didn't have to suppress my outside voice alone inside the lighting booth.

Peace is practically a foreign country for you right now.

"This too shall pass. Along with you, hopefully."

You're arguing with me now?

"No, but maybe it's time we had a little chat." I brought the house lights up for intermission.

The moment this show is over, you'll be back in that mess with them. If I were you, I'd leave campus and never look back.

"I'm not leaving with a mystery poisoner on campus. You're just a voice in my head. What do you know?"

Plenty. And don't make assumptions about me or what I know.

I chewed on that, not daring to utter a response. If the voice's implication was true, it either had its own sentience or an origin outside my own mind. In the case of the former, a mental health crisis was imminent. In the latter, I'd been invaded by something incorporeal with an unknown agenda. Either way, I couldn't handle it on my own. How many of my friends had I sent to get professional help? Why couldn't I take my own advice?

You like having me around. I'm not all bad.

"Okay, fine. You're helpful sometimes. Broken clocks are right twice a day."

That's just incredibly rude. Perhaps I'll shut my figurative mouth indefinitely.

"Wait."

The voice made no response. Intermission had ended, so I dimmed the house lights. Backstage, the twins pulled the curtains, and I turned on the spotlight at center stage. Hal Hawkins wore a red satin tuxedo jacket with a white shirt and black tie. Faith stood behind him, smiling and waving, wearing a green and gold sequined gown slit to the knee. There was a box behind them on its side atop some sort of rolling frame. They began their magic show, not the extrahuman kind, but the illusionist type.

Hal and Faith had an entire routine where he did most of the prestidigitation and she assisted. Scarves flowed endlessly from one of his pockets and then her hair, and linked rings joined and separated. He even pulled Seth and Nin out of a hat.

Their finale involved the box, of course. Everyone expected him to make Faith disappear, and he did, for a moment. He opened the box the second time, but somehow they'd switched places, so she stood holding the lid while he climbed out of the box. After that, the pair bowed. I brought the lights down when the applause ended, which took a good bit of time. People had loved the twist ending.

I looked down at my list, seeing there was only one act left to go: Cadence, with a vocal performance. At the dress rehearsal, she hadn't played the music or revealed the title of her selection, just gotten up on the stage in a majorette outfit and done a mic check.

At first, I didn't recognize the opening bars of the music Elanor played. And yes, she was up there, a Hawthorn student providing backing music for one of the Gallows Hill students. We weren't supposed to collaborate since this was one event where the schools competed against each other, but that didn't matter because everyone forgot who was playing a moment later.

When Cadence opened her mouth, singing about how she can't make him stay, I understood immediately what she was doing: using *Famous Last Words* by My Chemical Romance to win the talent show and provoke her flaky ex-boyfriend, Crow. I saw him in the wings, jaw dropped and eyes wide.

When she finished, even I stood up and applauded. The power of her performance lifted me from my seat, an unseen force but absolutely real. Cadence's voice worked a bit like psychic empathy when she sang but was a rare magical mermaid gift that mimicked mind magic when spoken. I moved under my own power. A mermaid's singing voice worked by inspiring latent emotions into action, like the ultimate motivational speaker. She'd affected the entire audience because they all stood to cheer.

Other students joined Crow in the wings, and almost every one of them applauded. Bar stood there scratching his head. Changelings with strong enough glamour could resist Cadence's mojo. Something didn't sit well with him about her performance, but because I was affected, I had no idea what it was.

I kept the stage lights up, and the rest of the performers came back on the stage. The judges in the front row, who consisted of performers from town, stepped up on the apron and handed a score-card to Nurse Smith, who'd been the MC. He read each one, then held the tally sheet out in front of him.

"Third place, *The Chain* by Piercing Whisper." A round of applause from the audience broke out, strong enough to demonstrate our home-team enthusiasm.

"Second place, *Vampire Club* by Izzy and Jonah."

More applause followed, heavier this time. It subsided as everyone waited to hear who won.

"And the winner, *Famous Last Words* by Cadence."

Had the Gallows Hill kids used megaphones? When I opened the door to check, the crowd was so loud I had to cover my ears. I guess Cadence's performance was its own kind of magic.

Let's just hope no one accuses her of cheating.

"Thought you were shutting your mouth?"

"What's that?"

I stepped back into the booth, hands covering my mouth and eyes widening as I stared into Alex Onassis's face. The skin under his eyes looked puffy and dark like he hadn't slept well in weeks, and he wore a full face of makeup. I almost mistook the bruise on his left cheek-bone for a contouring effect. He stood in the doorway of my light booth, pulling a set of clunky noise-canceling headphones off. They weren't turned on.

"What are you doing here?"

"Running the sound." He rolled his eyes. "And overhearing you talk to yourself."

"Fine. But you hate me, so why are you here?" I gestured at the space between us.

"Everyone's still whammied like she said they'd be." He gestured at the headphones. "Except me. I don't have much time. Watch out for Temperance. She's planning something horrible."

"What is she going to do, Alex?"

He reached toward the breast pocket in his blazer where his basilisk usually stayed, but she wasn't there. His eyes widened for a moment, but he caught himself and smoothed his expression.

"She's been writing things down, stuff about where you and your friends go every day. Who's on what team, which competition. And all the upcoming events."

"How do we prepare?"

He opened his mouth, but it closed almost immediately after. When he tried again, his lips moved, but no sound came out.

"I *can't* say it." He bared his teeth, clenching his fists. "Dammit. Damn *her*."

His eyes widened and he stepped back, pressing his hand against his left ear and sagging against his booth's doorway. Had something hurt him? Nothing and no one was present in the room except us and Ember, who still slept. Unless, somewhere, someone was hurting his familiar.

"How did she do this to you?"

"I can't *say*." He sucked in a breath. "I can't do this. Shouldn't have done any of it." He straightened shakily, then staggered out of my light booth, slamming the door behind him.

I opened the door, intending to go after him, but by the time I did, the hallway was empty. I opened the sound booth and looked inside, but he wasn't there. When I went downstairs from the tech floor, the crowd was too thick. I'd lost him.

"What did he mean?" I asked Ember, who'd woken up and was peeping insistently in my ear.

She tugged my hair on my left side. I turned in that direction, only to find Temperance in the corner, grinning at me. Her grundylow peered out from behind her hair, eyes gleaming in the darkness.

She doesn't even have to touch that boy to harm him. I told you to leave campus.

In my head, I replied, *My friends need me. I'm not going anywhere. I can't save anyone by abandoning them.*

That girl's got the look of a killer. Act soon.

I hadn't feared her until that moment despite everything I heard Faith accuse her of over the orb, but now, Temperance Fairbanks terrified me.

CHAPTER FORTY

I walked into the bathroom the night after the talent show. Faith swam laps in the pool, while Seth relaxed on a folded towel nearby. Ember glided down from my shoulder and sat beside him, curling her tail around her feet like a cat. I wasn't there to swim, so I stood where Faith could see me and waited.

At the end of her next lap, she crossed her arms on the edge of the pool and stared up at me.

"Is Temperance an extramagus? Specifically with mind magic?"

"That's a lead-pipe level of blunt." Faith shook water off her hand, then dragged it through her hair. "I don't think so. Her water came in early, but that's all I've seen her conjure."

"How early?" I put my hands on my hips. "Uncle Richard's fire came in grade school. Mom says he got water the year after that."

Faith sighed. "What gave you this idea?"

I paced along the side of the pool, telling her what had happened in the light booth and right afterward.

"Look, she's terrifying, but you can't go around accusing a Fairbanks of being an unregistered extramagus. My parents are horrible too."

"I don't want to poke the hornet's nest, but how else do you explain someone literally unable to talk like that?"

"Tell me again what Alex said."

"First he couldn't make a sound, and then it was 'I *can't* say it, I can't *say*' and he damned her. After that, he grabbed his ear and almost fell over."

"Yeah, that sounds like magic." She gripped the side of the pool, knuckles pale.

"And his familiar wasn't with him."

"That's why he doesn't dump her. If she's threatening his basilisk..." Faith slapped the water. "She's a monster."

"That explains a lot, but not everything. It looked like compulsion."

"I have one idea, but it's out there. We should check other possibilities first, like faerie stuff. A vow or something."

"I'll ask Cadence. She might not know, but she'll know who does." I sighed. "Sorry for ruining your swim, Faith."

"It's okay. It was important." Faith prepared to launch into a backstroke, but she stopped. "So's this. Tempe got her own room."

"How do you know?"

"Lena thanked me."

I gave her a grin. "You rescued her."

"Yeah, but I probably doomed Alex. When Temperance loses a victim, whoever's left suffers more."

I shivered. "I'm sorry. Enjoy the rest of your swim, and try to have a good night."

"You too."

I left the bathroom and went to find Cadence. She was in the fourth-floor hall, headed for the restroom with a bucket of toiletries. We went in together, and she took a minute to wash and dry her face. Afterward, Cadence glanced at me in the mirror while unscrewing a jar of moisturizer.

"What's up, Aliyah?"

"I have questions about glamour."

"I'm a mermaid, but I'll try to help. Go on."

"Can glamour work like mind magic? Make it so a person can't speak freely?"

"No, not at the changeling level. Not even most faeries. That's monarch-level stuff, like the queen and king."

"Oh."

"But Aliyah," she lowered her voice, "I've done it."

"Mind control?"

"It's a voice thing. I have to be direct—dot the Is and cross the Ts."

"How would Temperance Fairbanks manage it?"

"What?" Cadence stepped back, knocking her basket off the counter and spilling toiletries on the floor. "To whom?"

"Sorry." I bent down, retrieving tubes and brushes before they rolled away. "Alex Onassis."

"He's got big magic. You think she whammied someone that powerful?" Cadence bent over to help me. "Is she an extramagus?"

"Faith says no." I dropped the last tube of lip balm into the bucket. "So how could she manage it?"

We leaned against the counter, thinking. Finally, Cadence clapped her hands.

"What about a magipsychic device?"

"We're banned from bringing those on campus."

"That didn't stop you last year."

"Good point."

"I think you're looking for a gadget, Aliyah."

"Should I hit the library?"

"Are they open at this hour?"

"Yeah, all through December because of exams."

"So, let's go."

"Are you sure? I don't want to keep you from your beauty rest."

"I don't need it. I'm already gorgeous." She winked.

We headed out of the bathroom.

We weren't the first students in Hawthorn Academy history to hit the books in pajamas, but we were the only ones that night. The December Dance was on everyone's minds. I had a mystery to figure out.

I led Cadence to the giant index. Once we found listings on magipsychic gadgets, we ventured into the stacks. We took three volumes to a table and sat, flipping through them.

"What about this?" Cadence turned the book, tapping the illustration. "It blocks memories until people with trauma can work through them."

"I don't think it fits." I sighed, resting my chin on my hand. "He knew what he wanted to say, he just couldn't get the words out."

"What about something like this?" She flipped a handful of pages back to a different entry.

"Muffler?" I chewed my lower lip, scanning the item's description. "This turns the volume of voices down, either the user's or everyone around them. But it's a scarf, and he wasn't wearing one."

"I'm out of ideas from this book." Cadence shrugged. "What about that one?"

I opened another tome, turning to the index. We scanned the list, looking at the names and the brief descriptions of functions, but none of them fit.

"Is there anything I can help you find?" I looked up to see Mrs. Ashford, an infrequent helper in the library. She sat in a magipsychic assistive chair that glided above the floor.

"Yes, actually. You must know lots about this subject." I grinned. "We're looking for a particular type of magipsychic gadget, one that can do mind magic or ban a person from speaking on a certain topic."

"You won't find anything like that in these alternative therapies tomes." Mrs. Ashford sighed. "You want history books from the Second World War."

"Oh." Cadence blinked. "You think it's a banned device?"

"Likely banned worldwide if it channels compulsive magic. Those are nasty inventions, and they have a steep cost to use. Professor Luciano's doctoral theses are all on that subject. They're in collegiate libraries, unfortunately." Mrs. Ashford said. "The only advanced material we have is *A History of Axis Extrahumans*, and it's upstairs."

"Thanks, Mrs. Ashford."

"I'm a librarian, so it's my duty to keep you informed." She grinned, but it didn't touch her eyes this time. She wasn't old enough to have lived during World War II, but she must've heard stories from people who'd been there. Like Bubbe's dad.

Cadence and I brought the alternative therapies books to the desk, setting them in the return bin. *A History of Axis Extrahumans* was easy to find. We both yawned our heads off as I checked the book out.

Back in my room, I tried to read by the light of my solar magic, which Grace slept soundly through, but I fell asleep with my head pillowed on the pages.

I brought *A History of Axis Extrahumans* to class the next day. During Creatives, I flipped through it instead of working on art. Hal came to see what I was doing.

"Why are you researching Nazi magi?" he asked.

"To counter a bad apple." I mumbled Temperance's name while clearing my throat and Hal nodded. "They had some nasty gadgets back then. If only there was one that shut their effects down."

"Wait a minute." He scratched his head. "My Magicpsych Fair project was a switch, remember?"

"Yeah, but this is way more complicated than lights and bathtubs."

"Ooh!" Hal's eyes lit up. I'd almost forgotten how much he loved fixing things. "Tell me more."

"It's sensitive information."

"For my ears, or this location?"

"Location." I glanced around. "I'm trying to help someone unpopular."

"Okay." He reached for the book. "Let me see."

"I'm trying to see if one's being used on a person." I leaned my head on my hand. "And find something to stop it."

"Does this book have an index?"

I showed him. Hal speed-read the listings, with one finger under the words. Most were in German, with a handful in a less obvious language.

"I couldn't figure it out, so maybe you know. Why Greek?"

"Golden Dawn." Hal rolled his eyes. "Their magi helped the Axis back then."

"Ugh."

"I'm going to need a lexicon. Want to look it over during library time?"

"Sure." I looked him in the eye. "But only if you don't wear yourself out over this."

"I'm having a good day, so it should be fine. I promise to go straight to Nurse Smith if I start flagging."

"Okay, then."

We still had half an hour, so I got my clay container from the day before and sat with Lee, sharing tools to carve a brick pattern. I missed the cobblestone streets and brick architecture of Salem on this campus made of wood. Time passed quickly, but the design took shape under my hands until the bell rang. It went so well, maybe I'd have an entry for the Craft Expo in February.

I let Hal select a lexicon and retreated to a corner, settling into a tufted leather chair across from two more with a table between them. When Hal joined me, he had Faith in tow. I handed the book over.

"You and Cadence are smart. You two guessed my theory," Faith said. "I asked Tempe about a gadget. It was in my parents' basement five years ago, but it vanished the day after I asked her about it. She could have brought it here. If it's in this book, I'll recognize it."

I sat staring at her, but Hal's face went hard, eyes coldly bright like the day he'd discovered his illness. Hal Hawkins seemed mostly harmless, but his closest friends knew otherwise. He was prone to random bouts of righteous fury, and heaven wouldn't help whoever invoked it.

"We should call the FBE."

"We don't have proof." Faith sighed. "Calling them now is a boy-who-cried-wolf problem waiting to happen."

"Okay." Hal set the book on the table and opened it. "Let's see if anything looks familiar."

Faith studied each picture as we flipped through, searching in a more direct fashion than the night before. On page after page, she shook her head, but Hal stopped to peer at a gadget in a sidebar.

"This one's an Allied device, something they fought back with." He tapped the page. "It's constructed similarly to my project, but it nullifies magic when you flip the switch."

I wrote the page number in my notebook and we kept going. About two-thirds of the way through, Faith shuddered, wrapping her arms around herself.

"That's what I saw." She leaned forward to read without touching the page. "Says it stores all types of magic and drains energy when used."

"Whoa." My hand trembled when I moved to pat Faith's shoulder. "So, it hurts the person using it? That sounds counterproductive."

"It's not, though." Hal pointed at the text. "One Axis magus used it to firebomb a tank and chose to drain his entire platoon of mundane soldiers. They all died. No wonder it's banned."

"God." I put my hand over my mouth. I tried not to take the Almighty's name in vain, but this was horrifying. "How do we stop something like that?"

"What about that Allied nullifier?" Hal leaned his chin on his hand. "What do you think it'd do? Break Tempe's device?"

Faith grabbed my notebook and flipped the book to the page I'd marked down before.

"No." She read the description. "But see this? If she used it to ban someone from talking about her, it can shut that effect off."

"One-time use." Hal sighed. "Null magi can shut down any magic. Too bad there's none here."

"Well, can we modify your switch, Hal?"

"Maybe, but before I agree, I need to know." Hal looked at Faith, then me. "Who are you trying to save with this thing?"

The love of his life didn't tell him what she's up to? Oh, this is rich.

"You don't know?" I ignored the Evil Inside Voice.

"It's not Michelina Zanelli. I know she's out of the woods."

"Nobody deserves what he's going through," I confessed. "It's Alex."

His name hung in the air between us. Hal examined it, judging the worth of the magus who bore it.

"Yeah, he sucks." I sighed. "But we need more information. He tried to tell me, but he can't unless we fix his problem."

"I can't judge him for his screwy world view." Faith hung her head. "I'd be right there with him if it hadn't been for you, Hal."

"If you *both* agree the depressive demon nightmare boy needs rescuing, I can't argue." Hal nodded. "Let's do this."

We worked in silence for the rest of library time, checking every resource we could think of for information about nullification switches. We found a surprisingly comprehensive schematic in a magipsychic engineering manual referenced in the back of the first alternative therapies volume I'd flipped through with Cadence the night before.

Hal checked both books out and headed to Lab with the rest of us. I partnered with Dylan and Faith with Logan. Hal wanted us to give them a heads up in case we needed their help. Most gadgets required multiple contributors, and this one was no exception. Logan insisted on joining us, so we included him in the evening's plans.

Dylan, on the other hand, just nodded and changed the subject. I'd never seen him so focused on classwork. We'd moved on from recording the plant's growth to a perpetual motion device, so maybe that was it.

Why not ask about that new guitar?

I did.

"It's the Lyceum." He glued a blade on the fan at the top of the device. "One of the, uh, regulars is a fan, I guess, and she gave me an enormous tip the week before the talent show."

"Wow." I blinked. "She must really like you. Or something."

"I guess." The blade clattered to the bench. "A little help here?"

I didn't bother continuing that conversation.

After Lab, Hal stayed behind. Logan, Faith, and I waited in the hall, overhearing him ask Professor Luciano if he could bring his Magipsych Fair project back to his room.

"You'd like to do further study, is that it?" The professor raised an eyebrow, glancing at the doorway where we waited. "And you've got the time and energy?"

Faith turned her back on them, pretending to chat with me about my necklace.

"Yes. I'd like to explore alternate applications with some of my classmates. I think magical switches are fascinating. They have so many potential uses."

"That sounds brilliant, Harold. Of course I'll allow it." He sighed, reaching up to rub his temple. "But you must return it before winter break."

"I might want to work with it longer than that."

"Then you can request it again when the second semester begins."

"I understand, sir."

"Sir?" Professor Luciano gave Hal a worn grin. "You haven't called me that in ages, Mr. Hawkins."

The professor turned toward a closet and rummaged around for a moment, then produced a box labeled with Hal's name and exchanged it for a word of thanks. We met in the hall and walked toward the lobby.

Faith shrugged. "That was easy."

"Too easy." Hal glanced from one side of the hall to the other. "Do you get the impression something's not right with him?"

"He seems exhausted." I nodded. "And his familiar wasn't on his shoulder."

"Aren't exams stressful for professors?" Faith asked.

"Probably." I shrugged. "But he wasn't like this last year."

"Maybe he thinks we're doing the right thing." Hal hefted the box. "If he's got any idea."

"I wouldn't trust an adult advising against helping people, anyway." Faith rolled her eyes. "I'm glad he's our professor."

"Me too." I grinned.

Hal and Faith took the device up to his room while Logan and I went to Penelope's window to order four dinners to go. We'd work through the meal and have privacy. Lee was playing Truncheons and Flagons in Kitty's room that night.

I also stopped by the café to get pastries, teabags, and some apples for later. Logan helped me carry everything to the stairs. I called out our floor. Hal let us into the room, and I passed the food around.

"Thanks." Faith opened her dinner bag. "I'm starving."

We took a few minutes to eat because hangry studying wasn't productive. After that, we spread the books out on the floor, with the switch set out on a large piece of cardboard.

"I thought we were making a magic gadget?" Logan scratched his head. "That looks done."

"Modifying." Hal tapped the manual with the schematics. "We already have half the steps done if we start with this."

"So, it's like your project is the base unit?" Logan raised an eyebrow.

"Yeah." Hal nodded.

We finished the food and got to work, following the instructions. The manual restated that this device was for one-time use and would have to be recharged to nullify effects a second time.

"I'm not sure I'm comfortable with one shot." Faith brushed a lock of chestnut hair away from her face. "When Tempe retaliates, it'll be major-league."

"We have to work smarter," Hal urged. "Someone gets Alex alone before using it. She won't know how he broke out if we do that."

"But who?" I asked.

"Not you, Aliyah," Hal said. "You said he came to you twice. She'll be watching you."

"Wait." Logan looked up from the connection he just soldered. "Aren't you worried? I mean, it's Alex."

"Yeah." I nodded. "An agenda to escape. You didn't see him at the talent show, Logan. When he realized Asceco wasn't with him, he looked terrified."

"I'll do it," Hal said.

"No way." Faith shook her head. "You're about as stealthy as a bull in a china shop."

"Temperance will notice any of us," Logan said.

"Except Grace. Who can be invisible." I stood. "Should I get her?"

Everyone agreed, so I headed down the hall to fetch my roommate. Then I realized it was still dinner time, so she'd be in the dining hall. I was about to turn my back on the door to our room, but it opened.

"Hey." Azrael Ambersmith emerged, pausing halfway through.

"Hi." I blinked. "Is Grace in there?"

"Yeah." He leaned back, summoning her. I heard a muffled reply that she'd be there in a minute. He stepped all the way into the hall, closing the door behind him.

"Are you her date to the dance, Az?"

"No." He gazed at his shoes. "I just asked. She's going with someone else."

"Oh." It seemed pretty obvious to me that they liked each other. "Who?"

"You're not going to like it."

"What's up, Aliyah?" Grace came out of the room.

"I'm working on something with Logan, Hal, and Faith. We could use your help."

"Okay." She nodded, shutting the door. "Thanks for the glamour help, Az. See you later."

"Yeah, see you."

He went to the stairs and called for his floor. Grace insisted on fetching a smoothie for Hal to keep his strength up. I figured that was a good time to get the biggest sticking point out of the way.

"Look, we're doing this to help Alex, so if you've got a problem with that, I'll find someone else."

"Help him get away from Tempe?"

"Yeah."

"Count. Me. In." Her grin was so feral I almost jumped. "This is awesome." She ordered five pineapple smoothies.

"I didn't expect that response." I lowered my voice as we approached the crowded café. "He's your enemy, right?"

"He's been looking defanged lately. The enemy of my enemy is my frenemy."

"What's that?" I blinked.

"An It Girl mantra. It's catty, but I've got to do whatever works." Her smile didn't touch her eyes.

With the smoothies nestled in two trays, we ascended the stairs. At Hal's room, we walked in on a discussion about infusing the device.

"It's already got all the glamour and psychic energy it needs." Hal tapped the diagram. "Here and here, so we need to connect those parts to the barrel."

"What's it for?"

Everyone else drank their smoothies as I filled Grace in on the aftermath of the talent show. I included my conversations with Faith and Cadence afterward. She narrowed her eyes, then clenched her fists and paced in front of the door.

I let her be. That was how Grace put things together, and something had the wheels in her head turning on overdrive.

Faith and Logan made the physical connections as Hal instructed, but they called me over to help finish them with a little heat to reduce drying time.

Finally, Grace looked it over using the monocle Hal had in his toolkit, the one that let us see all the energies infused in the device.

"We need Cadence."

"We're trying to keep this as secret as possible." Faith shook her head. "And she's the biggest gossip on campus."

"Doesn't matter." Grace gave the monocle back to Hal. "Alex had no trouble talking to Aliyah until after Cadence sang in the show. I think Tempe put that power in her gadget somehow."

Grace handed the monocle over, and I peered through it.

"There aren't mind magi here, so she couldn't have gotten it that way, but what if she managed to meet one off-campus?"

"That is a theory question." Logan reached for the monocle and had a look. "A similar power can counter mind energy, like psychic empathy. Merfolk magic isn't well-documented, but Doris knows it. Cadence's voice ability is close enough."

"I get it." I nodded. "We only have one shot, but we can't risk her mentioning it because our entire plan hinges on Tempe not knowing how we're canceling her magic."

"There's only one way without telling her," Logan said. "Get her to do the mermaid voice thing in front of whoever's carrying the switch while it's hidden."

"But when?" I scratched my head.

"The dance." Faith answered. "She'll be totally distracted, trying to outdo Grace. And the sooner we do this, the better for Alex and us."

"The dance is tomorrow night." Hal sighed. "That crunches our time. We've still got loads to do."

"It'll go faster now that I'm here." Grace sat on the floor between Faith and Logan. "Crafting is my jam."

"I'm on self-care and rehydration duty." I opened the panel to the grooming station, fetched water, and heated it with solar magic to make tea.

The extra help did speed things up, though it was exhausting. Faith took Hal's hands during breaks, bolstering him with her undead energy. I passed food and drinks around like a waitress. When we ran out, I dropped by Kitty's to see if she had extra snacks at Truncheons and Flagons.

"We finished our dungeon crawl almost an hour ago." She handed me a bag of tortilla chips and a jar of salsa. "You guys are burning the midnight oil. Taking exams seriously?"

"I guess we are."

"Awesome." She peered under the round table. "Yes! Dorian left the rest of his Mountain Dew."

"Will he mind, do you think?"

"Nah. I'll tell him Logan needed it. Magic words." Kitty got a brown paper bag, plucked the salsa from my hand, and put it inside with the soda cans. She added a half-full bag of mandarin oranges. "Oh, and Faith donated these to my game, so I'm just giving them back."

"Thanks, Kitty."

Since it was Friday, we still had another hour to work. Our familiars had all zonked out during the last snack break. Hal switched from hands-on conjuring to reading the manual and supervising. Fortunately, the extra food helped us keep going, which we needed. The dance was in less than twenty-four hours at that point. It felt almost anticlimactic when we finished fifty minutes later.

We all yawned our heads off as we said goodnight only minutes before lights out. I was asleep before my head hit the pillow, while Grace sat up in bed, reading about Tempe's device in *A History of Axis Extrahumans*. She'd polished off the Mountain Dew.

CHAPTER FORTY-ONE

I sat at breakfast with Hal, Faith, Grace, and Logan. All of our familiars dozed in the critter-friendly area in the corner. Grace was the only one without bleary eyes. I had no idea where her energy came from. She didn't even have a cup of coffee like the rest of us. Logan's arm stretched halfway across the table, supporting his head. He blinked wearily at me.

"I can't believe we built the whole thing," he mumbled.

"Modified, technically." Hal leaned against the wall inside the booth, using his hand as a pillow.

"Will it work, do you think?" Grace raised an eyebrow.

"Yeah." Faith rubbed her eyes. "If you shoot your shot at the right time."

"Thanks, guys." I yawned, stretching an arm overhead like I wanted a nonexistent teacher's attention. At second glance, I realized teachers were in the cafeteria. Professor Luciano sat in the corner with Messing's Dean Adelphi over a pot of tea.

"That's what friends are for." Logan grinned.

"I didn't do much, but I'm glad I'm not the only one willing to help our old enemy."

"He doesn't deserve it." Grace shrugged. "And we need to maintain our winning streak."

"Yeah." Faith nodded. "She won't stop, but it'll be hard for her, losing an asset."

"Don't you care what happens to Alex after all this?"

"Not really," Hal said. "He took major advantage of you last year, Aliyah. Don't expect that snake to change his stripes."

Did you really think all their intentions mirrored your own?

I shook my head, putting three heaping spoonfuls of sugar into my coffee and stirring. I didn't care about their reasons, which weren't as informed as mine. I was the only one who'd seen the look on Alex's face that night.

His sense of helpless distress in the light booth had been pitiful, and he was unable to escape on his own. I couldn't save the guy I cared for, so I'd help the one I used to be with instead.

He didn't ask for help.

"Tzedakah is the greatest mitzvah." I blinked and put my hand over my mouth. "Oops."

"That's not a thing from Passover, is it?" Grace sipped her orange juice.

"No, but it's been on my mind since Yom Kippur." I wrapped cold fingers around my warm cup. "We've been so focused on winning everything, I worry I'll forget that helping is important."

They didn't freeze in place, but everyone got quiet and still. And stared at me.

"That'll never happen," Logan said.

"Yeah." Faith snorted. "That's like saying a fish forgot to swim."

"Or the sun forgot to rise," Grace added.

"As long as you don't let your guard down." Hal tilted his head, reminding me of his dad. "You can help Alex, but don't go trusting him afterward."

"No worries." I sipped my blissfully hot coffee. "He'll probably turn his nose up in the air and call me a do-gooder."

"Oooh, big insults." Grace made a duck face and waggled her fingers at me. "Aliyah, the Good Witch of the South."

"Salem's in the north." Logan scratched his head.

"Sorry." Grace winked, amping up her accent. "It's southern to me, don't you know."

Everybody laughed.

"Hey," Faith said. "Wasn't there a null magus in the papers a few years back?"

"Yeah." I nodded, then took a big slug of coffee. It was the perfect temperature, warm enough that it comforted my throat but cool enough to not burn. "Al Dunstable. He saved his faerie girlfriend from iron poisoning by canceling her troll magic. Nixed his Sidhe variety, too. Now they're regular magi."

Hal sat bolt upright in his seat, staring with eyes like twin moons. Faith put her arm around him. My sleep-deprived brain couldn't imagine why.

"Sounds interesting." Logan leaned over his coffee and inhaled deeply. "Tell it while I fall asleep? Like a bedtime story?"

"Yeah, tell us," Faith said.

"I think I'll doze off before getting a sentence out." I nodded. "I've got everything I know about it in a scrapbook at home. We can go over it another time."

They nodded, still leaning together with their arms around each other. Moments passed. Logan nodded a few times, then shook exhaustion off long enough to remember his coffee. Finally, it occurred to me why the story of Al Dunstable and Gemma Tolland would hit super close to home for Hal and Faith, and maybe even give them hope.

"How will you guys get through the dance?" Grace broke the silence.

"With a good long nap," Hal said.

"Why are you drinking all this then?" Grace pointed at the coffee.

"Because we don't have whatever you're using to look so chipper." Faith pointed at Grace's face, with its distinct lack of circles under the eyes. Then I realized how she did it.

"It's Umbral magic. She's as tired as we are, just hides it better. Am I right?"

"You got me." Grace smiled and tapped her nose. "I'm wearing this enhancement for an errand. After that, it's dreamland for a few hours."

"Beauty sleep," Logan said. "I need that."

We all had a laugh, then finished our beverages and breakfast. When we got up to bus our table, a snarky voice called out behind us.

"Look at the pajama crew. Field trip to Walmart later?" I turned to find Dylan.

"What?" I blinked, staring at my friend.

"You heard me. Looks like you spent all night with books, but there's nothing to study for right now. What were you up to, anyway?" He crossed his arms over his chest and raised his eyebrow.

"We'll talk later, Dylan." I approached him but he shook his head, glaring at me.

"Not now, Aliyah." He addressed me but glared at Grace. "I don't have the energy for your psychobabble."

Logan and Hal blinked blearily at Dylan and Faith rubbed her chin, but Grace slipped her arm through mine and led us all toward the dishwashing window.

"Don't mind him." Grace shook her head, sighing. "He probably just needs more time."

"No, Grace." I turned my head, staring at her. "He's had plenty of that. Plus time working on his music and hanging out with friends in his band. He's waiting for something. Maybe an apology?"

"It's been almost six months since we broke up. And what do I need to apologize for?"

"I don't know." I shrugged. "He's been through more than you think, what with discovering he's an extramagus."

"Look, I get it. It hurts to break up." Grace sighed. "But I had nothing to do with the extramagus thing. His attitude's gotten ridiculous."

"It's worse than you think for him. I can't say more than that."

"Why?" She shook her head. "Look, maybe you're a sanity unicorn. What if Dylan's just normal for an extramagus and having a mental break?"

I froze, stung as if she'd just slapped me in the face. Logan dropped his coffee spoon. Hal blinked.

"Holy shit, Grace, I can't believe you said that." Faith rounded on her, putting her hands on her hips.

"It didn't sound good." Hal shook his head.

"I'm sorry." Grace pressed both hands to her chest.

"Save it for Dylan." My face flushed, or at least it felt hot. Maybe it was my hand, channeling solar magic. I took three deep breaths before continuing, "Just two words. I'm. Sorry. That's it. Why is that so hard for you to understand?"

"Because I owned my issues last year, and part of that was refusing to take the blame for stuff that's not my fault."

"How about I give you a reading, Grace?" None of us had noticed Izzy approach, which made sense considering how tired we were.

"I don't believe in those."

"For amusement then." She shrugged. "Maybe it'll be relaxing."

The rest of us stared like we were at a CW drama-watch party.

"If the rest of you get off my case, fine."

"If you don't mind, I need to hit the hay." Hal shuffled toward the critter area, looking for Nin. "Before I have to hit the infirmary."

"The rest of you go back to sleep," Izzy said. "You all look like something the mercat dragged in."

We left, sleepily waving goodbye. On the way out, I glanced at Professor Luciano. Had he noticed Dylan's disdain and our subsequent argument? No. He hadn't gone to Dean Adelphi for social time. Cards covered the table between them, the tea pushed to the side. He was getting a reading, and at the center of it all sat the Tower.

Ouch.

Death wasn't the worst card to get in a tarot reading by itself. Two made it scarier: the Tower and the Chariot reversed. I glanced at the other cards surrounding the Tower. Mostly, they were cups and swords and not too bad. But there was the Chariot reversed in a future position, and Death was beside it.

The Professor didn't glance up, even though I'd been staring for a while. Dean Adelphi did, and she narrowed her eyes. I didn't wait around to see what she'd do next.

That reading was foretelling a catastrophe.

After seeing that, it should have been harder to rest, but I was almost asleep when Grace came in and went directly to bed. If we didn't sleep now, carrying out a covert plan to hoodwink Temperance at the dance would get dangerous.

I wore my dress from Parents' Night. It was amazing looking and comfortable, plus I didn't mind wearing the same special-event dress twice. Grace chose something completely different. It was a lavender and gold chiffon confection that draped across her body with no discernible fastenings, and it had a neckline that plunged to her solar plexus. Her footwear seemed risky.

At first, I wasn't sure why she'd picked six-inch platforms. I wondered how she'd dance in them. Kitty and Faith came by our room to get ready, joined by Cadence and Izzy later. The hour before the dance consisted of a flurry of preening, plus a few panicked moments where Cadence helped Grace struggle with dress tape.

Grabbing a handful of spare dress tape strips, I took advantage of her distraction. Grace's handbag sat on her bed, out of her view, so I headed toward it with the tape. Faith saw what I was doing immediately.

"Hey Cadence, if your voice isn't too tired, I'd love to hear another song." Faith stepped up to the mirror beside Grace with her eyeshadow palette and started applying.

"Okay."

Instead of a showstopping vocal showcase, Cadence regaled us with a sedate rendition of an old song her mother loved: *Tiny Dancer* by Elton John. I turned Grace's bag so it pointed at Cadence, opened it, and stuffed the wardrobe malfunction fixers inside.

Cadence had her back to the switch, but the space between it and her was unobstructed, a direct line of sight. I stood by the bag, keeping it open as long as I could. As she reached the end of the last verse, I closed it and went about the business of applying lipstick.

Let's hope it's enough.

A knock at the door made us all freeze in our tracks. At that point, we weren't expecting anyone. I went to answer it, hand glowing faintly because I worried it was Temperance. She'd been too quiet, and our wins against her so far suddenly felt too easy. I needn't have worried.

Logan stood outside the door, hanging his head and blushing.

"Hey, Aliyah? Can I go in your group of friends to the dance?"

"Of course." I nodded, banishing my magic. "You told Dorian no, huh?"

"Yeah, guess I chickened out." He sighed. "But I said he can ask me to dance once we're there."

"Do you want to talk about it?" I stepped into the hall, closing the door behind me and lowering my voice.

"I don't know." Logan tilted his head, peering at my face without meeting my eyes as if he expected to find something there he didn't like, but the tightness in his expression eased and the blush faded.

"It's all good if you don't."

"No, I should get it off my chest." Logan leaned against the wall, staring across the hall instead of looking at me. He had an easier time if he didn't have to make eye contact. "This is gonna sound stupid, but the way he asked, well, it felt almost insulting."

"Definitely not stupid. And I agree." One corner of my mouth tilted up. "Someone gave me advice that might also work for you. Here goes." I cleared my throat. "Your someone special should worship the ground you walk on and make you feel happy."

"My brain knows that." He sighed, gazing down the hall toward Dorian's room. "But my heart's another story. It feels like nobody understands what it's like."

"I absolutely do." I leaned close beside him, whispering, "I've had a crush on Dylan for a year and a half."

Logan's lower lip trembled as if he might cry. My breath caught in my throat, which choked up with tears I refused to allow to ruin my makeup. So I turned and reached out, and we ended up in a shaky sort of bear hug.

We'd done that before multiple times a day when he'd stayed in the room at Bubbe's office. This time, something was different. Not emotionally or in any weird hormonal way; physically, something was wrong. I glanced down briefly, then at his face again.

"You need to go back to your room before the dance, Logan." I loosened my grip, holding him at arm's length.

"Why?"

"Pants. You've still got pajama bottoms on."

"Oh!" His face turned red, like the first day we'd met. Logan's social gaffes and mistakes had diminished since then, at least around his friends. "Yeah, I'd better fix that. See you soon, Aliyah."

"Yeah, see you."

I headed back into the room and told everyone Logan would join us. Grace looked away, collecting her bag. We left minutes after that. Everyone else was ready, and the dance was about to start.

I stood in the third-floor hallway, waiting for the folks I'd invited to go in this group. Faith had gone to get Hal, and they showed up with Kitty and Eston. That made sense because they were on dates.

The rest arrived one by one, except for Izzy, who arrived with Lee, of course. Bar and Brianna showed up, Crow at their heels. Cadence smiled, and I was in the middle of a relieved sigh until the bird shifter headed for Grace. She passed her bag, nullifying switch and all, to me.

"It's up to you to save the prince of darkness," she murmured and stepped forward.

That was when I noticed his distinctively designed suit, complete with lavender vest and tie. Crow cleaned up extremely well, to the point where casting directors at Lifetime or the Hallmark Channel might clamor to give him romantic leads in teen movies. They linked arms.

Everyone's favorite it girl is about to make some unexpected waves.

"Grace?" I put a hand on her free arm, stopping her. "Are you seriously doing this?"

"Sorry." She looked me in the eye, at least. The regret there shocked me into letting her go. "I'm countering something. You'll see when we get downstairs."

She let Crow call out the first floor to the staircase. Hal and Faith followed them, along with Kitty and Eston. Their movements revealed Dorian, who'd been standing behind them. He stared and blinked, watching the stairs carry them away. After that, he hurried to my side.

"Aliyah, I've got to tell you something." His eyes were wide. "I just found out."

"Listen, we've got to go, or we'll be late." I sighed.

"But it's about—"

"We're going. Now." Cadence's voice cut through Dorian's like a knife.

We all followed her, although I wanted to wait for Dylan. It was as if her voice had moved my body. I could have resisted if I hadn't been so shocked by Grace and exhausted from the night before, but maybe I wouldn't have. Cadence was one of my best friends, and I'd never seen her this hurt. She needed me.

I stepped off the first floor too late to kick off the dancing as I had at all the other dances here. Music already played *I'm With You* by Avril Lavigne. As expected, Grace was out there with Crow, Hal with Faith, and Kitty with Eston. Noah had paired up with Jonah. Elanor stepped up to our group and asked Brianna to dance.

I looked around for Dylan, intending to drag him out there, but Logan put a hand on my arm and pointed past the other couples on the floor. My heart nearly stopped.

"No."

Dylan was out there already, dancing with Temperance Fairbanks.

I shook out of Logan's grip and hurried away, turning my back on the dance floor. I couldn't watch this. Thankfully, there were plenty of chairs in the corner. I headed toward them, but a voice I couldn't divorce from authority stopped me.

"Miss Morgenstern, may I have this dance?"

"Professor Luciano?" I glanced over my shoulder, and sure enough, he stood there, elbow out. I blinked.

Izzy stood behind him, between Lee and Cadence, holding a tarot card: the King of Cups. She nodded and I trusted her, but I still had doubts. A professor couldn't rescue me from a broken heart.

Perhaps he's got wisdom to impart.

I nodded and took his arm, wondering why the Evil Inside Voice reassured me. Mostly it expected the worst from everyone. Had it always been sympathetic toward my professor? A few gasps and whispers followed us, but they cut out at a word from Cadence.

"Professor, what's this about?"

"This." He pulled the lapel on his jacket, revealing a faintly yellowed letter in the pocket, with a familiar return address: 10-1/2 Hawthorne Street.

"Oh." I blinked. "But my great uncle's letters are in my room. I've been reading them."

"This is one of their counterparts."

"You're Bert?"

"Filberto. I only allowed Noah the elder to call me that." He nodded. "And you, just this once."

"Why are you telling me now?"

"It will come up in the near future." He sighed. "Inevitable events, I'm afraid."

"What do you mean? What's going to happen?"

"Further investigation." He sighed. "Due to the fear and turmoil on this campus. But you're an extramagus, in tune with more magic than your fellows. You can feel it if you focus." We reached the edge of the dance floor, so he spun me to turn us around.

I let him lead, and we locked gazes. He blinked slowly as though waiting for me to do something.

"How?"

"Close your eyes and clear your mind. Consider well what comes unbidden to it."

I tried, worried I'd trip or bump into someone. Making it through this dance without incident was important, but so was discovering the effects of all the drama this semester. All I could think of was Dylan and how he'd been that morning. Had Temperance gotten her hooks into him right after that? Or much sooner?

If I had any money, I'd wager his new guitar.

"Keep practicing, and it will come through eventually. I believe you've got the basic idea."

"How do you know?"

"Finish reading all the letters." He risked a fragile grin. "Your great uncle and I had much in common. Your worries aren't unfounded."

"How bad do you think it'll get?"

"I'm not sure. I believe you're stuck in a coincidental pattern, along with some of your cohorts."

"So, you're telling me to be on guard?"

"And prepared. Practice the exercise you attempted today each morning or every night. Perhaps both is best." The song ended, and he escorted me off the dance floor.

"Thanks, Professor."

"Thank me by continuing your studies and vigilance." He bowed.

"I will." I curtsied.

"May your evening be fruitful." He turned on his heel and headed for the punch bowl, where he filled a cup before merging into the crowd of assorted faculty.

I walked in the opposite direction, unsure how I'd manage to find Alex. Temperance's gambit, bringing Dylan as her date, meant he might not have bothered coming. All the same, I had a mission, one best accomplished in shadows I'd never felt comfortable navigating.

On any other night I would have conjured light, but I couldn't draw attention to myself now, especially while Grace still distracted Temperance by shooting dirty looks at her over Crow's shoulder on the dance floor. The music changed to *Three Libras* by A Perfect Circle, a sufficiently seething soundtrack to their rivalry.

"Watch it."

Just like that, I found Alex—by tripping over his feet.

I tumbled to the floor on my back, twisting an ankle on the way and ending up beside him. He didn't catch me, not that I expected it. Ember peeped overhead, swooping toward me. Moments later, she wove to her left instead, as though she'd spotted something. Her white-hot flash of anger made a searing mark in my mind.

"Aren't you getting up, Morgenstern?"

I tried to get up and winced. "Not on my own, so you're stuck with me for now." I grabbed Grace's handbag, pulling it open. Luckily, my eyes had adjusted to the darkness by then.

"Am not." He bent his knees, getting his feet under him. "You know I can't talk to you."

"Wait." I reached in, grabbing the switch. "I've got something for you."

"If it's not a flask of bourbon, I'm not interested."

"It's freedom." I pulled the device out of the bag.

"No," he whimpered.

Alex flung his arms up, crossing them in front of his face, palms out. His eyes widened, whites like ghosts of crescent moons. I realized he thought I'd come here to murder him with a magipsychic device because one like it had hurt him before.

Look what that she-devil is capable of. Who's next?

Three things happened at once. I flipped the switch. Ember dive-bombed him, dropping something long and limp into his lap, and Alex burst into tears, clutching it against his chest and sobbing.

The music covered our confrontation, but it wouldn't for long if this kept up.

"Need help?" Logan stood between us, Doris mewing at whatever Alex held in his arms. No, not a what, a who. His familiar.

He's just a boy under all that venom and self-importance, one who loves his familiar like the rest of you.

"Nurse Smith. For Asceco." I answered. "And we're having a chat later about whatever you couldn't say after the talent show, Alex."

Logan chirped at Doris, who took off running, then held his hand down, and I took it. By the time Nurse Smith arrived, we'd moved far enough away from Alex to avoid getting detained and questioned.

"Why didn't you go to the infirmary with him?" Logan asked.

"We've got to stick around in case Dylan needs us. There's no way he went on this date for real."

Logan glanced around to see who was nearby before saying, "The thingamabob's a one-shot deal."

"We don't need it." I shook my head. "He must have had a plan, like, to get information or something."

Oh, you sweet summer child.

I stopped near the refreshment table. The voice's words confused me. Surely, it didn't think Dylan actually wanted to be around the mean girl? Maybe the best way to ignore it was to do something else.

I decided to give the professor's mysterious extramagus technique another try. Logan stared as I closed my eyes. This time, I managed to visualize a flat, nearly blank horizon like the winter ocean at twilight, and floating across it came the answer to all the turmoil.

Noah and Jonah, dancing together. They gazed into each other's eyes like the rest of the world had ceased to exist.

When I opened my eyes and looked at the dance floor, I saw them in the flesh. Instead of a gaze, their lips met, which caused an unexpected ruckus.

Even at Hawthorn, where we had chaperons and curfews, a kiss like that wouldn't raise faculty hackles. The sound and fury didn't come from the adults in the room.

Temperance Fairbanks let out a frustrated little scream, disgust twisting her face as she dragged Dylan off the dance floor. The humidity level rose as she approached, which meant she was angry enough to conjure without meaning to.

Beside me, Logan narrowed his eyes, humming slightly. The cloying air relaxed its grip as the extra moisture dissipated. Precious the grundylow shot him a dirty look from under Tempe's hair as she retreated to the corner Alex had occupied earlier.

"Uh-oh." Logan winced. "She's gonna get even angrier."

"It's her own fault." Dorian held three cups of punch. "You two look like you need refreshments."

I took one. "Thanks."

"No." Logan refused. "I need to dance." He took both cups from

Dorian and set them on the table, then grabbed his hand. "Come on. I promised you at least one."

I settled into a chair. Logan Pierce was a stress-dancer, so he might stay on the floor with Dorian until the music stopped for the night. I watched everybody on the floor. Even though the as-friends group had been my idea, it seemed like they'd all partnered up out there. Even Cadence had gone to cut a rug with Azrael Ambersmith.

"Hey." The chair beside me creaked.

"Hi, Bar."

"You don't sound happy."

"It's not you."

"I get it. Your dude had a date, even though he accepted the invitation. And she's nothing nice."

"What do you think happened with Crow?"

"He says Grace spent a week begging him to go with her. I don't know why."

You do. But you can hardly tell him about all that.

"So why aren't you out there dancing with Cadence?"

"She said no. Doesn't like me that way."

"Are you okay?"

"I'll live. At least I asked, right?"

"Yeah. You did."

"Who was the guy the nurse took out of here?"

"Alex Onassis."

"Did you know him?"

"He's my ex."

"Are you okay?"

I thought about that for a moment. The mission had been accomplished. We'd thwarted Temperance, but I'd lost my shot at telling Dylan how I felt. She must have decided to use him against us while she could. Maybe the voice had a point about the guitar. The Fairbanks family was extremely wealthy, and they frequented the Lyceum. Bribery with a musical instrument wasn't out of character for them.

But this wasn't over. Tempe could do much worse to Dylan than bribery, and still might. We'd freed Alex in the hope he'd have more information about her larger plans, so I still had work to do. That meant another chance, maybe.

"I'm not, but I'll get better eventually."

"I'm not a good talker. Or a good dancer either." Bar stood. "But I'm around if you need a listener. Tomorrow. I'm heading back to my room."

"Thanks, Bar."

He left.

The music changed to *Everybody Hurts* by REM. I recognized the music from Bubbe's office and it was a huge downer, so a lot of people left the dance floor. I sat, intending to drink the remaining two cups of punch Logan had left on the table.

Grace had other ideas. She sat in the seat Bar had just vacated.

"I'm sorry for pushing the device thing on you at the last minute."

"I managed. But are you going to apologize for the other thing?"

"What do you mean by that?"

"How long did you know about Temperance asking Dylan?"

"About a week. What's the big deal?"

"We're going to have to do all this work again and in as little time. Break's coming up. What if she whammies him?"

"Oh, no, Aliyah." She shook her head. "She won't have to."

"What?" I blinked. "I figured he's here because of that guitar. The only way he could afford that was if she paid for it."

"You're probably right about that." She nodded. "But whatever's been eating him, it's about to go toxic."

"Because he's an extramagus?"

"No." She sighed. "Just, since he got in trouble with the headmaster, he's been on a downward spiral."

"You noticed, and you still refused to apologize?"

"I can't lose face. None of us can afford that."

"It must be so hard being popular."

"Actually, it is. I have to look flawless, can't mess anything up, and have to say the perfect thing in the exact tone. I thought you'd understand because you have it harder as an extramagus."

"Boo-fricking-hoo, Grace. You chose to do the It Girl thing. I never opted in."

"I didn't know it'd be like this. Fake image, fake boyfriends, fake everything. At least you get to be real."

"You know what being real is? It's helping your friends. Making sure they don't fall so far they hurt themselves. How many times did you thank me for being there last year?"

"You know. You saved my life."

"And you didn't save Dylan's? Why? Because you used to be a couple?"

"He's not suicidal."

"What do you think Tempe's about then? Handing out guitars with no strings?"

"Hate crimes." She hung her head. "Against half the people on this campus. Shit. I've been wrong this whole time."

"It's okay. We can fix it."

"What do we do?"

"Finish this dance." I stood, and she joined me. "At least you do. I'm going back to our room and making a list."

"I'm not sure I want to be here either. Crow's intense."

"Then dance with someone else. Cadence would probably love to take him off your hands."

"Yeah, I owe her an apology, along with some other people."

"Do you want me to go with you?"

"Nah, I've got this. You go make the list."

We parted ways. As I headed toward the stairs, I ran into Faith and Hal.

"It worked." I held the bag out toward him.

"Great." He took it. "I'll be tweaking it again over the break. We might want it again in the spring."

"Are you leaving already?" Faith asked. "You barely danced."

"I did plenty. I'm exhausted." I yawned.

"So are we," Hal said.

We headed up the stairs together.

CHAPTER FORTY-TWO

The next morning, Logan knocked on our door. Grace had come in sometime after I'd gone to sleep, and he wanted to see her. Apparently, he'd danced a hole into his shoe, but she wasn't remotely ready to wake up. We left his dress shoes in my room and went down to the café for pastry and magical bean juice. The place was deserted except for us.

"So, how'd it go with Dorian?" I asked, settling into one of the tufted chairs by the fireplace. It wasn't lit, but I fixed that as we sat down.

"It didn't." Logan stared into his Americano.

"Oh?" I dunked a biscotti in my latte.

"I think I liked the idea of Dorian more than, you know, *him*." He glanced at his chocolate croissant. "If that makes sense."

"No, I get it. So you were stress-dancing?"

"Nobody's ever called it that." He snorted. "But yeah. I wore him out."

"Who'd you dance with after that?"

"Grace, and then a guy from Gallow's Hill. He had no trouble keeping up, even though he had two left feet. Big guy, but nice. I think we're going to be friends." Logan finally took a bite of his croissant.

"Bar?"

"How'd you know?"

"Lucky guess." I dunked my cookie again. "What happened with Cadence?"

"Oh, she's back together with Crow."

"Well then, the evening turned out all right for her, at least."

"And Alex."

"But he was in tears last time we saw him."

"We helped him, though. He must be better off now, so let's visit him."

I had my doubts, but the only way to know for sure was directly from him. We finished our pastries and caffeinated drinks, got a blueberry muffin and herbal tea to go, then headed down the ramp to the infirmary. It was quiet, and Nurse Smith wasn't at his desk. Ezekiel Brown, the vampire CNA, was on duty instead.

"Hi, Zeke."

"Mr. Pierce. Miss Morgenstern. What do you need?"

"We're checking on Alex Onassis," Logan said.

"Ah, I remember." He nodded. "It was your familiar who alerted the nurse to his condition. He's here. I'll see if he's awake."

Moments later, Zeke returned, nodding. He opened the door to one of the exam rooms, and we went inside. Alex sat up on the edge of a bed, his familiar curled up in his lap, asleep. Despite the night in the infirmary, he didn't look well-rested, and he sneered at us.

Logan smiled anyway, setting the tea and muffin on the bedside table. I stood there with my arms crossed, leaning in the doorway. In this case, Logan was the optimist. We'd done the right thing for Alex, even if we'd had our own motives. I wasn't waiting for an about-face.

"Why are you being so nice to me?" He snorted, but quietly.

"Not nice, good," I answered. "There's a difference. One's for people you like, the other's doing the right thing for whoever needs it."

"That's fair."

"Exactly." Logan nodded. Doris paced over to the bed, hopped up, and sat there peering at Asceco as he slept.

"I'll rephrase. Why did you help me?"

"You needed it. Wasn't that why you went to Aliyah twice?" Logan answered.

"There's got to be a *káti gia káti*." He sighed, shaking his head. "Quid pro quo."

"If it makes you feel better, fine." I tilted my head. "What were you trying to tell me up in the light booth?"

"Oh." He paled, making the circles under his eyes look darker than before. "Not here."

"I'm not going into your room or letting you in mine."

"I meant off-campus."

"Fine. When?"

"How about we walk you to the train?" Logan offered. "When you leave for break, I mean."

"That works." He nodded. "But there's something I can say that you need to know. About *her*."

"Go on." I waved my hand, trying to look nonchalant even though his impending warning spooked me. Ember stirred on my shoulder, peeping softly.

"Don't let her bring Dylan back to New York with her." He sighed, closing his eyes. "I went at Thanksgiving. It was all downhill from there."

Logan and I stood silent and staring. His jaw dropped. Had his gut crashed too, like mine? The danger was clear to both of us, at least.

"But how?" I finally managed. "He's barely talking to most of us."

"I have some ideas," Logan said. "Whatever we try, we'll do our best."

"Thanks for the snack, Pierce. Now leave me alone. I'm going back to sleep."

We parted ways upstairs, with Logan heading back to his room. It had something to do with those ideas, which he didn't explain to me. I spent the rest of the day in the gym, running the track and doing drills. It was the only thing that came close to quelling my new and unwelcome sense of foreboding.

Everyone spent the last week before break studying. Lab didn't have exams, but we'd be tested on lecture material. The second-year students worked overtime on catching up. We'd been awfully distracted. Dylan refused help from everyone except Logan, who became his constant companion. Dorian gave them space, tagging along with me instead.

It eased my fears about winter break. I'd come to trust Logan Pierce like family. He'd do his best to convince Dylan to stay on campus for the winter. Alex's untold story hung over our heads like razor wire, and my fraying self-control made my hands glow at random. The last thing I needed was to stir up any extramagus hatred.

I wore myself out physically, both at the gym and in the baths, swimming morning and night. If I was too tired for anxiety, maybe it'd leave me alone. Faith noticed. She must have squealed on me to Izzy because she showed up on Wednesday night, towel in hand.

"Have you tried meditation?" She gave me a hand out of the pool.

"No. The last thing I want is more time to think."

"It's not like that." Izzy tossed the towel at my head. "I do it all the time. At least try it. I don't like how thin you're getting."

"Excuse me?" I blinked.

"You've lost what looks like ten pounds in a week. I can see your ribs."

I stood at the mirror. Hip bones jutted under the hem on my tank-ini, which draped a little in front. I agreed to try meditating but during break. I stopped swimming in the mornings and added protein smoothies at breakfast and lunch to appease her.

The exam on Monday was the least of my worries. I answered every question with little trouble. Much of it was on topics we'd studied on our own time.

People leaving campus packed and prepared. Most were heading out on Tuesday, with extramural students taking a detour by their campuses before traveling out of town. Alex's flight back to Greece was a Monday night red-eye, so he left campus after lunch. I waited ten minutes, then helped Logan gather bags for Bubbe's, which was our pretense for leaving when we did. We'd meet Alex at the Witch's Brew.

"How did it go with Dylan?"

"He's staying here." Logan pulled the door to the hallway open. "But I didn't convince him. Noah did."

I blinked. We continued down the hall, pushing through the exit into the street. We paused to put on gloves and hats, and Logan continued as we walked down Essex Street.

"Your brother asked Dylan to play some gigs with him in town over the break. Paying ones." Logan paused, adjusting the strap on his satchel. "Apparently, Tempe bought that Paul Reed Smith guitar Dylan's had since the talent show. Noah made it clear he didn't like that."

I nodded. "I guess Dylan respects him, then."

Alex stood outside the coffee shop. He'd been inside though, because he had hot chocolates for both of us. When I asked why he bothered, he said, "It's only money."

We went the rest of the way down Essex Street, turning right on Washington toward the train station. The streets were largely deserted, the only people hurrying through the cold on brisk errands. He made sure nobody was nearby before speaking.

"She wants to make an example of a lesser extrahuman."

"'Lesser?'" I stared at him.

"Look, I don't know how else to say what that means." He sighed. "I'm not sure who or how, but whatever she does to them, it'll be extremely humiliating. Probably painful, too."

"Any idea who she might choose? Or when she'll do it?"

"The Craft Expo, maybe?" Logan asked.

"Spirit Week and Bishop's Row are both higher-profile events. Probably during one of those." He shuddered. "She knows how to bide her time."

"Was she always planning this?"

"If so, she didn't tell me until after Thanksgiving." He reached inside his coat, stroking Asceco's head. She hissed softly in response. "When she had leverage."

"Did she poison Clementine? And Seth?"

"Yeah. Somehow, she used poison that felt just like her roommate's. I don't know how she did it because she insists she's not an extramagus."

I nodded. "I've got that figured out."

"Can you sense each other or something?" Alex blinked. "On second thought, don't answer that."

"Did you know she had a secret boyfriend?"

"Oh, gods, yes. Asceco smelled him on her all the time. I didn't care." His breath caught in his throat. "I was never into her, but I was okay with us using each other. Tolerated all her lying. But then she—"

"We know she hurt you." Logan patted his arm. "Faith told us how bad she could be."

"She's half my size, but her magic's like a tsunami. And that grundylow." He shivered. "We were lopsided from the start, but once she had the upper hand, it got brutal."

"What did he smell like?" Logan asked. "The boyfriend, I mean?"

"I don't see how that'll help. Dragonets and mercats don't have the same senses as a basilisk."

"Noah's got a tallin," I offered.

"Oh, gods, he's not in on this?" Alex's attempted laugh turned into a sob. "Not after what I did to him last year?"

"My brother holds crazy grudges, so no." I sighed. "We're trying to find out who he is."

"I can talk to Asceco," Logan said. "I've got a weird ability. If that's okay with you."

"Rare. And yeah, okay." Alex nodded, opening his coat again. Logan and Asceco peered at each other for almost a minute, sticking their tongues out a few times in the process.

"All set." He nodded. "Thanks, Alex."

"No." He shook his head. "Don't thank me for throwing a thimble of water on a house fire I helped set."

"I don't take returns on thank yous." Logan grinned. "It's a big gesture, coming from you."

"We're even now, so don't expect any more."

"Noted." I jerked my chin at the train, which had just pulled in. "That's your ride. Don't miss it."

He nodded, then turned his back on us and headed up the stairs to the platform.

"Have a good break," Logan called after him.

He threw one hand up in farewell and got on the train. After that, Logan and I headed to Bubbe's, where we stowed his bags in the spare room. She was busy with a patient, so we only said hello and goodbye before heading back to campus and having dinner with our friends.

The next day was a flurry of goodbyes. Arick and Lena went to the airport at the same time since they were on the same Lufthansa flight to Frankfurt, where they'd catch trains to Bergen and Genoa. Hailey and Bailey caught their Acela to New York, the same one Temperance took, though they got on a different car. Kitty and Eston left together, headed to Portland so he could meet her mothers. They all departed after breakfast.

Faith stayed on campus that year, along with Hal, Dylan, Lee, and Grace, who promised to keep her from getting bored. Dorian got on the commuter rail after lunch. Providence wasn't far and he missed his parents, but he promised to let us know when he was on the way back so we could meet him at Salem station.

Elanor stayed longest, leaving while the rest of us were on the way to dinner. She was almost at the door, where Noah waited to walk her out. I thought she'd leave without saying goodbye, but she turned and sprinted toward Logan, lifting him off the floor in a bear hug. Their eyes were bright and shiny, though they didn't weep.

"You take care of my baby brother, Morgenstern," she told me.

I nodded and she was gone.

Noah came to me in the living room after breakfast on the third day of break. Logan and I were playing video games.

"I'm in love," he said. "With Jonah Arnold."

"That's awesome." I hugged him. "I'm so happy for you!"

"We're going on a date tonight, to the movies."

"Cool!" Logan smiled. "We're walking around to look at everyone's holiday decorations."

"So, you two?" Noah raised an eyebrow. "Like, alone together?"

"No." Logan shook his head. "Most of the gang from school, plus Izzy and Cadence."

"No Crow?" He didn't ask about Dylan, who hadn't been over yet.

"They broke up again." I shrugged. "I kinda hope they stay that way," I said, and I told Noah about what I'd heard at the Lyceum.

"That's the Merlini family business for you. Cadence can do better."

But she didn't. They got back together that night.

Most of break went on the same way, hanging around with friends and doing whatever the weather and our budgets allowed around Salem. I kept offering Logan some of my allowance, but he refused.

"I'm working for Bubbe. She's paying me. It's only a little, but enough for pocket money."

Noah and I invited everyone still at Hawthorn over for the first night of Hanukkah, the Festival of Lights. And Jonah, who couldn't share our meal with us or come until an hour after sunset. Mom, Dad, and Bubbe agreed to have dinner first, despite our usual tradition.

Hal and Faith were in Boston at the hospital, but everybody else showed up. Even Dylan, who seemed happy to be there all through dinner. That made sense, considering how much he loved food.

"These are amazing!" he exclaimed over dessert. "What are they?"

"*Sufganya.*" I passed him another fried confection of jelly-filled dough. "Noah made them."

"Even better."

Since the holiday was all about hope and endurance, I wanted him to have a good time. So I went to a lot of effort, making another batch of *sufganya*. He said he wasn't hungry anymore, but put most of it in his backpack for later.

After that, I made sure to include him in the group playing dreidel. The rules were simple enough for everyone to follow, though Grace confused the letters on most of her spins.

"That was *Nun*." I tapped the Hebrew letter. "You get nothing."

"Sorry, thought it was *Gimmel*." She put back the pile of foil-wrapped chocolate gelt she'd raked in by mistake.

"Easy mistake to make." I shrugged. "They're similar. Noah used to deliberately mix them up."

"Hey!" he protested. "I was six."

"Yeah. You're all grown up now." Dylan grinned, watching his spin. "*Hei*, right? That means I take half?"

"Uh-huh." I nodded.

"Do they all mean something?" Lee picked the top up, turning it in his hand to look at the letters before taking his turn.

"*Nes gadol hayah sham*." Noah chanted.

"A great miracle happened here." I translated. "After Judah won the temple back, the oil lasted eight nights instead of one. It's why we make all the fried food."

"Why didn't they just make more oil?" Lee spun, watched, then shrugged. "*Nun*." He passed the dreidel to me.

"They couldn't let the light go out, or the temple would have stayed desecrated." I spun. "*Shin*. Put one in."

I tossed a piece of gelt into the pot between us and passed the dreidel, but before Logan could spin, someone knocked on the door. Noah jumped up, opening it to let Jonah in. They hugged, pecking each other on both cheeks like they do in Europe, but they held hands as Noah led him out of the living room and into the kitchen to meet our parents.

After that, Dylan's mood soured. He collected his things and made excuses, preparing to leave. I tried to stop him.

"At least stay for the *Menorah*."

"Yeah, Dylan," Grace added. "Remember what we talked about?"

He blinked. "All right, fine. But as soon as that's done, I'm going."

We gathered in the dining room by the window facing the back yard. Dad set the candles out beside the matchbook, one for the first night and the other the *shamash*, which was the candle in the middle that brought light to the others. On the first night, we said three blessings.

"*Baruch Atah Adonai Elohenu Melech haolam asher kideshanu bemitzvotav vetzivanu lehadlik ner Chanukah*," Dad sang.

"Blessed are You, Lord our God, King of the universe, who has sanctified us with His commandments and commanded us to kindle the Chanukah light," Noah murmured beside Jonah, squeezing his hand.

"*Baruch Atah Adonai Elohenu Melech Haolam sheasa nisim laavotenu bayamim hahem bizman hazeh*," Bubbe sang. Logan joined in, pronouncing the Hebrew almost exactly like my grandma. He must have asked for her help practicing.

"Wow," I said. He blushed.

"Blessed are You, Lord our God, King of the universe, who performed miracles for our forefathers in those days at this time." Dylan recited under his breath, arms crossed over his chest. "I studied too."

"Shh." Lee elbowed him.

"It's okay. I remember what it was like, learning these when I was your age. Right here in this room, too," Mom said. Then she sang the third blessing. "*Baruch Atah Adonai Elohenu Melech Haolam shehecheyanu vekiyimanu vehigianu lizman hazeh*."

"Blessed are You, Lord our God, King of the universe, who has granted us life, sustained us, and enabled us to reach this occasion." I translated for Grace, who sighed, nodding. I figured the third prayer, said only on the first night, would resonate especially well with her.

My father struck a match, lit the *shamash*, and touched the flame to the wick on the first candle. It sat vigil for a moment until Dad set the *shamash* in the middle. The flames stabilized, pushing the darkness back from the window if only just a little.

The flames guttered, flickering briefly in the wake of Dylan's passage. He left without saying goodbye. Grace and I both glanced over our shoulders, listening to the front door closing behind him.

"I apologized. We're good."

"What's his problem, then?"

"Beats me. Ask your brother. They hang out all the time."

I didn't. Not because I spaced and forgot to, either.

It's because you don't want to. Not really.

Being with my family and friends let me ignore the Evil Inside Voice for a good while longer.

CHAPTER FORTY-THREE

Classes should have gotten back to normal after the break in January. Everyone was back, including the extramural groups from the other schools. Something felt off, though, like the stillness ahead of a Nor'easter. I resumed my frantic levels of physical training from the week before break. This time I avoided Izzy so she wouldn't notice.

Dylan trained at the same time, conjuring and throwing orbs in the middle of the gym. I circled him, running around my crush in an ironic parallel to avoiding my emotions. I'd ruined last year's team dynamic with relationship drama. Fear of the same outcome stopped me.

Maybe it wasn't for the best. I hadn't felt this unstable since I'd first started hearing the Evil Inside Voice and randomly conjuring solar magic. I needed something to control, and training, especially with Bishop's Row coming at the end of February, was the most constructive option.

I'd have to stick to a strategy of steady meals. That shouldn't have been hard at a boarding school with scheduled dining, or so I thought.

The unease I'd witnessed in Professor Luciano had grown so much that even Dorian noticed. Usually sharp and quick like Ember on a sunny day, our teacher reminded me of flat soda. By Monday of the third week, I couldn't stand it and headed to my room after Lab. I sat cross-legged on the floor, clearing my mind to see what showed up. Instead of visualizing him or any classmate, I got the Evil Inside Voice.

It's the poisonings. You forgot to meet with the headmaster.

"Crap on a crap cracker."

I stood up so quickly I got dizzy. Leaning on my desk, I waited for the feeling to pass. The moment it did, I rushed out of the room, Ember flapping along behind me until she managed to grab my blazer and cling on. In moments, my feet carried me down the stairs, which I'd activated for an even bigger speed boost. The lobby flew by in a blur.

A convenient column helped me turn the corner ahead of the academic wing, which led to the headmaster's office. I skidded to a stop, reaching out to pull the door open. As my fingers made contact with it, I heard a voice from the shadows to my right.

"That was fast." Hal stepped forward. "I just sent Nin to your room to fetch you."

"She's there alone, then." I panted to catch my breath. "Because I'm here for my own reasons."

"Hmm." He tilted his head. "That might get complicated. My dad wants to ask you a few questions."

"As long as it's not about Professor Luciano."

"It is, actually. He's already in there." He sighed. "I've got to fetch Nin. Good luck in there, Aliyah."

My hand trembled as it reached to open the door, almost like it wasn't part of me anymore. The wood was feverishly warm, or maybe my hand was cold, but I pulled it open anyway.

Once inside, I sat in the chair to the right of my professor. The other one was already occupied by Professor DeBeer.

"Miss Morgenstern, perhaps you can enlighten us."

"I'll try, Headmaster."

"Professor DeBeer thinks she saw Professor Luciano in the café after your last period on the day Clementine was poisoned. Hal tells me that you were the last student to leave the laboratory that day. Do you happen to remember which way he went after closing up the room?"

"I don't." I sighed. "I didn't see him lock up."

"Then we're at an impasse, I'm afraid. Unless you know anything that could help us clear this up."

"I might. What sort of thing do you mean?"

"The whereabouts of any ice or poison magus, especially if you saw one of each together near the cafe it would be helpful, in addition to any troubling statements they might have made."

My brain went into overdrive. Alex had come down from upstairs. Dorian and Lena had gone straight to the infirmary with me. Dylan was working in the café but they already knew that and had cleared him. Were there any faculty besides Luciano with poison? And what about ice?

"I only saw Dylan." How was I supposed to help Professor Luciano? And why was he under suspicion?

What about that stained glass mural? Fire with poison ice? Am I ringing a bell?

My professor had taught me to sense magic as an extramagus as though he'd done it himself. Great-Uncle Noah hadn't gotten his second element until long after graduation, in the Coast Guard. After Filberto Luciano was back in Italy, writing letters overseas. My eyes widened.

"I certainly didn't see Professor Luciano in there. He wasn't in the lobby, not before or after Familiar Bonding. Professor DeBeer must have been mistaken."

"How dare you?" She whirled, staring daggers at me. "Call in a different student, sir. Miss Morgenstern's got a natural bias."

I knew what she meant but refused to disclose my revelation about the man who in kinder times might have been my great uncle-in-law.

"Which was what you said earlier about my son, Professor DeBeer."

Block her throw.

"The lobby was packed. There should be lots of students to ask."

Not like that. With Seth. But don't rat your friends out.

"Another familiar was poisoned a month later." Headmaster Hawkins raised an eyebrow. "Was Professor Luciano there for that?"

I shook my head. "No."

"Where did it happen, then?"

These waters are shark-infested. Tread them carefully.

"I'm not sure. You'd have to ask Faith. I wasn't with her when it happened."

"Then how do you know he wasn't with her?"

Don't lie, just skirt the truth. It's the only way to protect them all.

"The same way I knew Seth was in trouble. Something I tried after a lot of research."

Both true. Now digress.

"I'm an extramagus. We have this quirk, sort of. To sense, like, disturbances in the Force."

Good job.

"Is that true? Can extramagi trace the flow of magic?"

"Yes, Headmaster." Professor Luciano nodded. "Like tanuki trace luck, though the ability to manipulate it is limited to their particular elements. And of course, their coincidental drawback."

He meant the limitation in power. Every extramagus was supposed to have one. Uncle Richard's was the only one I'd heard about in detail. It was geographic, limiting everything but his initial element of fire to Rhode Island.

"Thank the gods for those." Professor DeBeer traced a sigil I couldn't identify in the air.

"Have you discovered your drawback yet, Miss Morgenstern?"

"No, but I haven't tried."

"Noted." Headmaster Hawkins waved his hand at the door. "Miss Morgenstern, Professor Luciano. You're both free to go. I've got more to discuss with Professor DeBeer, however."

"This isn't over, Lucy." Susan DeBeer glared. "We'll find out who's been inappropriate with students eventually, and you're not off my radar yet."

I opened the door for my teacher and closed it behind him, too. He looked wearier than before but not as weighed down.

"What did she mean, inappropriate with students?" I led him to the other end of the short hallway, away from the door. "If it's about the dance, I'll go in there and explain it to her."

"There was an anonymous tip." He leaned against the column I'd used to pivot with earlier.

"And of course, she blames the ex—" I cleared my throat. "Er, ex-boyfriend of my great-uncle first."

"Ah." He nodded. "You understand."

"Yeah, but why didn't you just tell me?" I scratched my head, a spot behind my left ear. It stung like a slice of jalapeno except not on the tongue.

"Didn't I?" He raised an eyebrow.

"I'm not talking about Noah the elder." The stinging sensation intensified like angry bees.

"Neither am I, but I can't directly mention the other thing."

"Why?" I reached up again. The stinging buzz ramped up, along with a strange whine in my ear.

"Sealed records."

The bottom dropped out of my world, and I toppled. The professor wasn't quick enough to catch me. The last thing I remembered for a while was concern creasing his face and Ember's frantic shriek.

I woke in the infirmary with Ember's upside-down head before me as she peered into my face.

"Peep?"

"Yeah, I'm awake." I sighed, turning my head to look around. Hal was in the next bed for his infusion, Faith by his side.

"What are you in for?" Hal asked. "Never mind. We were here when they brought you, so we know."

"I don't."

"You collapsed." Faith picked a paper cup with a lid and a straw off my bedside table and handed it to me. "Dehydration, stress, and insufficient caloric intake. Don't get up, you're on an IV."

"What about Professor Luciano? Is he okay?" I peered at the cup, unable to determine its contents.

"Besides worrying about you, he's fine." Hal pointed at the beverage. "It's banana berry. Jonah brought it; he says it's full of potassium."

"Jonah?" I took a sip. It felt like heaven and tasted like manna from that neighborhood too. I drank more. "Noah's boyfriend? Jonah Arnold?"

"Yeah." Faith answered. "Noah was with him, rolling his eyes and everything. Jonah insisted it was Noah's idea."

"No way." I blinked.

"Yeah." Hal grinned. "He actually got Noah to admit he cares."

"Wow. Sounds familiar."

Hal smiled like a window full of sunbeams while Faith blushed.

"We've got the Craft Expo, then Spirit Week with all the school monarch business and games in less than a month." Faith tapped the cup, then pointed at me. "Drink up, and keep a food journal or something. Don't make me come off reserves and steal your glory."

"Okay."

"I'd love to tell you not to be a stranger, Aliyah." Hal grinned. "But I don't want you visiting during infusion time like this again. Just walk in like everyone else."

We all had a laugh at that. I was good to go at about the same time they were, so we left together. The cafeteria was closed, so I got another smoothie and some croissants at the cafe and ate them in my room. Grace was out, where I didn't know. Popularity kept her busy.

I didn't wait up for my roommate. After brushing my teeth and getting into PJs, I remembered what the professor had said right before I passed out.

Sealed records. Dorian had mentioned those in his story. The unidentified male conspirator had mentioned them also, which lined up with Tempe's secret boyfriend. Was this a clue that could reveal his identity?

I got into bed. Just before dropping off to sleep, I thought I had it, but when my eyes closed, all I dreamed of was Bishop's Row, accompanied by the sound of regulation whistles.

The rest of January flew by. I had to share my extra time in the gym with each school's cheer squad. I hadn't thought of them since the beginning of the year, which seemed like it had been before the Common Era, but they persisted, cranking music and practicing routines to commands shouted by their coaches.

The Hawthorn group was Coach Chen's project. He'd handed the reins of captain over to Logan Pierce, who had way more dancing talent than I'd imagined. The twins, Kitty, Grace, and Arick filled out the rest of the team. The second day they practiced during my track time, Alex showed up. Coach Chen and Logan spent a good twenty minutes in conversation I couldn't hear, and he ended up on the squad.

Messing's faculty coach was a willowy brunette woman with a pixie by her side, which meant she was a psychic summoner and that she knew performance art since pixies loved song and dance. The student captain was Jacinta, a memory psychic cousin of Azrael's. I didn't know why she passed wristbands to each squad member, but when they performed their routine for the first time at levels approaching perfect, I understood. She'd impressed the routine into the bands, likely with her coach's help.

Gallows Hill blew me away. I stopped running a few times just to watch them. Cadence was the captain, and instead of dancing, she'd leaned heavily into gymnastics. Her squad of shifters and changelings practiced backflips and danced on their hands, tossing each other into the air on multiple occasions. Stephanie Hawkins was technically coaching, but she left everything to Cadence, who clearly knew her squad's abilities.

Logan burned the candle at both ends. He had to captain the cheer squad but also finish his paintings for the Craft Expo, which came first. I checked on him, eventually settling into a routine of getting smoothies between meals.

"Something's got to give." Logan sighed. "I can't do everything."

"Grace said something like that before break." I twirled the straw in my banana berry smoothie. "Why not delegate? Nobody can do your artwork for you, but how about appointing a lieutenant for the cheer squad?"

"That's not a bad idea." He perked up. "They all know the routine now. If someone could supervise them running through it, I could spend some extra time in the Creatives room. But who?"

"How about Kitty? She's got experience keeping people on track, what with Truncheons and Flagons every week."

"I'll ask her. Thanks!"

After that, I saw less of Logan in the gym at odd hours, and he seemed more content. He finished all three of his paintings in time for the Expo. It was held in the gym, so I let Ember fly around all she wanted.

We'd all been encouraged to dress business casual or better. Logan chose his navy-blue suit, the one Grace had made, and he told everyone who his designer was, including the student visitors and the judges who came by to view his work. I heard it all, sitting with my brick design kiln-fired mugs at the next table.

"You're being too nice," Alex interrupted. "Stop it."

"It's true, though." Logan shrugged.

"Don't promote yourself, then." Alex sauntered off. "Doesn't matter to me."

"Maybe he's right." I sighed. "I don't like admitting that, but this expo is about showing your own work."

"I'm not going to stop saying nice things that are true about my friends just because there are judges, Aliyah."

"I get it."

After that, I let Logan be himself, but I took a page out of his book and talked his paintings up to anyone who even glanced at my pottery. Maybe I was biased because one depicted Ember stuck in my hair. Even though Logan hadn't been there when it happened, he'd loved the story enough to spend weeks painting his vision of it.

Everybody expected the press to be there. We'd been given release forms, with one specific publication listed: the Extrahuman Examiner, the social paper Cadence's mother worked for. She clicked around the room on heels so high and spindly they reminded me of church spires, taking notes and pictures with a MagPad, the only device guaranteed to work in the Under and its adjacent places.

She stopped in front of Logan's table, too far away for him to make conversation. I watched her tapping furiously on the screen, pausing between sentences like she was conversing with someone else. In the end, she didn't talk to Logan. Or me, either.

"That's weird." I scratched my head.

"Doris said the same thing." Logan reached down to pat her.

"Peep!" Ember darted through the air, making a figure eight above my head before landing on my table, where she hopped up and down, peeping excitedly at Logan.

"Oh!" He blinked. "Really, Ember?"

Before I could ask what just happened, a man approached the table. He wore his tan tweed suit like an afterthought, but the smile on his face as he gazed at Logan's work was genuine.

"Hello!" He stuck out his hand. "I'm Jim Howard from the Boston Globe. Mrs. DelMar sent me."

"Logan Pierce." They shook. "Are you a judge?"

"I edit the extrahuman Interest section. Every year, we do a series on student art in Massachusetts, and I'd like to interview you about those paintings if you don't mind."

"Of course! I mean, I don't mind at all."

"I'll keep an eye on your table, Logan." I grinned.

Logan led Mr. Howard toward the café, where they ordered coffee and sat down. He ended up missing the judges. By the time he returned, they'd tallied the scores, and Headmaster Hawkins was ready to make the announcement.

Even though no other artist had gotten press attention, Logan placed third. He stayed up at the podium to wait for the other winners and cheered each of them. Grace came in second with her fashion collection, which didn't surprise me. Neither did the first place winner, Azrael Ambersmith.

I had a look after the fact at his chess set, crafted from myriad found items and upcycled materials. It followed the traditional faerie division of Seelie and Unseelie, facing each other across the board. Most chess sets along a fae theme didn't include any other extrahumans, but Azrael's was diverse. Surprising to many, but not me, who'd known him for so long.

His pawns were shifters; wolves on the Unseelie side faced lions across the board. The rooks were magi, representing fire on the Seelie side across from ice. Knights were familiars, golden dragonets countering Unseelie jet gryphons. Clairvoyant bishops carried satchels and brandished cards at Unseelie telekinetics with projectiles hovering over their heads.

The monarchs took my breath away. The Seelie king had golden hair, with eyes glancing to one side. His queen's hair was longer and ruddy, and she faced the board with grim determination. I had no idea who'd inspired Azrael, but they were clearly patterned after people he knew.

I recognized the Unseelie king immediately, though I wasn't sure how Azrael had managed to capture both love and pain on such a small face. I put a hand over my chest, blinking back tears.

"It's Hal."

"And of course his queen is Faith," Grace murmured as she pointed at the figure, which wore the dress she'd made for our friend.

"Why?"

"Az wanted to give them a tribute after he heard nobody was doing stained glass this year."

"How?" I sniffled. "He doesn't go around talking about it."

"That's my fault," Grace said. "I couldn't help it, Aliyah. I told Azrael about Hal's illness back in October."

"No, I understand." I hugged her. "You really care about him, huh?"

"We've got to keep fighting." She sniffled, arms still around me. "It doesn't matter how I feel."

"It does. The whole reason we're working so hard is so everyone can be who they are and follow their hearts, including you."

"You're too nice." She pulled back, looking me in the eye.

Déjà vu.

"Promise me you'll be kind to yourself. And soon, Grace."

"When I'm sure we're winning, yeah."

We dropped our arms, letting go. After that, I worked even harder.

CHAPTER FORTY-FOUR

Noah came out to run during the last week of January. It reminded me of how we used to circle Salem Commons through middle school, with one exception: he smiled almost constantly. I was sure Jonah's presence on the bleachers had something to do with it.

My brother's vampire boyfriend was on Messing's team, but that didn't stop him from cheering us on and supplying us with water when we needed it. He sat with Hal, who'd taken to timing us.

"Why aren't you training?" I asked him between laps.

"I don't need to do cardio anymore." He grinned.

"So why help the competition?" I raised an eyebrow.

"I don't see it that way. Extramurals are about coming together and recognizing how we're all awesome."

"I feel the same," Hal added. "We're stronger together."

"Thanks for the smoothie, by the way."

"Glad to help. Before this happened, I trained too hard a few times myself."

"I'm glad you and Noah found each other, Jonah."

"I'm a lucky guy. My boyfriend's amazing, and his sister approves."

"You've got one up on Hal." Faith strode over. "And I hear you on the amazing boyfriend thing. I might have to fight you if you say Noah's the best, though."

"We can agree to disagree," Jonah replied. "Until one of them ends up as Hawthorn's Spirit Week Monarch."

We all had a laugh.

Then Faith joined our supplemental track runs.

I tried to ignore the Monarch business, which wasn't easy with Grace as my roommate. She was campaigning for one of the two Hawthorn crowns, of course.

"We can't let Tempe win this."

"After all the times we thwarted her socially, do you even think she has a chance?"

"I wouldn't put it past her to get votes by coercion."

I thought about Professor Luciano's sealed record and had to agree. She had access to reputation-damaging information through her conspirator. Dorian was supposed to be investigating the secret boyfriend, and I approached him that day at lunch and cut right to the chase.

"Have you found anything in Coach Pickman's files? About you-know-who's boyfriend?"

"Nobody seems likely, last time I checked."

"When was that, Dorian."

"December." He winced. "Sorry. I'm not sure whether you feel this, but something's been off since we came back."

"I have. It's distracting, but we can't drop the ball. If we do, the abusive bigot will terrorize everyone."

"Yeah, I know, but we've defeated her pretty soundly on all fronts. I'm not sure what more we can do."

"Grace's latest thing is making sure she doesn't get a Monarch crown."

"That's easy."

"How? When Grace is the only major candidate, the second crown could go to anyone."

"You make Alex Onassis a poster child."

"Huh?"

"She pretty much brutalized the poor kid, and her entire year knows it. They're scared of her, so we need to either make them brave or humiliate her. Which do you want?"

"Bravery." I shook my head. "She's the horrible one, so we go high."

"We remind them that Alex Onassis survived her bullshit."

"He'll never admit weakness, not even to say he came through it alive."

"Someone else should speak for him—a charismatic individual who stands up when it matters."

"You?"

"Nah, I'm a coward. I'm talking about you."

"Bishop's Row practice is no joke. You've got spare time."

"I gave you the idea. Find someone else."

I tried but came up with nothing. Eston and Logan weren't built for that kind of social maneuvering. Kitty was way too nice to pull off public criticism. Lee was Switzerland. In Tempe's own year, the only people I trusted were Lena, who was too timid, and Arick, who needed to study. I asked Izzy for advice.

"Yeah, no." She stared at the cards spread across the floor in her room. "It's not going to work without Dorian."

"Or me?"

"No. You can't pull it off. See this Empress reversed? It might even backfire and make Tempe look sympathetic. You're Alex's ex, and you're intimidating, Aliyah."

"So, how do I convince Dorian to buck up?"

She flipped The Fool reversed and stared at it. "You don't. It's up to him. The only thing you can reasonably do is say you didn't find anyone and leave it at that."

I followed her advice, expecting the worst, which I assumed happened when Dorian shook his head at my news. Right afterward, I saw him talking to Alex in the hall.

Neither of them came forward with a public statement, but something happened—a rumor about Temperance, one that had everyone laughing at her. He'd gone with humiliation after all.

Arick told me the story. Tempe had threatened Alex while they dated, forcing him to dress and act like a gnome during their intimate time. I knew that wasn't true, but it was an extremely damaging rumor to an open magisupremacist.

Snickers and snorts followed Tempe everywhere. Her face seemed constantly red and her fists were eternally clenched. Dorian had utterly wrecked her reputation, along with any chance at a Monarch crown.

He's kicked a hornet's nest. Beware her sting.

I tried to corner Dorian, hoping he'd get another reading from Izzy, but he avoided me. I wasn't sure why. I couldn't even talk to him long enough for a simple warning.

The votes were in and the results given on the last Friday in February. At the end of Spirit Week, they'd crown the Monarchs at the Cheer Squad competition, the night before the Bishop's Row games. The extramural guests and the entire Hawthorn student body sat in the gym's bleachers, waiting. Stephanie Hawkins made the announcement for Gallows Hill.

"We've heard your voices, and they chose two of our most talented. Your Monarchs are Cadence DelMar and Brianna Collins!"

The girls hurried off the bleachers, rushing to her side to curtsy and bow. Once the cheers died down, they moved back to their seats to let Dean Adelphi make the announcement for Messing Academy.

"You're all Monarchs in my book, but the students representing you are Jonah Arnold and Isabella Mendez!" All the Messing Academy kids snapped their fingers instead of clapping like they were at a poetry slam instead of a pep rally. In moments, cheers from both Gallows Hill and Hawthorn drowned them out. That made sense because Jonah and Izzy both moved in circles outside their schools.

You could have heard a pin drop as Headmaster Hawkins stepped to the middle of the gym. He held the paper with the results almost like an afterthought, and I was shocked by his announcement.

"At Hawthorn Academy, we see ourselves as an extended family. That's why I'm so pleased to announce that our crowns go to a pair of blood relatives."

I blinked because Grace Dubois was an only child.

"Noah and Aliyah Morgenstern!"

It was all I could do to keep from tripping over my own feet while descending the bleachers. Once on the floor, I glanced back up at Grace, who winked and gave me a thumbs-up.

"Grace campaigned for you, not herself," Noah said, taking my hand. "She swore me to secrecy."

I stood with my brother, applause, hoots, and whistles washing over me, speechless with joyful tears running down my face.

It was the last moment of pure happiness I had that year.

CHAPTER FORTY-FIVE

Spirit Week was a sequence of theme days, and Grace had made five outfits for me to wear. On Monday for school colors, she had me in a pencil-skirted plum suit with gold trim and buttons. Tuesday's retro day ensemble was from the eighties, an iridescent taffeta bubble skirt with an off-the-shoulder sequined top in gold.

I feared Wednesday's mascot day because hawthorn was the tree our school was named after. But Grace managed this by putting me in a purple t-shirt printed with the words March of the Ents and the image of a tree tearing a wall down.

On Thursday's pajama day, she gave me a golden satin nightgown with a purple lace dressing gown to go over it. Friday I was in my Bishop's Row uniform, with one addition: a Rocky Balboa-style robe with my number on the back.

"It should have been you," I said. "We both heard about Temperance last year, but you're the one who put together a plan. At the expense of your own happiness."

"Nah," she replied. "Everyone laughs at her now. Nobody will take her hatred seriously anymore. Finally, it feels like I can rest."

"Still. Wouldn't you rather show all these creations off by wearing them yourself?"

"My dream was always other people wearing them. I can get out of the spotlight, be myself," she said. "This was way harder than I thought it'd be."

After dinner, everyone headed to the gym again for a pep rally. Ezekiel and Nurse Smith teamed up at a DJ table to introduce the Bishop's Row teams. After that, the Monarchs would get their crowns on a platform under the scoreboard and the cheer squads would compete.

Peering out from the curtain in front of the locker room entrance, I spotted the Cheer Squad judges in the front row. Brianna tugged my sleeve, and we geeked out over a blonde woman in a powder-pink dress. She was Jeannie LaMontaigne, a Gallows Hill alumnus and member of the Tinfoil Hat pack from Providence Paranormal. Izzy's abuela sat out there too. She'd been a ballroom dance champ in her young adulthood. Azrael's oldest brother, a four-year dancer at the Boston Ballet, rounded out the judges.

We grouped by teams, waiting for our schools and numbers to be announced. Dylan elbowed me as they called Gallows Hill.

"Congratulations. Didn't get a chance to say it before."

"Thanks." I grinned.

"Must have been a near thing, competing with Grace's ego."

"That's not what happened," I told him.

"Oh." He blinked.

"You really thought she'd go low?"

"Didn't she? I mean, have you heard the rumors about Tempe?"

"Those didn't come from Grace."

"Huh." He shook his head. "Well, my mind's blown."

The voice on the PA called Messing Academy.

Tell him. If this isn't your moment, I don't know what is.

"Um. Maybe not yet."

"Please, Aliyah." He groaned. "Don't drop another devastating shoe. I can't handle it."

"No, no. This is a good thing. I hope."

"So say it."

398

"Dylan Khan." I took a breath as deep as the Atlantic Ocean. "For the last year and a half, I've had—"

The PA announcer boomed out, "Hawthorn Academy!"

And just like that, my moment evaporated.

I sat on the platform in the gym beside my brother, a heavy gilded crown on my head. The other four Monarchs did the same, with Cadence in front for her performance. An enormous banner hung behind us, emblazoned with the words Extramural Monarchs' Court. We watched as the Gallows Hill Cheer Squad took their places.

Born This Way by Lady Gaga boomed over the speakers and they launched into their routine, their energy breaching the stratosphere. The entire squad hugged afterward before returning to the bleachers. Cadence broke off to take her place beside Brianna afterward.

It took five minutes for Jacinda's squad to prepare since they had a set with screens to either side. The music started before they did.

"That's Portugal. The Man," Noah blinked. "Unconventional for cheering."

He called it. The Messing Squad's performance pushed the norm, from their entrance to the props. They leaped out from behind the screens, ribbons trailing from their wrists to the tune of *Feel it Still*. The routine combined dance styles and trappings from different eras and genres. It was totally unique and skillfully performed.

Hawthorn's squad went traditional, except for their music choice. Only Alex would have picked *Victorious* by Panic! At the Disco. Logan favored sure things and stability, and that showed in the classic cheer-leading choreography. He'd made it a foundation for his performers to incorporate individual flourishes. The twins flung jazz hands every-where. Grace executed splits and backflips in front of them. Alex and Logan tossed Kitty in the air like she weighed nothing, and their victory formation at the end built a tree instead of a pyramid with Arick at the top, augmented by Skinner the bookwyrm and Asceco the basilisk to represent branches.

After the tallies were in, Messing Academy won. All of the perfor-
mances were so solid, it would have been a tough call if the judges had
scored subjectively, but cheering had categories with numeric points.
Jacinda's squad had scored ten points for creativity and also coordina-
tion, so they squeaked a win over Logan's by two points. Cadence's
was only behind his by one, so they almost had a three-way tie.

The rally was over, and our coaches all wanted us to get plenty of
rest before the games the next day. Most of the students and the
others headed out into the halls. Many of the Bishop's Row players
did too, but I noticed Noah and Jonah sneak away to the locker room.

Rat them out.

"No."

"Huh?" Cadence said. "Didn't catch that."

"Inside voice got out, sorry."

She threw her head back and laughed. I joined in, mostly to mask
the sudden nervousness I felt. My friends had all gotten their chances
to show off, put their talents out there, and be judged. Grace with her
fashion, Izzy at the talent show, and Cadence here. Logan and Hal had
had success at the Magipsych fair, and Noah had finally found
someone to love who returned his feelings.

The next day would test my talents on the court against some of
those same friends. That had to be the reason for my queasy stomach
and shaky hands.

What if you're wrong?

"Hey, Aliyah!" Dylan flagged me down from the doors leading to
the hall. "Smoothies?"

I sprinted after him. Maybe I'd get another moment after all.

The café was packed with Gallows Hill kids. I had to squeeze past
what felt like an entire pack of wolf shifters before Bar spotted me
and got them to make way.

"Royalty coming through!"

"Your Highness." One of them bowed.

"Oh, no. Just a joke," I insisted.

"If the troll's giving you fealty, I'm not gonna argue."

We laughed, and I finally made it to the counter. Dylan held a pair of banana berry smoothies, just like the one I'd had on the day I collapsed.

He said something, but I couldn't hear him. I beckoned him into the corner Noah had sat in with Jonah on the first day I'd seen them together, figuring a little good luck couldn't hurt. He leaned over the small round table, close enough for me to hear.

"What did you want to say? Back in the locker room, I mean?"

The bottom dropped out of my courage. I took a sip of the smoothie, closing my eyes in an attempt to calm myself, and it backfired as spectacularly as July Fourth firework because that magic sight ability kicked in. Behind my eyelids, I saw Noah and Jonah cowering in fear someplace with tiles, and somehow there was fire and rain.

Go back to the gym. Now.

"I'm sorry. I've got to go." I stood up, leaving both Dylan and the smoothie behind and prepared to fight my way back through the crowd.

Cadence saw.

"Everybody move!"

Her voice created a path and I took it immediately, lifting knees and elbows to sprint away at top speed. Noah would probably laugh in my face or get angry if I interrupted an epic makeout session.

I didn't care.

If he was in trouble and I didn't barge in, I'd never forgive myself. I'd do anything to stop my brother from getting hurt, a fact made clear on my first day at Hawthorn when I threatened the third-year's It Girl to defend his integrity.

I'd save his life alone if I had to, but as I ran, I felt someone behind me—a powerful presence.

I glanced over my shoulder to find Ember flapping madly to keep up with me. Nobody else was there.

You're never alone.

"You're. Not. Real," I panted.

I couldn't be haunted. Ghosts couldn't manifest on the Hawthorn campus, but the feeling persisted. I continued on, holding my hands out to fling open the academic wing's doors.

For a moment, I worried about breaking the stained glass mural crafted by Hal's grandmother, but it held even under my panic-induced motions.

As I ran down the hall to the gym, my body responded perfectly to my demands on it like I was made for this specific action at this particular moment.

Coincidence is on your side. Don't squander it.

The gym was dark. The platform with the Monarchs' seats was still standing, but the banner was missing. Someone stood by the bleachers, a tall and lanky figure that froze as I passed. I had no time for whoever it was. My gut felt like lead, but my arms and legs only moved faster toward the locker room.

Inside, I skidded to a stop in the common space. A shower was running, but I couldn't tell where it was over the sound of my ragged gasps for air. One glance at the floor told me I needed the gender-neutral section. A scrap of purple and gold fabric lay by the doorway, emblazoned with a two—Noah's jersey number.

I paced ahead, stepping softly and slowly. Whoever had orches-trated my brother's distress didn't deserve the courtesy of a warning. Ember landed on my shoulder, clinging to it like a life raft in a stormy sea.

It was Temperance, of course, and her behavior defied the meaning of her name. She held the Axis device I'd only seen on paper in front of her, pointing it at my brother and Jonah, who sat under one of the showerheads, soaked to the bone.

Above them hung the banner that had recently been in the gym. She'd changed the words to read Least Likely to Succeed.

And I smelled blood.

CHAPTER FORTY-SIX

Blood Like Water
Temperance

Their meddling had made me sick, from the first day when DuBois upstaged me to winter break when Dylan Khan refused to step into my parlor like a good little fly. What had me steamed was that tale-bearing coward, Spanos. I knew he'd been behind the gnome rumor, which was infuriating.

The sissy ice magus wouldn't escape my wrath. He and that trash gryphon were getting boiled away as soon as I had the chance.

I had other prey to stalk first, a parentally imposed duty that now fell to me. Charity was weak, refused to get her hands dirty, and Faith had gone off the rails, siding with the inferiors. I'd always known exterminating parasites was my destiny. More than that, it was my calling in life, according to my parents.

Why else had they given me this marvelous toy?

I hid with Precious in the shadows behind the bleachers, watching the leech hold hands with his favorite blood bag. It was disgusting how vampires carried on with living people. You didn't fall in love with a cheeseburger. Leeches were lying vermin, incapable of love, mocking life. People like Noah Morgenstern were worse, making it look normal to date predators.

Samuel Ives and I hadn't been anything like that, of course. We were pure magi, no weak psychics, savage shifters, or Unseelie faeries in our heritage. We'd made a natural match until someone ratted us out. I wasn't sure who, but that was the only explanation for Faith's hissy fit after the Magipsych Fair.

After that, I deliberately dropped hints at the most biased faculty member. Susan DeBeer had gone to undergrad with my mother, so I knew all about how her advisor, an extramagus with poison and mind magic, had taken advantage of her. Luciano was supposed to take the fall in her "inappropriate behavior" witch hunt and get blamed for poisoning Clementine and Seth.

Aliyah Morgenstern had cleared him and doomed my relationship. Samuel broke up with me at the end of January and resigned the next day. I'd lost my boyfriend, so now she'd lose a brother. If I did everything perfectly, nobody would suspect me, either.

"Go in the locker room already," I murmured, rolling my eyes.

Precious caressed my cheek with one cold webbed hand. I'd be patient like him. He hadn't gotten up to any mischief since exacting my revenge on Bailey Overton for defecting to the inferiors.

Finally, they went in, laughing, with their arms around each other. I took my time unfastening the banner and making modifications to it by wetting the ink and moving it around. I checked my bag for my secret weapon, ensuring it was fully charged with every magical element I'd need so nobody could pin this on me. If we struck too early, the vermin could escape. Besides, I wanted everything to be perfect for my first act of righteous justice.

The altered sign would make as much of a statement as the pile of ashes and the dead snake. Noah's familiar would be collateral damage.

I sent Precious in first. He got into the pipes through the drain in the steam room, using the water inside to locate the leech and his supper. They were in the gender-neutral showers with the water off. As I snuck in, Precious opened the pipes, covering them with enough water to give me the upper hand.

The undead thing took a step toward me.

"Freeze, leech!" I twirled my hand, twisting water around his feet, giving it maximum cohesion and immobilizing him.

"What the f—" I swung a punch, my magic calling water to slap Noah across the face.

"On your knees, both of you." I pulled out the device my parents had given me. "Or you both die. This makes me an extramagus. Don't make me demonstrate it."

Precious took off, dashing after something scaly that slithered across the floor. I couldn't look away from the vermin in front of me, but I checked Morgenstern's shoulder. His familiar still clung there, though his uniform had torn and was hanging askew.

The leech mumbled something about time.

"Did I say you could talk?"

"No." Noah snorted. "Fine, we're getting down. Come on, Jonah. We can pretend we're on a picnic. In a rainstorm."

"That's right, but only the leech is getting anything to eat. He's turning you, Morgenstern."

"No." The vamp kneeled but shook his head. "I won't take away his choice."

I held one hand up, drawing water out of the air around it until I had enough to drown a man. I flung it at Morgenstern, pushing it down his nose and throat.

"Turn him or he dies."

Noah's eyes bulged, and he clawed at his throat in vain. I almost thought the leech wouldn't go through with it, but he caved when Noah toppled over. I called the water back, not wanting to kill Morgenstern too soon.

My lip curled into a sneer as I watched the leech drink. It was every bit as nasty as I'd imagined, and the fact that I'd forced them into it had my heart racing. I chortled, finally victorious, owning the undesirables.

Until that leech raised his eyebrow at me because of course, his unnatural hearing let him hear my heartbeat.

"Stop." I splashed the coldest water I could find at them.

"I'm sorry," the vermin said, but not to me.

"It's okay," Morgenstern croaked, tears running down his face. "I forgive you."

"Now drink from the leech, Morgenstern."

"Noah, don't." The leech's eyes filled with what could only be crocodile tears.

"Listen up, parasite." I patted my device. "I'm giving you ten seconds to say farewell to Morgenstern's humanity. If he's not vamped by then, I'm frying both of you."

I punctuated that long goodbye with my voice, counting their last moments down.

CHAPTER FORTY-SEVEN

Aliyah

I stood transfixed by the scene before me, frozen in time and space as Temperance spoke.

"Time's up. Any last words?"

"Go hump a gnome." Noah rolled his eyes.

"Lies!" she screamed. "Fake news!"

"Protest much, Gertrude?" My brother was a master of sass and awe. "Wait. Hamlet's mom didn't get nasty with gnomes."

"You took everything from me," she snarled. "Now drink!"

"Please don't." Jonah sobbed. "Let him go. Just kill me instead."

"Shut up, leech!" She stamped her foot, splashing in maybe six inches of water. "You both die."

I stepped forward.

"You have to get through me first."

Temperance turned her head, took one look at me, and sneered.

"Grace's pet extramagus? Fire and sunlight, all out of control. Try taking me down without killing them both in the process. I dare you."

"Okay." I held my hands in conjuring position, stepping closer to Noah and Jonah. "Ember!"

My dragonet reared up, letting out a throaty roar as she mingled her magic with mine. I took a deep breath, preparing to superheat her weapon so she'd drop it, but Ember's roar turned into a yawn, and she sat back on her haunches.

She drained your familiar just now.

Tempe pointed the device at me. As she pulled the trigger, I experienced an all-too-familiar feeling.

"Poison?" My legs wavered. "Is that all you've got?"

I turned my fire inward, sending it through my veins and burning the toxin out of my blood. I resumed my stance, inching forward to put more of my body between the device and the boys. Jonah tried to push Noah toward the door.

"Precious!" Temperance called. "Make sure he's turned!"

The grundylow emerged from a drain in a disturbing fashion, squeezing up through the holes to head Noah off. Precious leaped at my brother's bloodstained neck with his webbed hands outstretched.

A cry pierced the air, and a streak of white feathers and fur flashed toward the grundylow in mid-leap, knocking him aside.

Precious hissed, retreating under the shower spray. Mercy the gryphon circled, trapping him in the corner.

"Aliyah!" Dorian called from the doorway. He wheezed, and the water in the air made his shirt cling to something under it in the front. "Run defense!"

"You lying bitch!" Temperance pointed the device at Dorian.

Mercy's wings stopped flapping and she dropped out of the air, hitting the wet tile with a sickening smack.

Dorian's eyes widened and his lip trembled, but he conjured ice anyway, trying to block her attack. It melted because she'd shot him with a copy of my fire. The resulting water knocked him face-down in the puddle, the remainder of the flames burned away the back of his hair and shirt, revealing a binder.

Everything seemed to happen at once, like when I freed Alex at the dance. Tempe's device let out another blast of flame, at my brother this time. Precious thrust Jonah's bloodied wrist into Noah's mouth. Mercy's wing flapped once, weakly. Temperance raised her free hand, then punched down, flattening the gryphon with a watery hammer.

"Murderer!" I pointed at her.

"Pest control." Tempe narrowed her eyes. "And I'm not done yet."

I'd never seen a vampire Rage and had no idea how primal a force they channeled.

Jonah tore free of Precious's grasp, flinging the grundylow away. His eyes glowed a baleful red, his bared fangs sharp and long. He crouched, hissing, prepared to pounce.

I leaped in front of Jonah, expecting her to use the device to incinerate him. I held my hands out, a small orb with both my elements in front of me.

Bishop's Row was the closest thing I knew to battle tactics. My defensive play might have worked, but Temperance had watched me all year. She knew my biggest weakness on the court—the classic fakeout.

She aimed at Noah instead. He should have perished on the spot because even Jonah's vampiric dash back to his side wasn't as fast as lightning, but he didn't die.

The bolt hit him, fanning out along the water. The lightning paralyzed him and it had the same effect on Jonah, so he was turned.

Water arced over Tempe's head, forming what looked like a Faraday cage, but its deadly bolt continued toward Dorian and me.

Ice crashed through the room in a shimmering glacial wall and the lightning shattered it. My hair crackled and stood on end, but it absorbed enough of the charge to save us.

The ice was purple like in the mural, but nobody had conjured that since my great-uncle's time here with Filberto Luciano.

Bert became an extramagus when he fell in love, and his powers had reverted once Noah the elder died. That's what's in his sealed record.

"Stop, Miss Fairbanks." Professor Luciano stepped forward, shaking purple ice off his fingers. "I won't let you hurt them."

She laughed.

"Look at them." She smirked. "Slavering monsters. I'm defending myself."

"We're all witnesses. You'll go to prison." He held out his hand. "It's not too late to do the right thing, Tempe. Let me help you. Give me the device."

"If I kill you all, I write this story and win my family's legacy." Her grin was sharp and painful. "I've got all the power here. You just want to steal it."

"Love is my power." He stepped beside me. "My love for this school and everyone in it is a strength beyond your imagination. You will do no more harm. Miss Morgenstern, get them to safety."

I wanted to defy his orders and make this stand with him because nobody should have to fight evil alone, but Noah gasped and Dorian groaned. They needed me more.

The heat and light had driven Jonah to the brink, and his closest, most vulnerable target was Dorian.

Noah wasted no time. He squinted, wincing at the solar flares in his hands, but managed to keep Jonah at bay.

I dashed for Dorian, grabbing him under the arms and dragging him into the common room before going back in.

Tempe blasted Noah's hands with more solar energy, overloading him. If I couldn't help him banish it, we'd all get incinerated.

Jonah's hands were on fire, and he wasn't in the shower spray any longer. He shrieked, the Rage transforming into a flight response. I could see the bones in his fingers.

Professor Luciano pulled ice from the floor and encased Jonah's hands, dousing the blaze. The injured vampire dashed into the dark cave of the changing area. I hurried to my brother's side.

"Aliyah, get out." He sobbed, staring at the twin suns in his hands. "I can't banish it. I'm going to kill everyone."

"We'll stop it together." I stared at his eyes. "Look at me."

I knelt beside him and took his hands, using the same banishing technique Elanor had taught me. He finally met my gaze, nodding. I took a deep breath and remembered every time we'd saved each other in much smaller ways. They flashed through the blinding light between us in an instant.

The night I was sure the Kraken hid under my bed, and he let me sleep in his room.

The day he came home from middle school friendless, and I said I'd always love him.

The Sukkot he'd shared his sleeping bag so I'd be brave enough to sleep outside all night.

The Passover he came out as gay, and I was the first one to hug him.

The day he helped me pack for my first year at Hawthorn.

"I love you, Noah. No matter what."

"Forever, Aliyah."

That was supposed to be our goodbye to each other and the world because all that effort wasn't enough. This amount of energy was impossible for us to banish on our own.

Through the light, I saw a feathery shadow diving. It flew at Tempe's face, and she flung her hands up to fend off the strix's poisoned claws. The professor lunged forward, grabbing the device. He clutched it to his chest, then turned his head to look at me.

"Professor, no." My eyes widened. "It drains life."

"I choose whose."

Professor Luciano pointed the device at the impossible globe of light. He staggered, knees splashing on ice, water, and tile. He pulled the trigger with one hand and clutched his heart with the other.

I gripped my brother's hands tighter, still contributing my effort to banish what felt like the sun. The light diminished, damping back down to normal levels for the human eye. Noah's hands were colder than a winter ocean. A stain darkened the front of his jersey, red rimmed his eyes, and blood caked his lips. He wasn't breathing.

We locked gazes, me and my brother the vampire.

Temperance lay on the floor with her eyes open, a single shallow scratch on her cheek. I could tell by the way her chest rose and fell and how Precious held her head between his webbed hands that she was paralyzed.

Professor Luciano curled motionless, still clutching the Axis device. His strix hopped toward him, waterlogged feathers temporarily grounding her. She preened a tuft of hair behind his ear, then let out three mournful hoots.

Ember swooped off my shoulder, landing beside the professor's familiar. She keened, as she had on the day we all thought Doris had died.

"No."

My brother ran toward the door. I rushed to the professor's side. There had to be hope. I pulled his shoulder, turning him from his side to his back, and he opened his eyes.

"Thank you." His hand remained on his chest over his heart.

"I got you hurt." I sniffled, my face wetter than it had been. "Bad."

"Badly," he corrected with a final raised eyebrow. "I banished the sun to spare all of you."

Noah returned. "Hold on. Help is coming."

"Stay with me, Bert." I pulled his hands away from the device, wrapping mine around them, but they were almost as cold as Noah's.

"We all die, but love doesn't." He gasped. "Keep fighting. Heed the magic. Its tone is harsh but never wrong."

"Is that the voice I hear in my head?"

He glanced down at my *Shema Yisrael* pendant, then back at my face. He smiled, somehow looking through me as though he'd just recognized an old friend.

Professor Filberto Luciano had no more answers for me or anyone else in this world.

He'd left it.

CHAPTER FORTY-EIGHT

Pulling the purple and gold robe off, I used it to cover Professor Luciano's head and shoulders.

Some part of me would never stop shaking and crying, even after the physical feelings had passed. That sorrow felt vast and eternal, just like love. Maybe that was why it loomed so large, because grief is the space our loved ones leave behind.

Turning to Noah didn't come close to filling it, but it helped. We embraced, leaning together in the dank shower's relative quiet.

"Peep." Ember nestled against me, curling her tail around my shoulders.

"Hiss." Lotan slithered away from him and on to my shoulder with Ember, though I couldn't fathom why. She'd always comforted him through sadness before. Noah clung more tightly to me, sobbing harder. I hoped she was just cold, not rejecting him.

A quartet of adults arrived, but I only noticed one at first. I was mesmerized by Stephanie Hawkins saving Jonah Arnold, something only a dhampyr could do. She deliberately cut her wrist and used it to coax Jonah out of the changing room and down from his Rage. He reached up, pulling the arm close and covering it with his lips.

All the polish and poise, the wide-eyed cheer and positivity about her person vanished as though her ex-husband had transported it away with space magic. Mrs. Hawkins was exactly as dour as Hal had described. As Jonah drank from her, flesh knitted over the charred bone of his fingertips and the blisters on his face faded. Stephanie sobbed, eyes focused on something or someone not here.

She must have been a blood doll.

"Hold me back." Noah lunged, so I caught him.

Like before, he felt colder than he should have, but the biggest difference between now and then was a drastic increase in strength. No matter how hard I held on, I couldn't fight him. Not even with all the extra training. My grip slipped and he dashed toward Stephanie, fangs out. Somewhere behind me, a dog barked.

"Hold!" Faith called behind me.

My brother froze in place, jaw dropped, bicuspids impossibly long.

"March." She stepped into view, holding her hand out to Noah, who followed her command.

The air shimmered between them, but I knew better. I was watching undeath magic at work. She continued, accompanying him until they both got out of the room.

"You murdered my colleague." Professor DeBeer glared. "And this poor gryphon. Do you have anything to say for yourself?"

Temperance held her hands in front of her, bound by a set of black metal cuffs. Precious muttered glumly inside what looked like a fishbowl with a lid made of the same black metal.

"I should have thought bigger. Exterminated the inferiors, not just the vermin who infected them."

Professor DeBeer sniffed. "I hope they throw the book at you."

"You would have taken the fall." Tempe giggled. "The way you carry on about extramagi, you sound almost exactly like them."

"Keep talking if you want," Azrael's aunt from Salem PD said from the doorway, "but you have the right to remain silent."

Kim Ichiro stepped out from behind her with a contingent of local MCSIs.

The squeak of a knob turning caught my attention. Headmaster Hawkins stood by the shower's control with a blue nitrile glove on his hand and turned it off, his face covered with water, dark and still like welder's glass. Whether it was from the spray or tears, I couldn't tell. He reached down, touching Jonah's head. Stephanie put her free hand on his arm. He snapped his fingers, and they all vanished.

"Poor Dorian." Nurse Smith shook his head. I watched his back as he bent down, scooping the gryphon up.

"Mercy?" I asked.

"She's gone." He turned, revealing the tears on his face. "Are you the one who moved him?"

I nodded, unable to speak past the lump in my throat.

"Probably saved his life. He could have drowned face down in this water."

I couldn't hold myself together anymore and collapsed to the floor, ears ringing. Somewhere in the distance, a woman sobbed. When I took a breath, it paused. *I* was making that noise.

The karkinos crawled out of Nurse Smith's pocket and enlarged, then lifted me to his back. The rocking motion of his stride was the last thing I remembered before passing out.

I woke in my room instead of the infirmary. Oddly, I felt good, until the memory of what had happened crashed like a wave against my consciousness.

My eyes stung as I went through motions. Get the bathroom bag. Put on the robe. Walk to the restroom. Brush teeth, wash face, shower. Back to the room to dress, not paying attention to which clothes go on the body. Open the door again.

"Aliyah?" Elanor stood in the hall, her uniform on, including ankyr, ballistae, and cestus. "I brought a spare uniform. Whistle's in a half hour. Are you going to make it?"

"Is Noah?"

"He can't." She shook her head.

"I'll make it. For him."

"Are you sure?"

"If it were Logan, what would you say?"

"Same thing."

After changing, I followed her down the hall, the stairs, through the lobby. Faith joined us, also wearing her uniform and walking over from the café.

"Drink this." Faith handed me a smoothie, then took a swig from her cup.

"Not banana berry."

Noah will never drink banana berry smoothies again.

"No. Green tea and coconut."

"Good. Thanks." I slugged it down so fast I got an ice cream headache.

We pushed through the doors to the academic wing. *Long Division.* The mural held a different meaning for me now, just like its counterpart, *Fire and Ice.* Together and separate. Opposite and intimate. Contributions from students like us, two generations ago by people learning in the same halls. Maybe we didn't have to repeat their mistakes.

"Where's everyone else?"

"Either the locker room or the bleachers," Elanor answered. "You remember who we're playing?"

"Messing." I nodded. "Gallows Hill after."

"Just checking." She held her hands against the gym's doors. "You ready?"

"Just a sec." I went to pull my hair back but realized I didn't have an elastic.

"Here." Faith handed me a familiar-looking one.

"Thanks for letting me borrow—"

"That's your lucky one, remember? I'm returning it. Now put your hair up, and let's go."

I did. We went.

Izzy played reverse point instead of Jonah, who remained in the infirmary with my brother. I'd taken Noah's place as first defense, with Faith off reserves at my usual mid position. Before the starting whistle, Dylan glanced at me. He said nothing, but the puffy redness around his eyes spoke volumes. We shared this grief.

"For Noah," I said.

He nodded.

Elanor did the coin toss with Izzy, and Messing got first throw.

The cestus the psychics wore gave their orbs colors. On the surface, the gameplay looked the same, but it felt totally different for one major reason: none of the psychic energy mingled with our elemental magic. That meant we couldn't absorb orbs. They either bounced off or canceled each other out.

That was how it had always worked for the Messing kids, who seemed used to it. We suffered due to the learning curve. A psychic orb bounced off Dylan's ice defense, tagging Faith out on the first throw, but after that, we didn't repeat the mistake. All the same, we lost the first match against Messing.

Fortunately, today was best two out of three. We won the second match quickly but by the skin of our teeth, still adapting to the gameplay difference. It was a real nail-biter, with just Izzy and Elanor left at the end.

The third game went much longer. Faith hung in for a long time, undeath magic enhancing her endurance, but in the end she went out, taking their second defense with her. Messing still had four players, with their remaining mid left recharging her orb. Only Dylan, Elanor, and I remained on our side. It looked bleak. As soon as Izzy finished her conjure, we'd be toast unless we played perfectly.

Messing's last salvo before Elanor's final gambit was a trio of orbs thrown at the same time. I got tagged out leaping into the air to absorb two with my body and left the last for Dylan, the only way for two defense to counter three throws at once.

That was a move Noah would be proud of.

"Thanks."

"You're welcome?" Messing's first defense blinked.

The buzzer sounded. Izzy was out, tagged by Elanor's throw. We'd won.

Everything else about our victory went by in a blur of purple and gold. I only remember the roar of the crowd, a sense of being carried, and Elanor's face: a smile on lips under tear-streaked eyes, embracing Coach Pickman.

All of us celebrated and mourned at the same time in some way. Dylan alone, howling with his face turned heavenward. Lee off the bench, leaning on Izzy's shoulders, the green and orange of her uniform clashing with his. Faith sobbing openly, her arm linked with mine. My eyes had no more tears, so I cried on the inside.

Like everything else for me that day, the victory was hollow. In the locker room, that same sense of futile routine motion took over. Shower, dry, change. Head out. I avoided looking in the direction of the gender-neutral area, but a flutter of yellow caught my eye there.

"Police line, do not cross." I read.

"Come on, Aliyah." Dylan linked hands with me. "You don't need to be here."

He led me back out into the now-empty gym.

"I've had a crush on you." I blurted. "For ages."

"I'm gay."

We stopped, let go, and stared at each other. I blinked first.

"But Grace?"

"That was awkward because I loved her, but physically, nothing was there."

"I get it." I nodded. "You can be in love without sex."

"I'm surprised you understand."

"It's the way I feel about you."

"Aliyah." He shook his head. "You're like a sister."

"I'll live." I nodded. "I'm going to the infirmary. Come with me?"

"Sure."

We stopped at the cafe for sandwiches, got them to go, and headed down.

The only other person in the room with Noah was Dorian, who slept on his side, hooked up to some kind of beeping machine.

Professor Luciano's strix perched on the headboard, head under her wing. A white box sat on his bedside table, surrounded by flowers. I'd seen one of those every time Bubbe lost a patient. Mercy was inside. Her earthly remains, anyway.

"Where's Jonah?" I blinked back tears. "Didn't Stephanie save him?"

"Salem Jail." Noah sighed. "They arrested him because of my new sun allergy."

"Tempe forced you!" Dylan slammed his hand on the bedside table. "Don't they make exceptions for that here?"

"Did." I leaned back in my chair. "During and right after the Reveal, but those days are long gone, and the laws changed."

"Jonah's stuck unless Tempe's convicted of coercing him. You need a permit ahead of time and clear consent with witnesses when it happens." Noah picked at the edge of his blanket. "Believe me, I checked. Recently."

"What about you?" Dylan asked. "Will they let you out in time for the game tomorrow?"

"They're giving me blood every half hour. New vamps need that until their bodies adjust to being undead." He sighed. "It usually takes twenty-four hours, but even when I'm out, I can't play."

"Why not?"

"I have to leave Hawthorn." He closed his eyes. "No vampire students allowed. The only reason I'm still on campus is that it's dangerous to move me for at least the next eight hours."

"Headmaster Hawkins wouldn't kick you out."

"He didn't." Alex Onassis walked through the door, holding a bouquet of lilies. "The Board of Trustees makes the rules for admission. All the headmaster decides on his own is faculty, staff, and events. The board's meeting after the game with Gallows Hill. They might vote to replace him."

"What are you doing here?" Noah's eyes gleamed red.

"These are for Dorian." He crossed the room, placing the flowers in a jar at Dorian's bedside. "I was about to head in there last night. He stopped me and sent me to get a professor because I could run faster."

"It would have been me in that bed." Alex turned his back on us and sniffled before continuing, "Asceco in that box. I owe Dorian Spanos an enormous debt, so leave me alone, Noah."

"He saved us too, then." I sniffled. "Because Professor Luciano wouldn't have gotten there in time without either of them."

"And I called him selfish." Dylan hung his head. "Lazy. A coward."

"Jerk," Dorian croaked.

"What?" Dylan looked up.

Dorian reached for water but missed. Alex got it for him. After taking a sip, he spoke again.

"You forgot 'jerk.'"

"Yeah, I did." Dylan looked up. "And I'm sorry. It was easier to blame you for my problems instead of dealing with them."

"Dorian, I'm so sorry." I stood, clenching my fists. "You might not know it yet—"

"Mercy's gone." He closed his eyes, cradling the water glass in his hands. "The headmaster told me last night."

"Oh. Thought you just woke up."

"Nah."

"What's the beepy thing for then?" Dylan asked.

"Heart monitor." Dorian opened his eyes. "It stopped."

"Dude." Dylan blinked.

"I was dead for like thirty seconds."

Everyone sniffled, noses and faces wet—even Alex.

"Guys, it's okay." One corner of his mouth turned up. "Nobody can beat me in the goth cred department now."

"You're taking all this extremely well." Noah raised an eyebrow.

"No. With snark is how I take everything." He set the glass down. "But mostly, it's because your grandma visited this morning for over an hour while they fed Noah in the other room."

"Ah." I nodded.

"Now, if you all wouldn't mind keeping it down, me and my resuscitated ticker need more rest." He jerked a thumb at the strix on the headboard. "And the weird owl, too."

Noah shooed us out, insisting he was just getting to the good part in the latest installment of his favorite space opera series. We left our friends in whatever peace they could salvage.

We played Gallows Hill the next day, trouncing them rapidly in two matches. I'm not sure whether we had more ferocity because of Noah's being kicked out or if Brianna's team just didn't have the heart to compete after all the tragedy.

Azrael was especially off his game, which wasn't surprising when I thought about it later. He'd grown up idolizing Noah and had been excited about competing against him on the court. Without that aspect, he lost focus.

After the final whistle, Brianna rushed over and hugged each of us in turn instead of the usual post-game series of handshakes. All of the other Gallows Hill players followed suit, even Crow, who swallowed his bad-boy demeanor for once. At the end of the line, when I came to Bar, he lifted me off the ground.

"Your friends, your brother, and your professor deserved better than what they got. I'm sorry, Aliyah." He put me back down.

As the crowd dispersed, that hollow feeling returned, but Logan came over and stood by my side.

"Whatever happens, I'm here."

He took my hand and squeezed, gaze on the floor away from my face. Eye contact wasn't the same for him as other people, but that little hand squeeze was worth a thousand intensely cinematic gazes. It gave me just as much comfort as hugging Noah back in the locker room in the wake of all that tragedy.

"Thanks, Logan." I squeezed back. "For everything."

I could end by telling you that Grace got hired on all summer at Amber-smith Fashions, or that Logan got an internship at Bubbe's office.

Or that Elanor Pierce rented a basement apartment in the Point with Noah before the ink on her diploma was dry.

But I won't. None of those had the same impact on my year as the first day back on Monday morning, when life at Hawthorn went on without Noah, Mercy, and Professor Luciano.

It started with a special announcement before breakfast by Headmaster Hawkins in the lobby. He stood at the podium, waving us toward the rows of chairs as we descended the stairs. Once everyone was seated, he spoke.

"First, it is with great sorrow that I officially announce the passing of Professor Luciano, who graced us with his wisdom and guidance. He lost his life heroically, banishing a magical threat that could have caused mass casualties on campus. During this effort, Mercy, the gryphon familiar of Mr. Dorian Spanos, also perished. They will be sorely missed."

Headmaster Hawkins clapped his hands, activating the magipsychic display behind him. Pictures of Mercy and Professor Luciano appeared, with the words In Memoriam between them.

"As a direct consequence of this tragedy, Mr. Noah Morgenstern has been deemed ineligible to continue attending classes. The nature of his condition is private at his own request. A student was responsible for this deliberate threat to our campus. Temperance Fairbanks was expelled and turned over to the Federal Bureau of Extrahumans, where her actions and motives will be investigated and prosecuted in accordance with national law."

He cleared his throat before continuing.

"The Board of Trustees held an emergency meeting last night. I am instructing section one of the second-year cohort for the remainder of this semester in addition to my other duties. That said, I'll be stepping out of the headmaster's role at the end of this academic year, remaining to serve as a professor to that same group of students next fall."

He raised his hand, quelling the voices that rose in protest.

"The Board of Trustees voted to demote me but keep me on. They were generous, and the paperwork is already signed. A letter will go out this summer with the name of the new headmaster, selected from a list of candidates I have compiled for them. I will forever be honored by each and every one of my students. Thank you."

After the meeting, we sat together in the biggest booth over breakfast.

"Trustees?" Grace wrinkled her nose. "Doesn't that include one of Faith's parents?"

"Yeah, my father." Faith opened her mouth and mimed sticking her finger down her throat.

"Mine too," Logan added.

"And Mrs. Onassis." Hailey wrinkled her nose.

"There are four more, you know." Bailey stirred her coffee.

"That's why my dad's still teaching. Miss Dunstable and Mr. Thurston are his godparents, and Mr. Gauthier went to college with him."

"What about trustee number seven?" Dorian asked.

"I don't know him, but he's an undeath magus from upstate New York." Hal sighed. "I overheard Dad say he voted to spite Mr. Fairbanks. They don't get along."

The string of words out of Faith's mouth made everyone stop and stare.

"What?" I asked.

"Temperance. I bet she was under orders."

"Isn't that kind of paranoid?" Kitty tossed her head.

"No." Faith and Logan answered in chorus.

"This spells trouble next year for sure." I leaned my chin on my hand. "What if the new headmaster is Mrs. Pierce or something? No offense, Logan."

"That won't happen." Hal tapped his temple. "Dad's smart. One of his terms for resignation was the list he mentioned. It says that any new headmaster must be one of the people on that list. We won't know what we're dealing with until the board chooses, though."

"For now, let's just try to get through the week, okay?" Lee said. "And actually eat our breakfasts." It was good advice, so we took it.

I wondered whether the headmaster would give us a reading

assignment in the library or send us to Creatives, but neither happened. He taught us as promised, but did nothing as tone-deaf or heartless as attempting to take Filberto Luciano's place.

He assigned us to make our own tribute as a class to our mentor and to Mercy. Logan sketched them both from memory, adding Mercy to his right shoulder instead of his strix. Faith made paper cranes, passing them around for everyone to decorate. Dylan wrote poems about courage and lost love, then dragged out his guitar and set them to music. Hal asked me what the professor's last words were, then wrote them out on parchment with calligraphic ink, adding his thumbprint as punctuation at the end.

Dorian didn't have the heart to do much besides watch. I overheard the headmaster telling him about the academic track. My classmate walked to the front of the room, his head held high, and announced that he'd be back to graduate with us next year, no matter what. We each went over and hugged him. Yes, even Dylan.

At the last minute before the bell, the strix woke and swooped down from a rafter. She landed on the desk, hooting at the other familiars, and they assembled in a semicircle on the floor, howling, keening, caterwauling, and squeaking in their own mourning ritual, aimed at Dorian. For Mercy. Logan stood beside me, weeping. When the critters stopped, the strix hooted at Logan, then blinked at Dorian, hopping toward him.

"What?"

"She's offering you her sympathies," Logan said. "And her name is Julia."

"Thanks, Julia." Dorian held out his hand. "My condolences. He was the best teacher I ever had. You must miss him terribly."

She tapped his hand with her beak, then peered at him and hooted.

"Yeah, sure, if you don't mind the gym." He held out his arm, but Julia fluttered to his shoulder. "It kinda reeks in there, but you know that already."

"I think they'll be okay, Logan." I patted his arm. "Thanks to you."

He nodded, wiping away tears.

Before we left, the door to Professor Luciano's classroom was covered from top to bottom with our handiwork. Finally, I added my own tribute: a single white feather and an envelope postmarked Genoa, Italy 1982, to Noah Morgenstern at 10-1/2 Hawthorne Street, Salem, Massachusetts. I'd keep the letter, but the envelope on the door would always be filled with love.

The End

I hope you enjoyed Hawthorn Year Two. The ending was bittersweet, but this series is not complete. Year Three is in progress already, and I'm beginning to discover just how much impact the trustees and the incoming headmaster will have on Aliyah and her classmates.

Stay tuned for more. And if you're curious about my other work, you can find it on my Author Central page.

Thank you!
D.R. Perry

The story continues with Hawthorn Academy Year Three, available for order now at Amazon and through Kindle Unlimited.

AUTHOR'S NOTES

Thank you so much for reading continuing with Hawthorn Academy with Year Two. In this book, we see life getting more complicated for Aliyah and her friends. Each one learns more about their world and themselves, and I feel lucky to watch them grow.

The holidays we celebrate with the Morgensterns this time are Sukkot, Festival of Booths, and Hanukkah, Festival of Lights. I give a full accounting of three blessings on the first night of Hanukkah, but text does not do them justice since they are traditionally sung. Here's a link to the Chabad website with recordings, in case you're curious about how they sound.

https://www.chabad.org/holidays/chanukah/article_cdo/aid/103874/jewish/Blessings-on-the-Menorah.htm

One of the heavier subjects I tackle in year two is abuse, which we see in a few different forms through the eyes of Aliyah's classmates. I wanted to give some resources to any readers who might need them or know someone who does. The Hotline helps people experiencing domestic violence and abuse, with a survivor-centered focus. For minor children in danger, ChildHelp provides both prevention and intervention, and HAVOCA is a group for adult survivors run by survivors.

http://www.thehotline.org
http://www.childhelp.org/
http://www.havoca.org/

Once again, thanks for opening this book and stepping into the Revealed World with me again. Aliyah has one more year at Hawthorn, so look for the third volume in the future. Beyond that, I'm considering where in this world I'll go next.

Perhaps I'll explore what life is like at Gallows Hill, Messing, or even Trout in Rhode Island. There's a chance I might follow Aliyah and her classmates to college. I'd love to hear what you think about the possibilities. You can find all of my social media contacts and my mailing list at my website, https://www.drperryauthor.com/, and reach out through one of them.

With Gratitude,
D.R. Perry

PROVIDENCE PARANORMAL COLLEGE

Who's enrolled? Students who are a bit different: vampires, were-wolves, changelings, shifters, psychics, and magi.

For one-hundred years, the college has taught and trained only psychics or magi, and for the first time, it's opening the doors to those not different: regular humans.

At this Ivy-League school, the students are expected to learn their powers and keep high grades.

Unfortunately, grades are slipping, but that's what happens when a mysterious villain is hunting you down…

Because someone is angry about this new admissions policy and they'll kill to stop integration. To defeat this rising evil, the students must band together and master their strange powers – because if they don't..

Well, it's pretty hard to graduate when you're dead.

Includes the first five books plus four brand new short stories inside the college.

"I spent more than a couple of late nights reading through these stories to find out what was going to happen to my new friends!" – Michael Anderle, Best-Selling Author of The Kurtherian Gambit

This series is for fans of Harry Potter, Jaymin Eve, and all academy books.

Get it today at Amazon and through Kindle Unlimited

THANK YOU!

Thank you for reading! If you loved this book, please leave a review. You can find my other work by clicking the links below, going to **my website** or visiting my **Author Central page**.

CONNECT WITH THE AUTHOR

Website: https://www.drperryauthor.com/

Join her newsletter!

Find more of D.R. Perry's books on Amazon.

OTHER LMBPN PUBLISHING BOOKS

To be notified of new releases and special promotions from LMBPN publishing, please join our email list:

http://lmbpn.com/email/

For a complete list of books published by LMBPN please visit the following pages:

https://lmbpn.com/books-by-lmbpn-publishing/

All LMBPN Audiobooks are Available at Audible.com and iTunes. For a complete list of audiobooks visit:

www.lmbpn.com/audible

www.ingramcontent.com/pod-product-compliance
Lightning Source LLC
Chambersburg PA
CBHW020230110726
47898CB00004B/1217